New Orleans Noir

The Classics

EDITED BY JULIE SMITH

This collection is comprised of works of fiction. All names, characters, places, and incidents are the product of the authors' imaginations. Any resemblance to real events or persons, living or dead, is entirely coincidental.

Published by Akashic Books
©2016 Akashic Books

Series concept by Tim McLoughlin and Johnny Temple
New Orleans map by Sohrab Habibion

ISBN: 978-1-61775-384-8
Library of Congress Control Number: 2015934071
All rights reserved

First printing

Grateful acknowledgment is made for permission to reprint the stories in this anthology. See page 316 for details.

Akashic Books
Twitter: @AkashicBooks
Facebook: AkashicBooks
E-mail: info@akashicbooks.com
Website: www.akashicbooks.com

ALSO IN THE AKASHIC NOIR SERIES

NEW ORLEANS

61

10

90

PIGEON TOWN

VERSAILLES BOULEVARD

UPTOWN

MISSISSIPPI RIVER

AUDUBON
PARK

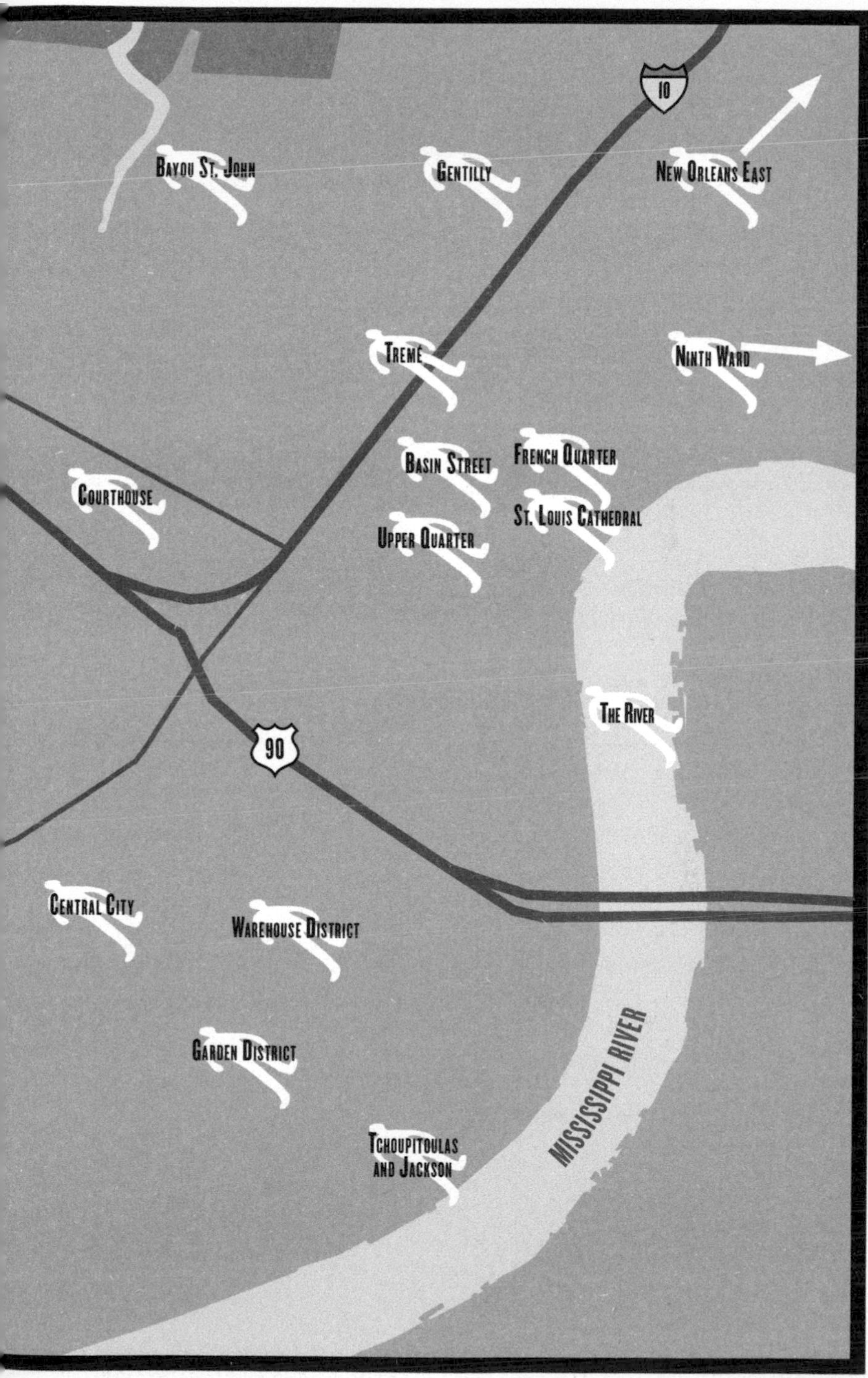
Bayou St. John
Gentilly
New Orleans East
10
Tremé
Ninth Ward
Basin Street
French Quarter
Courthouse
St. Louis Cathedral
Upper Quarter
The River
90
Central City
Warehouse District
Garden District
Mississippi River
Tchoupitoulas and Jackson

TABLE OF CONTENTS

PART III: THE THANATOS SYNDROME

INTRODUCTION
The Many Ways It Can All Go Away

J ust after Hurricane Katrina, when New Orleans was at its most noir moment (and so were we all), I was invited by Akashic Books to put together a volume of original stories for the first *New Orleans Noir*. It perfectly suited all our moods down here, which might account for the extremely high quality of the stories the authors produced. The collection has remained so popular that, almost ten years later, we're coming back for *The Classics*, reprinted stories by some of the finest writers who ever walked the rough-and-tumble streets of the City that Care Forgot—a pretty funny sobriquet when you consider what they wrote.

Listen to a character herein: "He had it made. Then it all went away . . . it always goes away. If you know anything, you know that." So wrote John William Corrington in "Pleadings," one of the stories collected herein. It's one of my favorite quotes about the noir tradition. Maybe it doesn't apply to everyone in a noir tale, or even always to the protagonist, but you can bet it perfectly describes *someone's* fate.

With one exception, each of these stories reflects that scenario in some way or other—in every case there's a terrible loss, sometimes an unbearable loss. Much like in our lives. Most of us, I hope, will deal with our losses in less murderous, self-destructive, and downright horrific ways, but stories like this, even as they make us wince, let us identify with others who've been there.

Sometimes you can practically feel the author's own losses, his or her own desires for revenge or oblivion. And what a magnificent array of authors to choose from! It was a thrill to stroll through two centuries of stories written in a city as rich as delta dirt in literary tradition.

A glittering constellation of writers has passed through New Orleans—including Mark Twain, Sherwood Anderson, O. Henry, and even Walt Whitman, to name some of the not-so-usual suspects. Then there are the ones whose sojourns here are better known, the ones on whom we pride ourselves, such as Tennessee Williams, William Faulkner, Eudora Welty, Ellen Gilchrist, and James Lee Burke.

It was an anthologist's feast—just about everybody who came to New Orleans wrote about it. But there were surprises as well.

Here's what became apparent almost immediately: our well-known fascination with death and funerals and cemeteries and the dark side in general, coupled with our unfortunate notoriety for being Murder Central, hasn't produced a lot of crime stories. So in many cases I've had to content myself with the dark and brooding. You don't mind, do you? It's *very* dark and brooding.

But considering the detective story as we know it now wasn't even invented till 1841, nineteenth-century writers in New Orleans probably transferred more than their share of dark thoughts to paper. I noticed right away that many of our early authors were concerned with race and injustice. That's no surprise, since race is always on our minds here and most of our neighborhoods are either mixed or cheek-by-jowl. Creole, that early word for mixed Spanish or French heritage, now means almost exclusively African American and white.

Many of our nineteenth-century writers were concerned specifically with injustice against people of color, yet most of them, at first glance, were white. My guess is this doesn't mean black people weren't writing, just that they didn't find easy avenues to publication. One who did was Armand Lanusse, a well-off and well-educated free man of color who published the first collection of poetry by African Americans in the United States. He was a member of a literary group of men of similar background called Les Cenelles, which was also the name of the collection.

The story of his I've included is about plaçage, possibly nineteenth-century Louisiana's most fascinating social custom. It was a contract much like marriage, but always between a white man and a Creole woman. Here's how it was different from conventional marriage: the man was usually also married to someone else! (Invariably someone white.) Though it no doubt had advantages for some women—the men were often required to buy them houses and educate their children—Lanusse took a dim view. You could even say a noir view.

Grace King, far from being an advocate for African Americans, started writing to rebut the work of George Washington Cable, whose sympathy toward black people she considered objectionable. Given that, it's hard to know how to interpret "The Little Convent Girl." But I'd forgotten her opinions when I read the story, which moved me in a way that may have been different from the way King intended. Rather than try to deconstruct it, I'm going to take the view that there's more than one truth in a strong tale.

Kate Chopin was a writer famed for her early feminist novel *The Awakening*, from which the first section of this anthology takes its name. In "The Story of an Hour" she writes again about the female role of the time. This one, like many of Chopin's stories, is set on a "plantation," and several nineteenth-century New Orleans neighborhoods were made up of plantations. A distinguished literature professor I consulted informs me that the setting for this one couldn't be New Orleans, but I'm going off the reservation here—I think it could be. This plantation sounds exactly like the setting of another Chopin story called "Bayou St. John." Therefore, I deduce and decree (for purposes of this anthology) that Bayou St. John is the neighborhood where this tale takes place.

William Sidney Porter (a.k.a. O. Henry) fled to New Orleans in 1896 to avoid trial for embezzlement and ended up setting five stories here. Although his writing career was well along at the time, "Whistling Dick's Christmas Stocking," written in prison, was the first story he published under his famous pseudonym. This is the one story in the collection that has a happy ending, but Porter's fascination with crime, hoboes, and the down-and-out surely qualifies it as semi-noir, at least!

The middle twentieth century produced more iconic writers with, luckily for the reader, some very creepy perspectives. "Desire and the Black Masseur," by Tennessee Williams, and Eudora Welty's "The Purple Hat" may not be so much noir as gothic, but they both evoke that wonderfully unsettling feeling you get from a good story that freaks you out partly because you know the writer had something in mind that you don't quite understand, and that you'll never understand. So your half-delicious nightmares can just go on and on as you think of endless possible interpretations. Both stories are about sex and violence, said the critics, and that seems obvious enough. The critics said quite a bit more, but I think noir readers may just prefer to know they'll give you a good case of the shivers.

In Shirley Ann Grau's "Miss Yellow Eyes," "all roads lead to despair," wrote one critic. There's no crime in it, but if noir is about a life—or a predicament—in which everything's gone to hell and there's no way out, "Miss Yellow Eyes" is the genuine article. "Ritual Murder," a short play about so-called senseless murder by Tom Dent, an African American poet revered in these parts, is as true today as it was when it was written thirty-eight years ago. (It really ought to be taught in schools.)

With John William Corrington's lawyer story, "Pleadings," we start to get more into the contemporary noir mode. Though originally published in a literary magazine, this is possibly the most bruising yarn in the collection, brutally hyperrealistic, so full of human pain and suffering it'll make you want to pull the covers over your head.

I organized the anthology chronologically because I thought it was fascinating to see how ways of talking about violence, brutality, despair, and injustice have evolved over nearly two centuries. It has always been curious to me that New Orleans, with all its mystery and crime, has produced so few detective series. John Dickson Carr once set a trilogy here. But other than that, if there were any at all before Chris Wiltz introduced her Neal Rafferty series in 1981, I can find no record of it. Wiltz was first, but then came a small deluge, including John and Joyce Corrington, O'Neil De Noux, Ace Atkins, James Colbert, Barbara Colley, J.M. Redmann, Barbara Hambly, James Sallis, Tony Fennelly, Greg Herren, Robert Skinner, D.J. Donaldson, David Fulmer, Dick Lochte, Tony Dunbar, me, and, a few years later, Bill Loehfelm. There was also, of course, James Lee Burke, but he is *sui generis*, partly because he's a titan and partly because, aside from *The Neon Rain*, he really writes about Southwest Louisiana, with the occasional New Orleans chapter included—to which we cling desperately! (Disclaimer here: I'm not counting any series set outside Orleans Parish, like Charlaine Harris's Sookie Stackhouse series, nor am I counting exclusively self-published series.)

I mention all this to put fictional Big Easy crime in perspective. Of the distinguished group above, I'm lucky to have found excellent stories by Burke, De Noux, and Atkins, and I've unearthed a few other goodies as well. Ellen Gilchrist's "Rich" has become a modern classic. Poppy Z. Brite came up with a historical— and slightly supernatural—angle in "Mussolini and the Axeman's Jazz." In the tiny but poignant "Rose," John Biguenet delves into the devastating psychological effects of a crime. Valerie Martin in "Spats," and Nevada Barr in "GDMFSOB," explore similar themes of love gone wrong. (Incidentally, though Barr is a favorite hometown writer to many—since her Anna Pigeon series takes place in a different national park each time—her home base is New Orleans.)

No contemporary New Orleans anthology is complete without a Hurricane Katrina story, since that's our reality now, our way of reckoning with time and measuring our reclaimed lives, much the same way 9/11 remains a reality for most New Yorkers. Like the Holocaust, it's not something we want to forget, no matter how painful the memory. James Lee Burke's "Jesus Out to Sea" manages both to evoke that terrible time and the whole world of beauty (and crime) that preceded it.

Last is the tragic tale of a fourteen-year-old already in enough trouble to have an ankle bracelet. It's by Maurice Carlos Ruffin, a stunning new writer who's been making waves around his hometown ever since he turned up in James Nolan's fabled writing class a few years ago. Baby, as the kid in the story is called, is a product of his neighborhood—and isn't that what this book's all about?

If you're from New Orleans, the neighborhood theme will resonate like Tibetan temple bells. And yet, surely every city has similar hoods, similar behavior patterns, similar travails—and has had them forever. "Indeed," wrote Voltaire, "history is nothing more than a tableau of crimes and misfortunes."

Julie Smith
New Orleans, LA
January 2016

PART I

The Awakening

A MARRIAGE OF CONSCIENCE

BY ARMAND LANUSSE

St. Louis Cathedral

(Originally published in 1843)

One Sunday morning, when I returned to this town after a few days away, I was strolling aimlessly through the streets when the sound of the bells of the old cathedral drew me to the holy temple. Let us join, I told myself, the crowd of the faithful who always fill the sanctuary when the Lord's day returns; let us go hear the voice of the ministers of a tolerant and merciful God praising his infinite greatness; let us go listen to the holy, eloquent words of the wise priest who is temporarily replacing the respectable parish priest that death has just taken from us. A few young men were gathered at the church door and as I walked past them, the words *schism, priests,* and *churchwardens* struck my ear. I crossed the threshold of the temple and was astonished when I saw only two or three people kneeling on the stone floor instead of the crowd I thought I would encounter; instead of the holy hymns and evangelical words I came to hear, absolute silence reigned inside this vast edifice.

I tried to imagine what could possibly cause such abandonment of this holy place, which has been so greatly venerated for so long by the people of Louisiana. I was thinking about the few words I had gathered at the entrance when I saw a beautiful young woman with wild hair and disheveled clothing run in through one of the side doors of the temple, cross the balustrade that separates the nave from the sanctuary, and prostrate herself on the steps of the altar devoted to the comforter of the afflicted, that tender and poetic Mary, mother of the savior of mankind. I approached the balustrade and leaned against it, unnoticed by this stranger, so absorbed were all the faculties of her being in the prayer she was murmuring. Suddenly, she raised her eyes bathed in tears toward the image of the queen of martyrs and cried out: "O holy Mary, my patron saint, take pity on me. While the story of my sufferings makes my sisters smile and my mother herself calls me a madwoman when she sees my tears flowing, O you, virgin full of indulgence, now that I have prayed and a little tranquility has slipped into my heart, please listen kindly to what I need to tell you in the hopes of lightening my sorrow."

After collecting herself for a moment, the young woman continued in these terms:

"Up to the age of sixteen, my life was as calm as the innocent thoughts that then filled my mind. I obeyed the lessons of a pious aunt who loved me tenderly and with whom I had lived since I was a very small child, and I lovingly practiced the admirable precepts of the Christian religion. Alas, death came to rob me of that good relative and I had to go live with my mother, whom I sincerely loved, but the noisy life there was not at all in harmony with the peaceful habits I had acquired since early childhood.

"I had lived in my mother's house for a year and I still could not accustom myself to the silly language of my elder sisters, who were only interested in balls, feasts, and finery. They went to every party and always wanted me to accompany them. Up to then I had resisted all temptations, but at the end of the last carnival, my mother, who said she did not like my stubbornness, demanded that I enter a world that was utterly new to me.

"So to obey her, I made up my mind to go to several of those balls, which always made me shiver with horror; for in the midst of a crowd of men speaking a different language, with impudent looks and bold gestures, not one girl had a brother under whose protection she could take shelter; not one woman had a legitimate husband whose honorable name could impress that vulgar crowd avid for crude pleasures.

"At one of these strange gatherings, I had retired, according to my custom, to the least conspicuous part of the room, disposed to refuse all the invitations to dance that I might receive. I had already turned down several of them when a young man whose manners were full of distinction, quite unlike those of the other dancers, came up to me and with exquisite politeness insisted that I grant him the favor, he said, of giving him the waltz that was about to begin. I wanted to refuse again but I did not have the strength to do so, unfortunately for me. At that moment, the orchestra began to warm up, his hand grasped mine, I gave myself entirely to him, and we were soon immersed in the crowd of dancers.

"Little by little, the ball lost its repulsive features to my eyes. It is true that I could see only Gustave: that was the name of my attentive partner. We danced together all night and when I left I carried away in my heart sentiments quite different from the ones I had when I left the previous balls.

"Gustave and I saw each other frequently after that. With all my heart, I shared the love I thought I had truly inspired in him, so often did he repeat it. One day, my mother informed me that the man I loved, having first obtained her consent, had asked her to propose our union to me. I did not dissimulate my joy and answered that I would be happy to become Gustave's wife. But when the woman who brought me into the world wanted me to understand that this young man, who occupied a position in society well above ours, could not unite with me in a legitimate way, I hid my head in my hands and wept with an indignant heart, for it was only as a mistress and not as a wife that Gustave wanted me.

"I did not wish to see him anymore.

"Some time had passed when one day my mother told me: 'But my dear daughter, since you are repulsed by a condition that so many young ladies seek in this country, why don't you contract a marriage of conscience? Gustave is proposing this to you.' 'What is a marriage of conscience?' I asked my mother. 'It is,' she answered, 'a pact which is outside the law, but to which a priest gives all the character of a legitimate engagement.' 'Well then, Mother, I have no further objection,' I told her. 'An engagement taken at the foot of the altar must always suffice, it seems to me; who would dare violate its sanctity? I do not understand why one must have the sanction of the law in that case.' My mother, full of joy, agreed with me and left our home immediately.

"A few days later I was united with my lover.

"My happiness did not last. Hardly a year had gone by after our union when Gustave, whose inconstant character had become clear to me, seemed to be doing his best to fill my heart with all the anguish of the most frightful jealousy, for I was madly in love with that man. How many times did I follow him to those balls I have already mentioned, not to find ease for my pain but to make it more harrowing still? There I would see Gustave lavish his attention on other women, perhaps less pretty than me, while I, not daring to confess my suffering to anyone and blushing to see myself thus disdained by my husband, would withdraw, alone and pensive, to a corner of the room. I found myself repeating to myself these verses I had read somewhere and that were engraved in my memory, as they seemed to have been written to paint the state of my own soul:

In all these salons, why say that I suffer?
Each man gives himself only to pleasure;
It's all joyful waltzes and gambling and dances
That charm everyone and no one chances
To think that these balls make me cry and suffer . . .

"At last, I joyfully welcomed the day I became a mother, and I thought that this sacred title I had just acquired would make my husband's affections return to me. Alas, it was only an illusion, and reality was soon to drive it quickly from my heart . . .

"I soon learned that Gustave, regardless of the vows that united us, was about to contract another marriage. I did not want to believe it. But when I spoke to him about it, he confessed that financial motives were forcing him to take on this new engagement, but as for the rest, he would never cease to have for me all the attentions that could make a woman happy. 'Oh,' I said to him bitterly, 'do you really think that I could be happy if I must live with the certitude that I have a rival whom you yourself have acknowledged? Besides, you cannot abandon me like this. The priest received our vows, did he not? Is it in your power to untie the indissoluble knot that binds us to each other? Can you be so ignorant of the duties imposed on us by the laws of marriage?' 'You are forgetting,' he answered smiling, 'that we are united only by a marriage of conscience.' 'So your conscience does not trouble you?' I asked him. 'No,' he answered coldly. Then I threw myself at his feet. To bring him back to more honorable feelings, I showed him our child, that angel who only yesterday flew out of my arms to increase the cohorts of those who ceaselessly praise the name of the Creator. Annoyed by my moans and sobs, Gustave banished me from his presence.

"I never saw him again.

"A week ago I learned that his new marriage was celebrated with great pomp; a week ago God stripped me of the little reason that I still retained; and whenever I happen to regain some sanity, it is only to measure the extent of my misfortune."

Then, suddenly, the madwoman's tears dried up. She let out a frightful laugh that disturbed the sanctity of the place in which we stood. She crossed the balustrade again and hurried out of the temple as quickly as she had come in, through the door facing the altar to Mary.

I followed her as she stopped on the sidewalk in front of the church. At this moment, an elegant carriage drawn by two spirited horses passed rapidly by on the street. A young lady of great beauty and an elegantly dressed gentleman were sitting inside. After staring into the carriage, the madwoman cried out, "That's him!" and I saw her rush out in front of the horses.

"Stop!" people cried from all sides. It was too late. The coachman was able to control his horses and they stopped, but not before they horribly trampled the body of the unfortunate woman writhing under their hooves. I looked at the people inside the carriage; the young lady appeared to be shuddering in pity; an extreme pallor covered the face of the elegant man, whose whole body was frighteningly motionless at this moment.

The bloody corpse of the young woman was soon carried under the peristyle of City Hall.

"Was she demented?" asked the lady in the carriage with a voice full of compassion.

"Yes, madam," I cried, "she went mad because a coward took advantage of her naiveté and shamefully deceived her; and that coward, madam, is—"

"Whip the horses! Go!" shouted the pale man, suddenly emerging from his stupor.

The coachman obeyed this order, the horses galloped off . . . and the young lady leaned out vainly in my direction to grasp the last words I had just pronounced . . .

Translated from the French by David and Nicole Ball

THE LITTLE CONVENT GIRL

BY GRACE KING

The River

(Originally published in 1893)

She was coming down on the boat from Cincinnati, the little convent girl. Two sisters had brought her aboard. They gave her in charge of the captain, got her a state-room, saw that the new little trunk was put into it, hung the new little satchel up on the wall, showed her how to bolt the door at night, shook hands with her for good-by (good-bys have really no significance for sisters), and left her there. After a while the bells all rang, and the boat, in the awkward elephantine fashion of boats, got into midstream. The chambermaid found her sitting on the chair in the state-room where the sisters had left her, and showed her how to sit on a chair in the saloon. And there she sat until the captain came and hunted her up for supper. She could not do anything of herself; she had to be initiated into everything by someone else.

She was known on the boat only as "the little convent girl." Her name, of course, was registered in the clerk's office, but on a steamboat no one thinks of consulting the clerk's ledger. It is always the little widow, the fat madam, the tall colonel, the parson, etc. The captain, who pronounced by the letter, always called her the little convent girl. She was the beau-ideal of the little convent girl. She never raised her eyes except when spoken to. Of course she never spoke first, even to the chambermaid, and when she did speak it was in the wee, shy, furtive voice one might imagine a just-budding violet to have; and she walked with such soft, easy, carefully calculated steps that one naturally felt the penalties that must have secured them—penalties dictated by a black code of deportment.

She was dressed in deep mourning. Her black straw hat was trimmed with stiff new crape, and her stiff new bombazine dress had crape collar and cuffs. She wore her hair in two long plaits fastened around her head tight and fast. Her hair had a strong inclination to curl, but that had been taken out of it as austerely as the noise out of her footfalls.

Her hair was as black as her dress; her eyes, when one saw them, seemed blacker than either, on account of the bluishness of the white surrounding the pupil. Her eyelashes were almost as thick as the black veil which the sisters had fastened around her hat with an extra pin the very last thing before leaving. She had a round little face, and a tiny pointed chin; her mouth was slightly protuberant from the teeth, over which she tried to keep her lips well shut, the effort giving them a pathetic little forced expression. Her complexion was sallow, a pale sallow, the complexion of a brunette bleached in darkened rooms. The only color about her was a blue taffeta ribbon from which a large silver medal of the Virgin hung over the place where a breastpin should have been. She was so little, so little, although she was eighteen, as the sisters told the captain; otherwise they would not have permitted her to travel all the way to New Orleans alone.

Unless the captain or the clerk remembered to fetch her out in front, she would sit all day in the cabin, in the same place, crocheting lace, her spool of thread and box of patterns in her lap, on the handkerchief spread to save her new dress. Never leaning back—oh, no! always straight and stiff, as if the conventual back board were there within call. She would eat only convent fare at first, notwithstanding the importunities of the waiters, and the jocularities of the captain, and particularly of the clerk. Everyone knows the fund of humor possessed by a steamboat clerk, and what a field for display the table at meal-times affords. On Friday she fasted rigidly, and she never began to eat, or finished, without a little Latin movement of the lips and a sign of the cross. And always at six o'clock of the evening she remembered the angelus, although there was no church bell to remind her of it.

She was in mourning for her father, the sisters told the captain, and she was going to New Orleans to her mother. She had not seen her mother since she was an infant, on account of some disagreement between the parents, in consequence of which the father had brought her to Cincinnati, and placed her in the convent. There she had been for twelve years, only going to her father for vacations and holidays. So long as the father lived he would never let the child have any communication with her mother. Now that he was dead all that was changed, and the first thing that the girl herself wanted to do was to go to her mother.

The mother superior had arranged it all with the mother of the girl, who was to come personally to the boat in New Orleans, and receive her child from the captain, presenting a letter from the mother superior, a facsimile of which the sisters gave the captain.

It is a long voyage from Cincinnati to New Orleans, the rivers doing their best to make it interminable, embroidering themselves *ad libitum* all over the country. Every five miles, and sometimes oftener, the boat would stop to put off or take on freight, if not both. The little convent girl, sitting in the cabin, had her terrible frights at first from the hideous noises attendant on these landings—the whistles, the ringings of the bells, the running to and fro, the shouting. Every time she thought it was shipwreck, death, judgment, purgatory; and her sins! her sins! She would drop her crochet, and clutch her prayer-beads from her pocket, and relax the constraint over her lips, which would go to rattling off prayers with the velocity of a relaxed windlass. That was at first, before the captain took to fetching her out in front to see the boat make a landing.

Then she got to liking it so much that she would stay all day just where the captain put her, going inside only for her meals. She forgot herself at times so much that she would draw her chair a little closer to the railing, and put up her veil, actually, to see better. No one ever usurped her place, quite in front, or intruded upon her either with word or look; for everyone learned to know her shyness, and began to feel a personal interest in her, and all wanted the little convent girl to see everything that she possibly could.

And it was worth seeing—the balancing and *chasséeing* and waltzing of the cumbersome old boat to make a landing. It seemed to be always attended with the difficulty and the improbability of a new enterprise; and the relief when it did sidle up anywhere within rope's-throw of the spot aimed at! And the roustabout throwing the rope from the perilous end of the dangling gang-plank! And the dangling roustabouts hanging like drops of water from it— dropping sometimes twenty feet to the land, and not infrequently into the river itself. And then what a rolling of barrels, and shouldering of sacks, and singing of Jim Crow songs, and pacing of Jim Crow steps; and black skins glistening through torn shirts, and white teeth gleaming through red lips, and laughing, and talking and—bewildering! entrancing! Surely the little convent girl in her convent walls never dreamed of so much unpunished noise and movement in the world!

The first time she heard the mate—it must have been like the first time woman ever heard man—curse and swear, she turned pale, and ran quickly, quickly into the saloon, and—came out again? No, indeed! not with all the soul she had to save, and all the other sins on her conscience. She shook her head resolutely, and was not seen in her chair on deck again until the captain not only reassured her, but guaranteed his reassurance. And after that, whenever the boat was about to make a landing, the mate would first glance up to the guards, and if the little convent girl was sitting there he would change his invective to sarcasm, and

politely request the colored gentlemen not to hurry themselves—
on no account whatever; to take their time about shoving out the
plank; to send the rope ashore by post-office—write him when it
got there; begging them not to strain their backs; calling them mis-
ter, colonel, major, general, prince, and your royal highness, which
was vastly amusing. At night, however, or when the little convent
girl was not there, language flowed in its natural curve, the mate
swearing like a pagan to make up for lost time.

The captain forgot himself one day: it was when the boat ran
aground in the most unexpected manner and place, and he went
to work to express his opinion, as only steamboat captains can, of
the pilot, mate, engineer, crew, boat, river, country, and the world
in general, ringing the bell, first to back, then to head, shouting
himself hoarser than his own whistle—when he chanced to see
the little black figure hurrying through the chaos on the deck; and
the captain stuck as fast aground in midstream as the boat had
done.

In the evening the little convent girl would be taken on the
upper deck, and going up the steep stairs there was such confusion, to keep the black skirts well over the stiff white petticoats;
and, coming down, such blushing when suspicion would cross the
unprepared face that a rim of white stocking might be visible; and
the thin feet, laced so tightly in the glossy new leather boots, would
cling to each successive step as if they could never, never make another venture; and then one boot would (there is but that word)
hesitate out, and feel and feel around, and have such a pause of
helpless agony as if indeed the next step must have been wilfully
removed, or was nowhere to be found on the wide, wide earth.

It was a miracle that the pilot ever got her up into the pilot-
house; but pilots have a lonely time, and do not hesitate even at
miracles when there is a chance for company. He would place a
box for her to climb to the tall bench behind the wheel, and he
would arrange the cushions, and open a window here to let in

air, and shut one there to cut off a draft, as if there could be no tenderer consideration in life for him than her comfort. And he would talk of the river to her, explain the chart, pointing out eddies, whirlpools, shoals, depths, new beds, old beds, cut-offs, caving banks, and making banks, as exquisitely and respectfully as if she had been the River Commission.

It was his opinion that there was as great a river as the Mississippi flowing directly under it—an underself of a river, as much a counterpart of the other as the second story of a house is of the first; in fact, he said, they were navigating through the upper story. Whirlpools were holes in the floor of the upper river, so to speak; eddies were rifts and cracks. And deep under the earth, hurrying toward the subterranean stream, were other streams, small and great, but all deep, hurrying to and from that great mother-stream underneath, just as the small and great overground streams hurry to and from their mother Mississippi. It was almost more than the little convent girl could take in: at least such was the expression of her eyes; for they opened as all eyes have to open at pilot stories. And he knew as much of astronomy as he did of hydrology, could call the stars by name, and define the shapes of the constellations; and she, who had studied astronomy at the convent, was charmed to find that what she had learned was all true. It was in the pilot-house, one night, that she forgot herself for the first time in her life, and stayed up until after nine o'clock. Although she appeared almost intoxicated at the wild pleasure, she was immediately overwhelmed at the wickedness of it, and observed much more rigidity of conduct thereafter. The engineer, the boiler-men, the firemen, the stokers, they all knew when the little convent girl was up in the pilot-house: the speaking-tube became so mild and gentle.

With all the delays of river and boat, however, there is an end to the journey from Cincinnati to New Orleans. The latter city, which at one time to the impatient seemed at the terminus of the never, began, all of a sudden, one day to make its nearingness felt; and from that period every other interest paled before the interest in the immanence of arrival into port, and the whole boat was seized with a panic of preparation, the little convent girl with the others. Although so immaculate was she in person and effects that she might have been struck with a landing, as some good people might be struck with death, at any moment without fear of results, her trunk was packed and repacked, her satchel arranged and rearranged, and, the last day, her hair was brushed and plaited and smoothed over and over again until the very last glimmer of a curl disappeared. Her dress was whisked, as if for microscopic inspection; her face was washed; and her fingernails were scrubbed with the hard convent nailbrush, until the disciplined little tips ached with a pristine soreness. And still there were hours to wait, and still the boat added up delays. But she arrived at last, after all, with not more than the usual and expected difference between the actual and the advertised time of arrival.

There was extra blowing and extra ringing, shouting, commanding, rushing up the gangway and rushing down the gangway. The clerks, sitting behind tables on the first deck, were plied, in the twinkling of an eye, with estimates, receipts, charges, countercharges, claims, reclaims, demands, questions, accusations, threats, all at topmost voices. None but steamboat clerks could have stood it. And there were throngs composed of individuals every one of whom wanted to see the captain first and at once; and those who could not get to him shouted over the heads of the others; and as usual he lost his temper and politeness, and began to do what he termed "hustle."

"Captain! Captain!" a voice called him to where a hand plucked his sleeve, and a letter was thrust toward him. "The cross, and the name of the convent." He recognized the envelope of the mother superior. He read the duplicate of the letter given by the sisters.

He looked at the woman—the mother—casually, then again and again.

The little convent girl saw him coming, leading someone toward her. She rose. The captain took her hand first, before the other greeting, "Good-by, my dear," he said. He tried to add something else, but seemed undetermined what. "Be a good little girl—" It was evidently all he could think of. Nodding to the woman behind him, he turned on his heel, and left.

One of the deck-hands was sent to fetch her trunk. He walked out behind them, through the cabin, and the crowd on deck, down the stairs, and out over the gangway. The little convent girl and her mother went with hands tightly clasped. She did not turn her eyes to the right or left, or once (what all passengers do) look backward at the boat which, however slowly, had carried her surely over dangers that she wot not of. All looked at her as she passed. All wanted to say good-by to the little convent girl, to see the mother who had been deprived of her so long. Some expressed surprise in a whistle; some in other ways. All exclaimed audibly, or to themselves, "Colored!"

It takes about a month to make the round trip from New Orleans to Cincinnati and back, counting five days' stoppage in New Orleans. It was a month to a day when the steamboat came puffing and blowing up to the wharf again, like a stout dowager after too long a walk; and the same scene of confusion was enacted, as it had been enacted twelve times a year, at almost the same wharf for twenty years; and the same calm, a death calmness by contrast, followed as usual the next morning.

The decks were quiet and clean; one cargo had just been delivered, part of another stood ready on the levee to be shipped. The captain was there waiting for his business to begin, the clerk was in his office getting his books ready, the voice of the mate could be heard below, mustering the old crew out and a new crew in; for if steamboat crews have a single principle—and there are those who deny them any—it is never to ship twice in succession on the same boat. It was too early yet for any but roustabouts, marketers, and church-goers; so early that even the river was still partly mist-covered; only in places could the swift, dark current be seen rolling swiftly along.

"Captain!" A hand plucked at his elbow, as if not confident that the mere calling would secure attention. The captain turned. The mother of the little convent girl stood there, and she held the little convent girl by the hand. "I have brought her to see you," the woman said. "You were so kind—and she is so quiet, so still, all the time, I thought it would do her a pleasure."

She spoke with an accent, and with embarrassment; otherwise one would have said that she was bold and assured enough.

"She don't go nowhere, she don't do nothing but make her crochet and her prayers, so I thought I would bring her for a little visit of *How d'ye do* to you."

There was, perhaps, some inflection in the woman's voice that might have made known, or at least awakened, the suspicion of some latent hope or intention, had the captain's ear been fine enough to detect it. There might have been something in the little convent girl's face, had his eye been more sensitive—a trifle paler, maybe, the lips a little tighter drawn, the blue ribbon a shade faded. He may have noticed that, but—and the visit of *How d'ye do* came to an end.

They walked down the stairway, the woman in front, the little convent girl—her hand released to shake hands with the captain—following, across the bared deck, out to the gangway, over to the middle of it. No one was looking, no one saw more than a flutter of white petticoats, a show of white stockings, as the little convent girl went under the water.

The roustabout dived, as the roustabouts always do, after the drowning, even at the risk of their good-for-nothing lives. The mate himself jumped overboard; but she had gone down in a whirlpool. Perhaps, as the pilot had told her whirlpools always did, it may have carried her through to the underground river, to that vast, hidden, dark Mississippi that flows beneath the one we see; for her body was never found.

THE STORY OF AN HOUR

BY KATE CHOPIN

Bayou St. John

(Originally published in 1894)

Knowing that Mrs. Mallard was afflicted with a heart trouble, great care was taken to break to her as gently as possible the news of her husband's death.

It was her sister Josephine who told her, in broken sentences; veiled hints that revealed in half concealing. Her husband's friend Richards was there too, near her. It was he who had been in the newspaper office when intelligence of the railroad disaster was received, with Brently Mallard's name leading the list of "killed." He had only taken the time to assure himself of its truth by a second telegram, and had hastened to forestall any less careful, less tender friend in bearing the sad message.

She did not hear the story as many women have heard the same, with a paralyzed inability to accept its significance. She wept at once, with sudden, wild abandonment, in her sister's arms. When the storm of grief had spent itself she went away to her room alone. She would have no one follow her.

There stood, facing the open window, a comfortable, roomy armchair. Into this she sank, pressed down by a physical exhaustion that haunted her body and seemed to reach into her soul.

She could see in the open square before her house the tops of trees that were all aquiver with the new spring life. The delicious breath of rain was in the air. In the street below a peddler was crying his wares. The notes of a distant song which someone was singing reached her faintly, and countless sparrows were twittering in the eaves.

There were patches of blue sky showing here and there through the clouds that had met and piled one above the other in the west facing her window.

She sat with her head thrown back upon the cushion of the chair, quite motionless, except when a sob came up into her throat and shook her, as a child who has cried itself to sleep continues to sob in its dreams.

She was young, with a fair, calm face, whose lines bespoke repression and even a certain strength. But now there was a dull stare in her eyes, whose gaze was fixed away off yonder on one of those patches of blue sky. It was not a glance of reflection, but rather indicated a suspension of intelligent thought.

There was something coming to her and she was waiting for it, fearfully. What was it? She did not know; it was too subtle and elusive to name. But she felt it, creeping out of the sky, reaching toward her through the sounds, the scents, the color that filled the air.

Now her bosom rose and fell tumultuously. She was beginning to recognize this thing that was approaching to possess her, and she was striving to beat it back with her will—as powerless as her two white slender hands would have been.

When she abandoned herself a little whispered word escaped her slightly parted lips. She said it over and over under her breath: "Free, free, free!" The vacant stare and the look of terror that had followed it went from her eyes. They stayed keen and bright. Her pulses beat fast, and the coursing blood warmed and relaxed every inch of her body.

She did not stop to ask if it were or were not a monstrous joy that held her. A clear and exalted perception enabled her to dismiss the suggestion as trivial.

She knew that she would weep again when she saw the kind,

tender hands folded in death; the face that had never looked save with love upon her, fixed and gray and dead. But she saw beyond that bitter moment a long procession of years to come that would belong to her absolutely. And she opened and spread her arms out to them in welcome.

There would be no one to live for her during those coming years; she would live for herself. There would be no powerful will bending hers in that blind persistence with which men and women believe they have a right to impose a private will upon a fellow-creature. A kind intention or a cruel intention made the act seem no less a crime as she looked upon it in that brief moment of illumination.

And yet she had loved him—sometimes. Often she had not. What did it matter! What could love, the unsolved mystery, count for in face of this possession of self-assertion which she suddenly recognized as the strongest impulse of her being!

"Free! Body and soul free!" she kept whispering.

Josephine was kneeling before the closed door with her lips to the keyhole, imploring for admission. "Louise, open the door! I beg; open the door—you will make yourself ill. What are you doing, Louise? For heaven's sake open the door."

"Go away. I am not making myself ill." No; she was drinking in a very elixir of life through that open window.

Her fancy was running riot along those days ahead of her. Spring days, and summer days, and all sorts of days that would be her own. She breathed a quick prayer that life might be long. It was only yesterday she had thought with a shudder that life might be long.

She arose at length and opened the door to her sister's importunities. There was a feverish triumph in her eyes, and she carried herself unwittingly like a goddess of Victory. She clasped her sister's waist, and together they descended the stairs. Richards stood waiting for them at the bottom.

Someone was opening the front door with a latchkey. It was Brently Mallard who entered, a little travel-stained, composedly carrying his grip-sack and umbrella. He had been far from the scene of accident, and did not even know there had been one. He stood amazed at Josephine's piercing cry; at Richards's quick motion to screen him from the view of his wife.

But Richards was too late.

When the doctors came they said she had died of heart disease—of joy that kills.

WHISTLING DICK'S CHRISTMAS STOCKING

BY O. HENRY

French Quarter

(Originally published in 1899)

I t was with much caution that Whistling Dick slid back the door of the box-car, for Article 5716, City Ordinances, authorized (perhaps unconstitutionally) arrest on suspicion, and he was familiar of old with this ordinance. So, before climbing out, he surveyed the field with all the care of a good general.

He saw no change since his last visit to this big, alms-giving, long-suffering city of the South, the cold weather paradise of the tramps. The levee where his freight-car stood was pimpled with dark bulks of merchandise. The breeze reeked with the well-remembered, sickening smell of the old tarpaulins that covered bales and barrels. The dun river slipped along among the shipping with an oily gurgle. Far down toward Chalmette he could see the great bend in the stream, outlined by the row of electric lights. Across the river Algiers lay, a long, irregular blot, made darker by the dawn which lightened the sky beyond. An industrious tug or two, coming for some early sailing ship, gave a few appalling toots, that seemed to be the signal for breaking day. The Italian luggers were creeping nearer their landing, laden with early vegetables and shellfish. A vague roar, subterranean in quality, from dray wheels and streetcars, began to make itself heard and felt; and the ferryboats, the Mary Anns of water craft, stirred sullenly to their menial morning tasks.

Whistling Dick's red head popped suddenly back into the car. A sight too imposing and magnificent for his gaze had been added to the scene. A vast, incomparable policeman rounded a pile of rice sacks and stood within twenty yards of the car. The daily miracle of the dawn, now being performed above Algiers, received the flattering attention of this specimen of municipal official splendor. He gazed with unbiased dignity at the faintly glowing colors until, at last, he turned to them his broad back, as if convinced that legal interference was not needed, and the sunrise might proceed unchecked. So he turned his face to the rice bags, and, drawing a flat flask from an inside pocket, he placed it to his lips and regarded the firmament.

Whistling Dick, professional tramp, possessed a half-friendly acquaintance with this officer. They had met several times before on the levee at night, for the officer, himself a lover of music, had been attracted by the exquisite whistling of the shiftless vagabond. Still, he did not care, under the present circumstances, to renew the acquaintance. There is a difference between meeting a policeman on a lonely wharf and whistling a few operatic airs with him, and being caught by him crawling out of a freight-car. So Dick waited, as even a New Orleans policeman must move on some time—perhaps it is a retributive law of nature—and before long "Big Fritz" majestically disappeared between the trains of cars.

Whistling Dick waited as long as his judgment advised, and then slid swiftly to the ground. Assuming as far as possible the air of an honest laborer who seeks his daily toil, he moved across the network of railway lines, with the intention of making his way by quiet Girod Street to a certain bench in Lafayette Square, where, according to appointment, he hoped to rejoin a pal known as "Slick," this adventurous pilgrim having preceded him by one day in a cattle-car into which a loose slat had enticed him.

As Whistling Dick picked his way where night still lingered among the big, reeking, musty warehouses, he gave way to the habit that had won for him his title. Subdued, yet clear, with each note as true and liquid as a bobolink's, his whistle tinkled about the dim, cold mountains of brick like drops of rain falling into a hidden pool. He followed an air, but it swam mistily into a swirling current of improvisation. You could cull out the trill of mountain brooks, the staccato of green rushes shivering above chilly lagoons, the pipe of sleepy birds.

Rounding a corner, the whistler collided with a mountain of blue and brass.

"So," observed the mountain calmly, "you are already pack. Und dere vill not pe frost before two veeks yet! Und you haf forgotten how to vistle. Dere was a valse note in dot last bar."

"Watcher know about it?" said Whistling Dick, with tentative familiarity. "You wit' yer little Gherman-band nixcumrous chunes. Watcher know about music? Pick yer ears, and listen agin. Here's de way I whistled it—see?"

He puckered his lips, but the big policeman held up his hand.

"Shtop," he said, "und learn der right way. Und learn also dot a rolling shtone can't vistle for a cent."

Big Fritz's heavy mustache rounded into a circle, and from its depths came a sound deep and mellow as that from a flute. He repeated a few bars of the air the tramp had been whistling. The rendition was cold, but correct, and he emphasized the note he had taken exception to.

"Dot p is p natural, und not p vlat. Py der vay, you petter pe glad I meet you. Von hour later, und I vould haf to put you in a gage to vistle mit der chail pirds. Der orders are to bull all der pums after sunrise."

"To which?"

"To bull der pums—eferybody mitout fisible means. Dirty days is der price, or fifteen tollars."

"Is dat straight, or a game you givin' me?"

"It's der pest tip you efer had. I gif it to you pecause I pelief you are not so bad as der rest. Und pecause you gan visl 'Der Freis-chütz' bezzer dan I myself gan. Don't run against any more bol-icemans aroundt der corners, but go away from town a few tays. Good-pye."

So Madame Orleans had at last grown weary of the strange and ruffled brood that came yearly to nestle beneath her chari-table pinions.

After the big policeman had departed, Whistling Dick stood for an irresolute minute, feeling all the outraged indignation of a delinquent tenant who is ordered to vacate his premises. He had pictured to himself a day of dreamful ease when he should have joined his pal; a day of lounging on the wharf, munching the ba-nanas and coconuts scattered in unloading the fruit steamers; and then a feast along the free-lunch counters from which the easy-going owners were too good-natured or too generous to drive him away; and afterward a pipe in one of the little flowery parks and a snooze in some shady corner of the wharf. But here was a stern order to exile, and one that he knew must be obeyed. So, with a wary eye open for the gleam of brass buttons, he began his retreat toward a rural refuge. A few days in the country need not nec-essarily prove disastrous. Beyond the possibility of a slight nip of frost, there was no formidable evil to be looked for.

However, it was with a depressed spirit that Whistling Dick passed the old French market on his chosen route down the river. For safety's sake he still presented to the world his portrayal of the part of the worthy artisan on his way to labor. A stall-keeper in the market, undeceived, hailed him by the generic name of his ilk, and "Jack" halted, taken by surprise. The vendor, melted by this proof of his own acuteness, bestowed a foot of frankfurter and half a loaf, and thus the problem of breakfast was solved.

When the streets, from topographical reasons, began to shun the riverbank the exile mounted to the top of the levee, and on its well-trodden path pursued his way. The suburban eye regarded him with cold suspicion, individuals reflected the stern spirit of the city's heartless edict. He missed the seclusion of the crowded town and the safety he could always find in the multitude.

At Chalmette, six miles upon his desultory way, there suddenly menaced him a vast and bewildering industry. A new port was being established; the dock was being built, compresses were going up; picks and shovels and barrows struck at him like serpents from every side. An arrogant foreman bore down upon him, estimating his muscles with the eye of a recruiting-sergeant. Brown men and black men all about him were toiling away. He fled in terror.

By noon he had reached the country of the plantations, the great, sad, silent levels bordering the mighty river. He overlooked fields of sugar-cane so vast that their farthest limits melted into the sky. The sugar-making season was well advanced, and the cutters were at work; the waggons creaked drearily after them; the Negro teamsters inspired the mules to greater speed with mellow and sonorous imprecations. Dark-green groves, blurred by the blue of distance, showed where the plantation-houses stood. The tall chimneys of the sugar-mills caught the eye miles distant, like light-houses at sea.

At a certain point Whistling Dick's unerring nose caught the scent of frying fish. Like a pointer to a quail, he made his way down the levee side straight to the camp of a credulous and ancient fisherman, whom he charmed with song and story, so that he dined like an admiral, and then like a philosopher annihilated the worst three hours of the day by a nap under the trees.

When he awoke and again continued his hegira, a frosty sparkle in the air had succeeded the drowsy warmth of the day, and as this portent of a chilly night translated itself to the brain of Sir Peregrine, he lengthened his stride and bethought him of shelter. He travelled a road that faithfully followed the convolutions of the levee, running along its base, but whither he knew not. Bushes and rank grass crowded it to the wheel ruts, and out of this ambuscade the pests of the lowlands swarmed after him, humming a keen, vicious soprano. And as the night grew nearer, although colder, the whine of the mosquitoes became a greedy, petulant snarl that shut out all other sounds. To his right, against the heavens, he saw a green light moving, and, accompanying it, the masts and funnels of a big incoming steamer, moving as upon a screen at a magic-lantern show. And there were mysterious marshes at his left, out of which came queer gurgling cries and a choked croaking. The whistling vagrant struck up a merry warble to offset these melancholy influences, and it is likely that never before, since Pan himself jigged it on his reeds, had such sounds been heard in those depressing solitudes.

A distant clatter in the rear quickly developed into the swift beat of horses' hoofs, and Whistling Dick stepped aside into the dew-wet grass to clear the track. Turning his head, he saw approaching a fine team of stylish grays drawing a double surrey. A stout man with a white mustache occupied the front seat, giving all his attention to the rigid lines in his hands. Behind him sat a placid, middle-aged lady and a brilliant-looking girl hardly arrived at young ladyhood. The lap-robe had slipped partly from the knees of the gentleman driving, and Whistling Dick saw two stout canvas bags between his feet—bags such as, while loafing in cities, he had seen warily transferred between express waggons and bank doors. The remaining space in the vehicle was filled with parcels of various sizes and shapes.

As the surrey swept even with the sidetracked tramp, the bright-eyed girl, seized by some merry, madcap impulse, leaned out toward him with a sweet, dazzling smile, and cried, "Mer-ry Christmas!" in a shrill, plaintive treble.

Such a thing had not often happened to Whistling Dick, and he felt handicapped in devising the correct response. But lacking time for reflection, he let his instinct decide, and snatching off his battered derby, he rapidly extended it at arm's length, and drew it back with a continuous motion, and shouted a loud, but ceremonious, "Ah, there!" after the flying surrey.

The sudden movement of the girl had caused one of the parcels to become unwrapped, and something limp and black fell from it into the road. The tramp picked it up, and found it to be a new black silk stocking, long and fine and slender. It crunched crisply, and yet with a luxurious softness, between his fingers.

"Ther bloomin' little skeezicks!" said Whistling Dick, with a broad grin bisecting his freckled face. "W'ot d' yer think of dat, now! Mer-ry Chris-mus! Sounded like a cuckoo clock, dat's what she did. Dem guys is swells too, bet yer life, an' der old 'un stacks dem sacks of dough down under his trotters like dey was common as dried apples. Been shoppin' for Chrismus, and de kid's lost one of her new socks w'ot she was goin' to hold up Santy wid. De bloomin' little skeezicks! Wit' her *Mer-ry Chris-mus!* W'ot d' yer t'ink! Same as to say, *Hello, Jack, how goes it?* and as swell as Fift' Av'noo, and as easy as a blowout in Cincinnat."

Whistling Dick folded the stocking carefully, and stuffed it into his pocket.

It was nearly two hours later when he came upon signs of habitation. The buildings of an extensive plantation were brought into view by a turn in the road. He easily selected the planter's residence in a large square building with two wings, with numerous good-sized, well-lighted windows, and broad verandas running around its full extent. It was set upon a smooth lawn, which was faintly lit by the far-reaching rays of the lamps within. A noble grove surrounded it, and old-fashioned shrubbery grew thickly about the walks and fences. The quarters of the hands and the mill buildings were situated at a distance in the rear.

The road was now enclosed on each side by a fence, and presently, as Whistling Dick drew nearer the house, he suddenly stopped and sniffed the air.

"If dere ain't a hobo stew cookin' somewhere in dis immediate precinct," he said to himself, "me nose has quit tellin' de trut'."

Without hesitation he climbed the fence to windward. He found himself in an apparently disused lot, where piles of old bricks were stacked, and rejected, decaying lumber. In a corner he saw the faint glow of a fire that had become little more than a bed of living coals, and he thought he could see some dim human forms sitting or lying about it. He drew nearer, and by the light of a little blaze that suddenly flared up he saw plainly the fat figure of a ragged man in an old brown sweater and cap.

"Dat man," said Whistling Dick to himself softly, "is a dead ringer for Boston Harry. I'll try him wit' de high sign."

He whistled one or two bars of a rag-time melody, and the air was immediately taken up, and then quickly ended with a peculiar run. The first whistler walked confidently up to the fire. The fat man looked up, and spake in a loud, asthmatic wheeze:

"Gents, the unexpected but welcome addition to our circle is Mr. Whistling Dick, an old friend of mine for whom I fully vouches. The waiter will lay another cover at once. Mr. W.D. will join us at supper, during which function he will enlighten us in regard to the circumstances that gave us the pleasure of his company."

"Chewin' de stuffin' out 'n de dictionary, as usual, Boston," said Whistling Dick. "But t'anks all de same for de invitashun. I guess I finds meself here about de same way as yous guys. A cop gimme de tip dis mornin'. Yous workin' on dis farm?"

"A guest," said Boston, sternly, "shouldn't never insult his entertainers until he's filled up wit' grub. 'Tain't good business sense. Workin'!—but I will restrain myself. We five—me, Deaf Pete, Blinky, Goggles, and Indiana Tom—got put on to this scheme of Noo Orleans to work visiting gentlemen upon her dirty streets, and we hit the road last evening just as the tender hues of twilight had flopped down upon the daisies and things. Blinky, pass the empty oyster-can at your left to the empty gentleman at your right."

For the next ten minutes the gang of roadsters paid their un-divided attention to the supper. In an old five-gallon kerosene can they had cooked a stew of potatoes, meat, and onions, which they partook of from smaller cans they had found scattered about the vacant lot.

Whistling Dick had known Boston Harry of old, and knew him to be one of the shrewdest and most successful of his brother-hood. He looked like a prosperous stock-drover or solid merchant from some country village. He was stout and hale, with a ruddy, always smoothly shaven face. His clothes were strong and neat, and he gave special attention to his decent-appearing shoes. Dur-ing the past ten years he had acquired a reputation for working a larger number of successfully managed confidence games than any of his acquaintances, and he had not a day's work to be counted against him. It was rumored among his associates that he had saved a considerable amount of money. The four other men were fair specimens of the slinking, ill-clad, noisome genus who carried their labels of "suspicious" in plain view.

After the bottom of the large can had been scraped, and pipes lit at the coals, two of the men called Boston aside and spake with him lowly and mysteriously. He nodded decisively, and then said aloud to Whistling Dick:

"Listen, sonny, to some plain talky-talk. We five are on a lay. I've guaranteed you to be square, and you're to come in on the profits equal with the boys, and you've got to help. Two hundred hands on this plantation are expecting to be paid a week's wages to-morrow morning. To-morrow's Christmas, and they want to lay off. Says the boss: *Work from five to nine in the morning to get a train load of sugar off, and I'll pay every man cash down for the week and a day extra.* They say: *Hooray for the boss! It goes.* He drives to Noo Orleans to-day, and fetches back the cold dollars. Two thousand and seventy-four fifty is the amount. I got the figures from a man who talks too much, who got 'em from the bookkeeper. The boss of this plantation thinks he's going to pay this wealth to the hands. He's got it down wrong; he's going to pay it to us. It's going to stay in the leisure class, where it belongs. Now, half of this haul goes to me, and the other half the rest of you may divide. Why the difference? I represent the brains. It's my scheme. Here's the way we're going to get it. There's some company at supper in the house, but they'll leave about nine. They've just happened in for an hour or so. If they don't go pretty soon, we'll work the scheme anyhow. We want all night to get away good with the dollars. They're heavy. About nine o'clock Deaf Pete and Blinky'll go down the road about a quarter beyond the house, and set fire to a big cane-field there that the cutters haven't touched yet. The wind's just right to have it roaring in two minutes. The alarm'll be given, and every man Jack about the place will be down there in ten minutes, fighting fire. That'll leave the money sacks and the women alone in the house for us to handle. You've heard cane burn? Well, there's mighty few women can screech loud enough to be heard above its crackling. The thing's dead safe. The only danger is in being caught before we can get far enough away with the money. Now, if you—"

"Boston," interrupted Whistling Dick, rising to his feet, "t'anks for the grub yous fellers has given me, but I'll be movin' on now."

"What do you mean?" asked Boston, also rising.

"W'y, you can count me outer dis deal. You oughter know that. I'm on de bum all right enough, but dat other t'ing don't go wit' me. Burglary is no good. I'll say good night and many t'anks fer—"

Whistling Dick had moved away a few steps as he spoke, but he stopped very suddenly. Boston had covered him with a short revolver of roomy caliber.

"Take your seat," said the tramp leader. "I'd feel mighty proud of myself if I let you go and spoil the game. You'll stick right in this camp until we finish the job. The end of that brick pile is your limit. You go two inches beyond that, and I'll have to shoot. Better take it easy, now."

"It's my way of doin'," said Whistling Dick. "Easy goes. You can depress de muzzle of dat twelve-incher, and run 'er back on de trucks. I remains, as de newspapers says, *in yer midst*."

"All right," said Boston, lowering his piece, as the other returned and took his seat again on a projecting plank in a pile of timber. "Don't try to leave; that's all. I wouldn't miss this chance even if I had to shoot an old acquaintance to make it go. I don't want to hurt anybody specially, but this thousand dollars I'm going to get will fix me for fair. I'm going to drop the road, and start a saloon in a little town I know about. I'm tired of being kicked around."

Boston Harry took from his pocket a cheap silver watch, and held it near the fire.

"It's a quarter to nine," he said. "Pete, you and Blinky start. Go down the road past the house, and fire the cane in a dozen places. Then strike for the levee, and come back on it, instead of the road, so you won't meet anybody. By the time you get back the men will all be striking out for the fire, and we'll break for the house and collar the dollars. Everybody cough up what matches he's got."

The two surly tramps made a collection of all the matches in the party, Whistling Dick contributing his quota with propitiatory alacrity, and then they departed in the dim starlight in the direction of the road.

Of the three remaining vagrants, two, Goggles and Indiana Tom, reclined lazily upon convenient lumber and regarded Whistling Dick with undisguised disfavor. Boston, observing that the dissenting recruit was disposed to remain peaceably, relaxed a little of his vigilance. Whistling Dick arose presently and strolled leisurely up and down keeping carefully within the territory assigned him.

"Dis planter chap," he said, pausing before Boston Harry,

"w'ot makes yer t'ink he's got de tin in de house wit' 'im?"

"I'm advised of the facts in the case," said Boston. "He drove to Noo Orleans and got it, I say, to-day. Want to change your mind now and come in?"

"Naw, I was just askin'. W'ot kind o' team did de boss drive?"

"Pair of grays."

"Double surrey?"

"Yep."

"Women folks along?"

"Wife and kid. Say, what morning paper are you trying to pump news for?"

"I was just conversin' to pass de time away. I guess dat team passed me in de road dis evenin'. Dat's all."

As Whistling Dick put his hands in his pockets and continued his curtailed beat up and down by the fire, he felt the silk stocking he had picked up in the road.

"Ther bloomin' little skeezicks," he muttered, with a grin.

As he walked up and down he could see, through a sort of natural opening or lane among the trees, the planter's residence some seventy-five yards distant. The side of the house toward him exhibited spacious, well-lighted windows through which a soft radiance streamed, illuminating the broad veranda and some extent of the lawn beneath.

"What's that you said?" asked Boston, sharply.

"Oh, nuttin' 't all," said Whistling Dick, lounging carelessly, and kicking meditatively at a little stone on the ground. "Just as easy," continued the warbling vagrant softly to himself, "an' sociable an' swell an' sassy, wit' her *Mer-ry Chris-mus*. W'ot d'yer t'ink, now!"

Dinner, two hours late, was being served in the Bellemeade plantation dining-room.

The dining-room and all its appurtenances spoke of an old regime that was here continued rather than suggested to the memory. The plate was rich to the extent that its age and quaintness alone saved it from being showy; there were interesting names signed in the corners of the pictures on the walls; the viands were of the kind that bring a shine into the eyes of gourmets. The service was swift, silent, lavish, as in the days when the waiters were assets like the plate. The names by which the planter's family and their visitors addressed one another were historic in the annals of two nations. Their manners and conversation had that most difficult kind of ease—the kind that still preserves punctilio. The planter himself seemed to be the dynamo that generated the larger portion of the gaiety and wit. The younger ones at the board found it more than difficult to turn back on him his guns of raillery and banter. It is true, the young men attempted to storm his works repeatedly, incited by the hope of gaining the approbation of their fair companions; but even when they sped a well-aimed shaft, the planter forced them to feel defeat by the tremendous discomfiting thunder of the laughter with which he accompanied his retorts. At the head of the table, serene, matronly, benevolent, reigned the mistress of the house, placing here and there the right smile, the right word, the encouraging glance.

The talk of the party was too desultory, too evanescent to follow, but at last they came to the subject of the tramp nuisance, one that had of late vexed the plantations for many miles around. The planter seized the occasion to direct his good-natured fire of raillery at the mistress, accusing her of encouraging the plague. "They swarm up and down the river every winter," he said. "They overrun New Orleans, and we catch the surplus, which is generally the worst part. And, a day or two ago, Madame New Orleans, suddenly discovering that she can't go shopping without brushing her skirts against great rows of the vagabonds sunning themselves on the banquettes, says to the police, *Catch 'em all,* and the police catch a dozen or two, and the remaining three or four thousand overflow up and down the levee, and Madame there"—pointing tragically with the carving-knife at her—"feeds them. They won't work; they defy my overseers, and they make friends with my dogs; and you, Madame, feed them before my eyes, and intimidate me when I would interfere. Tell us, please, how many to-day did you thus incite to future laziness and depredation?"

"Six, I think," said Madame, with a reflective smile; "but you know two of them offered to work, for you heard them yourself."

The planter's disconcerting laugh rang out again. "Yes, at their own trades. And one was an artificial-flower maker, and the other a glass-blower. Oh, they were looking for work! Not a hand would they consent to lift to labor of any other kind."

"And another one," continued the soft-hearted mistress, "used quite good language. It was really extraordinary for one of his class. And he carried a watch. And had lived in Boston. I don't believe they are all bad. They have always seemed to me to rather lack development. I always look upon them as children with whom wisdom has remained at a standstill while whiskers have continued to grow. We passed one this evening as we were driving home who had a face as good as it was incompetent. He was whistling the intermezzo from *Cavalleria* and blowing the spirit of Mascagni himself into it."

A bright-eyed young girl who sat at the left of the mistress leaned over, and said in a confidential undertone: "I wonder, Mamma, if that tramp we passed on the road found my stocking, and do you think he will hang it up to-night? Now I can hang up but one. Do you know why I wanted a new pair of silk stockings when I have plenty? Well, old Aunt Judy says if you hang up two that have never been worn, Santa Claus will fill one with good things, and Monsieur Pambe will place in the other payment for all the words you have spoken—good or bad—on the day before Christmas. That's why I've been unusually nice and polite to every-one to-day. Monsieur Pambe, you know, is a witch gentleman; he—"

The words of the young girl were interrupted by a startling thing.

Like the wraith of some burned-out shooting star, a black streak came crashing through the window-pane and upon the table, where it shivered into fragments a dozen pieces of crystal and china ware, and then glanced between the heads of the guests to the wall, imprinting therein a deep, round indentation, at which, to-day, the visitor to Bellemeade marvels as he gazes upon it and listens to this tale as it is told.

The women screamed in many keys, and the men sprang to their feet, and would have laid their hands upon their swords had not the verities of chronology forbidden.

The planter was the first to act; he sprang to the intruding missile, and held it up to view.

"By Jupiter!" he cried. "A meteoric shower of hosiery! Has communication at last been established with Mars?"

"I should say—ahem—Venus," ventured a young-gentleman visitor, looking hopefully for approbation toward the unresponsive young-lady visitors.

The planter held at arm's length the unceremonious visitor—a long dangling black stocking. "It's loaded," he announced.

As he spoke, he reversed the stocking, holding it by the toe, and down from it dropped a roundish stone, wrapped about by a piece of yellowish paper. "Now for the first interstellar message of the century!" he cried; and nodding to the company, who had crowded about him, he adjusted his glasses with provoking deliberation, and examined it closely. When he finished, he had changed from the jolly host to the practical, decisive man of business. He immediately struck a bell, and said to the silent-footed mulatto man who responded: "Go and tell Mr. Wesley to get Reeves and Maurice and about ten stout hands they can rely upon, and come to the hall door at once. Tell him to have the men arm themselves, and bring plenty of ropes and plough lines. Tell him to hurry." And then he read aloud from the paper these words:

To the Gent of de Hous:

Dere is five tuff hoboes xcept meself in the vaken lot near de road war de old brick piles is. Dey got me stuck up wid a gun see and I taken dis means of communication. 2 of der lads is gone down to set fire to de cain field below de hous and when yous fellers goes to turn de hoes on it de hole gang is goin to rob de hous of de money yoo gotto pay off wit say git a move on ye say de kid dropt dis sock in der rode tel her mery crismus de same as she told me. Ketch de bums down de rode first and den sen a relefe core to get me out of soke youres truly,
Whistlen Dick

There was some quiet, but rapid maneuvering at Bellemeade during the ensuing half hour, which ended in five disgusted and sullen tramps being captured, and locked securely in an outhouse pending the coming of the morning and retribution. For another result, the visiting young gentlemen had secured the unqualified worship of the visiting young ladies by their distinguished and heroic conduct. For still another, behold Whistling Dick, the hero, seated at the planter's table, feasting upon viands his experience had never before included, and waited upon by admiring femininity in shapes of such beauty and "swellness" that even his ever-full mouth could scarcely prevent him from whistling. He was made to disclose in detail his adventure with the evil gang of Boston Harry, and how he cunningly wrote the note and wrapped it around the stone and placed it at the toe of the stocking, and, watching his chance, sent it silently, with a wonderful centrifugal momentum, like a comet, at one of the big lighted windows of the dining-room. The planter vowed that the wanderer should wander no more; that his was a goodness and an honesty that should be rewarded, and that a debt of gratitude had been made that must be paid; for had he not saved them from a doubtless imminent loss, and maybe a greater calamity? He assured Whistling Dick that he might consider himself a charge upon the honor of Bellemeade; that a position suited to his powers would be found for him at once, and hinted that the way would be heartily smoothed for him to rise to as high places of emolument and trust as the plantation afforded.

But now, they said, he must be weary, and the immediate thing to consider was rest and sleep. So the mistress spoke to a servant, and Whistling Dick was conducted to a room in the wing of the house occupied by the servants. To this room, in a few minutes, was brought a portable tin bathtub filled with water, which was placed on a piece of oiled cloth upon the floor. There the vagrant was left to pass the night.

By the light of a candle he examined the room. A bed, with the covers neatly turned back, revealed snowy pillows and sheets. A worn but clean red carpet covered the floor. There was a dresser with a beveled mirror, a washstand with a flowered bowl and pitcher; the two or three chairs were softly upholstered. A little table held books, papers, and a day-old cluster of roses in a jar. There were towels on a rack and soap in a white dish.

Whistling Dick set his candle on a chair and placed his hat carefully under the table. After satisfying what we must suppose to have been his curiosity by a sober scrutiny, he removed his coat, folded it, and laid it upon the floor, near the wall, as far as possible from the unused bathtub. Taking his coat for a pillow, he stretched himself luxuriously upon the carpet.

When, on Christmas morning, the first streaks of dawn broke above the marshes, Whistling Dick awoke, and reached instinctively for his hat. Then he remembered that the skirts of Fortune had swept him into their folds on the night previous, and he went to the window and raised it, to let the fresh breath of the morning cool his brow and fix the yet dreamlike memory of his good luck within his brain.

As he stood there, certain dread and ominous sounds pierced the fearful hollow of his ear.

The force of plantation workers, eager to complete the shortened task allotted to them, were all astir. The mighty din of the ogre Labor shook the earth, and the poor tattered and forever disguised Prince in search of his fortune held tight to the window-sill even in the enchanted castle, and trembled.

Already from the bosom of the mill came the thunder of rolling barrels of sugar, and (prison-like sounds) there was a great rattling of chains as the mules were harried with stimulant imprecations to their places by the waggon-tongues. A little vicious "dummy" engine, with a train of flat cars in tow, stewed and fumed on the plantation tap of the narrow-gauge railroad, and a toiling, hurrying, hallooing stream of workers were dimly seen in the half darkness loading the train with the weekly output of sugar. Here was a poem; an epic—nay, a tragedy—with work, the curse of the world, for its theme.

The December air was frosty, but the sweat broke out upon Whistling Dick's face. He thrust his head out of the window, and looked down. Fifteen feet below him, against the wall of the house, he could make out that a border of flowers grew, and by that token he overhung a bed of soft earth.

Softly as a burglar goes, he clambered out upon the sill, lowered himself until he hung by his hands alone, and then dropped safely. No one seemed to be about upon this side of the house. He dodged low, and skimmed swiftly across the yard to the low fence. It was an easy matter to vault this, for a terror urged him such as lifts the gazelle over the thorn bush when the lion pursues. A crash through the dew-drenched weeds on the roadside, a clutching, slippery rush up the grassy side of the levee to the footpath at the summit, and—he was free!

The east was blushing and brightening. The wind, himself a vagrant rover, saluted his brother upon the cheek. Some wild geese, high above, gave cry. A rabbit skipped along the path before him, free to turn to the right or to the left as his mood should send him. The river slid past, and certainly no one could tell the ultimate abiding place of its waters.

A small, ruffled, brown-breasted bird, sitting upon a dog-wood sapling, began a soft, throaty, tender little piping in praise of the dew which entices foolish worms from their holes; but suddenly he stopped, and sat with his head turned sidewise, listening.

From the path along the levee there burst forth a jubilant, stirring, buoyant, thrilling whistle, loud and keen and clear as the cleanest notes of the piccolo. The soaring sound rippled and trilled and arpeggioed as the songs of wild birds do not; but it had a wild free grace that, in a way, reminded the small brown bird of something familiar, but exactly what he could not tell. There was in it the bird call, or reveille, that all birds know; but a great waste of lavish, unmeaning things that art had added and arranged, besides, and that were quite puzzling and strange; and the little brown bird sat with his head on one side until the sound died away in the distance.

The little bird did not know that the part of that strange warbling that he understood was just what kept the warbler without his breakfast; but he knew very well that the part he did not understand did not concern him, so he gave a little flutter of his wings and swooped down like a brown bullet upon a big fat worm that was wriggling along the levee path.

PART II
SWEET BIRD OF YOUTH

THE PURPLE HAT

BY Eudora Welty

Upper Quarter

(Originally published in 1941)

I t was in a bar, a quiet little hole in the wall. It was four o'clock in the afternoon. Beyond the open door the rain fell, the heavy color of the sea, in air where the sunlight was still suspended. Its watery reflection lighted the room, as a room might have lighted a mousehole. It was in New Orleans.

There was a bartender whose mouth and eyes curved downward from the divide of his baby-pink nose, as if he had combed them down, like his hair; he always just said nothing. The seats at his bar were black oilcloth knobs, worn and smooth and as much alike as six pebbles on the beach, and yet the two customers had chosen very particularly the knobs they would sit on. They had come in separately out of the wet, and had each chosen an end stool, and now sat with the length of the little bar between them. The bartender obviously did not know either one; he rested his eyes by closing them . . .

The fat customer, with a rather affable look about him, said he would have a rye. The unshaven young man with the shaking hands, though he had come in first, only looked fearfully at a spot on the counter before him until the bartender, as if he could hear silent prayer, covered the spot with a drink.

The fat man swallowed, and began at once to look a little cozy and prosperous. He seemed ready to speak, if the moment came . . .

There was a calm roll of thunder, no more than a shifting of the daily rain clouds over Royal Street.

Then—"Rain or shine," the fat man spoke, "she'll be there."

The bartender stilled his cloth on the bar, as if mopping up made a loud noise, and waited.

"Why, at the Palace of Pleasure," said the fat man. He was really more heavy and solid than he was simply fat.

The bartender leaned forward an inch on his hand.

"The lady will be at the Palace of Pleasure," said the fat man in his drowsy voice. "The lady with the purple hat."

Then the fat man turned on the black knob, put his elbow on the counter, and rested his cheek on his hand, where he could see all the way down the bar. For a moment his eyes seemed dancing there, above one of those hands so short and so plump that you are always counting the fingers . . . really helpless-looking hands for so large a man.

The young man stared back without much curiosity, looking at the affable face much the way you stare out at a little station where your train is passing through. His hand alone found its place on his small glass.

"Oh, the hat she wears is a creation," said the fat man, al- most dreamily, yet not taking his eyes from the young man. It was strange that he did not once regard the bartender, who after all had done him the courtesy of asking a polite question or two, or at least the same as asked. "A great and ancient and bedraggled purple hat."

There was another rumble overhead. Here they seemed to in- habit the world that was just beneath the thunder. The fat man let it go by, lifting his little finger like a pianist. Then he went on.

"Sure, she's one of those thousands of middle-aged women who come every day to the Palace, would not be kept away by anything on earth . . . Most of them are dull enough, drab old creatures, all of them, walking in with their big black purses held wearily by the handles like suitcases packed for a trip. No one has ever been able to find out how all these old creatures can leave their lives at home like that to gamble . . . what their husbands think . . . who keeps the house in order . . . who pays . . . At any rate, she is one like the rest, except for the hat, and except for the young man that always meets her there, from year to year . . . And I think she is a ghost."

"Ghost!" said the bartender—noncommittally, just as he might repeat an order.

"For this reason," said the fat man.

A reminiscent tone came into his voice which seemed to put the silent thin young man on his guard. He made the beginning of a gesture toward the bottle. The bartender was already filling his glass.

"In thirty years she has not changed," said the fat man. "Neither has she changed her hat. Dear God, how the moths must have hungered for that hat. But she has kept it in full bloom on her head, that monstrosity—purple too, as if she were beautiful in the bargain. She has not aged, but she keeps her middle age. The young man, on the other hand, must change—I'm sure he's not always the same young man. For thirty years," he said, "she's met a young man at the dice table every afternoon, rain or shine, at five o'clock, and gambles till midnight and tells him good-bye, and still it looks to be always the same young man—always young, but a little stale, a little tired . . . the smudge of a sideburn . . . She finds them, she does. She picks them. Where I don't know, unless New Orleans, as I've always had a guess, is the birthplace of ready-made victims."

"Who are you?" asked the young man. It was the sort of idle voice in which the greatest wildness sometimes speaks out at last in a quiet bar.

"In the Palace of Pleasure there is a little catwalk along beneath the dome," said the fat man. His rather small, mournful lips, such as big men often have, now parted in a vague smile. "I am the man whose eyes look out over the gambling room. I am the armed man that everyone knows to be watching, at all they do. I don't believe my position is dignified by a title." Nevertheless, he looked rather pleased. "I have watched her every day for thirty years and I think she is a ghost. I have seen her murdered twice," said the fat man.

The bartender's enormous sad black eyebrows raised, like hoods on baby carriages, and showed his round eyes.

The fat man lifted his other fat little hand and studied, or rather showed off, a ruby ring that he wore on his little finger. "That carpet, if you have ever been there, in the Palace of Pleasure, is red, but from up above, it changes and gives off light between the worn crisscrossing of the aisles like the facets of a well-cut ruby," he said, speaking in a declarative manner as if he had been waiting for a chance to deliver this enviable comparison. "The tables and chandeliers are far down below me, points in its interior . . . Life in the ruby. And yet somehow all that people do is clear and lucid and authentic there, as if it were magnified in the red lens, not made smaller. I can see everything in the world from my catwalk. You mustn't think I brag . . ." He looked all at once from his ring straight at the young man's face, which was as drained and white as ever, expressionless, with a thin drop of whiskey running down his cheek where he had blundered with his glass.

"I have seen this old and disgusting creature in her purple hat every night, quite plainly, for thirty years, and to my belief she has been murdered twice. I suppose it will take the third time." He himself smoothly tossed down a drink.

The bartender leaned over and filled the young man's glass.

"It's within the week, within the month, that she comes back. Once she was shot point-blank—that was the first time. The young man was hot-headed then. I saw her carried out bleeding from the face. We hush those things, you know, at the Palace. There are no signs afterward, no trouble . . . The soft red carpet . . . Within the month she was back—with her young man meeting her at the table just after five."

The bartender put his head to one side.

"The only good of shooting her was, it made a brief period of peace there," said the fat man. "I wouldn't scoff, if I were you." He did seem the least bit fretted by that kind of interruption.

"The second time took into account the hat," he went on. "And I do think her young man was on his way toward the right idea that time, the secret. I think he had learned something. Or he wanted it all kept more quiet, or he was a new one . . ." He looked at the young man at the other end of the bar with a patient, compassionate expression, or it may have been the inevitably tender contour of his round cheeks. "It is time that I told you about the hat. It is quite a hat. A great, wide, deep hat such as has no fashion and never knew there was fashion and change. It serves her to come out in winter and summer. Those are old plush flowers that trim it—roses? Poppies? A man wouldn't know easily. And you would never know if you only met her wearing the hat that a little glass vial with a plunger helps decorate the crown. You would have to see it from above . . . Or you would need to be the young man sitting beside her at the gambling table when, at some point in the evening, she takes the hat off and lays it carefully in her lap, under the table . . . Then you might notice the little vial, and be attracted to it and wish to take it out and examine it at your pleasure off in the washroom—to admire the handle, for instance, which is red glass, like the petal of an artificial flower."

The bartender suddenly lifted his hand to his mouth as if it held a glass, and yawned into it. The thin young man hit the counter faintly with his tumbler.

"She does more than just that, though," said the fat man with a little annoyance in his soft voice. "Perhaps I haven't explained that she is a lover too, or did you know that she would be? It is hard to make it clear to a man who has never been out to the Palace of Pleasure, but only serves drinks all day behind a bar. You see . . ." And now, lowering his voice a little, he deliberately turned from the young man and would not look at him anymore. But the young man looked at him, without lifting his drink—as if there were something hypnotic and irresistible even about his side face with the round, hiding cheek.

"Try to imagine," the fat man was saying gently to the bartender, who looked back at him. "At some point in the evening she always takes off the purple hat. Usually it is very late . . . when it is almost time for her to go. The young man who has come to the rendezvous watches her until she removes it, watches her hungrily. Is it in order to see her hair? Well, most ghosts that are lovers, and lovers that are ghosts, have the long thick black hair that you would expect, and hers is no exception to the rule. It is pinned up, of course—in her straggly vague way. But the young man doesn't look at it after all. He is enamored of her hat—her ancient, battered, outrageous hat with the awful plush flowers. She lays it down below the level of the table there, on her shabby old lap, and he caresses it . . . Well, I suppose in this town there are stranger forms of love than that, and who are any of us to say what ways people may not find to love? She herself, you know, seems perfectly satisfied with it. And yet she must not be satisfied, being a ghost . . . Does it matter how she seeks her desire? I am sure she speaks to him, in a sort of purr, the purr that is used for talking in that room, and the young man does not know what she seeks of him, and she is leading him on, all the time. What does she say? I do not know. But believe me . . . she leads him on . . ."

The bartender leaned on one hand. He had an oddly cheerful look by this time, as if with strange and sad things to come his way his outlook became more vivacious.

"To look at, she has a large-sized head," said the fat man, pushing his lip with his short finger. "Well, it is more that her face spreads over such a wide area. Like the moon's . . . Much as I have studied her, I can only say that all her features seem to have moved farther apart from each other—expanded, if you see what I mean." He brought his hands together and parted them.

The bartender leaned over closer, staring at the fat man's face interestedly.

"But I can never finish telling you about the hat!" the fat man cried, and there was a little sigh somewhere in the room, very young, like a child's. "Of course, to balance the weight of the attractive little plunger, there is an object to match on the other side of this marvelous old hat—a jeweled hatpin, no less. Of course the pin is there to keep the hat safe! Each time she takes off the hat, she has first to remove the hatpin. You can see her do it every night of the world. It comes out a regular little flashing needle, ten or twelve inches long, and after she has taken the hat off, she sticks the pin back through."

The bartender pursed his lips.

"What about the second time she was murdered? Have you wondered how that was done?" The fat man turned back to face the young fellow, whose feet drove about beneath the stool. "The young lover had learned something, or come to some conclusion, you see," he said. "It was obvious all the time, of course, that by spinning the brim ever so easily as it rested on the lady's not over-sensitive old knees, it would be possible to remove the *opposite* ornament. There was not the slightest fuss or outcry when the pin entered between the ribs and pierced the heart. No one saw it done . . . except for me, naturally—I had been watching for it, more or less. The old creature, who had been winning at that, simply folded all softly in on herself, like a circus tent being taken down after the show, if you've ever seen the sight. I saw her carried out again. It takes three big boys every time, she is so heavy, and one of them always has the presence of mind to cover her piously with her old purple hat for the occasion."

The bartender shut his eyes distastefully.

"If you had ever been to the Palace of Pleasure, you'd know it all went completely as usual—people at the tables never turn around," said the fat man.

The bartender ran his hand down the side of his sad smooth hair.

"The trouble lies, you see," said the fat man, "with the young lover. You are he, let us say . . ." But he turned from the drinking young man, and it was the bartender who was asked to be the lover for the moment. "After a certain length of time goes by, and love has blossomed, and the hat, the purple hat, is thrilling to the touch of your hand—you can no longer be sure about the little vial. There in privacy you may find it to be empty. It is her coquettishness, you see. She leads you on. You are never to know whether . . ."

The chimes of St. Louis Cathedral went somnambulantly through the air. It was five o'clock. The young man had risen somehow to his feet. He moved out of the bar and disappeared in the rain of the alley. On the floor where his feet had been were old cigarette stubs that had been kicked and raked into a little circle—a rosette, a clock, a game wheel, or something . . .

The bartender put a cork in the bottle.

"I have to go myself," said the fat man.

Once more the bartender raised his great hooded brows. For a moment their eyes met. The fat man pulled out an enormous roll of worn bills. He paid in full for all drinks and added a nice tip.

"Up on the catwalk you get the feeling now and then that you could put out your finger and make a change in the universe." His great shoulders lifted.

The bartender, with his hands full of cash, leaned confidentially over the bar. "Is she a real ghost?" he asked, in a real whisper.

There was a pause, which the thunder filled.
"I'll let you know tomorrow," said the fat man.
Then he too was gone.

DESIRE AND THE BLACK MASSEUR

BY TENNESSEE WILLIAMS

Tremé

(Originally published in 1948)

From his very beginning this person, Anthony Burns, had betrayed an instinct for being included in things that swallowed him up. In his family there had been fifteen children and he the one given least notice, and when he went to work, after graduating from high school in the largest class on the records of that institution, he secured his job in the largest wholesale company of the city. Everything absorbed him and swallowed him up, and still he did not feel secure. He felt more secure at the movies than anywhere else. He loved to sit in the back rows of the movies where the darkness absorbed him gently so that he was like a particle of food dissolving in a big hot mouth. The cinema licked at his mind with a tender, flickering tongue that all but lulled him to sleep. Yes, a big motherly Nannie of a dog could not have licked him better or given him sweeter repose than the cinema did when he went there after work. His mouth would fall open at the movies and saliva would accumulate in it and dribble out the sides of it and all his being would relax so utterly that all the prickles and tightenings of a whole day's anxiety would be lifted away. He didn't follow the story on the screen but watched the figures. What they said or did was immaterial to him, he cared about only the figures who warmed him as if they were cuddled right next to him in the dark picture house and he loved every one of them but the ones with shrill voices.

The timidest kind of a person was Anthony Burns, always scuttling from one kind of protection to another but none of them ever being durable enough to suit him.

Now at the age of thirty, by virtue of so much protection, he still had in his face and body the unformed look of a child and he moved like a child in the presence of critical elders. In every move of his body and every inflection of speech and cast of expression there was a timid apology going out to the world for the little space that he had been somehow elected to occupy in it. His was not an inquiring type of mind. He only learned what he was required to learn and about himself he learned nothing. He had no idea of what his real desires were. Desire is something that is made to occupy a larger space than that which is afforded by the individual being, and this was especially true in the case of Anthony Burns. His desires, or rather his basic desire, was so much too big for him that it swallowed him up as a coat that should have been cut into ten smaller sizes, or rather there should have been that much more of Burns to make it fit him.

For the sins of the world are really only its partialities, its incompletions, and these are what sufferings must atone for. A wall that has been omitted from a house because the stones were exhausted, a room in a house left unfurnished because the householder's funds were not sufficient—these sorts of incompletions are usually covered up or glossed over by some kind of makeshift arrangement. The nature of man is full of such makeshift arrangements, devised by himself to cover his incompletion. He feels a part of himself to be like a missing wall or a room left unfurnished and he tries as well as he can to make up for it. The use of imagination, resorting to dreams or the loftier purpose of art, is a mask he devises to cover his incompletion. Or violence such as a war, between two men or among a number of nations, is also a blind and senseless compensation for that which is not yet formed in human nature. Then there is still another compensation. This one is found in the principle of atonement, the surrender of self to violent treatment by others with the idea of thereby clearing one's self of his guilt. This last way was the one that Anthony Burns unconsciously had elected.

Now at the age of thirty he was about to discover the instrument of his atonement. Like all other happenings in his life, it came about without intention or effort.

One afternoon, which was a Saturday afternoon in November, he went from his work in the huge wholesale corporation to a place with a red neon sign that said, *Turkish Baths and Massage*. He had been suffering lately from a vague sort of ache near the base of his spine and somebody else employed at the wholesale corporation had told him that he would be relieved by massage. You would suppose that the mere suggestion of such a thing would frighten him out of his wits, but when desire lives constantly with fear, and no partition between them, desire must become very tricky; it has to become as sly as the adversary, and this was one of those times when desire outwitted the enemy under the roof. At the very mention of the word *massage*, the desire woke up and exuded a sort of anesthetizing vapor all through Burns's nerves, catching fear off guard and allowing Burns to slip by it. Almost without knowing that he was really going, he went to the baths that Saturday afternoon.

The baths were situated in the basement of a hotel, right at the center of the keyed-up mercantile nerves of the downtown section, and yet the baths were a tiny world of their own. Secrecy was the atmosphere of the place and seemed to be its purpose. The entrance door had an oval of milky glass through which you could only detect a glimmer of light. And even when a patron had been admitted, he found himself standing in labyrinths of partitions, of corridors and cubicles curtained off from each other, of chambers with opaque doors and milky globes over lights and sheathings of vapor. Everywhere were agencies of concealment. The bodies of patrons, divested of their clothing, were swatched in billowing tent-like sheets of white fabric. They trailed barefooted along the moist white tiles, as white and noiseless as ghosts except for their breathing, and their faces all wore a nearly vacant expression. They drifted as if they had no thought to conduct them.

But now and again, across the central hallway, would step a masseur. The masseurs were Negroes. They seemed very dark and positive against the loose white hangings of the baths. They wore no sheets, they had on loose cotton drawers, and they moved about with force and resolution. They alone seemed to have an authority here. Their voices rang out boldly, never whispering in the sort of apologetic way that the patrons had in asking directions of them. This was their own rightful province, and they swept the white hangings aside with great black palms that you felt might just as easily have seized bolts of lightning and thrown them back at the clouds.

Anthony Burns stood more uncertainly than most near the entrance of the bathhouse. Once he had gotten through the milky-paned door his fate was decided and no more action or will on his part was called for. He paid two-fifty, which was the price of a bath and massage, and from that moment forward had only to follow directions and submit to care. Within a few moments a Negro masseur came to Burns and propelled him onward and then around a corner where he was led into one of the curtained compartments.

Take off your clothes, said the Negro.

The Negro had already sensed an unusual something about his latest patron and so he did not go out of the canvas-draped cubicle but remained leaning against a wall while Burns obeyed and undressed. The white man turned his face to the wall away from the Negro and fumbled awkwardly with his dark winter clothes. It took him a long time to get the clothes off his body, not because he wilfully lingered about it but because of a dreamlike state in which he was deeply falling. A faraway feeling engulfed him and his hands and fingers did not seem to be his own, they were numb and hot as if they were caught in the clasp of someone standing behind him, manipulating their motions. But at last he stood naked, and when he turned slowly about to face the Negro masseur, the black giant's eyes appeared not to see him at all and yet they had a glitter not present before, a liquid brightness suggesting bits of wet coal.

Put this on, he directed and held out to Burns a white sheet.

Gratefully the little man enveloped himself in the enormous coarse fabric and, holding it delicately up from his small-boned, womanish feet, he followed the Negro masseur through another corridor of rustling white curtains to the entrance of an opaque glass enclosure which was the steam-room. There his conductor left him. The blank walls heaved and sighed as steam issued from them. It swirled about Burns's naked figure, enveloping him in a heat and moisture such as the inside of a tremendous mouth, to be drugged and all but dissolved in this burning white vapor which hissed out of unseen walls.

After a time the black masseur returned. With a mumbled command, he led the trembling Burns back into the cubicle where he had left his clothes. A bare white table had been wheeled into the chamber during Burns's absence.

Lie on this, said the Negro.

Burns obeyed. The black masseur poured alcohol on Burns's body, first on his chest and then on his belly and thighs. It ran all over him, biting at him like insects. He gasped a little and crossed his legs over the wild complaint of his groin. Then without any warning the Negro raised up his black palm and brought it down with a terrific whack on the middle of Burns's soft belly. The little man's breath flew out of his mouth in a gasp and for two or three moments he couldn't inhale another.

Immediately after the passing of the first shock, a feeling of pleasure went through him. It swept as a liquid from either end of his body and into the tingling hollow of his groin. He dared not look, but he knew what the Negro must see. The black giant was grinning.

I hope I didn't hit you too hard, he murmured.

No, said Burns.

Turn over, said the Negro.

Burns tried vainly to move but the luxurious tiredness made him unable to. The Negro laughed and gripped the small of his waist and flopped him over as easily as he might have turned a pillow. Then he began to belabor his shoulders and buttocks with blows that increased in violence, and as the violence and the pain increased, the little man grew more and more fiercely hot with his first true satisfaction, until all at once a knot came loose in his loins and released a warm flow.

So by surprise is a man's desire discovered, and once discovered, the only need is surrender, to take what comes and ask no questions about it: and this was something that Burns was expressly made for.

Time and again the white-collar clerk went back to the Negro masseur. The knowledge grew quickly between them of what Burns wanted, that he was in search of atonement, and the black masseur was the natural instrument of it. He hated white-skinned bodies because they abused his pride. He loved to have their white skin prone beneath him, to bring his fist or the palm of his hand down hard on its passive surface. He had barely been able to hold this love in restraint, to control the wish that he felt to pound more fiercely and use the full of his power. But now at long last the suitable person had entered his orbit of passion. In the white-collar clerk he had located all that he longed for.

Those times when the black giant relaxed, when he sat at the rear of the baths and smoked cigarettes or devoured a bar of candy, the image of Burns would loom before his mind, a nude white body with angry red marks on it. The bar of chocolate would stop just short of his lips and the lips would slacken into a dreamy smile. The giant loved Burns, and Burns adored the giant.

Burns had become absentminded about his work. Right in the middle of typing a factory order, he would lean back at his desk and the giant would swim in the atmosphere before him. Then he would smile and his work-stiffened fingers would loosen and flop on the desk. Sometimes the boss would stop near him and call his name crossly. Burns! Burns! What are you dreaming about?

Throughout the winter the violence of the massage increased by fairly reasonable degrees, but when March came it was suddenly stepped up.

Burns left the baths one day with two broken ribs.

Every morning he hobbled to work more slowly and painfully but the state of his body could still be explained by saying he had rheumatism.

One day his boss asked him what he was doing for it. He told his boss that he was taking massage.

It don't seem to do you any good, said the boss.

Oh, yes, said Burns, I am showing lots of improvement!

That evening came his last visit to the baths.

His right leg was fractured. The blow which had broken the limb was so terrific that Burns had been unable to stifle an outcry. The manager of the bath establishment heard it and came into the compartment.

Burns was vomiting over the edge of the table.

Christ, said the manager, what's been going on here?

The black giant shrugged.

He asked me to hit him harder.

The manager looked over Burns and discovered his many bruises.

What do you think this is? A jungle? he asked the masseur.

Again the black giant shrugged.

Get the hell out of my place! the manager shouted. Take this perverted little monster with you, and neither of you had better show up here again!

The black giant tenderly lifted his drowsy partner and bore him away to a room in the town's Negro section.

There for a week the passion between them continued.

This interval was toward the end of the Lenten season. Across from the room where Burns and the Negro were staying there was a church whose open windows spilled out the mounting exhortations of a preacher. Each afternoon the fiery poem of death on the cross was repeated. The preacher was not fully conscious of what he wanted nor were the listeners, groaning and writhing before him. All of them were involved in a massive atonement.

Now and again some manifestation occurred, a woman stood up to expose a wound in her breast. Another had slashed an artery at her wrist.

Suffer, suffer, suffer! the preacher shouted. Our Lord was nailed on a cross for the sins of the world! They led Him above the town to the place of the skull, they moistened his lips with vinegar on a sponge, they drove five nails through his body, and He was the Rose of the World as He bled on the cross!

The congregation could not remain in the building but tumbled out on the street in a crazed procession with clothes torn open.

The sins of the world are all forgiven! they shouted.

All during this celebration of human atonement, the Negro masseur was completing his purpose with Burns.

All the windows were open in the death chamber.

The curtains blew out like thirsty little white tongues to lick at the street which seemed to reek with an overpowering honey.

A house had caught fire on the block in back of the church. The walls collapsed and the cinders floated about in the gold atmosphere. The scarlet engines, the ladders and powerful hoses were useless against the purity of the flame.

The Negro masseur leaned over his still breathing victim.

Burns was whispering something.

The black giant nodded.

You know what you have to do now? the victim asked him. The black giant nodded.

He picked up the body, which barely held together, and placed it gently on a clean-swept table.

The giant began to devour the body of Burns.

It took him twenty-four hours to eat the splintered bones clean.

When he had finished, the sky was serenely blue, the passionate services at the church were finished, the ashes had settled, the scarlet engines had gone, and the reek of honey was blown from the atmosphere.

Quiet had returned and there was an air of completion.

Those bare white bones, left over from Burns's atonement, were placed in a sack and borne to the end of a car line.

There the masseur walked out on a lonely pier and dropped his burden under the lake's quiet surface.

As the giant turned homeward, he mused on his satisfaction.

Yes, it is perfect, he thought, it is now completed!

Then in the sack, in which he had carried the bones, he dropped his belongings, a neat blue suit to conceal his dangerous body, some buttons of pearl, and a picture of Anthony Burns as a child of seven.

He moved to another city, obtained employment once more as an expert masseur. And there in a white-curtained place, serenely conscious of fate bringing toward him another, to suffer atonement as it had been suffered by Burns, he stood impassively waiting inside a milky-white door for the next to arrive.

And meantime, slowly, with barely a thought of so doing, the earth's whole population twisted and writhed beneath the manipulation of night's black fingers and the white ones of day with skeletons splintered and flesh reduced to pulp, as out of this unlikely problem, the answer, perfection, was slowly evolved through torture.

MISS YELLOW EYES

BY SHIRLEY ANN GRAU

Pigeon Town

(Originally published in 1955)

P ete brought Chris home one evening after supper. I remember it was early spring, because the Talisman rosebush by the kitchen steps had begun to blossom out. For that time of year it was cool: there was a good stiff wind off the river that shook the old bush and creaked it, knocked the biggest flowers to bits, and blew their petals into a little heap against the side of the wood steps. The Johnsons, who lived in the house next door, had put their bedspread out to air and forgot to take it in. So it was hanging out there on the porch railing, a pink spread with a fan-tailed yellow peacock in the middle. I could hear it flapping—loud when the wind was up, and very soft when it fell. And from out on the river there were the soft low tones of the ships' whistles. And I could hear a mockingbird too, perched up on top the house, singing away, forgetting that it was nighttime. And in all this, Pete's steps in the side alley, coming to the kitchen door.

"Hi, kid!" Pete held open the door with one arm stretched behind him. Chris came in.

I thought at first: *That's a white man.* And I wondered what a white man would do coming here. I got a second look and saw the difference, saw I'd made a mistake. His skin wasn't dark at all, but only suntanned. (Lots of white men were darker.) His eyes were a pale blue, the color of the china Ma got with the Octagon soap coupons. He had brown hair—no, it was closer to red, and only slightly wavy. He looked like a white man, almost. But I saw the difference. Maybe it was just his way of carrying himself—that was like a Negro.

But he was the handsomest man I'd ever seen, excepting none. I could feel the bottom of my stomach roll up into a hard ball.

"This here's Celia," Pete said.

Chris grinned and his blue eyes crinkled up into almost closed slits. He sat down at the table opposite me, flipping shut the book I'd been reading. "Evening's no time to be busy, kid."

Pete picked up the coffeepot from where it always stood on the back of the stove and shook it gently. "There's some here all right," he said to Chris as he reached up to the shelf for a couple of cups. "You want anything in yours? I reckon there'd be a can of milk in the icebox."

"No," Chris said. "I like it black."

Pete lit the fire under the speckled enamel coffeepot. "Where's Ma?"

"They having a dinner tonight . . . she said she'll be real late." Ma worked as a cook in one of the big houses on St. Charles Avenue. When there was a dinner, it meant she'd have to stay around and clean up afterward and wouldn't get home till eleven or twelve maybe.

"She'll get tomorrow off, though," I told Chris.

"Good enough." He grinned and his teeth were very square and bright.

They sat down at the table with me and stretched out their legs. Holding the coffee cup to his mouth, Chris reached out one finger and rubbed the petals of the big yellow rose in the drinking glass in the center of the table. "That's real pretty."

"Lena's been putting them there," Pete said.

"That's sure the one I want to meet," Chris said, and grinned over at Pete, and I knew that he'd been talking about Lena.

* * *

She was the sort of girl you talk about, she was that beautiful—
with light brown hair that was shoulder-length and perfectly
straight and ivory skin and eyes that were light brown with flecks
of yellow in them. She was all gold-colored. Sometimes when she
stood in the sun you could almost think the light was shining right
through her.

She was near seventeen then, three years older than I was.
The boys in high school all followed her around until the other
girls hated her. Every chance they got they would play some mean
trick on her, kicking dust in her lunch, or roughing her up playing
basketball, or tearing pages out of her books. Lena hardly ever lost
her temper; she didn't really seem to care. "I reckon I know who
the boys are looking at," she told me. She was right. There was
always a bunch of them trying to sit next to her in class or walk
next to her down the hall. And when school was through, there
was always a bunch of them waiting around the door, wanting to
take her home, or for rides if they had cars. And when she finally
came sauntering out, with her books tucked up under one arm, she
wouldn't pay them much attention; she'd just give them a kind of
little smile (to keep them from going to the other girls) and walk
home by herself, with maybe a few of them trailing along behind. I
used to wait and watch her leave and then I'd go home a different
way. I didn't want to interfere.

But, for all that, she didn't go out very much. And never with
the same boy for very long. Once Hoyt Carmichael came around
and stood in the kitchen door, asking for her, just begging to see
her. She wouldn't even come out to talk to him. Ma asked her later
if there was something wrong and Lena just nodded and shrugged
her shoulders all at once. Ma hugged her then and you could see
the relief in her face; she worried so about Lena, about her being
so very pretty.

Pete said: "You sure got to meet her, Chris, man."

And I said to Chris: "She's over by the Johnsons'." I got up and opened the door and yelled out into the alley: "Lena!"

She came in a few minutes. We could hear her steps on the alley bricks, slow. She never did hurry. Finally she opened the screen and stood there, looking from one to the other.

I said: "This is my sister Magdalena."

"And this here is Chris Watkin," Pete said.

Chris had got up and bowed real solemnly. "I'm pleased to meet you."

Lena brushed the hair back from her forehead. She had long fingers, and hands so thin that the veins stood out blue on the backs. "Nobody calls me Magdalena," she said, "except Celia, now and then. Just Lena."

Chris's eyes crinkled up out of sight the way they had before. "I might could just call you Miss Yellow Eyes. Old Miss Yellow Eyes."

Lena just wrinkled her nose at him. In that light her eyes did look yellow, but usually if a man said something like that she'd walk out. Not this time. She just poured herself a cup of coffee, and when Chris pulled out a chair for her, she sat down, next to him.

I looked at them and I thought: *They look like a white couple.* And they did. Unless you had sharp trained eyes, like the people down here do, you would have thought they were white and you would have thought they made a handsome couple.

Chris looked over at me and lifted an eyebrow. Just one, the left one; it reached up high and arched in his forehead. "What you looking so solemn for, Celia?"

"Nothing."

And Lena asked: "You work with Pete at the railroad?"

"Sure," he said, and smiled at her. Only, more than his mouth was smiling. "We go swinging on and off those old tenders like hell afire. Jumping on and off those cars."

"I reckon that's hard work."

He laughed this time out loud. "I ain't exactly little." He bent forward and hunched his shoulders up a little so she could see the way the muscles swelled against the cloth of his shirt.

"You got fine shoulders, Mr. Watkin," she said. "I reckon they're even better than Pete there."

Pete grunted and finished his coffee. But she was right. Pete's shoulders were almost square out from his neck. Chris's weren't. They looked almost sloped and hunched the way flat bands of muscles reached up into his neck.

Chris shrugged and stood up. "Do you reckon you would like to walk around the corner for a couple of beers?"

"Okay," Pete said.

Lena lifted one eyebrow, just the way he had done. "Mr. Watkin, you do look like you celebrating something."

"I sure am," he said.

"What?" I asked.

"I plain tell you later, kid."

They must have been gone near two hours because Ma came home before they did. I'd fallen asleep. I'd just bent my head over for a minute to rest my eyes, and my forehead touched the soft pages of the book—*Treasure Island*. I'd got it from the library at school; it was dog-eared and smelled faintly of peanuts.

Ma was saying: "Lord, honey, why ain't you gone to bed?"

I lifted my head and rubbed my face until I could see Ma's figure in the doorway. "I'm waiting for them," I said.

Ma took off her coat and hung it up on the hook behind the door. "Who them?"

"Lena," I said, "and Pete. And Chris." I knew what she was going to say, so I answered first. "He's a friend of Pete, and Lena likes him."

Ma was frowning very slightly. "I plain wonder iffen he belong to that club."

"I don't know."

It was called the Better Days Club and the clubroom was the second floor of a little restaurant on Tulane Avenue. I'd never gone inside, though I had passed the place: a small wood building that had once been a house but now had a sign saying *Lefty's Restaurant and Café* in green letters on a square piece of board that hung out over the sidewalk and creaked in the wind. And I'd seen something else too when I passed: another sign, a small one tucked into the right center corner of the screen door, a sign that said *White Entrance to Rear.* If the police ever saw that they'd have found an excuse to raid the place and break up everything in it.

Ma kept asking Pete what they did there. Most times he didn't bother to answer. Once when she'd just insisted, he'd said, "We're fixing to have better times come." And sometimes he'd bring home little papers, not much more than book-size, with names like *New Day* and *Daily Sentinel* and *Watcher.*

Ma would burn the papers if she got hold of them. But she couldn't really stop Pete from going to the meetings. She didn't try too hard because he was so good to her and gave her part of his paycheck every week. With that money and what she made we always had enough. We didn't have to worry about eating, way some of our neighbors did.

Pete was a strange fellow—moody and restless and not happy. Sometimes—when he was sitting quiet, thinking or resting—there'd be a funny sort of look on his face (he was the darkest of us all): not hurt, not fear, not determination, but a mixture of all three.

Ma was still standing looking at me with a kind of puzzled expression on her face when we heard them, the three of them, coming home. They'd had a few beers and, what with the cold air outside, they all felt fine. They were singing too; I recognized the tune; it was the one from the jukebox around the corner in that bar.

Ma said: "They got no cause to be making a racket like that. Somebody might could call the police." Ma was terribly afraid of the police. She'd never had anything to do with them, but she was still afraid. Every time a police car passed in the street outside, she'd duck behind the curtain and peek out. And she'd walk clear around a block so she wouldn't come near one of the blue uniforms.

The three came in the kitchen door, Pete first and then Lena and Chris.

Pete had his arms full of beer cans; he let them all fall out on the table. "Man, I like to drop them sure."

"We brought some for you, Ma," Lena said.

"And Celia too," Chris added.

"It's plenty late," Ma said, looking hard at Chris.

"You don't have to work tomorrow," I said.

So we stayed up late. I don't know how late. Because the beer made me feel fine and sick all at once. First everything was swinging around inside my head and then the room too. Finally I figured how to handle it. I caught hold and let myself ride around on the big whooshing circles. There were times when I'd forget there was anybody else in the room, I'd swing so far away.

"Why, just you look at Celia there," Ma said, and everybody turned and watched me.

"You sure high, kid," Chris said.

"No, I'm not." I was careful to space the words, because I could tell by the way Ma had run hers together that she was feeling the beer too.

Pete had his guitar in his lap, flicking his fingers across the strings. "You an easy drunk." He was smiling, the way he seldom did. "Leastways you ain't gonna cost some man a lotta money getting you high."

"That absolutely and completely right." Ma bent forward,

with her hands one on each knee and the elbows sticking out, like a skinny football player. "You plain got to watch that when boys come to take you out."

"They ain't gonna want to take me out."

"Why not, kid?" Chris had folded his arms on the tabletop and was leaning his chin on them. His face was flushed so that his eyes only looked bluer.

"Not after they see Lena." I lifted my eyes up from his and let them drop over where I knew Lena was sitting. I just had time to notice the way the electric light made her skin gold and her eyes gold and her hair too, so that she seemed all one blurry color. And then the whole world tipped over and I went skidding off—but feeling extra fine because Chris was sitting just a little bit away next to Lena and she was looking at him like she'd never looked at anybody else before.

Next thing I knew, somebody was saying: "Celia, look." There was a photograph in front of me. A photograph of a young man, in a suit and tie, leaning back against a post, with his legs crossed, grinning at the camera.

I looked up. Ma was holding the photograph in front of me. It was in a wide silver-colored frame, with openwork, roses or flowers of some sort.

Pete began laughing. "Just you look at her," he said. "She don't even know her own daddy."

"I never seen that picture before," I said, loud as I could.

I'd never seen my daddy either. He was a steward on a United Fruit Lines ship, a real handsome man. He'd gone ashore at Antigua one day and forgot to come back.

"He looks mighty much like Chris," Ma said as she cleared a space on the shelf over between the windows. She put the picture there. And I knew then that she'd got it out from the bottom of a drawer somewhere, because this was a special occasion for her too.

"Chris," I said, remembering, "you never did tell us what you celebrating."

He had twisted sideways in his chair and had his arms wrapped around the back. "I going in the army."

Out of the corner of my eye I saw Pete staring at him, his mouth twisting and his face darkening.

Ma clucked her tongue against her teeth. "That a shame."

Chris grinned, his head cocked aside a little. "I got to leave tomorrow."

Pete swung back and forth on the two legs of his tilted chair. "Ain't good enough for nothing around here, but we good enough to put in the army and send off."

"Man"—Chris winked at him—"there ain't nothing you can do. And I plain reckon you gonna go next."

"No." Pete spoke the word so that it was almost a whistle.

"I'm a man, me," Chris said. "Can't run out on what I got to do." He tipped his head back and whistled a snatch of a little tune.

"I wouldn't like to go in the army," Lena said.

Chris went on whistling. Now we could recognize the song:

Yellow, yellow, yellow, yellow, yellow gal,
Yellow, yellow, yellow, yellow, yellow gal,
She's pretty and fine
Is the yellow gal . . .

Lena tossed her head. "I wouldn't like to none."

Chris stopped whistling and laughed. "You plain sound like Pete here."

Pete's face all crinkled up with anger. I thought: *He looks more like a Negro when he loses his temper; it makes his skin darker somehow.*

"Nothing to laugh about," he said. "Can't do nothing around here without people yelling *nigger* at you."

"Don't stay around here, man. You plain crazy to stay around here." Chris tilted back his chair and stared at the ceiling. "You plain crazy to stay a nigger. I done told you that."

Pete scowled at him and didn't answer.

Lena asked quickly: "Where you got to go?"

"Oregon." Chris was still staring at the ceiling and still smiling. "That where you cross over."

"You sure?"

Chris looked at her and smiled confidently. "Sure I'm sure."

Pete mumbled something under his breath that we didn't hear.

"I got a friend done it," Chris said. "Two years ago. He working out of Portland there, for the railroad. And he turn white."

Lena was resting her chin on her folded hands. "They don't look at you so close or anything?"

"No," Chris said. "I heard all about it. You can cross over if you want to."

"You going?" I asked.

"When I get done with the stretch in the army." He lowered his chair back to its four legs and stared out the little window, still smiling. "There's lots of jobs there for a railroad man."

Pete slammed the flat of his hand down against the table. Ma's eyes flew open like a door that's been kicked wide back. "I don't want to pretend I'm white," he said. "I ain't and I don't want to be. I reckon I want to be same as white and stay right here."

Ma murmured something under her breath and we all turned to look at her. Her eyes had dropped half-closed again and she had her hands folded across her stomach. Her mouth opened very slowly and this time she spoke loud enough for us all to hear. "Talking like that—you gonna do nothing but break you neck that way."

I got so sleepy then and so tired, all of a sudden, that I slipped sideways out of my chair. It was funny. I didn't notice I was slipping or moving until I was on the floor. Ma got hold of my arm and took me off to bed with her. And I didn't think to object. The last thing

I saw was Lena staring at Chris with her long light-colored eyes. Chris with his handsome face and his reddish hair and his movements so quick they almost seemed jerky.

I thought it would be all right with them.

I was sick the whole next day from the beer; so sick I couldn't go to school. Ma shook her head and Pete laughed and Lena just smiled a little.

And Chris went off to the army, all right. It wasn't long before Lena had a picture from him. He'd written across the back: *Here I am a soldier.* She stuck the picture in the frame of the mirror over her dresser.

That was the week Lena quit school. She came looking for me during lunchtime. "I'm going home," she said.

"You can't do that."

She shook her head. "I had enough."

So she walked out of school and didn't ever go back. (She was old enough to do that.) She bought a paper on her way home and sat down and went through the classified ads very carefully, looking for a job. It was three days before she found one she wanted: with some people who were going across the lake to Covington for the summer. Their regular city maid wouldn't go.

They took her on right away because they wanted to leave. She came back with a ten-dollar bill in her purse. "We got to leave in the morning," she said.

Ma didn't like it, her quitting school and leaving home, but she couldn't really stop her.

And Lena did want to go. She was practically jumping with excitement after she came back from the interview. "They got the most beautiful house," she said to Ma. "A lot prettier than where you work." And she told me: "They say the place over the lake is even prettier—even prettier."

I knew what she meant. I sometimes went to meet Ma at the

house where she worked. I liked to. It was nice to be in the middle of fine things, even if they weren't yours.

"It'll be real nice working there," Lena said.

That next morning, when she had got her things together and closed the lid of the suitcase, she told me to go down to the grocery at the corner, where there was a phone, and call a taxi. They were going to pay for it, she said.

I reckon I was excited; so excited that I called the wrong cab. I just looked at the back cover of the phone book where there was a picture of a long orange-color cab and a number in big orange letters. I gave them the address, then went back to the house and sat down on the porch with Lena.

The orange cab turned at the corner and came down our street. The driver was hanging out the window looking for house numbers; there weren't any except for the Stevenses' across the way. Bill Stevens had painted his number with big whitewash letters on his front door. The cab hit a rut in the street and the driver's head smacked the window edge. He jerked his head back inside and jammed the gears into second. Then he saw us: Lena and me and the suitcase on the edge of the porch.

He let the car move along slow in second with that heavy pulling sound and he watched us. As he got closer you could see that he was chewing on the corner of his lip. Still watching us, he went on slowly—right past the house. He said something once, but we were too far away to hear. Then he was down at the other corner, turning, and gone.

Lena stood and looked at me. She had on her best dress: a light blue one with round pockets in front. Both her hands were stuffed into the pockets. There was a handkerchief in the left one; you could see her fingers twisting it.

White cabs didn't pick up colored people: I knew that. But I'd forgot and called the first number, a white number, a wrong number. Lena didn't say anything, just kept looking at me, with her hand holding the handkerchief inside her pocket. I turned and ran all the way down to the corner and called the right number, and a colored cab that was painted black with gold stripes across the hood came and Lena was gone for the next four months, the four months of the summer.

It could have been the same cab brought her back that had come for her: black with gold stripes. She had on the same dress too, the blue one with round pockets; the same suitcase too, but this time in it was a letter of recommendation and a roll of bills she'd saved, all hidden in the fancy organdy aprons they'd given her.

She said: "He wanted me to stay on through the winter, but she got scared for their boy." And she held her chin stiff and straight when she said that.

I understood why that woman wanted my sister Lena out of the house. There wasn't any boy or man either that wouldn't look at her twice. White or colored, it didn't seem to make a difference, they all looked at her in the same way.

That was the only job Lena ever took. Because she hadn't been home more than a few days when Chris came back for her.

I remember how it was—early September and real foggy. It would close down every evening around seven and wouldn't lift until ten or ten thirty in the morning. All night long you could hear the foghorns and the whistles of the boats out on the river; and in the morning there'd be even more confusion when everybody tried to rush away from anchor. That Saturday morning Lena had taken a walk up to the levee to watch. Pete was just getting up. I could hear him in his room. Ma had left for work early. And me, I was scrubbing out the kitchen, the way I did every Saturday morning. That was when Chris came back.

He came around to the kitchen. I heard his steps in the alley—quickly coming, almost running. He came bursting in the door and almost slipped on the soapy floor. "Hi, kid," he said, took off his cap, and rubbed his hand over his reddish hair. "You working?"

"Looks like," I said.

He'd grown a mustache, a thin line. He stood for a moment chewing on his lip and the little hairs he had brushed so carefully into a line. Finally he said: "Where's everybody?"

"Lena went up on the levee to have a look at the river boats."

He grinned at me, flipped his cap back on, gave a kind of salute, and jumped down the two steps into the yard.

I sat back on my heels, picturing him and Lena in my mind and thinking what a fine couple they made. And the little picture of my father grinned down at me from the shelf by the window.

Pete called: "Seems like I heard Chris in there."

"He went off to look for Lena."

Pete came to the door; he was only half dressed and he was still holding up his pants with his one hand. He liked to sleep late Saturdays. "He might could have stayed to say hello."

"He wanted to see Lena, I reckon."

Pete grinned briefly and the grin faded into a yawn. "You ought to have let him look for her."

"Nuh-uh." I picked up the bar of soap and the scrubbing brush again. "I wanted them to get together, I reckon."

"Okay, kid," Pete said shortly, and turned back to his room. "You helped them out."

Chris and Lena came back after a while. They didn't say anything, but I noticed that Lena was kind of smiling like she was cuddling something to herself. And her eyes were so bright they looked light yellow, almost transparent.

Chris hung his army cap on the back of a chair and then sprawled down at the table. "You fixing to offer me anything to eat?"

"You can't be hungry this early in the morning," Lena said.

"Men are always hungry," I said. They both turned.

"You tell 'em, kid," Chris said. "You tell 'em for me."

"Let's us go to the beach," Lena said suddenly.

"Sure, honey," Chris said softly.

She wrinkled her nose at him and pretended she hadn't heard. "It's the last night before they close down everything for the winter."

"Okay—we gonna leave right now?"

"Crazy thing," Lena smiled. "Not in the morning. Let's us go right after supper."

"I got to stay here till then?"

"Not 'less you want to."

"Reckon I do," Chris said.

"You want to come, Celia?" Lena asked.

"Me?" I glanced over at Chris quickly. "Nuh-uh."

"Sure you do," Lena said. "You just come along."

And Chris lifted one eyebrow at me. "Come along," he said. "Iffen you don't mind going out with people old as me."

"Oh, no," I said. "Oh, no."

I never did figure out quite why Lena wanted me along that time. Maybe she didn't want to be alone with Chris because she didn't quite trust him yet. Or maybe she just wanted to be nice to me. I don't know. But I did go. I liked the beach. I liked to stare off across the lake and imagine I could see the shore on the other side, which of course I couldn't.

So I went with them, that evening after supper. It took us nearly an hour to get there—three changes of busses because it was exactly across town: the north end of the city. All the way, all along in the bus, Chris kept talking, telling stories.

"Man," he said, "that army sure is something—big—I never seen anything so big. Just in our little old camp there ain't a space of ground big enough to hold all the men, if they called them all out together . . ."

We reached the end of one bus line. He put one hand on Lena's arm and the other on mine and helped us out the door.

His hand was broad and hard on the palm and almost cool to the touch.

In the other bus we headed straight for the long seat across the back, so we could sit all three together. He sat in the middle and, leaning forward a little, rested both hands on his knees. Looking at him out the corner of my eye, I could see the flat broad strips of muscle in his neck, reaching up to under his chin. And once I caught Lena's eye, and I knew that on the other side she was watching too.

"All together like that," he said. "It gives you the funniest feeling—when you all marching together, so that you can't see away on either side, just men all together—it gives you a funny sort of feeling."

He turned to Lena and grinned; his bright square teeth flashed in the evening dusk. "I reckon you think that silly."

"No," she said quickly, and then corrected herself: "Of course I never been in the army."

"Look there," I said. We were passing the white beach. Even as far away as the road where we were, we could smell the popcorn and the sweat and the faint salt tingle from the wind off the lake.

"It almost cool tonight," Lena said.

"You ain't gonna be cold?"

"You don't got to worry about me."

"I reckon I do," he said.

Lena shook her head, and her eyes had a soft holding look in them. And I wished I could take Chris aside and tell him that he'd said just the right thing.

Out on the concrete walks of the white beach, people were jammed so close that there was hardly any space between. You could hear all the voices and the talking, murmuring at this distance. Then we were past the beach (the driver was going fast, grumbling under his breath that he was behind schedule), and the Ferris wheel was the only thing you could see, a circle of lights like a big star behind us. And on each side, open ground, low weeds, and no trees.

"There it is," Chris said, and pointed up through the window. I turned and looked and, sure enough, there it was; he was right: the lights, smaller maybe and dimmer, of Lincoln Beach, the colored beach.

"Lord," Lena said, "I haven't been out here in I don't know when. It's been that long."

We got off the bus; he dropped my arm but kept hold of Lena's. "You got to make this one night last all winter."

She didn't answer.

We had a fine time. I forgot that I was just tagging along and enjoyed myself much as any.

When we passed over by the shooting gallery Chris winked at Lena and me. "Which one of them dolls do you want?"

Lena wrinkled her nose. "I reckon you plain better see about getting 'em first."

He just shrugged. "You think I can do it, Celia?"

"Sure," I said. "Sure, sure you can."

"That's the girl for you," the man behind the counter said. "Thinks you can do anything."

"That my girl there all right." Chris reached in his pocket to pay the man. I could feel my ears getting red.

He picked up the rifle and slowly knocked down the whole row of green and brown painted ducks. He kept right on until Lena and I each had a doll in a bright pink feather skirt and he had a purple wreath of flowers hung around his neck. By this time the man was scowling at him and a few people were standing around watching.

"That's enough, soldier," the man said. "This here is just for amateurs."

Chris shrugged. We all turned and walked away.

"You did that mighty well," Lena said, turning her baby doll around and around in her hands, staring at it.

"I see lots of fellows better."

"Where'd you learn to shoot like that?" I tugged on his sleeve.

"I didn't learn—"

"Fibber!" Lena tossed her head.

"You got to let me finish. Up in Calcasieu parish, my daddy, he put a shotgun in my hand and give me a pocket of shells . . . I just keep shooting till I hit something or other."

It was hard to think of Chris having a father. "Where's he now?"

"My daddy? He been dead."

"You got a family?"

"No," Chris said. "Just me."

We walked out along the strip of sand, and the wind began pulling the feathers out of the dolls' skirts. I got out my handkerchief and tied it around my doll, but Lena just lifted hers up high in the air to see what the wind would do. Soon she just had a naked baby doll that was pink celluloid smeared with glue.

Lena and Chris found an old log and sat down. I went wading. I didn't want to go back to where they were, because I knew that Chris wanted Lena alone. So I kept walking up and down in the water that came just a little over my ankles.

It was almost too cold for swimmers. I saw just one, about thirty yards out, swimming up and down slowly. I couldn't really see him, just the regular white splashes from his arms. I looked out across the lake, the way I liked to do. It was all dark now; there was no telling where the lower part of the sky stopped and the water began. It was all the one color, all of it, out beyond the swimmer and the breakwater on the left where the waves hit a shallow spot and turned white and foamy. Except for that, it was all the same dark until you lifted your eyes high up in the sky and saw the stars.

I don't know how long I stood there, with my head bent back far as it would go, looking at the stars, trying to remember the names for them that I had learned in school: names like Bear and

Archer. I couldn't tell which was which. All I could see were stars, bright like they always were at the end of the summer and close; and every now and then one of them would fall.

I stood watching them, feeling the water move gently around my legs and curling my toes in the soft lake sand that was rippled by the waves. And trying to think up ways to stay away from those two who were sitting back up the beach, on a piece of driftwood, talking together.

Once the wind shifted a little suddenly or Chris spoke too loud, because I heard one word: "Oregon."

All of a sudden I knew that Lena was going to marry him. Just for that she was going to marry him; because she wanted so much to be white.

And I wanted to tell Chris again, the way I had wanted to in the bus, that he'd said just the right thing.

After a while Lena stood up and called to me, saying it was late; so we went home. By the time we got there, Ma had come. On the table was a bag of food she had brought. And so we all sat around and ate the remains of the party: little cakes, thin and crispy and spicy and in fancy shapes; and little patties full of oysters that Ma ran in the oven to heat up; and little crackers spread with fishy-tasting stuff, like sugar grains only bigger, that Ma called caviar; and all sorts of little sandwiches.

It was one nice thing about the place Ma worked. They never did check the food. And it was fun for us, tasting the strange things.

All of a sudden Lena turned to me and said: "I reckon I want to see where Oregon is." She gave Chris a long look out of the corner of her eyes.

My mouth was full and for a moment I couldn't answer.

"You plain got to have a map in your schoolbooks."

I finally managed to swallow. "Sure I got one—if you want to see it."

I got my history book and unfolded the map of the whole

country and put my finger down on the spot that said *Oregon* in pink letters. "There," I said. "That's Portland there."

Lena came and leaned over my shoulder; Pete didn't move; he sat with his chin in his hand and his elbows propped on the table.

"I want to stay here and be the same as white," he said, but we weren't listening to him.

Chris got out of the icebox the bottles of beer he had brought.

"Don't you want to see?" Lena asked him.

He grinned and took out his key chain, which had an opener on it, and began popping the caps off the bottles. "I looked at a map once. I know where it's at."

Ma was peering over my other shoulder. "It looks like it mighty far away."

"It ain't close," Chris said.

"You plain want to go there—" Ma was frowning at the map, straining to see without her glasses.

"Yes," Chris said, still popping the tops off bottles.

"And be white," Lena added very softly.

"Sure," Chris said. "No trouble at all to cross over."

"And you going there," Ma said again. She couldn't quite believe that anybody she was looking at right now could ever go that far away.

"Yea," Chris said, and put the last opened bottle with the others in a row on the table. "When I get out the army, we sure as hell going there."

"Who's we?" I asked.

"Lena and me."

Ma looked up at him so quickly that a hairpin tumbled out of her head and clicked down on the table.

"When we get married," he said.

Lena was looking at him, chewing her lower lip. "We going to do that?"

"Yea," he said. "Leastways if that what you want to do."

And Lena dropped her eyes down to the map again, though I'd swear this time she didn't know what she was seeing. Or maybe everywhere she'd look she was seeing Chris. Maybe that was it. She was smiling very slightly to herself, with just the corners of her lips, and they were trembling.

They got married that week in St. Michel's Church. It was in the morning—nine thirty, I remember—so the church was cold: biting empty cold. Even the two candles burning on the altar didn't look like they'd be warm. Though it only took a couple of minutes, my teeth were chattering so that I could hardly talk. Ma cried and Pete scowled and grinned by turns and Lena and Chris didn't seem to notice anything much.

The cold and the damp had made a bright strip of flush across Lena's cheeks. Old Mrs. Roberts, who lived next door, bent forward—she was sitting in the pew behind us—and tapped Ma on the shoulder. "I never seen her look prettier."

Lena had bought herself a new suit, with the money she'd earned over the summer: a cream-colored suit, with small black braiding on the cuffs and collar. She'd got a hat too, of the same color velvet. Cream was a good color for her; it was lighter than her skin somehow, so that it made her face stand out.

("She ought to always have clothes like that," Mayme Roberts said later, back at our house. She was old Mrs. Roberts's daughter, and seven kids had broken her up so that she wasn't even jealous of pretty girls anymore. "Maybe Chris'll make enough money to let her have pretty clothes like that.")

Lena and Chris went away because he had to get back to camp. And for the first time since I could remember, I had a room all to myself. So I made Lena's bed all nice and careful and put the fancy spread that Ma had crocheted on it—the one we hardly ever used. And put the little pink celluloid doll in the middle.

* * *

Sometime after the wedding, I don't remember exactly when, Pete had an accident. He'd been out on a long run, all the way up to Abiline. It was a long hard job and by the time he got back to town he was dead tired, and so he got a little careless. In the switch yards he got his hand caught in a loose coupling.

He was in the hospital for two weeks or so, in the colored surgical ward on the second floor of a huge cement building that said *Charity Hospital* in carved letters over the big front door. Ma went to see him on Tuesdays and Saturdays and I just went on Saturdays. Walking over from the bus, we'd pass Lefty's Restaurant and Café. Ma would turn her head away so that she wouldn't see it.

One time, the first Saturday I went with Ma, we brought Pete a letter, his induction notice. He read it and started laughing and crying all at once—until the ward nurse got worried and called an intern and together they gave him a shot. Right up till he passed out, he kept laughing.

And I began to wonder if it had been an accident . . .

After two weeks he came home. We hadn't expected him; we hadn't thought he was well enough to leave. Late one afternoon we heard steps in the side alley; Ma looked at me, quick and funny, and rushed over to open the door: it was Pete. He had come home alone on the streetcar and walked the three blocks from the car stop. By the time he got to the house he was ready to pass out: he had to sit down and rest his head on the table right there in the kitchen. But he'd held his arm careful so that it didn't start to bleed again. He'd always been afraid of blood.

Accidents like that happened a lot on the road. Maybe that was why the pay was so good. The fellows who sat around the grocery all day or the bar all had pensions because they'd lost an arm or a hand or a leg. It happened a lot; we knew that, but it didn't seem to make any difference.

Ma cried very softly to herself when she saw him so dizzy and weak he couldn't stand up. And I went out in the backyard, where he couldn't see, and was sick to my stomach.

He stayed in the house until he got some strength back and then he was out all day long. He left every morning just like he was working and he came back for dinner at night. Ma asked him once where he went, but he wouldn't say; and there was never any trouble about it. A check came from the railroad every month, regular; and he still gave Ma part of it.

Pete talked about his accident, though. It was all he'd talk about. "I seen my hand," he'd tell anybody who'd listen. "After they got it free, with the blood running down it, I seen it. And it wasn't cut off. My fingers was moving. I seen 'em. Was no call for them to go cut the hand off. There wasn't any call for them to do that, not even with all it hurting." (And it had hurt so bad that he'd passed out. They'd told us he just tumbled down all of a sudden—so that the cinders along the tracks cut in his cheek.)

He'd say: "Iffen it wasn't a man my color they wouldn't done it. They wouldn't go cut off a white man's hand."

He'd say: "It was only just one finger that was caught, they didn't have cause to take off the whole hand."

And when I heard him I couldn't help wondering. Wondering if maybe Pete hadn't tried to get one finger caught. The army wouldn't take a man with one finger missing. But just one finger gone wouldn't hamper a man much. The way Pete was acting wasn't like a man that had an accident he wasn't expecting. But like a man who'd got double-crossed somehow.

And looking at Ma, I could see that she was thinking the same thing.

Lena came home after a couple of months—Chris had been sent overseas.

She used to spend most of her days lying on the bed in our room, reading a magazine maybe, or writing to Chris, or just staring at the ceiling. When the winter sun came in through the window and fell on her, her skin turned gold and burning.

Since she slept so much during the days, often in the night she'd wake up and be lonesome. Then she'd call me. "Celia," she'd call real soft so that the sound wouldn't carry through the paper-board walls. "Celia, you awake?" And I'd tell her yes and wake up quick as I could.

Then she'd snap on the little lamp that Chris had given her for a wedding present. And she'd climb out of bed, wrapping one of the blankets around her because it was cold. And she'd sit on the cane-bottomed old chair and rock it slowly back and forth while she told me just what it would be like when Chris came back for her.

Sometimes Pete would hear us talking and would call: "Shut up in there." And Lena would only toss her head and say that he was an old grouch and not to pay any attention to him.

Pete had been in a terrible temper for weeks, the cold made his arm hurt so. He scarcely spoke anymore. And he didn't bother going out after supper; instead he stayed in his room, sitting in a chair with his feet propped up on the windowsill, looking out where there wasn't anything to see. Once I'd peeped in through the half-opened door. He was standing in the middle of the room, at the foot of the bed, and he was looking at his stub arm, which was still bright-red-colored. His lips were drawn back tight against his teeth, and his eyes were almost closed, they were so squinted.

Things went on this way right through the first part of the winter. Chris was in Japan. He sent Lena a silk kimono—green, with a red dragon embroidered across the back. He didn't write much, and then it was just a line saying that he was fine. Along toward the middle of January, I think it was, one of the letters mentioned fighting. It wasn't so bad, he said; and it wasn't noisy at all. That's what he noticed most, it seemed: the quietness. From the other letters we could tell that he was at the front all the rest of the winter.

It was March by this time. And in New Orleans March is just rain, icy splashing rain. One afternoon I ran the dozen or so blocks home from school and all I wanted to do was sit down by the stove. I found Ma and Pete in the kitchen. Ma was standing by the table, looking down at the two yellow pieces of paper like she expected them to move.

The telegram was in the middle of the table—the folded paper and the folded yellow envelope. There wasn't anything else, not even the big salt shaker which usually stood there.

Ma said: "Chris got himself hurt."

Pete was sitting across the room with his chair propped against the wall, tilting himself back and forth. "Ain't good enough for nothing around here," he said, and rubbed his stump arm with his good hand. "Ain't good enough for white people, but sure good enough to get killed."

"He ain't killed," Lena said from the next room. The walls were so thin she could hear every word. "He ain't got killed."

"Sure, Lena, honey," Ma said, and her voice was soft and comforting. "He going to be all right, him. Sure."

"Quit that," Ma told Pete in a fierce whisper. "You just quit that." She glanced over her shoulder toward Lena's room. "She got enough trouble without you adding to it."

Pete glared but didn't answer.

"You want me to get you something, Lena?" I started into our room. But her voice stopped me.

"No call for you to come in," she said.

Maybe she was crying, I don't know. Her voice didn't sound like it. Maybe she was though, crying for Chris. Nobody saw her.

Chris didn't send word to us. It was almost like he forgot. There was one letter from a friend of his in Japan, saying that he had seen him in a hospital there and that the nurses were a swell set of people and so were the doctors.

Lena left the letter open on the table for us all to see. That night she picked it up and put it in the drawer of her dresser with the yellow paper of the telegram.

And there wasn't anything else to do but wait.

No, there were two things, two things that Lena could do. The day after the telegram came, she asked me to come with her.

"Where?"

"St. Michel's." She was drying the dishes, putting them away in the cupboard, so I couldn't see her face, but I could tell from her voice how important this was.

"Sure," I said. "Sure, I'll come. Right away."

St. Michel's was a small church. I'd counted the pews once: there were just exactly twenty; and the side aisles were so narrow two people could hardly pass. The confessional was a single little recess on the right side in the back, behind the baptismal font. There was a light burning—Father Graziano would be back there.

"You wait for me," Lena said. And I sat down in the last pew while she walked over toward the light. I kept my head turned so that she wouldn't think I was watching her as she went up to the confessional and knocked very softly on the wood frame. Father Graziano stuck his gray old head out between the dark curtains. I didn't have to listen; I knew what Lena was asking him. She was asking him to pray for Chris. It only took her a minute; then she walked quickly up to the front, by the altar rail. I could hear her heels against the bare boards, each one a little explosion. There were three or four candles burning already. She lit another one—I saw the circle of light get bigger as she put hers on the black iron rack.

"Let's go," she said. "Let's go."

Father Graziano had come out of the confessional and was standing watching us. He was a small man, but heavy, with a big square head and a thick neck. He must have been a powerful man when he was young. Chris had a neck like that, muscled like that.

For a minute I thought he was going to come over and talk to us. He took one step, then stopped and rubbed his hand through his curly gray hair.

Lena didn't say anything until we reached the corner where we turned to go home. Without thinking, I turned.

"Not that way." She caught hold of my arm. "This way here." She went in the opposite direction.

I walked along with her, trying to see her face. But it was too dark and she had pulled the scarf high over her head.

"We got to go to Maam's," she said and her voice was muffled in the collar of her coat.

"To what?" not believing I'd heard her right.

"To Maam's."

Maam was a grisgris woman, so old nobody could remember when she'd been young or middle-aged even. Old as the river and wrinkled like it too, when the wind blows across.

She had a house on the *batture*, behind a clump of old thick hackberries. There was the story I'd heard: she had wanted a new house after a high water on the river had carried her old one away. (All this was fifty years ago, maybe.) So she'd walked down the levee to the nearest house, which was nearly a mile away: people didn't want to live close to her. She'd stood outside, looking out at the river and calling out: "I want a house. A fine new house. A nice new house. For me." She didn't say anything else, just turned and walked away. But the people inside had heard her and spread the word. Before they even began to fix the damage the flood had done to their own houses, the men worked on her house. In less than a week it was finished. They picked up their tools and left, and the next day they sent a kid down to spy and, sure enough, there was smoke coming out of the chimney. Maam had moved in: she must have been watching from somewhere close. Nobody knew where she had spent the week that she didn't have a house. And everybody was really too scared to find out.

She was still living in that house. It was built on good big solid pilings so that floodwaters didn't touch it. I'd seen it once; Pete had taken me up on the levee there and pointed it out: a two-room house that the air and the river damp had turned black, on top a flat tin roof that shone in the sun. At the beginning of the dirt path that led down to the house I saw a little pile of food people had left for her: some white pieces of slab bacon, some tin cans. Pete wouldn't let me get close. "No sense fooling with things you don't understand," he said.

Maam didn't leave her house often. But when she did, when she came walking down the streets or along the levee, people got out of her way. Either they slipped down into the *batture* bushes and waited until she passed by on the top of the levee, or, in town, they got off the banquette and into the street when she came by—an old woman with black skin that was nearly gray and eyes hidden in the folds of wrinkles, an old woman wearing a black dress, and a red shawl over her head and shoulders, a bright red shawl with silver and black signs sewed onto it. And always she'd be staring at the girls; what she liked best was to be able to touch them, on the arm or the hand, or catch hold of a little piece of their clothes. That didn't happen often, everybody was so careful of her.

And still Lena had said: "We going to Maam's."

"Lord," I said, "why?"

"For Chris."

There wasn't anything I could answer to that.

It was still early, seven thirty or eight, but nights don't seem to have time. The moon wasn't up yet; the sky was clear, with hard flecks of stars. Out on the river one ship was moving out—slipping between the riding lights of the other anchored ships that were waiting their turn at the docks below the point. You could hear the steady sound of the engines.

On top of the levee the river wind was strong and cold and heavy-wet. I shivered even with a coat and scarf. There was a heavy frost like mold on the riverside slant of the levee. I stopped and pulled a clover and touched it to my lips and felt the sting of ice.

There was a light in Maam's house. We saw that as we came down the narrow little path through the hackberry bushes, the way that Pete wouldn't let me go when I was little. She must have heard us coming—walking is noisy on a quiet night—because without our knocking Maam opened the door.

I never did see her face. She had the red scarf tied high around her head so that it stuck out far on the sides. She mightn't have had a face, for all I could tell. The house was warm, very warm; I could feel the heat rush out all around her. She was wearing a black dress without sleeves, of some light material with a sheen like satin. She had tied a green cord tight around her middle. Under it her stomach stuck out like a pregnant woman's.

"I came to fetch something," Lena said. Her voice was tight and hard.

Inside the house a round spot was shining on the far wall. I stared at it hard: a tray, a round tin tray, nailed to the wall. I couldn't see more than that because there wasn't much light; just a single kerosene lamp standing in the middle of the room, on the floor. Being low like that, it made the shadows go upward on the walls so that even familiar things looked strange.

"I came to fetch something," Lena said. "For somebody that's sick."

Maam didn't move.

"To make him well," Lena added.

Maam turned around, made a circle back through her cabin, ending up behind her half-open door, where we couldn't see. I suppose we could have stepped inside and watched her—but we didn't. And in a couple of seconds she was back at the doorway. She was holding both arms straight down against her sides, the hands clenched. And she kept looking from Lena to me and back again.

Lena took her left hand out of her coat pocket and I could see that she was holding a bill and a couple of coins. She moved them slowly back and forth; Maam's eyes followed but she did not move.

"You got to give it to me," Lena said. Her voice was high-pitched and rasping. I hadn't known it could be as rough as that.

Maam held out her hand: a thin black arm, all the muscles and tendons showing along the bone. She held out her arm, palm down, fist clenched. Then slowly, so that the old muscles under the thin skin moved in twisting lines, she turned the arm and opened the fingers. And in the palm there was a small bundle of cloth, white cloth. As we stared at it the three edges of the cloth, which had been pressed down in her hand, popped up slowly until they stuck straight up.

Lena reached out her right hand and took the three pointed edges of the cloth while her other hand dropped the money in its place. I could see how careful she was being not to touch the old woman.

Then we turned and almost ran back up the path to the top of the levee. I turned once near the top and looked back. Maam was still standing in the door, in her thin black sleeveless dress. She seemed to be singing something; I couldn't make out the words, just the sound. As she stood there, the lamplight all yellow behind her, I could feel her eyes reach out after us.

Lena had done all she could. She'd gone to the church and she'd prayed and lit a candle and asked the priest for special prayers. And she'd gone to the voodoo woman. She'd done all she could. Now there wasn't anything to do but wait.

You could see how hard waiting was for her. Her face was always thin, a little long, with fine features. And now you could almost see the strain lines run down her cheeks. The skin under her eyes turned blue; she wasn't sleeping. I knew that. She always lay very quiet in her bed, never tossing or turning. And that was just how I knew she was awake. Nobody lies stiff and still like that if they're really asleep; and their breathing isn't so shallow and quick.

I'd lie awake and listen to her pretending that she was asleep. And I'd want to get up and go over there and comfort her somehow. Only, some people you can't comfort. You can only go along with their pretending and pretend yourself.

That's what I did. I made out I didn't notice anything. Not the circles under her eyes; not the way she had of blinking rapidly (her eyes were so dry they burned); not the little zigzag vein that stood out blue on her left forehead.

One night we had left the shade up. There was a full moon, so bright that I woke up. Lena was really asleep then. I looked over at her: the light hadn't reached more than the side of her bed; it only reached her hand that was dangling over the edge of the bed, the fingers limp and curled a little. A hand so thin that the moonlight was like an X-ray, showing the bones.

And I wanted to cry for her if she couldn't cry for herself. But I only got up and pulled down the shade, and made the room all dark so I couldn't see anymore.

Chris died. The word came one Thursday late afternoon. Ma was out sweeping off the front steps and she took the telegram from the boy and brought it to Lena. Her hand was trembling when she held it out. Lena's thin hand didn't move even a little bit.

Lena opened the envelope with her fingernail, read it, cleared the kitchen table, and put it out there. (We didn't need to read it.)

She didn't make a sound. She didn't even catch her breath. Her face didn't change, her thin, tired face, with the deep circles under the eyes and the strain lines down the cheeks. Only there was a little pulse began to beat in the vein on her forehead—and her eyes changed, the light eyes with flecks of gold in them. They turned one color: dark, dull brown.

She put the telegram in the middle of the table. Her fingers let loose of it very slowly. Their tips brushed back and forth on the edges of the paper a couple of times before she dropped her arm to her side and very slowly turned and walked into the bedroom, her heels sounding on the floor, slow and steady. The bed creaked as she sat down on it.

Ma had been backing away from the telegram, the corner of her mouth twitching. She bumped into a chair and she looked down—surprised at its being there, even. Then, like a wall that's all of a sudden collapsing, she sat down and bent her head in her lap. She began to cry, not making a sound, her shoulders moving up and down.

Pete was balancing himself on his heels, teetering back and forth, grinning at the telegram like it was a person. I never saw his face look like that before; I was almost afraid of him. And he was Pete, my brother.

He reached down and flicked the paper edge with his fingers. "Good enough to die," he said. "We good enough to die."

There was a prickling all over me, even in my hair. I reckon I was shivering.

I tried to think of Chris dead. Chris shot. Chris in the hospital. Lying on a bed, and dead. Not moving. Chris, who was always moving. Chris, who was so handsome.

I stood and looked at the yellow telegram and tried to think what it would be like. Now, for Chris. I thought of things I had seen dead: dogs and mice and cats. They were born dead, or they died because they were old. Or they died because they were killed. I had seen them with their heads pulled aside and their insides spilled out red on the ground. It wouldn't be so different for a man.

But Chris . . .

"Even if you black," Pete was saying, "you good enough to get sent off to die."

And Ma said: "You shut you mouth!" She'd lifted her head up

from her lap, and the creases on her cheeks were quivering and her brown eyes stared—cotton eyes, the kids used to call them.

"You shut you mouth!" Ma shouted. She'd never talked that way before. Not to Pete. Her voice was hoarser even, because she had been crying without tears.

And Pete yelled right back, the way he'd never done before: "Sweet Jesus, I ain't gonna shut up for nobody when I'm talking the truth!"

I made a wide circle around him and went in the bedroom. Lena was sitting there, on the bed, with the pillows propped behind her. Her face was quiet and dull. There wasn't anything moving on it, not a line. There was no way of telling if she even heard the voices over in the kitchen.

I stood at the foot of the bed and put both hands on the cold iron railing. "Lena," I said, "you all right?"

She heard me. She shifted her eyes slowly over to me until they were looking directly at me. But she didn't answer. Her eyes, brown now and dark, stared straight into mine without shifting or moving or blinking or lightening. I stepped aside. The eyes didn't move with me. They stayed where they were, caught up in the air.

From the kitchen I could hear Pete and Ma shouting back and forth at each other until Ma finally gave way in deep dry sobbings that slowed and finally stopped. For a second or so everything was perfectly still. Then Ma said what had been in the back of our minds for months, only I didn't ever expect to hear her say it, not to her only boy.

"You no son of mine." She paused for a minute and I could hear the deep catching breath she took. "You no man even." Her voice was level and steady. Only, after every couple of words she'd have to stop for breath. "You a coward. A god-damn coward. And you made youself a cripple for all you life."

All of a sudden Pete began to laugh—high and thin and

ragged. "Maybe—maybe. But me, I'm breathing. And he ain't . . . Chris was fine and he ain't breathing."

Lena didn't give any sign that she'd heard. I went around to the side of the bed and took her hand: it was cold and heavy.

Pete was giggling; you could hardly understand what he was saying. "He want to cross over, him."

Ma wasn't interrupting him now. He went right ahead, choking on the words. "Chris boy, you fine and you brave and you ain't run out on what you got to do. And you ain't breathing neither. But you a man . . ."

Lena's hand moved ever so slightly.

"Lena," I said, "you all right?"

"Chris boy . . . you want to cross over . . . and you sure enough cross over . . . why, man, you sure cross over . . . but good, you cross over."

"Lena," I said, "don't you pay any mind to him. He's sort of crazy."

In the kitchen Pete was saying: "Chris, you a man, sure . . . sure . . . you sure cross over . . . but ain't you gonna come back for Lena? Ain't you coming back to get her?"

I looked down and saw that my hand was shaking. My whole body was. It had started at my legs and come upward. I couldn't see clearly either. Edges of things blurred together. Only one thing I saw clear: Chris lying still and dead.

"It didn't get you nowhere, Chris boy," Pete was giggling. "Being white and fine, where it got you? Where it got you? Dead and rotten."

And Lena said: "Stop him, Chris."

She said: "Stop him, Chris, please."

I heard her voice, soft and low and pleading, the way she wouldn't speak to anyone else, but only her husband.

Chris, dead on the other side of the world, covered with ground.

Pete was laughing. "Dead and gone, boy. Dead and gone."

"Stop him, Chris," Lena said, talking to somebody buried on the other side of the world. "Stop him, Chris."

But I was the only one who heard her. Just me; just me.

You could see her come back from wherever she'd been. Her eyes blinked a couple of times slowly and when they looked at me, they saw me. Really saw me, her little sister. Not Chris, just Celia.

Slowly she pushed herself up from the bed and went into the kitchen, where Pete was still laughing.

Ma was sitting at the table, arms stretched out, head resting on them. She wasn't crying anymore; it hardly looked like she was breathing.

"Dead and gone, man." Pete was teetering his chair back and forth, tapping it against the wall, so that everything on the little shelf over his head shook and moved. He had his mouth wide open, so wide that his eyes closed.

Lena hit him, hard as she could with the flat of her hand, hit him right across the face. And then she brought her left hand up, remembering to make a fist this time. It caught him square in the chest.

I heard him gasp; then he was standing up and things were falling from the shelf overhead. Lena stumbled back. And right where her hand struck the floor was the picture of our father, the picture in the silver metal frame, the one Ma had got out the night Chris first came.

She had it in her hand when she scrambled back to her feet. She was crying now, because he was still laughing. From far away I could hear her gasping: "Damn, damn, damn, damn." And she swung the picture frame in a wide arc at his laughing mouth. He saw it coming and forgot for just a moment and lifted his arm to cover his face. And the frame and glass smashed into his stub arm.

He screamed: not loud, just a kind of high-pitched gasp. And he turned and ran. I was in the way and he knocked me aside as he yanked open the door. He missed his footing on the steps and fell down into the alley. I could hear him out there, still screaming softly to himself with the pain: "Jesus, Jesus, Jesus, Jesus."

Lena stood in the middle of the room, her hands hanging down empty at her sides. Her lip was cut; there was a little trickle of blood down the corner of her mouth. Her tongue came out, tasted, and then licked it away.

PLEADINGS

BY JOHN WILLIAM CORRINGTON

Uptown

(Originally published in 1976)

I

Dinner was on the table when the phone rang, and Joan just stared at me.

—Go ahead, answer it. Maybe they need you in Washington.

—I don't want to get disbarred, I said.—More likely they need me at the Parish Prison.

I was closer than she was. It was Bertram Bijou, a deputy out in Jefferson Parish. He had a friend. With troubles. Being a lawyer, you find out that nobody has trouble, really. It's always a friend.

—Naw, on the level, Bert said.—You know Howard Bedlow?

No, I didn't know Howard Bedlow, but I would pretty soon.

They came to the house after supper. As a rule, I put people off when they want to come to the house. They've got eight hours a day to find out how to incorporate, write a will, pull their taxes down, or whatever. In the evening I like to sit quiet with Joan. We read and listen to Haydn or Boccherini and watch the light fade over uptown New Orleans. Sometimes, though I do not tell her, I like to imagine we are a late Roman couple sitting in our atrium in the countryside of England, not far from Londinium. It is always summer, and Septimus Severus has not yet begun to tax Britain out of existence. Still, it is twilight now, and there is nothing before us. We are young, but the world is old, and that is all right because the drive and the hysteria of destiny is past now, and we can sit and enjoy our garden, the twisted ivy, the huge caladiums, and if it is April, the daffodils that plunder our weak sun and sparkle across the land. It is always cool in my fantasy, and Joan crochets something for the center of our table, and I refuse to think of the burdens of administration that I will have to lift again tomorrow. They will wait, and Rome will never even know. It is always a hushed single moment, ageless and serene, and I am with her, and only the hopeless are still ambitious. Everything we will do has been done, and for the moment there is peace.

It is a silly fantasy, dreamed here in the heart of booming America, but it makes me happy, and so I was likely showing my mild irritation when Bert and his friend Howard Bedlow turned up. I tried to be kind. For several reasons. Bert is a nice man. An honest deputy, a politician in a small way, and perhaps what the Civil Law likes to call *un bon pere du famille*—though I think at Common Law Bert would be "an officious intermeddler." He seems prone to get involved with people. Partly because he would like very much to be on the Kenner City Council one day, but, I like to imagine, as much because there lingers in the Bijou blood some tincture of piety brought here and nurtured by his French sires and his Sicilian and Spanish maternal ascendants. New Orleans has people like that. A certain kindness, a certain sympathy left over from the days when one person's anguish or that of a family was the business of all their neighbors. Perhaps that fine and profound Catholic certainty of death and judgment which makes us all one.

And beyond approving Bert as a type, I have found that most people who come for law are in one way or another distressed: the distress of loss or fear, of humiliation or sudden realization. Or the more terrible distress of greed, appetite gone wild, the very biggest of deals in the offing, and O, my God, don't let me muff it.

Howard Bedlow was in his late forties. He might have been the Celtic gardener in my imaginary Roman garden. Taller than average, hair a peculiar reddish gold more suited to a surfing king than to an unsuccessful car salesman, he had that appearance of a man scarce half made up that I had always associated with European workmen and small tradesmen. His cuffs were frayed and too short. His collar seemed wrong; it fit neither his neck nor the thin stringy tie he wore knotted more or less under it. Once, some years ago, I found, he had tried to make a go of his own Rambler franchise, only to see it go down like a gunshot animal, month by month, week by week, until at last no one, not even the manager of the taco place next door, would cash his checks or give him a nickel for a local phone call.

Now he worked, mostly on commission, for one used car lot or another, as Bert told it. He had not gone bankrupt in the collapse of the Rambler business, but had sold his small house on the west bank and had paid off his debts, almost all of them dollar for dollar, fifty here, ten there. When I heard that, I decided against offering them coffee. I got out whiskey. You serve a man what he's worth, even if he invades your fantasies.

As Bert talked on, only pausing to sip his bourbon, Bedlow sat staring into his glass, his large hands cupping it, his fingers moving restlessly around its rim, listening to Bert as if he himself had no stake in all that was passing. I had once known a musician who had sat that way when people caught him in a situation where talk was inevitable. Like Bedlow, he was not resentful, only elsewhere, and his hands, trained to a mystical perfection, worked over and over certain passages in some silent score.

Bedlow looked up as Bert told about the house trailer he, Bedlow, lived in now—or had lived in until a week or so before. Bedlow frowned almost sympathetically, as if he could find some measure of compassion for a poor man who had come down so far.

—Now I got to be honest, Bert said at last, drawing a deep breath.—Howard, he didn't want to come. Bad times with lawyers.

—I can see that, I said.

—He can't put all that car franchise mess out of mind. Bitter, you know. Gone down hard. Lawyers like vultures, all over the place.

Bedlow nodded, frowning. Not in agreement with Bert on his own behalf, but as if he, indifferent to all this, could appreciate a man being bitter, untrusting after so much. I almost wondered if the trouble wasn't Bert's, so distant from it Bedlow seemed.

—I got to be honest, Bert said again. Then he paused, looking down at his whiskey. Howard studied his drink too.

—I told Howard he could come along with me to see you, or I had to take him up to Judge Talley. DWI, property damage, foul and abusive, resisting, public obscenity. You could pave the river with charges. I mean it.

All right. You could. And sometimes did. Some wise-ass tries to take apart Millie's Bar, the only place for four blocks where a working man can sit back and sip one without a lot of hassle. You take and let him consider the adamantine justice of Jefferson Parish for thirty days or six months before you turn him loose at the causeway and let him drag back to St. Tammany Parish with what's left of his tail tucked between his legs. Discretion of the Officer. That's the way it is, the way it's always been, the way it'll be till the whole human race learns how to handle itself in Millie's Bar.

But you don't do that with a friend. Makes no sense. You don't cart him off to Judge Elmer Talley who is the scourge of the working class if the working class indulges in what others call the curse of the working class. No, Bert was clubbing his buddy. To get him to an Officer of the Court. All right.

—He says he wants a divorce, Bert said.—Drinks like a three-legged hog and goes to low rating his wife in public and so on. Ain't that fine?

No, Bedlow acknowledged, frowning, shaking his head. It was *not* fine. He agreed with Bert, you could tell. It was sorry, too damned bad.

—I'm not going to tell you what he called his wife over to Sammie's Lounge last night. Sammie almost hit him. You know what I mean?

Yes I did. Maybe, here and there, the fire is not entirely out. I have known a man to beat another very nearly to death because the first spoke slightingly of his own mother. One does not talk that way about women folk, not even one's own. The lowly, the ignored, and the abused remember what the high-born and the wealthy have forgotten.

—Are you separated? I asked Bedlow.

—I ain't livin with the woman, he said laconically. It was the first time he had spoken since he came into my house.

—What's the trouble?

He told me. Told me in detail while Bert listened and made faces of astonishment and disbelief at me. Bert could still be astonished after seventeen years on the Jefferson Parish Sheriff's squad. You wonder that I like him?

It seemed that there had been adultery. A clear and flagrant act of faithlessness resulting in a child. A child that was not his, not a Bedlow. He had been away, in the wash of his financial troubles, watching the Rambler franchise expire, trying hard to do right. And she did it, swore to Christ and the Virgin she never did it, and went to confinement carrying another man's child.

—When? I asked—How old is . . . ?

—Nine, Bedlow said firmly.—He's . . . it's nine . . .

I stared at Bert. He shrugged. It seemed to be no surprise to him. Oh, hell, I thought. Maybe what this draggle-assed country needs is an emperor. Even if he taxes us to death and declares war on Guatemala. This is absurd.

—Mr. Bedlow, I said.—You can't get a divorce for adultery with a situation like that.

—How come?

—You've been living with her all that . . . nine years?

—Yeah.

—They . . . call it reconciliation. No way. If you stay on, you are presumed . . . what the hell. How long have you lived apart?

—Two weeks and two days, he answered. I suspected he could have told me the hours and minutes.

—I couldn't take it anymore. Knowing what I know . . .

Bedlow began to cry. Bert looked away, and I suppose I did. I have not seen many grown men cry cold sober. I have seen them mangled past any hope of life, twisting, screaming, cursing. I have seen them standing by a wrecked car while police and firemen tried to saw loose the bodies of their wives and children. I have seen men, told of the death of their one son, stand hard-jawed with tears running down their slabby sunburned cheeks, but that was not crying. Bedlow was crying, and he did not seem the kind of man who cries.

I motioned Bert back into the kitchen.—What the hell . . .

—This man, Bert said, spreading his hands,—is in trouble.

—All right, I said, hearing Bedlow out in the parlor, still sobbing as if something more than his life might be lost.—All right. But I don't think it's a lawyer he needs.

Bert frowned, outraged.—Well, he sure don't need one of . . . them.

I could not be sure whether he was referring to priests or psychiatrists. Or both. Bert trusted the law. Even working with it, knowing better than I its open sores and ugly fissures, he believed in it, and for some reason saw me as one of its dependable functionaries. I guess I was pleased by that.

—Fill me in on this whole business, will you?

Yes, he would, and would have earlier over the phone, but he had been busy mollifying Sammie and some of his customers who wanted to lay charges that Bert could not have sidestepped.

It was short and ugly, and I was hooked. Bedlow's wife was a good woman. The child was a hopeless defective. It was kept up at Pineville, at the Louisiana hospital for the feebleminded, or whatever the social scientists are calling imbeciles this year. A vegetating thing that its mother had named Albert Sidney Bedlow before they had taken it away, hooked it up for a lifetime of intravenous feeding, and added it to the schedule of cleaning up filth and washing, and all the things they do for human beings who can do nothing whatever for themselves. But Irma Bedlow couldn't let it go at that. The state is equipped, albeit poorly, for this kind of thing. It happens. You let the thing go, and they see to it, and one day, usually not long hence, it dies of pneumonia or a virus, or one of the myriad diseases that float and sift through the air of a place like that. This is the way these things are done, and all of us at the law have drawn up papers for things called "Baby So-and-so," sometimes, mercifully, without their parents having laid eyes on them.

Irma Bedlow saw it otherwise. During that first year, while the Rambler franchise was bleeding to death, while Bedlow was going half crazy, she had spent most of her time up in Alexandria, a few miles from the hospital, at her cousin's. So that she could visit Albert Sidney every day.

She would go there, Bert told me—as Bedlow had told him—and sit in the drafty ward on a hard chair next to Albert Sidney's chipped institutional crib, with her rosary, praying to Jesus Christ that He would send down His grace on her baby, make him whole, and let her suffer in his place. She would kneel in the twilight beside the bed stiff with urine, and stinking of such excrement as a child might produce who has never tasted food, amidst the bedlam of chattering and choking and animal sounds from bedridden idiots, cretins, declining mongoloids, microcephalics, and assorted other exiles from the great altarpiece of Hieronymus Bosch. Somehow, the chief psychologist had told Howard, her praying upset the other inmates of the ward, and at last he had to forbid Irma coming more than once a month. He told her that the praying was out altogether.

After trying to change the chief psychologist's mind, and failing, Irma had come home. The franchise was gone by then, and they had a secondhand trailer parked in a rundown court where they got water, electricity, and gas from pipes in the ground and a sullen old man in a prewar De Soto station wagon picked up garbage once a week. She said the rosary there, and talked about Albert Sidney to her husband who, cursed now with freedom by the ruin of his affairs, doggedly looking for some kind of a job, had nothing much to do or think about but his wife's abstracted words and the son he had almost had. Indeed, did have, but had in such a way that the having was more terrible than the lack.

It had taken no time to get into liquor, which his wife never touched, she fasting and praying, determined that no small imperfection in herself should stay His hand who could set things right with Albert Sidney in the flash of a moment's passing.

—And in that line, Bert said,—she ain't . . . they . . . never been man and wife since then. You know what I mean?

—Ummm.

—And she runs off on him. Couple or three times a year. They always find her at the cousin's. At least till last year. Her cousin won't have her around anymore. Seems Irma wanted her to fast for Albert Sidney too. Wanted the cousin's whole family to do it, and there was words, and now she just takes a room at the tourist court by the hospital and tries to get in as often as that chief psychologist will let her. But no praying, he holds to that.

—What does Bedlow believe?

—Claims he believes she got Albert Sidney with some other man.

—No, I mean . . . does he believe in praying?

—Naw. Too honest, I guess. Says he don't hold with beads and saying the same thing over and over. Says God stands on His own feet, and expects the same of us. Says we ain't here to s . . . around. What's done is done.

—Do you think he wants a divorce?

—Could he get one . . . ?

—Yes.

—Well, how do I know?

—You brought him here. He's not shopping for religious relics, is he?

Bert looked hurt. As if I were blaming him unfairly for some situation beyond his control or prevention.

—You want him in jail?

—No, I said.—I just don't know what to do about him. Where's he living?

—Got a cabin at the Bo-Peep Motel. Over off Veterans Highway. He puts in his time at the car lot and then goes to drinking and telling people his wife has done bastardized him.

—Why did he wait so long to come up with that line?

—It just come on him, what she must of done, he told me.

—That's right, Bedlow said, his voice raspy, aggressive.—I ain't educated or anything. I studies on it and after so long it come to me. I saw it wasn't *mine*, that . . . thing of hers. Look, how come she can't just get done mourning and say, well, that's how it falls out sometimes and I'm sorry as all hell, but you got to keep going. That's what your ordinary woman would say, ain't it?

He had come to the kitchen where Bert and I were standing, his face still wet with tears. He came in talking, and the flow went on as if he were as compulsive with his tongue as he was with a bottle. The words tumbled out so fast that you felt he must have practiced, this country man, to speak so rapidly, to say so much.

—But no. I tell you what: she's mourning for what she done to that . . . thing's real father, that's what she's been doing. He likely lives in Alex, and she can't get over what she done him when she got that . . . thing. And I tell you this, I said, look, honey, don't give it no name, 'cause if you give it a name, you're gonna think that name over and over and make like it was the name of a person and it ain't, and it'll ruin us just as sure as creaking hell. And she went and named it my father's name, who got it after Albert Sidney Johnston at Shiloh . . . look, I ain't laid a hand on that woman in God knows how many years, I tell you that. So you see, that's what these trips is about. She goes up and begs his pardon for not giving him a fine boy like he wanted, and she goes to see . . . the thing, and mourns . . . and g . . . . . . t to hell, I got to get shut of this . . . whole *thing*.

It came in a rush, as if, even talking, saying more words in the space of a moment than he had ever said before, Bedlow was enlarging, perfecting his suspicions—no, his certainty of what had been done to him.

We were silent for a moment.

—Well, it's hard, Bert said at last.

—Hard? Bedlow glared at him as if Bert had insulted him. —You don't even know hard . . .

—All right, I said.—We'll go down to the office in the morning and draw up and file.

—Huh?

—We'll file for legal separation. Will your wife contest it?

—Huh?

—I'm going to get you what you want. Will your wife go along?

—Well, I don't know. She don't . . . think about . . . things. If you was to tell her, I don't know.

Bert looked at him, his large dark face settled and serious. —That woman's a . . . Catholic, he said at last, and Bedlow stared back at him as if he had named a new name, and things needed thinking again.

A little while later they left, with Bedlow promising me and promising Bertram Bijou that he'd be in my office the next morning. For a long time after I closed the door behind them, I sat looking at the empty whiskey glasses and considered the course of living in the material world. Then I went and fixed me a shaker of martinis, and became quickly wiser. I considered that it was time to take Zeno seriously, give over the illusion of motion, of sequence. There are only a few moments in any life and when they arrive, they are fixed forever and we play through them, pretending to go on, but coming back to them over and over, again and again. If it is true that we can only approach a place but never reach it as the Philosopher claims, it must be corollary that we may almost leave a moment, but never quite. And so, as Dr. Freud so clearly saw, one moment, one vision, one thing come upon us, becomes the whole time and single theme of all we will ever do or know. We are invaded by our own one thing, and going on is a dream we have while lying still.

I thought, too, mixing one last shaker, that of the little wisdom in this failing age, Alcoholics Anonymous must possess more than its share. I am an alcoholic, they say. I have not had a drink in nine years, but I am an alcoholic, and the shadow, the motif of my living, is liquor bubbling into a glass over and over, again and again. That is all I really want, and I will never have it again because I will not take it, and I know that I will never really know why not.

—It's bedtime, Joan said, taking my drink and sipping it.

—What did they want?

—A man wants a divorce because nine years ago his wife had a feebleminded baby. He says it's not his. Wants me to claim adultery and unclaim the child.

—Nice man.

—Actually, I began. Then no. Bedlow did not seem a nice man or not a nice man. He seemed a driven man, outside whatever might be his element. So I said that.

—Who isn't? Joan sniffed. She is not the soul of charity at two thirty in the morning.

—What? Isn't what?

—Driven. Out of her . . . his . . . element?

I looked at her. Is it the commonest of things for men in their

forties to consider whether their women are satisfied? Is it a sign
of the spirit's collapse when you wonder how and with whom she
spends her days? What is the term for less than suspicion: a tiny
circlet of thought that touches your mind at lunch with clients or
on the way to the office, almost enough to make you turn back
home, and then disappears like smoke when you try to fix it, search
for a word or an act that might have stirred it to life?

—Are you . . . driven? I asked much too casually.

—Me? No, she sighed, kissing me.—I'm different, she said.
Was she too casual too?

—Bedlow isn't different. I think he wants it all never to have
happened. He had a little car franchise and a pregnant wife ten
years ago. Clover. He had it made. Then it all went away.

Joan lit a cigarette, crossed her legs, and sat down on the floor
with my drink. Her wrapper fell open, and I saw the shadow of her
breasts.—It always goes away. If you know anything, you know
that. Hang on as long as you can. 'Cause it's going away. If you
know anything . . .

I looked at her as she talked. She was as beautiful as the first
time I had seen her. It was an article of faith: nothing had changed.
Her body was still as soft and warm in my arms, and I wait for summer to see her in a bathing suit, and to see her take it off, water
running out of her blond hair, between her breasts that I love better than whatever it is that I love next best.

—Sometimes it doesn't go away, I said. Ponderously, I'm sure.

She cocked her head, almost said something, and sipped the
drink instead.

What made me think then of the pictures there in the parlor?
I went over them in the silence, the flush of gin, remembering
where and when we had bought each one. That one in San Francisco, in a Japanese gallery, I thinking that I would not like it long,
but thinking too that it didn't matter, since we were at the end of a
long difficult case with a fee to match. So if I didn't like it later, well . . .

And the Danish ship, painted on wood in the seventeenth century. I still liked it very much. But why did I think of these things? Was it that they stood on the walls, amidst our lives, adding some measure of substance and solidity to them, making it seem that the convention of living together, holding lovely things in common, added reality to the lives themselves? Then, or was it later, I saw us sitting not in a Roman garden in Britain, but in a battered house trailer in imperial America, the walls overspread with invisible pictures in the image of a baby's twisted unfinished face. And how would that be? How would we do then?

Joan smiled, lightly sardonic.—Ignore it, and it'll go away.

—Was there . . . something I was supposed to do? I asked.

The smile deepened, then faded.—Not a thing, she said.

II

The next morning, a will was made, two houses changed hands, a corporation, closely held, was born, seven suits were filed, and a deposition was taken from a whore who claimed that her right of privacy was invaded when the vice squad caught her performing an act against nature on one of their members in a French Quarter alley. Howard Bedlow did not turn up. Joan called just after lunch.

—I think I'll go over to the beach house for a day or two, she said, her voice flat and uncommunicative as only a woman's can be.

I guess there was a long pause. It crossed my mind that once I had wanted to be a musician, perhaps even learn to compose.—I can't get off till the day after tomorrow, I said, knowing that my words were inapposite to anything she might have in mind.—I could come Friday.

—That would be nice.

—Are you . . . taking the children?

—Louise will take care of them.

—You'll be . . . by yourself?

A pause on her side this time.

—Yes. Sometimes . . . things get out of hand.

—Anything you want to talk about?

She laughed.—You're the talker in the family.

—And you're what? The actor. Or the thinker?

—That's it. I don't know.

My voice went cold then. I couldn't help it.—Let me know if you figure it out. Then I hung up. And thought at once that I shouldn't have and yet glad of the miniscule gesture because however puny, it was an act, and acts in law are almost always merely words. I live in a storm of words: words substituting for actions, words to evade actions, words hinting of actions, words pretending actions. I looked down at the deposition on my desk and wondered if they had caught the whore *talking* to the vice squad man in the alley. Give her ten years: the utterance of words is an act against nature, an authentic act against nature. I had read somewhere that in Chicago they have opened establishments wherein neither massage nor sex is offered: only a woman who, for a sum certain in money, will talk to you. She will say anything you want her to say: filth, word-pictures of every possible abomination, fantasies of domination and degradation, sadistic orgies strewn out in detail, oaths, descriptions of rape and castration. For a few dollars you can be told how you molested a small child, how you have murdered your parents and covered the carcasses with excrement, assisted in the gang rape of your second grade teacher. All words.

The authentic crime against nature has finally arrived. It is available somewhere in Chicago. There is no penalty, for after all, it is protected by the first amendment. Scoff on, Voltaire, Rousseau, scoff on.

My secretary, who would like to speak filth to me, buzzed.

—Mr. Bijou.

—Good. Send him in.

—On the phone.

Bert sounded far away.—You ain't seen Howard, have you?

—No, I said.—Have you?

—Drunk somewhere. Called coughing and moaning something about a plot to shame him. Talking like last night. I think you ought to see Irma. You're supposed to seek reconciliation, ain't you?

—I think you're ripe for law school, Bert. Yes, that's what they say do.

—Well, he said.—Lemme see what I can do.

I was afraid of that. When I got home there was a note from Louise, the childrens' nurse. She had taken them to her place up in Livingston Parish for a day or two. They would like that. The house was deserted, and I liked that. Not really. I wondered what a fast trip to the Gulf coast would turn up, or a call to a friend of mine in Biloxi who specializes in that kind of thing. But worse, I wasn't sure I cared. Was it that I didn't love Joan anymore, that somewhere along the way I had become insulated against her acts? Could it be that the practice of law had slowly made me responsive only to words? Did I need to go to Chicago to feel real again?

I was restless and drank too many martinis and was involved so much in my own musings that time passed quickly. I played some Beethoven, God knows why. I am almost never so distraught that I enjoy spiritual posturing. Usually, his music makes me grin.

I tried very hard to reckon where I was and what I should do. I was in the twentieth century after Christ, and it felt all of that long since anything on earth had mattered. I was in a democratic empire called America, an officer of its courts, and surely a day in those courts is as a thousand years. I was an artisan in words, shaping destinies, allocating money and blame by my work. I was past the midpoint of my life and could not make out what it had meant so far.

Now amidst this time and place, I could do almost as I chose. Should it be the islands of the Pacific with a box of paints? To the Colorado mountains with a pack, beans, a guitar, pencils, and much paper? Or, like an anchorite, declare the longest of nonterminal hunger strikes, this one against God Almighty, hoping that public opinion forces Him to reveal that for which I was made and put in this place and time.

Or why not throw over these ambiguities, this wife doing whatever she might be doing on the coast of the Gulf, these anonymous children content with Louise up the country, contemplating chickens, ducks, and guinea-fowl. Begin again. Say every word you have ever said, to new people: Hello, new woman, I love you. I have good teeth and most of my mind. I can do well on a good night in a happy bed. Hello, new colleagues, what do we do this time? Is this a trucking firm or a telephone exchange? What is the desiderata? Profit or prophecy?

Bert shook my arm.—Are you okay? You didn't answer the door.

I studied him for a moment, my head soft and uncentered. I was nicely drunk, but coming back.—Yeah, I said.—I'm fine. What have you got tonight?

—Huh? Listen, can I turn down that music?

—Sure.

He doused the Second Symphony, and I found I was relieved, could breathe more deeply.—I brought her, he said.—She's kinda spaced out, like the kids say.

He frowned, watched me.—You sure you're all right?

I smiled.—All I needed was some company, Bert.

He smiled back.—All right, fine. You're probably in the best kind of shape for Irma.

—Huh?

He looked at the empty martini pitcher.—Nothing. She's just . . .

His voice trailed off and I watched him drift out of my line of sight. In the foyer, I could hear his voice, soft and distant, as if he were talking to a child.

I sobered up. Yes, I have that power. I discovered it in law school. However drunk, I can gather back in the purposely loosed strands of personality or whatever of us liquor casts apart. It is as if one were never truly sober, and hence one could claim back from liquor what it had never truly loosed. Either drunkenness or sobriety is an illusion.

Irma Bedlow was a surprise. I had reckoned on a woman well gone from womanhood. One of those shapeless bun-haired middle-aged creatures wearing bifocals, smiling out from behind the secrecy of knowing that they are at last safe from any but the most psychotic menaces from unbalanced males. But it was not that way. If I had been dead drunk on the one hand, or shuffling up to the communion rail on the other, she would have turned me around.

She was vivid. Dark hair and eyes, a complexion almost pale, a lovely body made more so by the thoughtless pride with which she inhabited it. She sat down opposite me, and our eyes held for a long moment.

I am used to a certain deference from people who come to me in legal situations. God knows we have worked long and hard enough to establish the mandarin tradition of the law, that circle of mysteries that swallows up laymen and all they possess like a vast desert or a hidden sea. People come to the law on tiptoe, watching, wishing they could know which words, what expressions and turns of phrase are *the ones* which bear their fate. I have smiled remembering that those who claim or avoid the law with such awe have themselves in their collectivity created it. But they are so far apart from one another in the sleep of their present lives that they cannot remember what they did together when they were awake.

But Irma Bedlow looked at me as if she were the counselor, her dark eyes fixed on mine to hold me to whatever I might say. Would I lie, and put both our cases in jeopardy? Would I say the best I knew, or had I wandered so long amidst the stunted shrubs of language, making unnatural acts in the name of my law, that words had turned from stones with which to build into ropy clinging undergrowth in which to become enmeshed?

I asked her if she would have a drink. I was surprised when she said yes. Fasts for the sake of an idiot child, trying to get others to do it, praying on her knees to Jesus beside the bed of Albert Sidney who did not know about the prayers, and who could know about Jesus only through infused knowledge there within the mansions of his imbecility. But yes, she said, and I went to fix it.

Of course Bert followed me over to the bar.—I don't know. I think maybe I ought to take care of Howard and let *her* be your client.

—Don't do that, I said, and wondered why I'd said it.

—She's fine, Bert was saying, and I knew he meant nothing to do with her looks. He was not a carnal man, Bert. He was a social man. Once he had told me he wanted either to be mayor of Kenner or a comedian. He did not mean it humorously and I did not take it so. He was the least funny of men. Rather he understood with his nerves the pathos of living and would have liked to divert us from it with comedy. But it would not be so, and Bert would end up mayor trying to come to grips with our common anguish instead of belittling it.

—I never talked to anyone like her. You'll see.

I think then I envisioned the most beautiful and desirable Jehovah's Witness in the world. Would we try conclusions over Isaiah? I warn you, Irma, I know the Book and other books beyond number. I am a prince in the kingdom of words, and I have seen raw respect flushed up unwillingly in the eye of other lawmongers, and have had my work mentioned favorably in appellate decisions which, in their small way, rule all this land.

—Here you are, I said.

She smiled at me as if I were a child who had brought his mother a cool drink unasked.

—Howard came to see you, she said, sipping the martini as if gin bruised with vermouth were her common fare.—Can you help me . . . help him?

—He wants a divorce, I said, confused, trying to get things in focus.

—No, she said. Not aggressively, only firmly. Her information was better than mine. I have used the same tone of voice with other attorneys many times. When you know, you know.

—He only wants it over with, done with. That's what he wants, she said.

Bert nodded. He had heard this before. There goes Bert's value as a checkpoint with reality. He believes her. Lordy.

—You mean . . . the marriage?

—No, not that. He knows what I know. If it *was* a marriage, you can't make it be over. You can only desert it. He wouldn't do that.

I shrugged, noticing that she had made no use of her beauty at all so far. She did not disguise it or deny it. She allowed it to exist and simply ignored it. Her femininity washed over me, and yet I knew that it was not directed toward me. It had some other focus, and she saw me as a moment, a crossing in her life, an occasion to stop and turn back for an instant before going on. I wondered what I would be doing for her.

—He *says* he wants a divorce.

She looked down at her drink. Her lashes were incredibly long, though it was obvious she used no makeup at all. Her lips were deep red, a color not used in lipsticks since the forties. I understood why Bedlow drank. Nine years with a beautiful woman you love and cannot touch. Is that your best idea?

—He told you . . . I'd been unfaithful.

Bert was shaking his head, blushing. Not negating what Howard had said, or deprecating it.

—He said that, I told her.

—And that our baby . . . that Albert Sidney wasn't . . . his?

—Yes, I said. Bert looked as if he would cry from shame.

She had not looked up while we talked. Her eyes stayed down, and while I waited, I heard the Beethoven tape, turned down but not off, running out at the end of the—Appassionata. It was a good moment to get up and change to something decent. I found a Vivaldi Chamber Mass, and the singers were very happy. The music was for God in the first instance, not for the spirit of fraternity or Napoleon or some other rubbish.

—What else? she asked across the room. I flipped the tape on, and eighteenth-century Venice came at us from four sides. I cut back the volume.

—He said you . . . hadn't been man and wife for nine years.

—All right.

I walked back and sat down again. I felt peculiar, neither drunk nor sober, so I poured another one. The first I'd had since they came.—Howard didn't seem to think so. He said . . . you wouldn't let him touch you.

She raised her eyes then. Not angrily, only that same firmness again.—That's not true, she said, no, whispered, and Bert nodded as though he had been an abiding presence in the marriage chamber for all those nine long years. He could contain himself no more. He fumbled in his coat pocket and handed me a crumpled and folded sheet of paper. It was a notice from American Motors canceling Howard Bedlow's franchise. Much boilerplate saying he hadn't delivered and so on. Enclosed find copy of agency contract with relevant revocation clauses underlined. Arrangements will be made for stock on hand, etc.

It was dated 9 May 1966. Bert was watching me. I nodded. —Eight years ago, I said.

—Not ten, Bert was going on.—You see . . .

—He lost the business . . . six months after . . . the . . . Albert Sidney.

We sat looking at the paper.

—I never denied him, Irma was saying.—After the baby . . . he couldn't. At first, we didn't think of it. What had we done? What had gone wrong? What were we . . . supposed to do? Was there something we were supposed to do?

—Genes were wrong . . . hormones, who knows? I said.

Irma smiled at me. Her eyes were black, not brown.—Do you believe that?

—Sure, I said, startled as one must be when he has uttered what passes for a common truth and it is questioned.—What else?

—Nothing, she said.—It's only . . .

She and Bert were both staring at me as if I had missed something. Then Irma leaned forward.—Will you go somewhere with me?

I was thinking of the Gulf coast, staring down at the face of my watch. It was almost one thirty. There was a moon and the tide was in, and the moon would be rolling through soft beds of cloud.

—Yes, I said.—Yes I will. Yes.

III

It was early in the morning when we reached Alexandria. The bus trip had been long and strange. We had talked about East Texas where Irma had grown up. Her mother had been from Evangeline Parish, her father a tool-pusher in the Kilgore fields until he lost both hands to a wild length of chain. She had been keeping things together working as a waitress when she met Howard.

On the bus, as if planted there, had been a huge black woman with a little boy whose head was tiny and pointed. It was so distorted that his eyes were pulled almost vertical. He made inarticulate noises and rooted about on the floor of the bus. The other passengers tried to ignore him, but the stench was very bad, and his mother took him to an empty seat in back and changed him several times. Irma helped once. The woman had been loud, aggressive, unfriendly when Irma approached her, but Irma whispered something, and the woman began to cry, her sobs loud and terrible. When they had gotten the child cleaned up, the black woman put her arms around Irma and kissed her.

—I tried hard as I could, miss, but I can't manage . . . oh, sweet Jesus knows I wisht I was dead first. But I can't manage the other four . . . I *got* to . . .

The two of them sat together on the rear seat for a long time, holding hands, talking so softly that I couldn't hear. Once, the boy crawled up and stopped at my seat. He looked up at me like some invertebrate given the power to be quizzical. I wondered which of us was in hell. He must have been about twelve years old.

In the station, Irma made a phone call while I had coffee. People moved through the twilit terminal, meeting, parting. One elderly woman in a thin print dress thirty years out of date even among country people kissed a young man in an army uniform good-bye. Her lips trembled as he shouldered his dufflebag and moved away.—Stop, she cried out, and then realized that he could not stop, because the dispatcher was calling the Houston bus. —Have you . . . forgotten anything? The soldier paused, smiled, and shook his head. Then he vanished behind some people trying to gather up clothes which had fallen from a cardboard suitcase with a broken clasp. Somewhere a small child cried as if it had awakened to find itself suddenly, utterly lost.

Irma came back and drank her coffee, and when we walked outside it was daylight in Alexandria, even as on the Gulf coast. An old station wagon with a broken muffler pulled up, and a thin man wearing glasses got out and kissed Irma as if it were a ritual and shook hands with me in that peculiar limp and diffident way of country people meeting someone from the city who might represent threat or advantage.

We drove for twenty minutes or so, and slowed down in front of a small white-frame place on a blacktop road not quite in or out of town. The yard was large and littered with wrecked and cannibalized autos. The metal bones of an old Hudson canted into the rubble of a '42 Ford convertible. Super deluxe. There was a shed which must have been an enlarged garage. Inside I could see tools, a lathe, work benches. A young man in overalls without a shirt looked out at us and waved casually. He had a piece of drive shaft in his hand. Chickens ambled stupidly in the grassless yard, pecking at oil patches and clumps of rust.

We had eggs and sausage and biscuits and talked quietly. They were not curious about me. They had seen a great deal during the years and there was nothing to be had from curiosity. You come to learn that things have to be taken as they come and it is no use to probe the gestations of tomorrows before they come. There is very little you can do to prepare.

It turned out there had been no quarrel between Irma and her sister's family. Her sister, plain as Irma was beautiful, who wore thick glasses and walked slowly because of her varicose veins, talked almost without expression, but with some lingering touch of her mother's French accent. She talked on as if she had saved everything she had seen and come to know, saved it all in exhaustive detail, knowing that someone would one day come for her report.

—It wasn't never any quarrel, and Howard had got to know better. Oh, we fussed, sure. My daddy always favored Irma and so I used to take after her over anything, you know. Jesus spare me, I guess I hated my own little sister. Till the baby come, and the Lord lifted the scales from my eyes. I dreamed He come down just for me. He looked like Mr. Denver, the station agent down to the L&N depot, and He said, "Elenor, I had enough stuff out of you, you hear? You see Albert Sidney? You satisfied now? Huh? Is that enough for you? You tell me that, 'cause I got to be getting on. I don't make nobody more beautiful or more smart or anything in this world, but I do sometimes take away their looks or ruin their minds or put blindness on 'em, or send 'em a trouble to break their hearts. Don't ask why 'cause it's not for you to know, but that's what I do. Now what else you want for Irma, huh?"

Tears were flowing down Elenor's face now, but her expression didn't change.—So I saw it was my doing, and I begged Him to set it right, told Him to strike me dead and set it right with that helpless baby. But He just shook His head and pushed up His sleeves like He could hear a through-freight coming. "It's not how it's done. It ain't like changing your mind about a hat or a new dress. You see that?"

—Well, I didn't, but what could I say? I said yes, and He started off and the place where we was began getting kind of fuzzy, then He turned and looked back at me and smiled. "How you know it *ain't* all right with Albert Sidney?" He asked. And I saw then that He loved me after all. Then, when I could hardly see Him, I heard Him say, "Anything you forgot, Elly?" but I never said nothing at all, only crossed myself the way Momma used to do.

Elenor touched her sister's shoulder shyly. Irma was watching me, something close to a smile on her lips.—Well, Elenor said, —We've prayed together since then, ain't we, hon? Irma took her sister's hand and pressed it against her cheek.

—We been close since then, Charlie, Elenor's husband said. —Done us all good. Except for poor Howard.

It seemed Howard had hardened his heart from the first. Charlie had worked for him in the Rambler franchise, manager of the service department. One day they had had words and Charlie quit, left New Orleans which was a plague to him anyway, and set up this little backyard place in Alex.

Why the fight? I asked Charlie. He was getting up to go out to work.—Never mind that, he said.—It . . . didn't have nothing to do with . . . this.

Elenor watched him go.—Yes it did, she began.

—Elenor, Irma stopped her.—Maybe you ought not . . . Charlie's . . .

Elenor was wiping her cheeks with her apron.—This man's a lawyer, ain't he? He knows what's right and wrong.

I winced and felt tired all at once, but you cannot ask for a pitcher of martinis at seven thirty in the morning in a Louisiana country house. That was the extent of my knowledge of right and wrong.

—A couple of months after Albert Sidney was born, I was at their place, Elenor went on.—Trying to help out. I was making the beds when Howard come in. It was early, but Howard was drunk and he talked funny, and before I knew, he pulled me down on the bed, and . . . I couldn't scream, I couldn't. Irma had the baby in the kitchen . . . and he couldn't. He tried to . . . make me . . . help him, but he couldn't anyhow. And I told Charlie, because a man ought to know. And they had words, and after that Charlie whipped him, and we moved up here . . .

Elenor sat looking out of the window where the sun was beginning to show over the trees.—And we come on up here.

Irma looked at her sister tenderly.—Elly, we got to go on over to the hospital now.

As we reached the door, Elenor called out.—Irma . . .

—Yes . . . ?

—Honey, you know how much I love you, don't you?

—I always did know, silly. You were the one didn't know.

We took the old station wagon and huffed slowly out of the yard. Charlie waved at us and his eyes followed us out of sight down the blacktop.

IV

Irma was smiling at me as we coughed along the road.—I feel kind of good, she said.

—I'm glad. Why?

—Like some kind of washday. It's long and hard, but comes the end, and you've got everything hanging out in the fresh air. Clean.

—It'll be dirty again, I said, and wished I could swallow the words almost before they were out.

Her hand touched my arm, and I almost lost control of the car. I kept my eyes on the road to Pineville. I was here to help her, not the other way around. There was too much contact between us already, too much emptiness in me, and what the hell I was doing halfway up the state with the wife of a man who could make out a showing that he was my client was more than I could figure out. Something to do with the Gulf.—There's another washday coming, she whispered, her lips close to my ear.

Will I be ready for washday? I wondered. Lord, how is it that we get ready for washday?

The Louisiana State Hospital is divided into several parts. There is one section for the criminally insane, and another for the feebleminded. This second section is, in turn, divided into what are called "tidy" and "untidy" wards. The difference is vast in terms of logistics and care. The difference in the moral realm is simply that between the seventh and the first circles. Hell is where we are.

Dr. Tumulty met us outside his office. He was a small man with a large nose and glasses which looked rather like those you can buy in a novelty shop—outsized nose attached. Behind the glasses, his eyes were weak and watery. His mouth was very small, and his hair thin, the color of corn shucks. I remember wondering then, at the start of our visit, whether one of the inmates had been promoted. It was a very bad idea, but only one of many.

—Hello, Irma, he said. He did not seem unhappy to see her.

—Hello, Monte, she said.

—He had a little respiratory trouble last week. It seems cleared up now.

Irma introduced us and Dr. Tumulty studied me quizzically. —A lawyer . . . ?

—Counselor, she said.—A good listener. Do you have time to show him around?

He looked at me, Charon sizing up a strange passenger, one who it seemed would be making a round trip.—Sure, all right. You coming?

—No, Irma said softly.—You can bring him to me afterward.

So Dr. Tumulty took me through the wards alone. I will not say everything I saw. There were mysteries in that initiation that will not go down into words. It is all the soul is worth and more to say less than all when you have come back from that place where, if only they knew, what men live and do asleep is done waking and in truth each endless day.

Yes, there were extreme cases of mongolism, cretins and im-beciles, dwarfs and things with enormous heads and bulging eyes, ears like tubes, mouths placed on the sides of their heads. There was an albino without nose or eyes or lips, and it sat in a chair, teeth exposed in a grin that could not be erased, its hands making a series of extremely complicated gestures over and over again, each lengthy sequence a perfect reproduction of the preceding one. The gestures were perfectly symmetrical and the repetition exact and made without pause, a formalism of mindlessness wor-thy of a Balinese dancer or a penance—performance of a secret prayer—played out before the catatonic admiration of three small blacks who sat on the floor before the albino watching its art with a concentration unknown among those who imagine themselves without defect.

This was the tidy ward, and all these inventions of a Bosch whose medium is flesh wore coveralls of dark gray cloth with a name patch on the left breast. This is Paul whose tongue, abnor-mally long and almost black and dry, hangs down his chin, and that, the hairless one with the enormous head and tiny face, who coughs and pets a filthy toy elephant, that is Larry. The dead-white one, the maker of rituals, is Anthony. Watching him are Edward and Joseph and Michael, microcephalics all, looking almost identi-cal in their shared malady.

—Does . . . Anthony, I began.

—All day. Every day, Dr. Tumulty said.—And the others watch. We give him tranquilizers at night. It used to be . . . all night too.

In another ward they kept the females. It was much the same there, except that wandering from one chair to another, watching the others, was a young girl, perhaps sixteen. She would have been pretty—no, she was pretty, despite the gray coverall and the pallor of her skin.—Hello, doctor, she said. Her voice sounded as if it had been recorded—cracked and scratchy. But her body seemed sound, her face normal except for small patches of what looked like eczema on her face. That, and her eyes were a little out of focus. She was carrying a small book covered in imitation red leather. *My Diary*, it said on the cover.

—Does she belong here? I asked Tumulty.

He nodded.—She's been here over a year.

The girl cuddled against him, and I could see that she was trying to press her breasts against him. Her hand wandered down toward his leg. He took her hand gently and stroked her hair.— Hello, doctor, she croaked again.

—Hi, Nancy, he answered.—Are you keeping up your diary?

She smiled.—For home. Hello, doctor.

—For home, sure, he said, and sat her down in a chair opposite an ancient television locked in a wire cage and tuned, I remember, to *Underdog*. She seemed to lose interest in us, to find her way quickly into the role of Sweet Polly, awaiting the inevitable rescue. Around her on the floor were scattered others of the less desperate cases. They watched the animated comedy on the snow-flecked, badly focused screen with absolute concentration. As we moved on, I heard Nancy whisper,—There's no need to fear . . .

—Congenital syphilis, Tumulty said.—It incubates for years, sometimes. She was in high school. Now she's here. It's easier for her now than at first. Most of her mind is gone. In a year she'll be dead.

He paused by a barred window, and looked out on the rolling Louisiana countryside beyond the distant fence.—About graduation time.

—There's no treatment . . . ?

—The cure is dying.

What I can remember of the untidy wards is fragmentary. The stench was very bad, the sounds were nonhuman, and the inmates, divided by sex, were naked in large concrete rooms, sitting on the damp floors, unable to control their bodily functions, obese mostly, and utterly asexual with tiny misshappen heads. There were benches along the sides of the concrete rooms, and the floors sloped down to a central caged drain in the center. One of the things—I mean inmates—was down trying slowly, in a fashion almost reptilian, to lick up filthy moisture from the drain. Another was chewing on a plastic bracelet by which it was identified. Most of the rest, young and older, sat on the benches or the floor staring at nothing, blubbering once in a while, scratching occasionally.

—Once, Dr. Tumulty said thoughtfully,—a legislator came. A budgetary inspection. We didn't get any more money. But he complained that we identified the untidy patients by number. He came and saw everything, and that's . . . what bothered him.

By then we were outside again, walking in the cool Louisiana summer morning. We had been inside less than an hour. I had thought it longer.

—It's the same everywhere. Massachusetts, Wyoming, Texas. Don't think badly of us. There's no money, no personnel, and even if there were . . .

—Then you could only . . . cover it.

—Cosmetics, yes. I've been in this work for eighteen years. I've never forgotten anything I saw. Not anything. You know what I think? What I really *know*?

—. . . ?

Tumulty paused and rubbed his hands together. He shivered a little, that sudden inexplicable thrill of cold inside that has no relationship to the temperature in the world, that represents, according to the old story, someone walking across the ground where your grave will one day be. A mockingbird flashed past us, a dark blur of gray, touched with the white of its wings. Tumulty started to say something, then shrugged and pointed at a small building a little way off.

—They're over there. One of the attendants will show you.

He looked from one building to another, shaking his head. —There's so much to do. So many of them . . .

—Yes, I said.—Thank you. Then I began walking toward the building he had indicated.

—Do . . . whatever you can . . . for her, Dr. Tumulty called after me.—I wish . . .

I turned back toward him. We stood perhaps thirty yards apart then.—Was there . . . something else you wanted to say? I asked.

He looked at me for a long moment, then away.—No, he said.—Nothing.

I stood there as he walked back into the clutter of central buildings, and finally vanished into one of them. Then, before I walked back to join Irma, I found a bench under an old magnolia and sat down for a few minutes. It was on the way to becoming warm now, and the sun's softness and the morning breeze were both going rapidly. The sky was absolutely clear, and by noon it would be very hot indeed. A few people were moving across the grounds. A nurse carrying something on a tray, two attendants talking animatedly to each other, one gesturing madly. Another attendant was herding a patient toward the medical building. It was a black inmate, male or female I could not say, since all the patients' heads were close-cropped for hygienic purposes, and the coverall obscured any other sign of sex. It staggered from one side of the cinder path to the other, swaying as if it were negotiating the deck of a ship in heavy weather out on the Gulf. Its arms flailed, seeking a balance it could never attain, and its eyes seemed to be seeking some point of reference in a world awash. But there was no point, the trees whirling and the buildings losing their way, and so the thing looked skyward, squinted terribly at the sun, pointed upward toward that brazen glory, almost fell down, its contorted black face now fixed undeviatingly toward that burning place in the sky which did not shift and whirl. But the attendant took its shoulder and urged it along, since it could not make its way on earth staring into the sky.

As it passed by my bench, it saw me, gestured at me, leaned in my direction amidst its stumblings, its dark face twinkling with sweat.

—No, Hollis, I heard the attendant say as the thing and I exchanged a long glance amidst the swirling trees, the spinning buildings, out there on the stormy Gulf. Then it grinned, its white teeth sparkling, its eyes almost pulled shut from the effort of grimace, its twisted fingers spieling a language both of us could grasp.

—Come on, Hollis, the attendant said impatiently, and the thing reared its head and turned away. No more time for me. It took a step or two, fell, and rolled in the grass, grunting, making sounds like I had never heard.—Hollis, I swear to God, the attendant said mildly, and helped the messenger to its feet once more.

The nurse in the building Tumulty had pointed out looked at me questioningly.—I'm looking for . . . Mrs. Bedlow.

—You'll have to wait . . . she began, and then her expression changed.—Oh, you must be the one. I knew I'd forgotten something. All right, straight back and to the left. Ward Three.

I walked down a long corridor with lights on the ceiling, each behind its wire cover. I wondered if Hollis might have been the reason for the precaution. Had he or she or it once leaped upward at the light, clawing, grasping, attempting to touch the sun? The walls were covered with an ugly pale yellow enamel which had begun peeling long ago, and the smell of cheap pine-scented deodorizer did not cover the deep ingrained stench of urine, much older than the blistered paint. Ward Three was a narrow dormitory filled with small beds. My eyes scanned the beds and I almost turned back, ready for the untidy wards again. Because here were the small children—what had been intended as children.

Down almost at the end of the ward, I saw Irma. She was seated in a visitor's chair, and in her arms was a child with a head larger than hers. It was gesticulating frantically, and I could hear its sounds the length of the ward. She held it close and whispered to it, kissed it, held it close, and as she drew it to her, the sounds became almost frantic. They were not human sounds. They were Hollis's sounds, and as I walked the length of the ward, I thought I knew what Tumulty had been about to say before he had thought better of it.

—Hello, Irma said. The child in her arms paused in its snufflings and looked up at me from huge unfocused eyes. Its tongue stood out, and it appeared that its lower jaw was congenitally dislocated. Saliva ran down the flap of flesh where you and I have lips, and Irma paid no mind as it dripped on her dress. It would have been pointless to wipe the child's mouth because the flow did not stop, nor did the discharge from its bulging, unblinking eyes. I looked at Irma. Her smile was genuine.

—This is . . . I began.

—Albert Sidney, she finished.—Oh, no. I wish it were. This is Barry. Say hello.

The child grunted and buried its head in her lap, sliding down to the floor and crawling behind her chair.

—You . . . wish . . . ?

—This is Albert Sidney, she said, turning to the bed next to her chair.

He lay there motionless, the sheet drawn up to what might

have been the region of his chin. His head was very large, and bulged out to one side in a way that I would never have supposed could support life. Where his eyes should have been, two blank white surfaces of solid cataract seemed to float lidless and intent. He had no nose, only a small hole surgically created, I think, and ringed with discharge. His mouth was a slash in the right side of his cheek, at least two inches over and up from where mouths belong. Irma stepped over beside him, and as she reached down and kissed him, rearranged the sheets, I saw one of his hands. It was a fingerless club of flesh dotted almost randomly with bits of fingernail.

I closed my eyes and then looked once more. I saw again what I must have seen at first and ignored, the thing I had come to see. On Albert Sidney's deformed and earless head, almost covering the awful disarray of his humanity, he had a wealth of reddish golden hair, rich and curly, proper aureole of a Celtic deity. Or a surfing king.

V

We had dinner at some anonymous restaurant in Alexandria, and then found a room at a motel not far from Pineville. I had bought a bottle of whiskey. Inside, I filled a glass after peeling away its sticky plastic cover that pretended to guard it from the world for my better health.

—Should I have brought you? Irma asked, sitting down on the bed.

—Yes, I said.—Sure. Nobody should . . . nobody ought to be shielded from this.

—But it . . . hasn't got anything to do with . . . us. What Howard wants to do, does it?

—No, I said.—I don't think so.

—Howard was all right. If things had gone . . . the way they do mostly. He wasn't . . . isn't . . . a weak man. He's brave, and he used to work . . . sometimes sixteen hours a day. He was very . . . steady. Do you know, I loved him . . .

I poured her a drink.—Sometimes, I said, and heard that my voice was unsteady.—None of us know . . . what we can . . . stand.

—If Howard had had just any kind of belief . . . but . . .

—. . . He just had himself . . . ?

—Just that. He . . . his two hands and a strong back, and he was quick with figures. He always . . . came out . . .

—. . . ahead.

She breathed deeply, and sipped the whiskey.—Every time. He . . . liked hard times. To work his way through. You couldn't stop him. And very honest. An honest man.

I finished the glass and poured another one. I couldn't get rid of the smells and the images. The whiskey was doing no good. It would only dull my senses prospectively. The smells and the images were inside for keeps.

—He's not honest about . . .

—Albert Sidney? No, but I . . . it doesn't matter. I release him of that. Which is why . . .

—You want me to go ahead with the divorce?

—I think. We can't help each other, don't you see?

—I see that. But . . . what will you do?

Irma laughed and slipped off her shoes, curled her feet under her. Somewhere back in the mechanical reaches of my mind, where I was listening to Vivaldi and watching a thin British rain fall into my garden, neither happy nor sad, preserved by my indifference from the Gulf, I saw that she was very beautiful and that she cared for me, had brought me to Alexandria as much for myself as for her sake, though she did not know it.

—. . . do what needs to be done for the baby, she was saying.

—I've asked for strength to do the best . . . thing.

—What do you want me to do?

—About the divorce? I don't know about . . . the legal stuff. I want to . . . how do you say it . . . ? Not to contest it?

—There's a way. When the other person makes life insupportable . . .

Irma looked at me strangely, as if I were not understanding.

—No, no. The other . . . what he says.

—Adultery?

—And the rest. About Albert Sidney . . .

—No. You can't . . .

—Why can't I? I told you, Howard is all right. I mean, he could be all right. I want to let him go. Can't you say some way or other what he claims is true?

I set my glass down.—In the pleadings. You can always accept what he says in your . . . answer.

—Pleadings?

—That's what they call . . . what we file in a suit. But I can't state an outright . . . lie . . .

—But you're his counsel. You have to say what he wants you to say.

—No, only in good faith. The Code of Civil Practice . . . if I pleaded a lie . . . anyhow, Jesus, after all this . . . I couldn't . . . Plead adultery . . . ? No way.

—Yes, Irma said firmly, lovingly. She rose from the bed and came to me.

—Yes, she whispered.—You'll be able to.

VI

The next evening the plane was late getting into New Orleans. There was a storm line along the Gulf, a series of separate systems, thin monotonous driving rain that fell all over the city and the southern part of the state. The house was cool and humid when I got home, and my head hurt. The house was empty, and that was all right. I had a bowl of soup and turned on something very beautiful. *La Stravaganza*. As I listened, I thought of that strange medieval custom of putting the mad and the demented on a boat, and keeping it moving from one port to another. A ship full of lunacy and witlessness and rage and subhumanity with no destination in view. *Furiosi*, the mad were called. What did they call those who came into this world like Irma's baby, scarce half made up? Those driven beyond the human by the world were given names and a status. But what of those who came damaged from the first? Did even the wisdom of the Church have no name for those who did not scream or curse or style themselves Emperor Frederic II or Gregory come again? What of those with bulbous heads and protruding tongues and those who stared all day at the blazing sun, all night at the cool distant moon? I listened and drank, and opened the door onto the patio so that the music was leavened with the sound of the falling rain.

It was early the next morning when Bert called me at home. He did not bother apologizing. I think he knew that we were both too much in it now. The amenities are for before. Or afterward.

—Listen, you're back.

—Yes.

—I got Howard straightened up. You want to talk to him?

—What's he saying?

—Well, he's cleared up, you see? I got him to shower and drink a pot of coffee. It ain't what he says is different, but he *is* himself and he wants to get them papers started. You know? You want to drop by Bo-Peep for a minute?

—No, I said,—but I will. I want to talk to that stupid bastard.

—Ah, Bert said slowly.—Un-huh. Well, fine, counselor. It's cabin 10. On the street to the right as you come in. Can't miss it.

I thought somebody ought to take a baseball bat and use it on Howard Bedlow until he came to understand. I was very tight about this thing now, no distance at all. I had thought about other things only once since I had been back. When a little phrase of

Vivaldi's had shimmered like a waterfall, and, still drunk, I had followed that billow down to the Gulf in my mind.

There were fantasies, of course. In one, I took Irma away. We left New Orleans and headed across America toward California, and she was quickly pregnant. The child was whole and healthy and strong, and what had befallen each of us back in Louisiana faded and receded faster and faster, became of smaller and smaller concern until we found ourselves in a place near the Russian River, above the glut and spew of people down below.

Acres apart and miles away, we had a tiny place carved from the natural wood of the hills. We labored under the sun and scarcely talked, and what there was, was ours. She would stand near a forest pool, nude, our child in her arms, and the rest was all forgotten as I watched them there, glistening, with beads of fresh water standing on their skin, the way things ought to be, under the sun.

Then I was driving toward Metairie amidst the dust and squalor of Airline Highway. Filling stations, hamburger joints, cut-rate liquor, tacos, wholesale carpeting, rent-a-car, people driving a little above the speed limit, sealed in air-conditioned cars, others standing at bus stops staring vacantly, some gesticulating in repetitive patterns, trying to be understood. No sign of life anywhere.

The sign above the Bo-Peep Motel pictured a girl in a bonnet with a shepherd's crook and a vast crinoline skirt. In her lap she held what looked from a distance like a child. Close, you could see that it was intended to be a lamb curled in her arms, eyes closed, hoofs tucked into its fleece, peacefully asleep. Bo-Peep's face, outlined in neon tubing, had been painted once, but most of the paint had chipped away, and now, during the day, she wore a faded leer of unparalleled perversity, red lips and china-blue eyes flawed by missing chips of color.

Bert sat in a chair outside the door. He was in uniform. His car was parked in front of cabin 10. The door was open, and just inside Howard Bedlow sat in an identical chair, staring out like a prisoner who knows there must be bars even though he cannot see them. He leaned forward, hands hanging down before him, and even from a distance he looked much older than I had remembered him.

Bert walked over as I parked.—How was the trip?

We stared at each other.—A revelation, I said,—He's sober?

—Oh, yeah. He had a little trouble last night down at the Kit-Kat Klub. Bert pointed down the road to a huddled cinder-block building beside a trailer court.

—They sent for somebody to see to him, and luck had it be me.

Howard looked like an old man up close. His eyes were crusted, squinting up at the weak morning sun, still misted at that hour. His hands hung down between his legs, almost touching the floor, and his forefingers moved involuntarily as if they were tracing a precise and repetitious pattern on the dust of the floor. He looked up at me, licking his lips. He had not shaved in a couple of days, and the light beard had the same tawny reddish color as his hair. He did not seem to recognize me for a moment. Then his expression came together. He looked almost frightened.

—You seen her, huh?

—That's right.

—What'd she say?

—It's all right with her.

—What's all right?

—The divorce. Just the way you want it.

—You mean . . . like everything I said . . . all that . . . ?

—She said maybe she owes you that much. For what she did.

—What she did?

—You know . . .

—What I said, told you?

—Wonder what the hell that is, Bert put in. He walked out into the driveway and stared down the street.

Bedlow shook his head slowly.—She owned up, told you everything?

—There was . . . a confirmation. Look, I said,—Bert will line you up a lawyer. I'm going to represent Ir . . . your wife.

—Oh? I was the one come to you . . .

I took a piece of motel stationery out of my pocket. There was a five-dollar bill held to it with a dark bobby pin. I remembered her hair cascading down, flowing about her face.—You never gave me a retainer. I did not act on your behalf.

I held out the paper and the bill.—This is my retainer. From her. It doesn't matter. She won't contest. I'll talk to your lawyer. It'll be easy.

—I never asked for nothing to be easy, Bedlow murmured.

—If you want to back off the adultery thing, which is silly, which even if it is true you cannot prove, you can go for rendering life insupportable . . .

—Life insupportable . . . ? I never asked things be easy . . .

—Yes you did, I said brutally.—You just didn't know you did.

I wanted to tell him there was something rotten and weak and collapsed in him. His heart, his guts, his genes. That he had taken a woman better than he had any right to, and that Albert Sidney . . . but how could I? Who was I to . . . and then Bert stepped back toward us, his face grim.

—S . . ., he was saying,—I think they've got a fire down to the trailer court. You all reckon we ought to . . .

—If it's mine, let it burn. Ain't nothing there I care about. I need a drink.

But Bert was looking at me, his face twisted with some pointless apprehension that made so little sense that both of us piled into his car, revved the siren, and fishtailed out into Airline Highway, almost smashing into traffic coming from both directions as he humped across the neutral ground and laid thirty yards of rubber getting to the trailer court.

The trailer was in flames from one end to the other. Of course it was Bedlow's. Bert's face was working, and he tried to edge the car close to the end of it where there were the least flames.

—She's back in Alex, I yelled at him.—She's staying in a motel back in Alex. There's nothing in there.

But my eyes snapped from the burning trailer to a stunted and dusty cottonwood tree behind it. Which was where the old station wagon was parked. I could see the tail pipe hanging down behind as I vaulted out of the car and pulled the flimsy screen door off the searing skin of the trailer with my bare hands. I was working on the inside door, kicking it, screaming at the pliant aluminum to give way, to let me pass, when Bert pulled me back.—You g . . . . . . d fool, you can't . . .

But I had smashed the door open by then and would have been into the gulf of flame and smoke inside if Bert had not clipped me alongside the head with the barrel of his .38.

Which was just the moment when Bedlow passed him. Bert had hold of me, my eyes watching the trees, the nearby trailers whirling, spinning furiously. Bert yelled at Bedlow to stop, that there was no one inside, an inspired and desperate lie—or was it a final testing?

—She is, I know she is, Bedlow screamed back at Bert.

I was down on the ground now, dazed, passing in and out of consciousness not simply from Bert's blow, but from exhaustion, too long on the line beyond the boundaries of good sense. But I looked up as Bedlow shouted, and I saw him standing for a split second where I had been, his hair the color of the flames behind. He looked very young and strong, and I remember musing in my semiconsciousness, maybe he can do it. Maybe he can.

—. . . And she's got my boy in there, we heard him yell as he vanished into the smoke. Bert let me fall all the way then, and I passed out for good.

VII

It was late afternoon when I got home. It dawned on me that I hadn't slept in over twenty-four hours. Huge white thunderheads stood over the city, white and pure as cotton. The sun was diminished, and the heat had fallen away. It seemed that everything was very quiet, that a waiting had set in. The evening news said there was a probability of rain, even small-craft warnings on the Gulf. Then, as if there were an electronic connection between the station and the clouds, rain began to fall just as I pulled into the drive. It fell softly at first, as if it feared to come too quickly on the scorched town below. Around me, as I cut off the engine, there rose that indescribable odor that comes from the coincidence of fresh rain with parched earth and concrete. I sat in the car for a long time, pressing Bert's handkerchief full of crushed ice against the lump on the side of my head. The ice kept trying to fall out because I was clumsy. I had not gotten used to the thick bandages on my hands, and each time I tried to adjust the handkerchief, the pain in my hands made me lose fine control. My head did not hurt so badly, but I felt weak, and so I stayed there through all the news, not wanting to pass out for the second time in one day, or to lay unconscious in an empty house.

—Are you just going to sit out here? Joan asked me softly.

I opened my eyes and peered up at her. She looked very different. As if I had not see her in years, as if we had lived separate lives, heights and depths in each that we could never tell the other.—No, I said.—I was just tired.

She frowned when I got out of the car.—What's the lump? And the hands? Can't I go away for a few days?

—Sure you can, I said a little too loudly, forcefully.—Any time at all. I ran into a hot door.

She was looking at my suit. One knee was torn, and an elbow was out. She sniffed.—Been to a firesale? she asked as we reached the door.

—That's not funny, I said.

—Sorry, she answered.

The children were there, and I tried very hard for the grace to see them anew, but it was just old Bart and tiny Nan trying to tell me about their holiday. Bart was still sifting sand on everything he touched, and Nan's fair skin was lightly burned. Beyond their prattle, I was trying to focus on something just beyond my reach.

Their mother came in with a pitcher of martinis and ran the kids back to the television room. She was a very beautiful woman, deep, in her thirties, who seemed to have hold of something— besides the martinis. I thought that if I were not married and she happened by, I would likely start a conversation with her.

—I ended up taking the kids with me, she said, sighing and dropping into her chair.

—Huh?

—They cried and said they'd rather come with me than stay with Louise. Even considering the ducks and chickens and things.

Hence the sand and sunburn. I poured two drinks as the phone rang.—That's quite a compliment, I said, getting up for it.

—You bet. We waited for you. We thought you'd be coming.

No, I thought as I picked up the phone. I had a gulf of my own. It was Bert. His voice was low, subdued.

—You know what? he was saying.—He made it. So help me Christ, he made it all the way to the back where . . . they were. Can you believe that?

—Did they find . . . ?

Bert's voice broke a little.—Yeah, he was right. You know how bad the fire was . . . but they called down from the state hospital and said she's taken the baby, child . . . out. Said must have had somebody help . . .

—No, I said.—I didn't, and as I said it I could see Dr. Tumulty rubbing his hands over nineteen years of a certain hell.

—Never mind, listen . . . when the fire boys got back there, it was . . . everything fused. They all formed this one thing. Said she was in a metal chair, and he was like kneeling in front, his arms . . . and they . . . you couldn't tell, but it had got to be . . .

I waited while he got himself back together.—It had got to be the baby she was holding, with Howard reaching out, his arms around . . . both . . .

—Bert, I started to say, tears running down my face.—Bert . . .

—It's all right, he said at last, clearing his throat. There was an empty silence on the line for a long moment, and I could hear the resonance of the line itself, that tiny lilting bleep of distant signals that you sometimes hear. It sounded like waves along the coast. —It really is. All right, he said.—It was like . . . they had, they was . . .

—Reconciled, I said.

Another silence.—Oh, s . . ., he said.—I'll be talking to you sometimes.

Then the line was empty, and after a moment I hung up.

Joan stared at me, at the moisture on my face, glanced at my hands, the lump on my head, the ruined suit.—What happened while I was gone? Did I miss anything?

—No, I smiled at her.—Not a thing.

I walked out onto the patio with my drink. There was still a small rain falling, but even as I stood there, it faded and the clouds began to break. Up there, the moon rode serenely from one cloud to the next, and far down the sky in the direction of the coast, I could see pulses of heat lightning above the rigolets where the lake flows into the Gulf.

RITUAL MURDER

BY TOM DENT

Courthouse

(Originally published in 1978)

CHARACTERS: Narrator, Joe Brown Jr., Bertha (Joe's wife), Mrs. Williams (Joe's teacher), Dr. Brayboy (a black psychiatrist), Mr. Andrews (Joe's boss), Mrs. Brown (Joe's mother), Mr. Brown (Joe's father), James Roberts (Joe's friend), Mr. Spaulding (anti-poverty program administrator), Chief of Police.

SETTING: New Orleans.

TIME: Now. It is important that the actors make their speeches in rhythm to the background music.

NARRATOR: Last summer, Joe Brown Jr., black youth of New Orleans, LA, committed murder. Play a special "Summertime" for him and play the same "Summertime" for his friend James Roberts who he knifed to death. [*We hear "Summertime" under the narrator's voice.*] In every black community of America; in the ghettos and neighborhood clubs where we gather to hear our music, we play "Summertime"; and in each community the bands play it differently. In no community does it sound like the "Summertime" of George Gershwin. It is blusier, darker, with its own beat and logic, its joys unknown to the white world. It is day now. The routine events of life have passed under the bridge. Joe Brown Jr. has been arrested, indicted, and formally charged with murder. It happened . . . it happened in a Ninth Ward bar—we need not name it for the purposes of this presentation. The stabbing was the culmination of an argument Joe Brown had with his friend. We have learned this, but the *Louisiana Weekly* only reported, "James Roberts is said to have made insulting remarks to Joe Brown, whereupon Brown pulled out a switchblade knife and stabbed Roberts three times in the chest before he could be subdued." The story received front page play in the *Louisiana Weekly*, and a lead in the crime-of-the-day section in the white *Times-Picayune*. After that, it received only minor news play, since there are other crimes to report in New Orleans. Play "Summertime" for Joe Brown Jr., and play the same "Summertime" for his friend James Roberts who he knifed to death. [*The music dies out.*] Why did this murder happen? No one really knows. The people who know Joe Brown best have ideas.

[*We see Bertha looking at TV. The sound is off, only the picture shows. Bertha is young, about twenty. She is Joe's wife. She is ironing while looking at the set—ironing baby things.*]

BERTHA: Joe just didn't have any sense. He is smart, oh yes, has a good brain, but didn't have good sense. The important thing was to settle down, get a good job, and take care of his three children. We been in the Florida Avenue project now for almost a year, and we never have enough money. Look at the people on TV, they make out okay. They fight, but they never let their fights destroy them. Joe didn't have control of his temper. He was a dreamer, he wanted things. But he wouldn't work to get them. Oh, he would take jobs in oyster houses, and he'd worked on boats ever since he was a kid. But he wouldn't come in at night, and sometimes he wouldn't get up in the morning to go to work. Sometimes he would come in and snap off the TV and say it was driving him crazy. It's not his TV—my father bought it, and besides, I like it, it's the only thing I have. This is just a seventeen-inch set, but I want a twenty-one-inch set. Now I'll never get one because he had to go out and do something foolish. You ask me why he killed that boy? I don't know. But I think he killed him because he had a bad temper and wouldn't settle down. Joe was a mild person, but he carried knives and guns—that's the way his family is. I used to tell him about it all the time. Once I asked him, *When are you gonna get a better job and make more money?* He said, *When I get rid of you and those snotty kids.* He could have done something if he had tried, if he had only tried; but instead, he wanted to take it out on us. I'll go see him, but now look; I have to do everything in this house myself: iron the clothes, cook the meals, buy the food, apply for relief, and get some help from my parents—and my father ain't working right now. Joe didn't want to have our last baby, Cynthia, but we couldn't murder her before she was even born and now I got to take care of her too. Joe knifed that boy because he was foolish, wouldn't settle down and accept things as they are, and because he didn't have common sense.

NARRATOR: Mrs. Williams, could you comment on your former student, Joe Brown Jr.?

MRS. WILLIAMS: I don't remember Joe Brown Jr. very well. I have so many children to try to remember. I had him three or four years ago just before he dropped out of school. I was his homeroom teacher. Joe was like all the others from the Ninth Ward, not interested in doing anything for themselves. You can't teach them anything. They don't want to learn, they *never* study, they won't sit still and pay attention in class. It's no surprise to me that he's in trouble. I try to do my best here, but I have only so much patience. I tell you, you don't know the things a teacher goes through with these kids. They come to class improperly dressed, from homes where they don't get any home training, which is why they are so ill-mannered. We try to teach them about America—about the opportunities America has to offer. We try to prepare them to get the best jobs they can—and you know a Negro child has to work harder. I teach History, Arithmetic, English, and Civics every day, and it goes in one ear and comes out the other. It gives me a terrible gas pain to have to go through it every day, and the noise these kids make is too, too hard on my ears. I've worked for ten years in this school, and I don't get paid much at all. But next month my husband and I will have saved enough money to buy a new Oldsmobile, which I'm happy to say will be the smartest, slickest, smoothest thing McDonough No. 81 has ever seen. Two boys got into a fight in the yard the other day and it was horrible. It pains me to hear the names they call each other—irritates my gas. Some of them even bring knives and guns to school. It's just terrible. I'm only relieved when I get home, turn on my TV, take my hair down and face off, drink a nice strong cup of coffee, look out at my lawn in Pontchartrain Park, and forget the day. You ask me why Joe Brown murdered his friend in a Negro bar on a Saturday night and I tell you it is because he was headed that way in the beginning. These kids just won't listen, and don't want to learn, and that's all there is to it.

[*Lights on Joe Brown Jr. He is wearing blue jeans and a T-shirt. He is seated. He faces the audience. There is a table in front of him. On the table is a small transistor radio, but the music we hear is Gil Evans's "Barbara Song."*]

Narrator: Here is Joe Brown Jr.

Joe Brown Jr.: Once I saw a feature about surfing on TV. Surfing on beautiful waves on a beach in Hawaii, or somewhere . . .

[*The lights shift to another man who is seated on the opposite side of the stage. He is a much older man, dressed in a business suit. He is a Negro. He is Dr. Brayboy, a psychiatrist. His chair does not face the audience; it faces Joe Brown Jr.*]

Narrator: A black psychiatrist, Dr. Thomas L. Brayboy.

Dr. Brayboy: At the core of Joe Brown's personality is a history of frustrations. Psychological, sociological, economic . . .

Joe Brown Jr.: . . . and I wanted to do that . . . surf. It was a dream I kept to myself. Because it would have been foolish to say it aloud. Nobody wants to be laughed at. And then I thought, I never see black people surfing . . .

Dr. Brayboy: We might call Joe Brown's homocidal act an act

of ritual murder. When murder occurs for no apparant reason but happens all the time, as in our race on Saturday nights, it is ritual murder. When I worked in Harlem Hospital in the emergency ward, I saw us coming in bleeding, blood seeping from the doors of the taxicabs . . . icepicks and knives . . .

[*These speeches must be slow, to the rhythm of music.*]

NARRATOR: Play "Summertime" for Joe Brown Jr., and a very funky "Summertime" for his friend James Roberts, who he knifed to death.

JOE BROWN JR.: . . . And then I thought, I don't see any black folks on TV, ever. Not any real black folks, anyway. There are those so-called black shows like *Good Times* and *The Jeffersons*, but they are so far removed from the kind of folks I know that they may as well be white too. I see us playing football, basketball, and baseball, and half the time I miss that because they be on in the afternoon, and I'm usually shelling oysters. *Where am I?* I asked my wife, and she answered, *In the Florida Avenue project where you are doing a poor job of taking care of your wife and children.* My boss answered, *On the job, if you would keep your mind on what you are doing . . . count the oysters.*

DR. BRAYBOY: . . . Ice picks and knives and frustration. My tests indicate that Joe Brown Jr. is considerably above average in intelligence. Above average in intelligence. *Above* average. Vocabulary and reading comprehension extraordinary . . .

NARRATOR: [*To audience*] Our purpose here is to discover why.

DR. BRAYBOY: . . . But school achievement extremely low. Dropped out at eighteen in the eleventh grade.

JOE BROWN JR.: I began watching all the TV sets I could, looking for my image on every channel, looking for someone who looked like me. I knew I existed, but I didn't see myself in the world of television or movies. Even the black characters were not me. All the black characters were either weak and stupid, or some kind of superman who doesn't really exist in my world. I couldn't define myself, and didn't know where to begin. When I listened to soul music on the radio I understood that, and I knew that was part of me, but that didn't help me much. Something was not right, and it was like . . . like I was the only cat in the whole world who knew it. Something began to come loose in me, like my mind would float away from my body and lay suspended on a shelf for hours at a time watching me open oysters. No one ever suspected, but my mind was trying to define me, to tell me who I was the way other people see me, only it couldn't because it didn't know where to begin.

[*The scene shifts to the desk of the Chief of Police. He may be played by a white actor, or a black actor in white face.*]

NARRATOR: The Chief of Police.

CHIEF OF POLICE: The rate of crime in the streets in New Orleans has risen sharply. We know that most of our colored citizens are wholesome, law-abiding, decent citizens. But the fact remains that the crime wave we are witnessing now across the nation is mostly nigger crime. Stop niggers and you will stop crime. The police must have more protection, more rights, and more weapons of all types to deal with the crime wave. We need guns, machine guns, multimachine guns, gas bombs, and reinforced nightsticks. Otherwise America is going to become a nightmare of black crime in the streets.

[*Lights up on Mr. Andrews, Joe's boss. He is sitting behind a terribly messy desk with papers stuck in desk holders. His feet are on the desk. He is eating a large muffuletta sandwich. His image must be one of a relaxed, informal interview at his office during lunchtime. If there are no white actors, the part can be played by a black actor in white face, but instead of eating lunch, he should be smoking a huge cigar.*]

NARRATOR: Joe Brown's employer, Mr. Andrews.

MR. ANDREWS: I have trouble with several of my nigra boys, but I likes 'em. [*He almost chokes on his sandwich.*] Joe was a little different from the rest . . . what would you say . . . dreamier . . .

more absentminded. Joe was always quitting, but he must have liked it here 'cause he always came back. You can't tell me anything about those people. One time, during lunch hour, they were singing and dancing outside to the radio and I snuck up to watch. If they had seen me they would've stopped. It was amazing. The way them boys danced is fantastic. They shore got rhythm and a sense of style about them. Yes sir . . . and guess who got the most style . . . ole Joe. [*Bites and eats.*] That boy sure can dance. I loves to watch him. [*Bites.*] Recently, he been going to the bathroom a lot and staying a long time. I ask the other boys, *Where's that doggone Joe?* They tell me. So one day I go to the john and there he is, sitting on the stool . . . readin'. I say, *Boy, I pay you to read or shell oysters?* He comes out all sulky. [*Smiling.*] He could be kind of sensitive at times, you know. I been knowing him since he was a kid . . . born around here . . . kind of touchy. [*Andrews has finished his sandwich. He takes his feet off the desk, throws the wrapper into the trash, and wipes his hands. A serious look comes over his face.*] As for why he killed that boy, I can't give you any answers. I think it has to do with nigras and the way they get wild on the weekend. Sometimes the good times get a little rough. And them [*pause*] you don't know what a boy like Joe can get mixed up in, or any of them out there. [*Waves toward the door.*] I don't understand it, and I know and likes 'em all, like they was my own family. My job is to keep 'em straight here . . . any trouble out of any of 'em and out the door they go.

[*The scene shifts to another white man. He is well dressed with his tie loosened, sitting behind an extremely disordered desk. Black actor can play in white face. He must, throughout his speech, wear a public relations smile. He must speak with a winning air.*]

NARRATOR: Mr. Richard Spaulding, director of the Poverty Program in New Orleans.

MR. SPAULDING: Last year we spent 3.5 million in five culturally deprived areas of New Orleans. This money has made a tremendous difference in the lives of our fine colored citizens. We have provided jobs, jobs, and more jobs. By creating, for the first time, indigenous community organizations controlled and operated by the people of the five target areas, we have, for the first time, provided a way to close the cultural and economic gap. Social service centers are going up in all these areas. We will develop a level of competency on par with American society as a whole. In the Desire area alone, 750 mothers go to our medical center each day. We have, in short, provided hope. Of course, there are still problems.

NARRATOR: Any insights into the murder of James Roberts last summer by Joe Brown Jr.?

MR. SPAULDING: We are building community centers, baseball diamonds, basketball courts, little leagues, golden-agers facilities, barbecue pits, swimming pools, badminton nets, and . . . if our dreams come true . . . well-supervised and policed bowling alleys. It is our firm hope that sociology will stay out of neighborhood bars.

NARRATOR: Thank you, Mr. Spaulding.

[*The scene shifts to a middle-aged woman sitting on a well-worn couch. She is wearing a plain dress. There is a small table with a lamp and Bible on it next to the couch. She is Mrs. Brown, Joe's mother. Across the stage, sitting in a big easy chair, is a middle-aged man in work clothes. He is Mr. Brown, Joe's father. He is drinking a large can of beer which, from time to time, he will place on the floor. He listens to what Mrs. Brown says intently, but there must be an air of distance in his attitude toward her and what she says, never affection. The audience must be made to believe they are in different places.*]

NARRATOR: [*Solemnly*] This is Joe Brown's mother. [*A spot focuses on Mrs. Brown. There is enough light, however, to see Mr. Brown.*]

MRS. BROWN: Joe was always a sweet kind boy, but Joe's problem is that he . . . stopped . . . going . . . to . . . church. I told him about that but it didn't make any difference. When we climb out of Christ chariot we liable to run into trouble. I tell the truth about my own children, like I tell it on anyone else. Once, before Joe got married, he came home in a temper about his boss and his job. Talking bad about the white folks. Said he wished something from another planet would destroy them all. Said he didn't like the way his boss talked to him, that he should be paid more, and like that. We all get mad at the white people, but there is no point in it. So many colored folks ain't even got a job. I told him, *If you think you can do better, go back and finish school.* But no, he didn't finish school, he just complained. *Stay in church,* I told him, but he started hanging around with bad friends. Bad friends lead to a bad end. Talking bad about white people is like busting your head against a brick wall.

NARRATOR: Mrs. Brown, do you feel your son would kill for no reason? There must have been a reason.

MRS. BROWN: When you hang around a bad crowd on Saturday nights, troubles are always gonna come. I told him to stay out of those bars. I don't know what happened or why. A friend told me the other boy was teasing Joe and Joe got mad. He was sensitive, you know, very serious and sensitive. He didn't like to be rubbed the wrong way.

NARRATOR: Mrs. Brown, the purpose of this program is to discover why your son knifed his friend. No one seems to have answers. We are using the scientific approach. Do *you* have any answers?

MRS. BROWN: [*Despairingly.*] I don't know why. I don't understand. You try to protect your children as best you can. It's just one of those things that happens on Saturday nights in a colored bar; like a disease. You hope you and nobody you know catches it. The Lord is the only protection.

NARRATOR: And your husband? Would he have any information, any ideas?

MRS. BROWN: [*Sharply.*] I haven't seen that man in four years.

[*Both Mrs. Brown and narrator look at Mr. Brown.*]

MR. BROWN: I plan to go see the boy . . . I just haven't had a chance yet. I have another family now and I can't find any work. I help him out when I can, but . . . [*pause*] . . . I can't understand why he would do a thing like that.

NARRATOR: If we could hear what James Roberts has to say.

[*We return to the summertime theme and the scene of the crime, the barroom where the play began with Joe Brown Jr. standing over James Roberts's body and all other actors frozen in their original positions as in the opening scene. After the narrator speaks the body of James Roberts begins to slowly arise from the floor aided by Joe Brown. It is important that Brown helps Roberts get up.*]

JAMES ROBERTS: [*Begins to laugh . . .*] It was all a joke. Nothing happened that hasn't happened between us before. Joe is still my best friend . . . if I were alive I would tell anyone that. That Saturday was a terrible one . . . not just because the lights went out for me. I heard a ringing in my ears when I woke up that morning. When I went to work at the hotel the first thing I had to do was take out the garbage. Have you ever smelled the stink of shrimp and oyster shells first thing in the morning? I hate that. The sounds of the street and the moan of the cook's voice; that's enough to drive anyone crazy, and I heard it every day. That day I decided to leave my job for real . . . one more week at the most.

JOE BROWN JR.: [*Getting up from the bunk into a sitting position.*] Damn. The same thing happened to me that day. I decided I was going to leave my job.

JAMES ROBERTS: [*Looking at Joe with disgust.*] Man, you are disgusting. You all time talking about leaving your job.

NARRATOR: [*To Roberts, then to Joe.*] Get to what happened at the café, please. We don't have all night.

JAMES ROBERTS: We were both very uptight . . . mad at our jobs—everybody . . . everything around us.

JOE BROWN JR.: [*Excitedly*] I know I was . . . I was ready to shoot somebody.

JAMES ROBERTS: Shut up. This is my scene.

JOE BROWN JR.: You won't even let anybody *agree* with you.

NARRATOR: Please.

JAMES ROBERTS: Joe went on and on all evening and all night. We were getting higher and higher, going from bar to bar. We went to Scotties, then to Shadowland, to the Havana . . . we had my sister's car . . . Joe getting mad and frustrated and talking 'bout what he was gonna do. By the time we got to the Ninth Ward Café, we was both stoned out of our minds. Joe getting dreamier and dreamier. He was talking about all his problems, his wife, his job, his children. I could understand that.

JOE BROWN JR.: You really couldn't because you don't have those problems.

[*We hear Otis Redding's "Satisfaction" from the album* Otis Redding Live.]

JAMES ROBERTS: Joe was screaming about the white man. He said he was $1,500 in debt . . . working like hell for the white man, then turning right around and giving it back to him. He said he couldn't laugh no more.

[*From this point on there must be little connection between Joe's thoughts and those of James Roberts. The Otis Redding recording continues, but must not drown out the speeches.*]

JOE BROWN JR.: I had a dream . . . I had a dream . . . I dreamed I had $66 million left to me by an unknown relative . . .

JAMES ROBERTS: [*Slow, to the music. As much pantomime as possible, as though he is reenacting the scene.*] We were in the Ninth Ward Café sitting in a booth by ourselves. There was something on the jukebox, I believe it was Otis Redding. It was a hot night. Joe was talking about how there was nowhere he could go to relax anymore. Then, suddenly, his mind would go off into outer space somewhere and I had to jerk him back. I would ask him what he was thinking about, and he would say he wasn't happy with himself. He didn't know himself or where he was headed to anymore.

JOE BROWN JR.: . . . I always get screwed up when I try to figure out the *first* thing I'm going to buy . . . a new car . . . maybe . . . Mark IV . . . a new house . . . a brick one with wood paneling . . . a new suit . . . a tailor-made three-piece . . . new shoes . . . some high steppers . . . a new transistor radio . . . a big Sony that plays loud with big sound . . . Then I'd give everybody a bill . . . but I can't figure out what I'm going to buy *first*.

JAMES ROBERTS: I said, *Man, what are you talking about?* I don't understand all this blues over what happens every day. He said he wanted to believe there is hope. I told him there is no hope. You a black motherfucker and you may as well learn to make the best of it.

JOE BROWN JR.: . . . People always tell me I can't make up my mind what I want, or I want things that don't make sense, or I want too much instead of being satisfied with just a little. People always tell me I ask too many questions . . . especially questions that no one can answer . . . and I am just frustrating myself because I can never find the answers. The way I figure it, you may as well dream 66 million as 66 thousand. The way I figure it, you may as well ask questions you *don't* have answers to; what's the point in asking questions everyone knows the answers to? Life is just a little thing anyway . . . doesn't really amount to much when you think about time and place.

JAMES ROBERTS: [*Intensely and quicker.*] Then he just blew. Screamed nobody calls him a black motherfucker. I just laughed. Everybody calls him that 'cause that's just what he is. There's nothing wrong with calling anyone a black motherfucker. We been doing it to each other all our lives, and we did it all evening while we were drinking. I just laughed. He jumps up, pulls out his blade, and goes for my heart. I could outfight Joe any day but . . .

JOE BROWN JR.: High steppers . . .

JAMES ROBERTS: . . . He got the jump on me and I couldn't get to my blade. It was ridiculous. He was like a crazy man . . . a wild man . . . turning on me for no reason when I done nothing to him at all . . . and shouting, *There is no hope!*

JOE BROWN JR.: High steppers . . .

JAMES ROBERTS: Before I knew it I was stunned and weak and there was blood all over the chest of my yellow polo shirt . . . I felt the lights darken, and my whole body turned to rubber . . .

JOE BROWN JR.: High steppers on a Saturday night . . .

JAMES ROBERTS: . . . But I couldn't move anything. [*Pause.*] Last thing I heard was Booker T. & the M.G.'s playing "Groovin'" . . . Joe . . . his eyes blazing . . . everything turned red.

NARRATOR: [*To Roberts after pause.*] You mean this caused such a brutal act? You called him a name?

JAMES ROBERTS: That's all it takes sometimes.

NARRATOR: And you think this makes sense? To lose your life at nineteen over such an insignificant thing?

JAMES ROBERTS: It happens all the time. I accept it. Joe is still my friend. Friends kill each other all the time . . . unless you have an enemy you can both kill.

NARRATOR: And you, Joe?

JOE BROWN JR.: What is there to say? It happened. It happens all the time. One thing I learned: when you pull a knife or gun, don't fool around, use it, or you might not have a chance to. Better him dead than me. He would say the same thing if it was the other way around.

NARRATOR: [*To Joe Brown Jr.*] What did you mean when you said there is no hope?

JOE BROWN JR.: [*Evenly.*] I don't know. *There is no hope.* Here in this jail, with my fate, I might be better off dead.

NARRATOR: One more question. [*To James Roberts.*] Do you feel you died for anything? Is there any meaning in it?

James Roberts: Yes, I died for something. But I don't know what it means.

Narrator: [To Joe Brown Jr.] And did your act mean anything?

Joe Brown Jr.: [Softly.] I suppose so. But I can't imagine what.

[The music of a bluesy "Summertime." The narrator comes out to downstage center, as in the beginning of the play. He addresses the audience directly in even tones.]

Narrator: Play "Summertime" for Joe Brown Jr. and play a very funky "Summertime" for his friend James Roberts who he knifed to death.

["Summertime" theme continues as narrator slowly scrutinizes the people he has just interviewed.]

Narrator: Our purpose here is to discover why. No one seems to have answers. Do you have any?

[Narrator moves to actors who plays Bertha, Mrs. Williams, Mrs. Brown, Joe Brown Sr., and Dr. Brayboy, asking the question, "Do you have answers?" To which they respond:]

Bertha: Joe knifed that boy because he was foolish, wouldn't settle down and accept things as they are, and because he didn't have common sense.

Mrs. Williams: You ask me why Joe Brown murdered his friend in a Negro bar on a Saturday night and I tell you it is because he was headed that way in the beginning. These kids just won't listen, and don't want to learn, and that's all there is to it.

Mr. Brown: I plan to go see the boy . . . I just haven't had a chance yet. I help him out when I can but [pause] I can't understand why he would do a thing like that.

Mrs. Brown: It's just one of those things that happens on a Saturday night in a colored bar . . . like a disease. You hope you and nobody you know catches it. The Lord is the only protection.

Dr. Brayboy: When murder occurs for no apparent reason, but happens all the time, as in our race on Saturday nights, it is ritual murder. That is, no apparent reason. There are reasons. The reasons are both personal and common. When a people who have no method of letting off steam against the source of their oppression exploit against each other, homicide, under these conditions, is a form of group suicide. When personal chemistries don't mix, just a little spark can bring about the explosion. Ice picks and knives and whatever happens to be lying around.

NARRATOR: When murder occurs for no apparent reason, but happens all the time, as in our race on a Saturday night, it is ritual murder.

[*The following lines should be distributed among the actors and delivered to the audience directly.*]

That is, no apparent reason. There are reasons. The reasons are both personal and common. When a people who have no method of letting off steam against the source of their oppression explode against each other, homicide, under these conditions, is a form of group suicide. When personal chemistries don't mix, just a little spark can bring about the explosion. Ice picks, knives and whatever happens to be lying around.

NARRATOR: [*Moving downstage facing audience directly.*] We have seen something unpleasant, but the play is over. Yes, we see this thing [*gesturing to stage behind him*] night after night, weekend after weekend. Only you have the power to stop it. It has to do with something in our minds. [*Pause. "Summertime" music gradually increases in volume.*] Play "Summertime" for Joe Brown Jr., and play a very funky "Summertime" for his friend James Roberts who he knifed to death.

[*Narrator walks over to Dr. Brayboy and shakes his hand as lights fade to black.*]

PART III

THE THANATOS SYNDROME

RICH

BY ELLEN GILCHRIST
Garden District
(Originally published in 1978)

Tom and Letty Wilson were rich in everything. They were rich in friends because Tom was a vice president of the Whitney Bank of New Orleans and liked doing business with his friends, and because Letty was vice president of the Junior League of New Orleans and had her picture in *Town and Country* every year at the Symphony Ball.

The Wilsons were rich in knowing exactly who they were because every year from Epiphany to Fat Tuesday they flew the beautiful green and gold and purple flag outside their house that meant that Letty had been queen of the Mardi Gras the year she was a debutante. Not that Letty was foolish enough to take the flag seriously.

Sometimes she was even embarrassed to call the yardman and ask him to come over and bring his high ladder.

"Preacher, can you come around on Tuesday and put up my flag?" she would ask.

"You know I can," the giant black man would answer. "I been saving time to put up your flag. I won't forget what a beautiful queen you made that year."

"Oh, hush, Preacher. I was a skinny little scared girl. It's a wonder I didn't fall off the balcony I was so sacred. I'll see you on Monday." And Letty would think to herself what a big phony Preacher was and wonder when he was going to try to borrow some more money from them.

Tom Wilson considered himself a natural as a banker because he loved to gamble and wheel and deal. From the time he was a boy in a small Baptist town in Tennessee he had loved to play cards and match nickels and lay bets.

In high school he read the *Nashville Banner* avidly and kept an eye out for useful situations such as the lingering and suspenseful illnesses of Pope Pius.

"Let's get up a pool on the day the Pope will die," he would say to the football team, "I'll hold the bank." And because the Pope took a very long time to die with many close calls there were times when Tom was the richest left tackle in Franklin, Tennessee.

Tom had a favorite saying about money. He had read it in the *Reader's Digest* and attributed it to Andrew Carnegie. "Money," Tom would say, "is what you keep score with. Andrew Carnegie."

Another way Tom made money in high school was performing as an amateur magician at local birthday parties and civic events. He could pull a silver dollar or a Lucky Strike cigarette from an astonished six-year-old's ear or from his own left palm extract a seemingly endless stream of multicolored silk chiffon or cause an ordinary piece of clothesline to behave like an Indian cobra.

He got interested in magic during a convalescence from German measles in the sixth grade. He sent off for books of magic tricks and practiced for hours before his bedroom mirror, his quick clever smile flashing and his long fingers curling and uncurling from the sleeves of a black dinner jacket his mother had bought at a church bazaar and remade to fit him.

Tom's personality was too flamboyant for the conservative Whitney Bank, but he was cheerful and cooperative and when he made a mistake he had the ability to turn it into an anecdote.

"Hey, Fred," he would call to one of his bosses. "Come have lunch on me and I'll tell you a good one."

They would walk down St. Charles Avenue to where it crosses Canal and turns into Royal Street as it enters the French Quarter.

They would walk into the crowded, humid excitement of the quarter, admiring the girls and watching the Yankee tourists sweat in their absurd spun-glass leisure suits, and turn into the side door of Antoine's or breeze past the maitre d' at Galatoire's or Brennan's.

When a red-faced waiter in funereal black had seated them at a choice table, Tom would loosen his Brooks Brothers tie, turn his handsome brown eyes on his guest, and begin.

"That bunch of promoters from Dallas talked me into backing an idea to videotape all the historic sights in the quarter and rent the tapes to hotels to show on closed-circuit television. Goddamnit, Fred, I could just see those fucking tourists sitting around their hotel rooms on rainy days ordering from room service and taking in the Cabildo and the Presbytere on TV." Tom laughed delightedly and waved his glass of vermouth at an elegantly dressed couple walking by the table.

"Well, they're barely breaking even on that one, and now they want to buy up a lot of soft-porn movies and sell them to motels in Jefferson Parish. What do you think? Can we stay with them for a few more months?"

Then the waiter would bring them cold oysters on the half shell and steaming *pompano en papillote* and a wine steward would serve them a fine Meursault or a Piesporter, and Tom would listen to whatever advice he was given as though it were the most intelligent thing he had ever heard in his life.

Of course he would be thinking, *You stupid, impotent son of a bitch. You scrawny little frog bastard, I'll buy and sell you before it's over. I've got more brains in my balls than the whole snotty bunch of you.*

"Tom, you always throw me off my diet," his friend would say, "damned if you don't."

"I told Letty the other day," Tom replied, "that she could just go right ahead and spend her life worrying about being buried in her wedding dress, but I didn't hustle my way to New Orleans all the way from north Tennessee to eat salads and melba toast. Pass me the French bread."

Letty fell in love with Tom the first time she laid eyes on him. He came to Tulane on a football scholarship and charmed his way into a fraternity of wealthy New Orleans boys famed for its drunkenness and its wild practical jokes. It was the same old story. Even the second-, third-, and fourth-generation blue bloods of New Orleans need an infusion of new genes now and then.

The afternoon after Tom was initiated, he arrived at the fraternity house with two Negro painters and sat in the low-hanging branches of a live oak tree overlooking Henry Clay Avenue, directing them in painting an official-looking yellow-and-white-striped pattern on the street in front of the property. "D-R-U-N-K," he yelled to his painters, holding on to the enormous limb with one hand and pushing his black hair out of his eyes with the other. "Paint it to say *D-R-U-N-K Z-O-N-E.*"

Letty stood near the tree with a group of friends watching him. He was wearing a blue shirt with the sleeves rolled up above his elbows, and a freshman beanie several sizes too small was perched on his head like a tipsy sparrow.

"I'm wearing this goddamn beanie forever," Tom yelled. "I'm wearing this beanie until someone brings me a beer," and Letty took the one she was holding and walked over to the tree and handed it to him.

One day a few weeks later, he commandeered a Bunny Bread truck while it was parked outside the fraternity house making a delivery. He picked up two friends and drove the truck madly around the Irish Channel, throwing fresh loaves of white and whole wheat and rye bread to the astonished housewives.

"Steal from the rich, give to the poor," Tom yelled, and his companions gave up trying to reason with him and helped him yell.

"Free bread, free cake," they yelled, handing out powdered

doughnuts and sweet rolls to a gang of kids playing baseball on a weed-covered vacant lot.

They stopped off at Darby's, an Irish bar where Tom made bets on races and football games, and took on some beer and left off some cinnamon rolls.

"Tom, you better go turn that truck in before they catch you," Darby advised, and Tom's friends agreed, so they drove the truck to the second-precinct police headquarters and turned themselves in. Tom used up half a year's allowance paying the damages, but it made his reputation.

In Tom's last year at Tulane a freshman drowned during a hazing accident at the Southern Yacht Club, and the event frightened Tom. He had never liked the boy and had suspected him of being involved with the queers and nigger lovers who hung around the philosophy department and the school newspaper. The boy had gone to prep school in the East and brought weird-looking girls to rush parties. Tom had resisted the temptation to blackball him as he was well connected in uptown society.

After the accident, Tom spent less time at the fraternity house and more time with Letty, whose plain sweet looks and expensive clothes excited him.

"I can't go in the house without thinking about it," he said to Letty. "All we were doing was making them swim from pier to pier carrying martinis. I did it fifteen times the year I pledged."

"He should have told someone he couldn't swim very well," Letty answered. "It was an accident. Everyone knows it was an accident. It wasn't your fault." And Letty cuddled up close to him on the couch, breathing as softly as a cat.

Tom had long serious talks with Letty's mild, alcoholic father, who held a seat on the New York Stock Exchange, and in the spring of the year Tom and Letty were married in the Cathedral of Saint Paul with twelve bridesmaids, four flower girls, and seven hundred guests. It was pronounced a marriage made in heaven, and Letty's mother ordered Masses said in Rome for their happiness.

They flew to New York on the way to Bermuda and spent their wedding night at the Sherry Netherland Hotel on Fifth Avenue. At least half a dozen of Letty's friends had lost their virginity at the same address, but the trip didn't seem prosaic to her.

She stayed in the bathroom a long time gazing at her plain face in the oval mirror and tugging at the white lace nightgown from the Lylian Shop, arranging it now to cover, now to reveal her small breasts. She crossed herself in the mirror, suddenly giggled, then walked out into the blue and gold bedroom as though she had been going to bed with men every night of her life. She had been up until three the night before reading a book on sexual intercourse. She offered her small unpainted mouth to Tom. Her pale hair smelled of Shalimar and carnations and candles. Now she was safe. Now life would begin.

"Oh, I love you, I love, I love, I love you," she whispered over and over. Tom's hands touching her seemed a strange and exciting passage that would carry her simple dreamy existence to a reality she had never encountered. She had never dreamed anyone so interesting would marry her.

Letty's enthusiasm and her frail body excited him, and he made love to her several times before he asked her to remove her gown.

The next day they breakfasted late and walked for a while along the avenue. In the afternoon Tom explained to his wife what her clitoris was and showed her some of the interesting things it was capable of generating, and before the day was out Letty became the first girl in her crowd to break the laws of God and the Napoleonic Code by indulging in oral intercourse.

Fourteen years went by and the Wilsons' luck held. Fourteen years is a long time to stay lucky, even for rich people who don't cause trouble for anyone.

Of course, even among the rich there are endless challenges, unyielding limits, rivalry, envy, quirks of fortune. Letty's father grew increasingly incompetent and sold his seat on the exchange, and Letty's irresponsible brothers went to work throwing away the money in Las Vegas and LA and Zurich and Johannesburg and Paris and anywhere they could think of to fly to with their interminable strings of mistresses.

Tom envied them their careless, thoughtless lives and he was annoyed that they controlled their own money while Letty's was tied up in some mysterious trust, but he kept his thoughts to himself as he did his obsessive irritation over his growing obesity.

"Looks like you're putting on a little weight there," a friend would observe.

"Good, good," Tom would say, "makes me look like a man. I got a wife to look at if I want to see someone who's skinny."

He stayed busy gambling and hunting and fishing and being the life of the party at the endless round of dinners and cocktail parties and benefits and Mardi Gras functions that consume the lives of the Roman Catholic hierarchy that dominates the life of the city that care forgot.

Letty was preoccupied with the details of their domestic life and her work in the community. She took her committees seriously and actually believed that the work she did made a difference in the lives of other people.

The Wilsons grew rich in houses. They lived in a large Victorian house in the Garden District, and across Lake Pontchartrain they had another Victorian house to stay in on the weekends, with a private beach surrounded by old moss-hung oak trees. Tom bought a duck camp in Plaquemines Parish and kept an apartment in the French Quarter in case one of his business friends fell in love with his secretary and needed someplace to be alone with her. Tom almost never used the apartment himself. He was rich in being satisfied to sleep with his own wife.

The Wilsons were rich in common sense. When five years of a good Catholic marriage went by and Letty inexplicably never became pregnant, they threw away their thermometers and ovulation charts and litmus paper and went down to the Catholic adoption agency and adopted a baby girl with curly black hair and hazel eyes. Everyone declared she looked exactly like Tom. The Wilsons named the little girl Helen and, as the months went by, everyone swore she even walked and talked like Tom.

At about the same time Helen came to be the Wilsons' little girl, Tom grew interested in raising Labrador retrievers. He had large wire runs with concrete floors built in the side yard for the dogs to stay in when he wasn't training them on the levee or at the park lagoon. He used all the latest methods for training Labs, including an electric cattle prod given to him by Chalin Perez himself and live ducks supplied by a friend on the Audubon Park Zoo Association Committee.

"Watch this, Helen," he would call to the little girl in the stroller, "watch this." And he would throw a duck into the lagoon with its secondary feathers neatly clipped on the left side and its feet tied loosely together, and one of the Labs would swim out into the water and carry it safely back and lay it at his feet.

As so often happens when childless couples are rich in common sense, before long Letty gave birth to a little boy, and then to twin boys, and finally to another little Wilson girl. The Wilsons became so rich in children the neighbors all lost count.

"Tom," Letty said, curling up close to him in the big walnut bed, "Tom, I want to talk to you about something important." The new baby girl was three months old. "Tom, I want to talk to Father Delahoussaye and ask him if we can use some birth control. I think we have all the children we need for now."

Tom put his arms around her and squeezed her until he wrinkled her new green linen B.H. Wragge, and she screamed for mercy.

"Stop it," she said, "be serious. Do you think it's all right to do that?"

Then Tom agreed with her that they had had all the luck with children they needed for the present, and Letty made up her mind to call the cathedral and make an appointment. All her friends were getting dispensations so they would have time to do their work at the Symphony League and the Thrift Shop and the New Orleans Museum Association and the PTAs of the private schools.

All the Wilson children were in good health except Helen. The pediatricians and psychiatrists weren't certain what was wrong with her. Helen couldn't concentrate on anything. She didn't like to share and she went through stages of biting other children at the Academy of the Sacred Heart of Jesus.

The doctors decided it was a combination of prenatal brain damage and dyslexia, a complicated learning disability that is a fashionable problem with children in New Orleans.

Letty felt like she spent half her life sitting in offices talking to people about Helen. The office she sat in most often belonged to Dr. Zander. She sat there twisting her rings and avoiding looking at the box of Kleenex on Dr. Zander's desk. It made her feel like she was sleeping in a dirty bed even to think of plucking a Kleenex from Dr. Zander's container and crying in a place where strangers cried. She imagined his chair was filled all day with women weeping over terrible and sordid things like their husbands running off with their secretaries or their children not getting into the right clubs and colleges.

"I don't know what we're going to do with her next," Letty said. "If we let them hold her back a grade it's just going to make her more self-conscious than ever."

"I wish we knew about her genetic background. You people have pull with the sisters. Can't you find out?"

"Tom doesn't want to find out. He says we'll just be opening a can of worms. He gets embarrassed even talking about Helen's problem."

"Well," said Dr. Zander, crossing his short legs and settling his steel-rimmed glasses on his nose like a tiny bicycle stuck on a hill, "let's start her on Dexedrine."

So Letty and Dr. Zander and Dr. Mullins and Dr. Pickett and Dr. Smith decided to try an experiment. They decided to give Helen five milligrams of Dexedrine every day for twenty days each month, taking her off the drug for ten days in between.

"Children with dyslexia react to drugs strangely," Dr. Zander said. "If you give them tranquilizers it peps them up, but if you give them Ritalin or Dexedrine it calms them down and makes them able to think straight.

"You may have to keep her home and have her tutored on the days she is off the drug," he continued, "but the rest of the time she should be easier to live with." And he reached over and patted Letty on the leg and for a moment she thought it might all turn out all right after all.

Helen stood by herself on the playground of the beautiful old pink-brick convent with its drooping wrought-iron balconies covered with ficus. She was watching the girl she liked talking with some other girls who were playing jacks. All the little girls wore blue-and-red-plaid skirts and navy blazers or sweaters. They looked like a disorderly marching band. Helen was waiting for the girl, whose name was Lisa, to decide if she wanted to go home with her after school and spend the afternoon. Lisa's mother was divorced and worked downtown in a department store, so Lisa rode the streetcar back and forth from school and could go anywhere she liked until five thirty in the afternoon. Sometimes she went home with Helen so she wouldn't have to ride the streetcar. Then Helen would be so excited, the hours until school let out would seem to last forever.

Sometimes Lisa liked her and wanted to go home with her and

other times she didn't, but she was always nice to Helen and let her stand next to her in lines.

Helen watched Lisa walking toward her. Lisa's skirt was two inches shorter than those of any of the other girls, and she wore high white socks that made her look like a skater. She wore a silver identification bracelet and Revlon nail polish.

"I'll go home with you if you get your mother to take us to get an Icee," Lisa said. "I was going last night but my mother's boyfriend didn't show up until after the place closed so I was going to walk to Manny's after school. Is that okay?"

"I think she will," Helen said, her eyes shining. "I'll go call her up and see."

"Naw, let's just go swing. We can ask her when she comes." Then Helen walked with her friend over to the swings and tried to be patient waiting for her turn.

The Dexedrine helped Helen concentrate and it helped her get along better with other people, but it seemed to have an unusual side effect. Helen was chubby and Dr. Zander had led the Wilsons to believe the drug would help her lose weight, but instead she grew even fatter. The Wilsons didn't want to force her to stop eating for fear they would make her nervous, so they tried to reason with her.

"Why can't I have any ice cream?" she would say. "Daddy is fat and he eats all the ice cream he wants." She was leaning up against Letty, stroking her arm and petting the baby with her other hand. They were in an upstairs sitting room with the afternoon sun streaming in through the French windows. Everything in the room was decorated with different shades of blue, and the curtains were white with old-fashioned blue-and-white-checked ruffles.

"You can have ice cream this evening after dinner," Letty said, "I just want you to wait a few hours before you have it. Won't you do that for me?"

"Can I hold the baby for a while?" Helen asked, and Letty

allowed her to sit in the rocker and hold the baby and rock it furiously back and forth crooning to it.

"Is Jennifer beautiful, Mother?" Helen asked.

"She's okay, but she doesn't have curly black hair like you. She just has plain brown hair. Don't you see, Helen, that's why we want you to stop eating between meals, because you're so pretty and we don't want you to get too fat. Why don't you go outside and play with Tim and try not to think about ice cream so much?"

"I don't care," Helen said, "I'm only nine years old and I'm hungry. I want you to tell the maids to give me some ice cream now," and she handed the baby to her mother and ran out of the room.

The Wilsons were rich in maids, and that was a good thing because there were all those children to be taken care of and cooked for and cleaned up after. The maids didn't mind taking care of the Wilson children all day. The Wilsons' house was much more comfortable than the ones they lived in, and no one cared whether they worked very hard or not as long as they showed up on time so Letty could get to her meetings. The maids left their own children with relatives or at home watching television, and when they went home at night they liked them much better than if they had spent the whole day with them.

The Wilson house had a wide white porch across the front and down both sides. It was shaded by enormous oak trees and furnished with swings and wicker rockers. In the afternoons the maids would sit on the porch and other maids from around the neighborhood would come up pushing prams and strollers and the children would all play together on the porch and in the yard. Sometimes the maids fixed lemonade and the children would sell it to passersby from a little stand.

The maids hated Helen. They didn't care whether she had dyslexia or not. All they knew was that she was a lot of trouble to take care of. One minute she would be as sweet as pie and cuddle up to them and say she loved them, and the next minute she wouldn't do anything they told her.

"You're a nigger, nigger, nigger, and my mother said I could cross St. Charles Avenue if I wanted to," Helen would say, and the maids would hold their lips together and look into each other's eyes.

One afternoon the Wilson children and their maids were sitting on the porch after school with some of the neighbors' children and maids. The baby was on the porch in a bassinet on wheels and a new maid was looking out for her. Helen was in the biggest swing and was swinging as high as she could go so that none of the other children could get in the swing with her.

"Helen," the new maid said, "it's Tim's turn in the swing. You been swinging for fifteen minutes while Tim's been waiting. You be a good girl now and let Tim have a turn. You too big to act like that."

"You're just a high-yeller nigger," Helen called, "and you can't make me do anything." And she swung up higher and higher.

This maid had never had Helen call her names before and she had a quick temper and didn't put up with children calling her a nigger. She walked over to the swing and grabbed the chain and stopped it from moving.

"You say you're sorry for that, little fat honky white girl," she said, and made as if to grab Helen by the arms, but Helen got away and started running, calling over her shoulder, "Nigger, can't make me do anything."

She was running and looking over her shoulder and she hit the bassinet and it went rolling down the brick stairs so fast none of the maids or children could stop it. It rolled down the stairs and threw the baby onto the sidewalk and the blood from the baby's head began to move all over the concrete like a little ruby lake.

The Wilsons' house was on Philip Street, a street so rich it even had its own drugstore. Not some tacky chain drugstore with everything on special all the time, but a cute drugstore made out of a frame bungalow with gingerbread trim. Everything inside cost twice as much as it did in a regular drugstore, and the grown people could order any kind of drugs they needed and a green Mazda pickup would bring them right over. The children had to get their drugs from a fourteen-year-old pusher in Audubon Park named Leroi, but they could get all the ice cream and candy and chewing gum they wanted from the drugstore and charge it to their parents.

No white adults were at home in the houses where the maids worked so they sent the children running to the drugstore to bring the druggist to help with the baby. They called the hospital and ordered an ambulance and they called several doctors and they called Tom's bank. All the children who were old enough ran to the drugstore except Helen. Helen sat on the porch steps staring down at the baby with the maids hovering over it like swans, and she was crying and screaming and beating her hands against her head. She was in one of the periods when she couldn't have Dexedrine. She screamed and screamed, but none of the maids had time to help her. They were too busy with the baby.

"Shut up, Helen," one of the maids called. "Shut up that goddamn screaming. This baby is about to die."

A police car and the local patrol service drove up. An ambulance arrived and the yard filled with people. The druggist and one of the maids rode off in the ambulance with the baby. The crowd in the yard swarmed and milled and swam before Helen's eyes like a parade.

Finally they stopped looking like people and just looked like spots of color on the yard. Helen ran up the stairs and climbed under her cherry four-poster bed and pulled her pillows and her eiderdown comforter under it with her. There were cereal boxes and an empty ice cream carton and half a tin of English cookies under the headboard. Helen was soaked with sweat and her little Lily playsuit was tight under the arms and cut into her flesh. Helen rolled up in the comforter and began to dream the dream of the heavy clouds. She dreamed she was praying, but the beads of the rosary slipped through her fingers so quickly she couldn't catch them and it was cold in the church and beautiful and fragrant, then dark, then light, and Helen was rolling in the heavy clouds that rolled her like biscuit dough. Just as she was about to suffocate they rolled her faceup to the blue air above the clouds. Then Helen was a pink kite floating above the houses at evening. In the yards children were playing and fathers were driving up and baseball games were beginning and the sky turned gray and closed upon the city like a lid.

And now the baby is alone with Helen in her room and the door is locked and Helen ties the baby to the table so it won't fall off.

"Hold still, Baby, this will just be a little shot. This won't hurt much. This won't take a minute." And the baby is still and Helen begins to work on it.

Letty knelt down beside the bed. "Helen, please come out from under there. No one is mad at you. Please come out and help me, Helen. I need you to help me."

Helen held on tighter to the slats of the bed and squeezed her eyes shut and refused to look at Letty.

Letty climbed under the bed to touch the child. Letty was crying and her heart had an anchor in it that kept digging in and sinking deeper and deeper.

Dr. Zander came into the bedroom and knelt beside the bed and began to talk to Helen. Finally he gave up being reasonable and wiggled his small gray-suited body under the bed and Helen was lost in the area of arms that tried to hold her.

Tom was sitting in the bank president's office trying not to let Mr.

Saunders know how much he despised him or how much it hurt and mattered to him to be listening to a lecture. Tom thought he was too old to have to listen to lectures. He was tired and he wanted a drink and he wanted to punch the bastard in the face.

"I know, I know," he answered, "I can take care of it. Just give me a month or two. You're right. I'll take care of it."

And he smoothed the pants of his cord suit and waited for the rest of the lecture.

A man came into the room without knocking. Tom's secretary was behind him.

"Tom, I think your baby has had an accident. I don't know any details. Look, I've called for a car. Let me go with you."

Tom ran up the steps of his house and into the hallway full of neighbors and relatives. A girl in a tennis dress touched him on the arm, someone handed him a drink. He ran up the winding stairs to Helen's room. He stood in the doorway. He could see Letty's shoes sticking out from under the bed. He could hear Dr. Zander talking. He couldn't go near them.

"Letty," he called, "Letty, come here, my god, come out from there."

No one came to the funeral but the family. Letty wore a plain dress she would wear any day and the children all wore their school clothes.

The funeral was terrible for the Wilsons, but afterward they went home and all the people from the Garden District and from all over town started coming over to cheer them up. It looked like the biggest cocktail party ever held in New Orleans. It took four rented butlers just to serve the drinks. Everyone wanted to get in on the Wilsons' tragedy.

In the months that followed the funeral Tom began to have sinus headaches for the first time in years. He was drinking a lot and smoking again. He was allergic to whiskey, and when he woke up in the morning his nose and head were so full of phlegm he had to vomit before he could think straight.

He began to have trouble with his vision.

One November day the high yellow windows of the Shell Oil Building all turned their eyes upon him as he stopped at the corner of Poydras and Carondelet to wait for a streetlight, and he had to pull the car over to a curb and talk to himself for several minutes before he could drive on.

He got back all the keys to his apartment so he could go there and be alone and think. One day he left work at two o'clock and drove around Jefferson Parish all afternoon drinking Scotch and eating potato chips.

Not as many people at the bank wanted to go out to lunch with him anymore. They were sick and tired of pretending his expensive mistakes were jokes.

One night Tom was gambling at the Pickwick Club with a poker group and a man jokingly accused him of cheating. Tom jumped up from the table, grabbed the man, and began hitting him with his fists. He hit the man in the mouth and knocked out his new gold inlays.

"You dirty little goddamn bond peddler, you son of a bitch! I'll kill you for that," Tom yelled, and it took four waiters to hold him while the terrified man made his escape. The next morning Tom resigned from the club.

He started riding the streetcar downtown to work so he wouldn't have to worry about driving his car home if he got drunk. He was worrying about money and he was worrying about his gambling debts, but most of the time he was thinking about Helen. She looked so much like him that he believed people would think she was his illegitimate child. The more he tried to talk himself into believing the baby's death was an accident, the more obstinate his mind became.

The Wilson children were forbidden to take the Labs out of the kennels without permission. One afternoon Tom came home earlier than usual and found Helen sitting in the open door of one of the kennels playing with a half-grown litter of puppies. She was holding one of the puppies and the others were climbing all around her and spilling out onto the grass. She held the puppy by its forelegs, making it dance in the air, then letting it drop. Then she would gather it in her arms and hold it tight and sing to it.

Tom walked over to the kennel and grabbed her by an arm and began to paddle her as hard as he could.

"Goddamn you, what are you trying to do? You know you aren't supposed to touch those dogs. What in the hell do you think you're doing?"

Helen was too terrified to scream. The Wilsons never spanked their children for anything.

"I didn't do anything to it. I was playing with it," she sobbed.

Letty and the twins came running out of the house and when Tom saw Letty he stopped hitting Helen and walked in through the kitchen door and up the stairs to the bedroom. Letty gave the children to the cook and followed him.

Tom stood by the bedroom window trying to think of something to say to Letty. He kept his back turned to her and he was making a nickel disappear with his left hand. He thought of himself at Tommie Keenen's birthday party wearing his black coat and hat and doing his famous rope trick. Mr. Keenen had given him fifteen dollars. He remembered sticking the money in his billfold.

"My god, Letty, I'm sorry. I don't know what the shit's going on. I thought she was hurting the dog. I know I shouldn't have hit her and there's something I need to tell you about the bank. Kennington is getting sacked. I may be part of the housecleaning."

"Why didn't you tell me before? Can't Daddy do anything?"

"I don't want him to do anything. Even if it happens it doesn't have anything to do with me. It's just bank politics. We'll say I quit. I want to get out of there anyway. That fucking place is driving me crazy."

Tom put the nickel in his pocket and closed the bedroom door. He could hear the maid down the hall comforting Helen. He didn't give a fuck if she cried all night. He walked over to Letty and put his arms around her. He smelled like he'd been drinking for a week. He reached under her dress and pulled down her pantyhose and her underpants and began kissing her face and hair while she stood awkwardly with the pants and hose around her feet like a halter. She was trying to cooperate.

She forgot that Tom smelled like sweat and whiskey. She was thinking about the night they were married. Every time they made love Letty pretended it was that night. She had spent thousands of nights in a bridal suite at the Sherry Netherland Hotel in New York City.

Letty lay on the walnut bed leaning into a pile of satin pillows and twisting a gold bracelet around her wrist. She could hear the children playing outside. She had a headache and her stomach was queasy, but she was afraid to take a Valium or an aspirin. She was waiting for the doctor to call her back and tell her if she was pregnant. She already knew what he was going to say.

Tom came into the room and sat by her on the bed.

"What's wrong?"

"Nothing's wrong. Please don't do that. I'm tired."

"Something's wrong."

"Nothing's wrong. Tom, please leave me alone."

Tom walked out through the French windows and onto a little balcony that overlooked the play yard and the dog runs. Sunshine flooded Philip Street, covering the houses and trees and dogs and children with a million volts a minute. It flowed down to hide in the roots of trees, glistening on the cars, baking the street, and lighting Helen's rumpled hair where she stooped over the puppy.

She was singing a little song. She had made up the song she was singing.

"The baby's dead. The baby's dead. The baby's gone to heaven."

"Jesus God," Tom muttered. All up and down Philip Street fathers were returning home from work. A jeep filled with teenagers came tearing past and threw a beer can against the curb.

Six or seven pieces of Tom's mind sailed out across the street and stationed themselves along the power line that zigzagged back and forth along Philip Street between the live oak trees.

The pieces of his mind sat upon the power line like a row of black starlings. They looked him over.

Helen took the dog out of the buggy and dragged it over to the kennel.

"Jesus Christ," Tom said, and the pieces of his mind flew back to him as swiftly as they had flown away and entered his eyes and ears and nostrils and arranged themselves in their proper places like parts of a phrenological head.

Tom looked at his watch. It said six fifteen. He stepped back into the bedroom and closed the French windows. A vase of huge roses from the garden hid Letty's reflection in the mirror.

"I'm going to the camp for the night. I need to get away. Besides, the season's almost over."

"All right," Letty answered. "Who are you going with?"

"I think I'll take Helen with me. I haven't paid any attention to her for weeks."

"That's good," Letty said, "I really think I'm getting a cold. I'll have a tray up for supper and try to get some sleep."

Tom moved around the room, opening drawers and closets and throwing some gear into a canvas duffel bag. He changed into his hunting clothes.

He removed the guns he needed from a shelf in the upstairs den and cleaned them neatly and thoroughly and zipped them into their carriers.

"Helen," he called from the downstairs porch, "bring the dog in the house and come get on some play clothes. I'm going to take you to the duck camp with me. You can take the dog."

"Can we stop and get beignets?" Helen called back, coming running at the invitation.

"Sure we can, honey. Whatever you like. Go get packed. We'll leave as soon as dinner is over."

It was past nine at night. They crossed the Mississippi River from the New Orleans side on the last ferry going to Algier's Point. There was an offshore breeze and a light rain fell on the old brown river. The Mississippi River smelled like the inside of a nigger cabin, powerful and fecund. The smell came in Tom's mouth until he felt he could chew it.

He leaned over the railing and vomited. He felt better and walked back to the red Chevrolet pickup he had given himself for a birthday present. He thought it was chic for a banker to own a pickup.

Helen was playing with the dog, pushing him off the seat and laughing when he climbed back on her lap. She had a paper bag of doughnuts from the French Market and was eating them and licking the powdered sugar from her fingers and knocking the dog off the seat.

She wasn't the least bit sleepy.

"I'm glad Tim didn't get to go. Tim was bad at school, that's why he had to stay home, isn't it? The sisters called Momma. I don't like Tim. I'm glad I got to go by myself." She stuck her fat arms out the window and rubbed Tom's canvas hunting jacket. "This coat feels hard. It's all dirty. Can we go up in the cabin and talk to the pilot?"

"Sit still, Helen."

"Put the dog in the back, he's bothering me." She bounced up and down on the seat. "We're going to the duck camp. We're going to the duck camp."

The ferry docked. Tom drove the pickup onto the blacktop road past the city dump and on into Plaquemines Parish.

They drove into the brackish marshes that fringe the Gulf of Mexico where it extends in ragged fingers along the coast below and to the east of New Orleans. As they drove closer to the sea the hardwoods turned to palmetto and water oak and willow.

The marshes were silent. Tom could smell the glasswort and black mangrove, the oyster and shrimp boats.

He wondered if it were true that children and dogs could penetrate a man's concealment, could know him utterly.

Helen leaned against his coat and prattled on.

In the Wilson house on Philip Street, Tim and the twins were cuddled up by Letty, hearing one last story before they went to bed.

A blue wicker tray held the remains of the children's hot chocolate. The china cups were a confirmation present sent to Letty from Limoges, France.

Now she was finishing reading a wonderful story by Ludwig Bemelmans about a little convent girl in Paris named Madeline who reforms the son of the Spanish ambassador, putting an end to his terrible habit of beheading chickens on a miniature guillotine.

Letty was feeling better. She had decided God was just trying to make up to her for Jennifer.

The camp was a three-room wooden shack built on pilings out over Bayou Lafouche, which runs through the middle of the parish.

The inside of the camp was casually furnished with old leather office furniture, hand-me-down tables and lamps, and a walnut poker table from Neiman-Marcus. Photographs of hunts and parties were tacked around the walls. Over the poker table were pictures of racehorses and their owners and an assortment of ribbons won in races.

Tom laid the guns down on the bar and opened a cabinet over the sink in the part of the room that served as a kitchen. The nigger hadn't come to clean up after the last party and the sink was piled with half-washed dishes. He found a clean glass and a bottle of Tanqueray gin and sat down behind the bar.

Helen was across the room on the floor finishing the beignets and trying to coax the dog to come closer. He was considering it. No one had remembered to feed him.

Tom pulled a new deck of cards out of a drawer, broke the seal, and began to shuffle them.

Helen came and stood by the bar. "Show me a trick, Daddy. Make the queen disappear. Show me how to do it."

"Do you promise not to tell anyone the secret? A magician never tells his secrets."

"I won't tell. Daddy, please show me, show me now."

Tom spread out the cards. He began to explain the trick.

"All right, you go here and here, then here. Then pick up these in just the right order, but look at the people while you do it, not at the cards."

"I'm going to do it for Lisa."

"She's going to beg you to tell the secret. What will you do then?"

"I'll tell her a magician never tells his secrets."

Tom drank the gin and poured some more.

"Now let me do it to you, Daddy."

"Not yet, Helen. Go sit over there with the dog and practice it where I can't see what you're doing. I'll pretend I'm Lisa and don't know what's going on."

Tom picked up the Kliengunther 7mm magnum rifle and shot the dog first, splattering its brains all over the door and walls. Without pausing, without giving her time to raise her eyes from the red and gray and black rainbow of the dog, he shot the little girl.

The bullet entered her head from the back. Her thick body rolled across the hardwood floor and lodged against a hat rack from Jody Mellon's old office in the Hibernia Bank Building. One of her arms landed on a pile of old *Penthouse* magazines and her disordered brain flung its roses north and east and south and west and rejoined the order from which it casually arose.

Tom put down the rifle, took a drink of the thick gin, and, carrying the pistol, walked out onto the pier through the kitchen door. Without removing his glasses or his hunting cap he stuck the .38 Smith & Wesson revolver against his palate and splattered his own head all over the new pier and the canvas covering of the Boston Whaler. His body struck the boat going down and landed in eight feet of water beside a broken crab trap left over from the summer.

A pair of deputies from the Plaquemines Parish sheriff's office found the bodies.

Everyone believed it was some terrible inexplicable mistake or accident.

No one believed that much bad luck could happen to a nice lady like Letty Dufrechou Wilson, who never hurt a flea or gave anyone a minute's trouble in her life.

No one believed that much bad luck could get together between the fifteenth week after Pentecost and the third week in Advent.

No one believed a man would kill his own little illegitimate dyslexic daughter just because she was crazy.

And no one, not even the district attorney of New Orleans, wanted to believe a man would shoot a $3,000 Labrador retriever sired by Super Chief out of Prestidigitation.

SPATS

BY VALERIE MARTIN

New Orleans East

(Originally published in 1988)

T he dogs are scratching at the kitchen door. How long, Lydia thinks, has she been lost in the thought of her rival dead? She passes her hand over her eyes, an unconscious effort to push the hot red edge off everything she sees, and goes to the door to let them in.

When Ivan confessed that he was in love with another woman, Lydia thought she could ride it out. She told him what she had so often told him in the turbulent course of their marriage, that he was a fool, that he would be sorry. Even as she watched his friends loading his possessions into the truck, even when she stood alone in the silent half-empty house contemplating a pale patch on the wall where one of his pictures had been, even then she didn't believe he was gone. Now she has only one hope to hold on to: he has left the dogs with her and this must mean he will be coming back.

When she opens the door Gretta hangs back, as she always does, but Spats pushes his way in as soon as she has turned the knob, knocking the door back against her shins and barreling past her, his heavy tail slapping the wood repeatedly. No sooner is he inside than he turns to block the door so that Gretta can't get past him. He lowers his big head and nips at her forelegs; it's play, it's all in fun, but Gretta only edges past him, pressing close to Lydia, who pushes at the bigger dog with her foot. "Spats," she says, "leave her alone." Spats backs away, but he is only waiting until she is gone; then he will try again. Lydia is struck with the inevitability of this scene. It happens every day, several times a day, and it is always the same. The dogs gambol into the kitchen, knocking against the table legs, turning about in ever-narrowing circles, until they throw themselves down a few feet apart and settle for their naps. Gretta always sleeps curled tightly in a semicircle, her only defense against attacks from her mate, who sleeps on his side, his long legs extended, his neck stretched out, the open, deep sleep of the innocent or the oppressor.

Lydia stands at the door looking back at the dogs. Sometimes Ivan got right down on the floor with Spats, lay beside him holding his big black head against his chest and talking to him. "Did you have a good time at the park today?" he'd croon. "Did you swim? Are you really tired now? Are you happy?" This memory causes Lydia's upper lip to pull back from her teeth. How often had she wanted to kick him right in his handsome face when he did that, crooning over the dog as if it were his child or his mistress. What about me? she thought. What about my day? But she never said that; instead she turned away, biting back her anger and confusion, for she couldn't admit that she was jealous of a dog.

Spats is asleep immediately, his jaws slack and his tongue lolling out over his black lips. As Lydia looks at him she has an unexpected thought: she could kill him. It is certainly in her power. No one would do anything about it, and it would hurt Ivan as nothing else could. She could poison him, or shoot him, or she could take him to a vet and say he was vicious and have him put away.

She lights a match against the grout in the countertop and turns the stove burner on. It is too cold, and she is so numb with the loss of her husband that she watches the flame wearily, hopelessly; it can do so little for her. She could plunge her hand into it and burn it, or she could stand close to it and still be cold. Then she puts the kettle over the flame and turns away.

She had argued with Ivan about everything for years, so often and so intensely that it seemed natural to her. She held him responsible for the hot flush that rose to her cheeks, the bitter taste that flooded her mouth at the very thought of him. She believed that she was ill; sometimes she believed her life was nearly over and she hated Ivan for this too, that he was killing her with these arguments and that he didn't care.

When the water is boiling she fills a cup with coffee and takes it to the table. She sits quietly in the still house; the only sound is the clink of the cup as she sets it back in the saucer. She goes through a cycle of resolutions. The first is a simple one: she will make her husband come back. It is inconceivable that she will fail. They always had these arguments, they even separated a few times, but he always came back and so he always would. He would tire of this other woman in a few weeks and then he would be back. After all, she asked herself, what did this woman have that she didn't have? An education? And what good was that? If Ivan loved this woman for her education, it wasn't really as if he loved her for herself. He loved her for something she had acquired. And Lydia was certain that Ivan had loved *her*, had married her, and must still love her, only for herself, because she was so apparent, so undisguised; there wasn't anything else to love her for.

So this first resolution is a calm one: she will wait for her husband and he will return and she will take him back.

She sets the cup down roughly on the table, for the inevitable question is upon her: how long can she wait? This has been going on for two months, and she is sick of waiting. There must be something she can do. The thought of action stiffens her spine, and her jaw clenches involuntarily. Now comes the terrible vision of her revenge, which never fails to take her so by surprise that she sighs as she lays herself open to it; revenge is her only lover now. She will see a lawyer, sue Ivan for adultery, and get every cent she can out of him, everything, for the rest of his life. But this is unsatisfactory, promising, as it does, nothing better than a long life without him, a life in which he continues to love someone else. She would do better to buy a gun and shoot him. She could call him late at night, when the other woman is asleep, and beg him to come over. He will come; she can scare him into it. And then when he lets himself in with his key she will shoot him in the living room. He left her, she will tell the court. She bought the gun to protect herself because she was alone. How was she to know he would let himself in so late at night? He told her he was never coming back and she had assumed the footsteps in the living room came from the man every lonely woman lies in bed at night listening for, the man who has found out her secret, who knows she is alone, whose mission, which is sanctioned by the male world, is to break the spirit if not the bones of those rebellious women who have the temerity to sleep at night without a man. So she shot him. She wasn't going to ask any questions and live to see him get off in court. How could she have known it was her husband, who had abandoned her?

Yes, yes, that would work. It would be easily accomplished, but wouldn't she only end up as she was now? Better to murder the other woman, who was, after all, the cause of all this intolerable pain. She knew her name, knew where she lived, where she worked. She had called her several times just to hear her voice, her cheerful hello, in which Lydia always heard Ivan's presence, as if he were standing right next to the woman and she had turned away from kissing him to answer the insistent phone. Lydia had heard of a man who killed people for money. She could pay this man, and then the woman would be gone.

The kettle is screaming; she has forgotten to turn off the flame. So she could drink another cup of coffee, then take a bath. But that would take only an hour or so and she has to get through the whole day. The silence in the house is intense, though she knows it is no more quiet than usual. Ivan was never home much in the daytime. What did she do before? It seems to her that that life was another life, one she will never know again, the life in which each day ended with the appearance of her husband. Sometimes, she admitted, she had not been happy to see him, but her certainty that she would see him made the question of whether she was happy or sad a matter of indifference to her. Often she didn't see him until late at night, when he appeared at one of the clubs where she was singing. He took a place in the audience and when she saw him she always sang for him. Then they were both happy. He knew she was admired, and that pleased him, as if she were his reflection and what others saw when they looked at her was more of him. Sometimes he gave her that same affectionate look he gave himself in mirrors, and when he did it made her lightheaded, and she would sing, holding her hands out a little before her, one index finger stretched out as if she were pointing at something, and she would wait until the inevitable line about how it was "you" she loved, wanted, hated, couldn't get free of, couldn't live without, and at that "you" she would make her moving hands be still and with her eyes as well as her hands she would point to her husband in the crowd. Those were the happiest moments they had, though neither of them was really conscious of them, nor did they ever speak of this happiness. When, during the break, they did speak, it was usually to argue about something.

She thinks of this as she stares dully at the dogs, Ivan's dogs. Later she will drive through the cold afternoon light to Larry's cold garage, where they will rehearse. They will have dinner together; Larry and Simon will try to cheer her up, and Kenneth, the drummer, will sit looking on in his usual daze. They will take drugs if anyone has any, cocaine or marijuana, and Simon will drink a six-pack of beer.

Then they will go to the club and she will sing as best she can. She will sing and sing, into the drunken faces of the audience, over the bobbing heads of the frenzied dancers; she will sing like some blinded bird lost in a dark forest trying to find her way out by listening to the echo of her own voice. The truth is that she sings better than she ever has. Everyone tells her so. Her voice is so full of suffering that hearing it would move a stone, though it will not move her husband, because he won't be there. Yet she can't stop looking for him in the audience, as she always has. And as she sings and looks for him she will remember exactly what it was like to find herself in his eyes. That was how she had first seen him, sitting at a table on the edge of the floor, watching her closely. He was carrying on a conversation with a tired-looking woman across from him but he watched Lydia so closely that she could feel his eyes on her. She smiled. She was aware of herself as the surprising creation she really was, a woman who was beautiful to look at and beautiful to hear. She was, at that moment, so self-conscious and so contented that she didn't notice what an oddity he was, a man who was both beautiful and masculine. Her attachment to his appearance, to his gestures, the suddenness of his smile, the coldness of his eyes, came later. At that moment it was herself in his eyes that she loved; as fatal a love match as she would ever know.

The phone rings. She hesitates, then gets up and crosses to the counter. She picks up the receiver and holds it to her ear.

"Hello," Ivan says. "Lydia?"

She says nothing.

"Talk to me!" he exclaims.

"Why should I?"

"Are you all right?"

"No."

"What are you doing?"

"Why are you calling me?"

"About the dogs."

"What about them?"

"Are they okay?"

She sighs. "Yes." Then, patiently, "When are you coming to get them?"

"I can't," he says. "I can't take them. I can't keep them here."

"Why?"

"There's no fenced yard. Vivian's landlord doesn't allow dogs."

At the mention of her rival's name, Lydia feels a sudden rush of blood to her face. "You bastard," she hisses.

"Baby, please," he says, "try to understand."

She slams the receiver down into the cradle. "Bastard," she says again. Her fingers tighten on the edge of the counter until the knuckles are white. He doesn't want the dogs. He doesn't want her. He isn't coming back. "I really can't stand it," she says into the empty kitchen. "I don't think I will be able to stand it."

She is feeding the dogs. They have to eat at either end of the kitchen because Spats will eat Gretta's dinner if he can. Gretta has to be fed first; then Spats is lured away from her bowl with his own. Gretta eats quickly, swallowing one big bite after another, for she knows she has only the time it takes Spats to finish his meal before he will push her away from hers. Tonight Spats is in a bad humor. He growls at Gretta when Lydia sets her bowl down. Gretta hangs her head and backs away. "Spats!" Lydia says. "Leave her alone." She pushes him away with one hand, holding out his bowl before him with the other.

But he growls again, turning his face toward her, and she sees that his teeth are bared and his threat is serious. "Spats," she says firmly, but she backs away. His eyes glaze over with something deep and vicious, and she knows that he no longer hears her. She drops the bowl. The sound of the bowl hitting the linoleum and the sight of his food scattered before him brings Spats back to himself. He falls to eating off the floor. Gretta lifts her head to watch him, then returns to her hurried eating.

Lydia leans against the stove. Her legs are weak and her heart beats absurdly in her ears. In the midst of all this weakness a habitual ambivalence goes hard as stone. Gretta, she thinks, certainly deserves to eat in peace.

She looks down at Spats. Now he is the big, awkward, playful, good fellow again.

"You just killed yourself," Lydia says. Spats looks back at her, his expression friendly, affable. He no longer remembers his fit of bad temper.

Lydia smiles at him. "You just killed yourself and you don't even have the sense to know it," she says.

It is nearly dawn. Lydia lies in her bed alone. She used to sleep on her back when Ivan was with her. Now she sleeps on her side, her legs drawn up to her chest. Or rather, she reminds herself, she lies awake in this position and waits for the sleep that doesn't come.

As far as she is concerned she is still married. Her husband is gone, but marriage, in her view, is not a condition that can be dissolved by external circumstances. She has always believed this; she told Ivan this when she married him, and he agreed or said he agreed. They were bound together for life. He had said he wanted nothing more.

She still believes it. It is all she understands marriage to be. They must cling to each other and let the great nightmarish flood of time wash over them as it will; at the end they would be found wherever they were left, washed onto whatever alien shore, dead or alive, still together, their lives entwined as surely as their bodies, inseparably, eternally. How many times in that last year, in the midst of the interminable quarrels that constituted their life together, had she seen pass across his face an expression that filled her with rage, for she saw that he knew she was drowning and he feared she would pull him down with her. So even as she raged at him, she clung to him more tightly, and the lovemaking that followed their arguments was so intense, so filled with her need of him that, she told herself, he must know, wherever she was going, he was going with her.

Now, she confesses to herself, she is drowning. Alone, at night, in the moonless sea of her bed, where she is tossed from nightmare to nightmare so that she wakes gasping for air, throwing her arms out before her, she is drowning alone in the dark and there is nothing to hold on to.

Lydia sits on the floor in the veterinarian's office. Spats lies next to her; his head rests in her lap. He is unconscious but his heart is still beating feebly. Lydia can feel it beneath her palm, which she has pressed against his side. His mouth has gone dry and his dry tongue lolls out to one side. His black lips are slack and there is no sign of the sharp canine teeth that he used to bare so viciously at the slightest provocation. Lydia sits watching his closed eyes and she is afflicted with the horror of what she has done.

He is four years old; she has known him all his life. When Ivan brought him home he was barely weaned and he cried all that first night, a helpless baby whimpering for his lost mother. But he was a sturdy, healthy animal, greedy for life, and he transferred his affections to Ivan and to his food bowl in a matter of days. Before he was half her size he had terrorized Gretta into the role he and Ivan had worked out for her: dog-wife, mother to his children. She would never have a moment's freedom as long as he lived, no sleep that could not be destroyed by his sudden desire for play, no meal that he did not oversee and covet. She was more intelligent than he, and his brutishness wore her down. She became a nervous, quiet animal who would rather be patted than fed, who barricaded herself under desks, behind chairs, wherever she could find a space Spats couldn't occupy at the same time.

Spats was well trained; Ivan saw to that. He always came when he was called and he followed just at his master's heel when they went out for their walks every day. But it ran against his grain;

every muscle in his body was tensed for that moment when Ivan would say, "Go ahead," and then he would spring forward and run as hard as he could for as long as he was allowed. He was a fine swimmer and loved to fetch sticks thrown into the water.

When he was a year old, his naturally territorial disposition began to show signs of something amiss. He attacked a neighbor who made the mistake of walking into his yard, and bit him twice, on the arm and on the hand. Lydia stood in the doorway screaming at him, and Ivan was there instantly, shouting at Spats and pulling him away from the startled neighbor, who kept muttering that it was his own fault; he shouldn't have come into the yard. Lydia had seen the attack from the start; she had, she realized, seen it coming and not known it. What disturbed her was that Spats had tried to bite the man's face or his throat, and that he had given his victim almost no notice of his intention. One moment he was wagging his tail and barking, she told Ivan; then, with a snarl, he was on the man.

Ivan made excuses for the animal, and Lydia admitted that it was freakish behavior. But in the years that followed, it happened again and again. Lydia had used this evidence against him, had convicted him on the grounds of it; in the last two years he had bitten seven people. Between these attacks he was normal, friendly, playful, and he grew into such a beautiful animal, his big head was so noble, his carriage so powerful and impressive, that people were drawn to him and often stopped to ask about him. He enjoyed everything in his life; he did everything—eating, running, swimming—with such gusto that it was a pleasure to watch him. He was so full of energy, of such inexhaustible force, it was as if he embodied life, and death must stand back a little in awe at the sight of him.

Now Lydia strokes his head, which seems to be getting heavier every moment, and she says his name softly. It's odd, she thinks, that I would like to die but I have to live, and he would like to live but he has to die.

In the last weeks she has wept for herself, for her lost love, for her husband, for her empty life, but the tears that fill her eyes now are for the dying animal she holds in her arms. She is looking straight into the natural beauty that was his life and she sees resting over it, like a relentless cloud of doom, the empty lovelessness that is her own. His big heart has stopped; he is gone.

THE MAN WITH MOON HANDS

BY O'NEIL DE NOUX

Tchoupitoulas and Jackson

(Originally published in 1993)

Before the meat wagon arrived, LaStanza went to take a look at the body. He didn't need a flashlight. The bright moon shined directly into that dirty New Orleans alley. Just inside the alley, LaStanza passed a young patrolman with sandy hair explaining to the other policemen, "He had a gun."

The body was about halfway down the dead-end alley. LaStanza's partner, Paul Snowood, stood over it. Next to him, a crime lab technician was reloading his camera.

"Come see this," Snowood twanged. "Got him through the pump with one shot." In his cowboy hat, rope tie around the neck of his western shirt, brown jeans, and snakeskin boots, Detective Snowood couldn't look more out of place if he tried.

"You sure you don't want me to take this?" LaStanza asked as he stepped up.

"You're up to your ass in murders already, boy," Snowood said. "This ain't nothin' but paperwork." Tilting his Stetson back, Snowood pointed to the body with his notepad and added, "Anyway, it looks like a good shootin'."

The body was on its side, legs straight out, arms contorted like soft pretzels. There were holes in the soles of both shoes and a worn spot on the man's jeans above the left knee. A stain of dark blood had gathered beneath the twisted torso. A small-caliber, blue-steel semiautomatic lay two feet from the man's head. It was a typical Saturday night special.

"You can handle the canvass for me, if you've a hankerin'."

"Sure," LaStanza said as he leaned over the body.

It was a white male, midtwenties, about five feet eight inches tall, one hundred and eighty pounds, with frizzy brown hair and a large gunshot wound in the center of his chest. Stepping out of the way of the technician, LaStanza paused and looked back at the body. There was something familiar about it. That was when he saw the hands.

He found some empty soft drink cases a few feet away and sat on them as his partner and the technician began taking measurements. Tugging angrily on his mustache, LaStanza stared at the pallid hands, at the limp fingers that looked like white goldfish left out to rot, and remembered . . .

LaStanza had been riding alone that night when the call came out.

"Headquarters—any Sixth District unit. Signal 103M with a gun. 2300 block of Rousseau."

A disturbance on Rousseau Street involving a mental case with a gun. There was only one appropriate thought: *Fuck me!*

It was a typically busy night in the bloody Sixth District. LaStanza was the only one available. He flipped on his blue lights, accelerated, and made it to Rousseau in less than two minutes. He found a small gathering in the 2300 block, about a dozen people standing in the street in front of an alley between a large warehouse and a junkyard. He was surprised to see a white face in the crowd.

As he climbed out, the white face approached and pointed to the alley and said, "My son's in there with a .25 automatic. He's a mental patient." The man was tall and very thin and wore thick spectacles.

"What's his problem?" LaStanza asked the spectacles.

"He's crazy."

"Who gave him the gun?"

"I did. I mean it's mine."

Crazy? It ran in the family. Now it was LaStanza's problem. There was a loony-tune in an alley with a gun. LaStanza withdrew his stainless steel .357 Smith & Wesson and approached the alley. He could see the young man clearly, standing under a light near the side door of the warehouse.

The man paid no attention to LaStanza moving into the alley. Looking up at the sky, the loony-tune ran his left hand through his frizzy hair. In his right hand he held a small, blue-steel automatic. He looked to be in his early twenties.

When he finally noticed LaStanza, he craned his neck forward and grinned. His large, bulbous eyes batted frantically at the approaching patrolman. He slowly raised the automatic and pointed it toward LaStanza, who ducked into the shadows.

The man went, "Zap. Zap." He followed this with a frightened laugh. His hand was shaking so hard, LaStanza thought the gun would fall.

The .357 magnum was cocked and pointed center on the man's chest.

"Put it down," LaStanza told the man as calmly as he could, "or I'll blow your brains out the back of your head." LaStanza's hands were steady, his voice flat and dry.

The man laughed again as his gun slowly inched forward until he let it drop to the ground. Then he raised his hands and said, "You see these hands?" The man glared at the huge white digits at the end of his palms. "They're not my hands. They're moon hands!"

LaStanza moved forward, stepped on the automatic, holstered his magnum, and slapped a handcuff across the loony's right wrist.

"These aren't my hands," the man complained as he tried to put his free hand in front of LaStanza's eyes. With a quick jerk,

LaStanza twisted the man around and cuffed both hands behind his back before picking up the automatic.

"They're *moon* hands!" the man cried.

On the way to Charity Hospital, the man told LaStanza he was a second-generation clone. Then he started pleading for LaStanza to take him to Tchoupitoulas and Jackson Avenue, to catch his flight—to Alpha Six.

"This one needs a ride," LaStanza told the standard-issue, heavyset, flat-faced admitting nurse. "Put him on the nonstop to Mandeville." It was nuthouse time, absolutely.

"Must be a full moon tonight," the bored nurse said. "All the loonies are out."

While LaStanza was filling out his report, a Seventh District patrolman came in with a howling man.

"What's his problem?" LaStanza asked.

"He thinks the world's being taken over by clones."

LaStanza couldn't resist. "Put him in with mine. He's a second-generation clone."

The patrolman eagerly obliged. LaStanza and the other cop watched the two men standing at opposite ends of the small trauma room, hissing and spitting at one another. LaStanza laughed so hard, his side ached. He'd been on the street long enough to not pass up an opportunity like that. Laughs were hard to find along the bloody streets of the Sixth District.

The Man with Moon Hands became one of LaStanza's favorite cop stories, especially after the man was released, as all nutcases inevitably were. The frizzy-haired loony began waiting every night at Tchoupitoulas and Jackson Avenue, for his flight—to Alpha Six. No matter the weather, he would be there, standing with his tattered brown suitcase in front of the old, abandoned New Orleans Cotton Exchange. No one bothered him. Most people probably figured he was just waiting in the wrong place for the Jackson Avenue Ferry.

One evening LaStanza watched the Man with Moon Hands for an hour and the man never moved a muscle. He stood patiently, the moon hands wrapped around the suitcase, the bulging eyes tilted upward at the dark sky, as he waited for his flight—to Alpha Six.

Then LaStanza got transferred to Homicide. Three years later, LaStanza was in a different alley.

"What's the matter wit' you?" Snowood yelled. "I thought you was gonna canvass!"

LaStanza climbed off the cases and started down the alley. He was still looking at the body.

"Mark and I are taking Wyatt Jr. here to the Bureau for his statement," Snowood said. To Snowood, a cop who shot someone had to be related, no matter how distantly, to Wyatt Earp himself.

LaStanza watched as the corpse was zipped into a black body bag and hauled off by the coroner's assistants. In the span of two minutes, he was alone. But there was nothing to canvass. It was a dead-end alley with no doors or windows, just brick walls and rusted dumpsters and bent-up garbage cans. It was a garbage alley.

It became very quiet. If he strained, LaStanza could hear cars in the distance, but it was silent in the alley. There was no movement except for the gnats circling over the fresh blood, and the rats crouching in anticipation of the moment when the detective would be gone.

On his way out of the alley, he remembered something else. He remembered yet another alley, back when he was a rookie. It was Mardi Gras morning and someone had killed a cop. LaStanza found the cop killer in a foggy alley. The man had a gun and it was over in less than a second. It was a good shooting, a clean shooting.

He'd shot the man without hesitation. And he wondered about that, about the intangible, about the unspoken reason a cop shoots one and not another. Maybe there was something in the moon man's frantic eyes that told LaStanza not to shoot. Maybe it was the frizzy hair. Or maybe it was the moon white hands.

"Looks like a good shooting," Sergeant Mark Land told LaStanza when he arrived at the Homicide office. "Looks like our man had no choice."

LaStanza sat heavily in his chair and didn't answer.

Big, burly, and Italian, with thick dark hair and a full mustache, Mark looked like an oversized version of LaStanza. Grinning broadly, the sergeant pulled up Snowood's chair and began to run down the patrolman's statement in detail, but LaStanza wasn't listening. He was thinking about the faded bricks of the old Cotton Exchange and the rusted drain pipes and all the lonely nights spent looking up at an empty sky.

When Mark finished, he yawned and said, "Shit, we'll be outta here in no time."

LaStanza leaned back in his chair and closed his eyes, but only for a moment.

"Say, boy, what's wrong wit' you?" Snowood called out as he approached. "You been acting spooky."

"It's nothing."

"Don't give me that shit. What's the matter?"

"Nothing, I told you." LaStanza scooped up his black coffee mug with its small inscription that read: *FUCK THIS SHIT!* He moved over to the coffeepot and poured the hot coffee-and-chicory into his mug, then filled his sergeant's cup when Mark stepped up. The young patrolman moved up with a Styrofoam cup. LaStanza put the pot down and turned away.

"Something wrong?" the patrolman asked in a shaky voice.

"No," Mark answered quickly.

LaStanza turned back and looked at the patrolman, noticing how the man's hand shook when he poured the coffee.

"He pulled the same gun on me a couple years ago," LaStanza said.

"What?" Mark said as he nearly spilled his coffee.

LaStanza took in a deep breath before adding, "That was the Man with Moon Hands."

"I'll be damned!" Mark did spill his coffee this time. Switching his cup to his other hand, he turned to the patrolman and said, "You killed a legend tonight, pal."

"What are y'all yakkin' about?" Snowood asked from his desk.

"Your victim was the Man with Moon Hands," Mark told him.

"No shit?"

LaStanza watched the patrolman's eyes. There was confusion there, along with a touch of fear.

"You never heard of the Man with Moon Hands?" Mark asked the patrolman.

"No," the man answered softly. "I've only been on the road six months."

"He was the most famous 103M in the city."

"At least we know who he is now," Snowood injected. "Sumbitch had no ID on him."

"He was a 103M?" the patrolman asked LaStanza, who did not respond. Turning back to Mark, the patrolman added, "He did look weird."

"What was his name?" Snowood asked his partner.

"I don't remember," LaStanza answered, still watching the patrolman, "but it's gotta be in the computer."

"Well I'll be," the patrolman sighed in relief. "He was crazy!"

LaStanza couldn't stop his voice from sounding vicious: "You couldn't see that?"

"What am I," the patrolman snapped back, "a psychiatrist?" He seemed stunned.

LaStanza gave him the Sicilian stare, the one that went

straight through to the back of the man's skull. Then he walked to his desk and flopped in his chair.

The exasperated patrolman continued explaining to Mark, "He looked right at me and pointed the gun and zapped me." The patrolman's voice began to rise as he followed the sergeant back into the interview room. "How'd he get the gun back anyway?"

"Goddamn courts release everything nowadays," Mark growled angrily.

LaStanza was finishing his daily report when the patrolman approached. Snowood had gone to the computer to try to identify the Man with Moon Hands.

"Excuse me, Detective LaStanza. Can I have a word with you?" The patrolman looked like a dog lost out in the rain.

LaStanza nodded to his partner's empty chair.

The patrolman's voice was almost a whisper: "I didn't know he was . . . a legend."

"He was a second-generation clone."

"What?"

"Forget it."

The patrolman's hands were shaking again. He looked like he wanted to run away. Gulping, he managed to say, "How was I supposed to know?"

LaStanza said nothing.

"He pointed a gun at me."

"You didn't see a tall man with thick glasses near the alley, did you?"

"No." The patrolman looked back anxiously.

LaStanza just nodded and returned to his daily.

After a minute, the whisper voice of the patrolman came back: "When he drew down on you, why didn't you shoot him?"

There it was again, the intangible. How do you explain what couldn't be explained? How do you explain what was incapable of even being comprehended by the mind, incapable of being distinguished by any of the senses? How do you explain something like that?

LaStanza knew he could not. You just knew.

Peering back into a pair of searching eyes, LaStanza recognized something. He recognized a look. It was a look that said, *I've got something to live with for the rest of my life.* He'd seen that same look in his own mirror.

"I passed the shoot-don't-shoot class with an A at the academy," the patrolman said in a strained voice.

"Some things can't be taught," LaStanza said finally. "Some things can't even be explained. You just know."

"You didn't shoot him and I did," the patrolman said. "Why?"

"I just knew."

It was as if he'd reached over and slapped the patrolman across the face. It took a second for the man to recover. He looked away from LaStanza's eyes and took in a couple breaths before asking, "Do you think I'll have any trouble with the grand jury?"

"Don't worry about it," LaStanza heard himself say. "It was a good shooting."

This story is for Josie.

ROSE

BY JOHN BIGUENET
Gentilly
(Originally published in 1999)

"It must have been, I think she said, two years after the kidnapping when your wife first came by." The voice on the phone sounded young. "What was that, '83, '84?"

"Kidnapping?"

"Yeah, she told me all about it, how it was for the private detective you hired after the police gave up."

"You mean the picture?"

"Right, the age progression."

"You could do it back then?"

"It was a pain in the ass. You had to write your own code. But, yeah, once we had the algorithms for stuff like teeth displacement of the lips, cartilage development in the nose and ears, stuff like that, all you had to do was add fat-to-tissue ratios by age, and you wound up with a fairly decent picture of what the face probably looked like. I mean, after you tried a couple different haircuts and cleaned up the image—the printers were a joke in those days."

"And you kept updating Kevin's . . ." He hesitated as he tried to remember the term. "Kevin's age progression?"

"Every year, like clockwork, on October 20. Of course, the new ones, it's no comparison. On-screen, we're 3-D now; the whole head can rotate. And if you've got a tape of the kid talking or singing, there's even a program to age the voice and sync it with the lips. You sort of teach it to talk, and then it can say anything you want, the head."

The voice was waiting for him to say something.

"I mean, we thought it was cool, Mr. Grierson, the way you two didn't lose hope you'd find your boy one day. Even after all these years."

He hung up while the man was still talking. On the kitchen table, the photo album Emily had used to bind the pictures, the age progressions, lay open to one that had the logo and phone number of Crescent CompuGraphics printed along its border. His son looked fifteen, maybe sixteen, in the picture.

He had found the red album the night before, after his wife's funeral. Indulging his grief after the desolate service and the miserly reception of chips and soft drinks at her sister's, he had sunk to his knees before Emily's hope chest at the foot of their bed, fingering the silk negligee bruised brown with age, inhaling the distant scent of gardenias on the bodice of an old evening gown, burying his arms in all the tenderly folded velvet and satin. It was his burrowing hand that discovered the album at the bottom of the trunk.

At first, he did not know who it was, the face growing younger and younger with each page. But soon enough, he began to suspect. And then, on the very last leaf of the red binder, he recognized the combed hair and fragile smile of the little boy who returned his gaze from a school photograph.

As he thought of Emily secretly thumbing through the age progressions, each year on Kevin's birthday adding a new portrait on top of the one from the year before, he felt the nausea rising in his throat and took a deep breath. It's just another kind of memory, he told himself, defending her.

He, for example, still could not forget the green clock on the kitchen wall that had first reminded him his son should be home from school already. Nor could he forget the pitiless clack of the

dead bolt as he had unlocked the door to see if the boy was daw-
dling down the sidewalk. And he would always remember stepping
onto the front porch and catching, just at the periphery of his vision, the first glimpse of the pulsing red light, like a flower bobbing
in and out of shadow.

In fact, turning his head in that small moment of uncertainty,
he took the light to be just that: a red rose tantalized by the afternoon's late sun but already hatched with the low shadows of the
molting elms that lined the street. And he remembered that as he
turned toward the flashing light, lifting his eyes over the roses trel-
lised along the fence—the hybrid Blue Girl that would not survive
the season, twined among the thick canes and velvet blossoms of
the Don Juan—and even as he started down the wooden steps
toward the front gate, slowly, deliberately, as if the people running
toward the house, shouting his name, had nothing to do with him,
he continued to think rose, rose, rose.

MUSSOLINI AND THE AXEMAN'S JAZZ

BY POPPY Z. BRITE

Basin Street

(Originally published in 1995)

Sarajevo, 1914

S tone turrets and crenelated columns loomed on either side of the Archduke's motorcade. The crowd parted before the open carriages, an indistinct blur of faces. Francis Ferdinand swallowed some of the unease that had been plaguing him all day: a bitter bile, a constant burn at the back of his throat.

It was his fourteenth wedding anniversary. Sophie sat beside him, a bouquet of scarlet roses at her bosom. These Serbs and Croats were a friendly crowd; as the heir apparent of Austria-Hungary, Francis Ferdinand stood to give them an equal voice in his empire. Besides, Sophie was a Slav, the daughter of a noble Czech family. Surely his marriage to a northern Slav had earned him the sympathy of these southern ones.

Yet the Archduke could not divest himself of the notion that there was a menacing edge to the throng. The occasional vivid detail—a sobbing baby, a flower tucked behind the ear of a beautiful woman—was lost before his eyes could fully register it. He glanced at Sophie. In the summer heat he could smell her sweat mingling with the *eau de parfum* she had dabbed on this morning.

She met his gaze and smiled faintly. Beneath her veil, her sweet face shone with perspiration. Back in Vienna, Sophie was snubbed by his court because she had been a lady in waiting when she met the Archduke, little better than a servant in their eyes. Francis Ferdinand's uncle, the old Emperor Francis Joseph, forbade the marriage. When the couple married anyway, Sophie was ostracized in a hundred ways. Francis Ferdinand knew it was sometimes a painful life for her, but she remained a steadfast wife, an exemplary mother.

For this reason he had brought her on the trip to Sarajevo. It was a routine army inspection for him, but for her it was a chance to be treated with the royal honors she deserved. On this anniversary of their blessed union, Sophie would endure no subtle slights, no calculated cruelties.

The Archduke had never loved another human being. His parents were hazy memories, his uncle a shambling old man whose time had come and gone. Even his three children brought him more distraction than joy. The first time he laid eyes on Sophie, he discerned in her an empathy such as he had never seen before. Her features, her mannerisms, her soft ample body—all bespoke a comfort Francis Ferdinand had never formerly craved, but suddenly could not live without.

The four cars approached the Cumuria Bridge. A pall of humidity hung over the water. The Archduke felt his skin steaming inside his heavy uniform, and his uneasiness intensified. He knew how defenseless they must look in the raised carriage, in the Serbian sun, the green feathers on his helmet drooping, Sophie's red roses beginning to wilt.

As they passed over the bridge, he saw an object arc out of the crowd and come hurtling toward him. In an instant his eye marked it as a crude hand bomb.

Francis Ferdinand raised his arm to protect Sophie and felt hot metal graze his flesh.

Gavrilo Princip's pistol left a smell on his palm like greasy coins, metallic and sour. It was a cheap thing from Belgium, as likely to blow his hand off as anything else. Still, it was all Gavrilo had, and he was the only one left to murder the villainous fool whose good intentions would crush Serbia.

He had known the other six would fail him. They were a young and earnest lot, always ready to sing the praises of a greater Serbia, but reluctant to look a man in the face and kill him. They spoke of the sanctity of human life, a short-sighted sentiment in Gavrilo's opinion. Human life was a fleeting thing, an expendable thing. The glory of a nation could endure through the ages. What his comrades failed to fully comprehend was that it must be oiled with human blood.

He raked his dirty hair back from his face and stared along the motorcade route. It looked as if the cars were finally coming. He took a deep breath. As the wet, sooty air entered his lungs, Gavrilo was seized with a racking cough that lasted a full minute. He had no handkerchief, so he cupped his hand over his mouth. When he pulled it away, his fingers were speckled with fresh blood. He and his six comrades were all tubercular, and none of them expected to live past thirty. The fevers, the lassitude, the night sweats, the constant tickling itch deep in the chest—all these made the cyanide capsules they carried in their pockets a source of comfort rather than of dread.

Now the task was left to him. Mohammed and Nedjelko, the first two along the route, were carrying hand bombs. One of them had heaved his bomb—Gavrilo had seen it go flying—but the motorcade had continued toward City Hall with no apparent damage. His comrades between Cumuria Bridge and City Hall—Vasco, Cvijetko, Danilo, Trifko—had done nothing.

The Archduke's carriage moved slowly through the crowd, then braked and came to a standstill less than five feet from Gavrilo. This struck him as nothing short of a miracle, God telling him to murder the villains for the glory of Serbia.

He fired twice. The pistol did not blow his hand off. He saw

Countess Sophie sag against her husband, saw blood on the Archduke's neck. The deed was done as well as he could do it.
Gavrilo turned the pistol on himself, but before he could fire, it
was knocked out of his hand. The crowd surged over him.

Gavrilo got his hand into his pocket, found the cyanide capsule and brought it to his mouth. Hundreds of hands were ripping
at him, pummeling him. His teeth cracked the capsule open. The
foul taste of bitter almonds flooded his mouth. He retched, swallowed, vomited, convulsed. The crowd would surely pull him to
pieces. He felt his guts unmooring, his bones coming loose from
their sockets, and still he could not die.

Sophie stood on the steps of City Hall between her husband and
Fehim Effendi Curcic, the burgomaster of Sarajevo. Though Sophie and several of her attendants were bleeding from superficial
cuts obtained from splinters of the bomb casing, and twelve spectators had been taken to hospital, Curcic obviously had no idea
that the motorcade had come close to being blown up. He was
surveying the crowd, a pleased look on his fat face. "Our hearts are
filled with happiness—" he began.

Francis Ferdinand was white with anger. He grabbed the burgomaster's arm and shouted into his face, "One comes here for a
visit and is received with bombs! Mr. Mayor, what do you say?"

Curcic still didn't understand. He smiled blandly at the Archduke and launched into his welcome speech again. The Archduke
let him continue this time, looking disgusted. Never once did Curcic
mention the bombing attempt.

Sophie gripped her husband's hand. She could see Francis Ferdinand gradually pulling himself together. He was a man of inflex-
ible opinions and sudden rages, painfully thin-skinned, capable of
holding a grudge for eternity. He was like a spoiled child, bragging
that he had shot five thousand stags, darkly hinting that he had
brought down as many political enemies. But Sophie loved him.

Not even her children fulfilled her vast need to be needed. This man did.

There was a delay while Francis Ferdinand sent a wire to the Emperor, who would have heard about the bomb. The army wanted to continue with the day's events, but the Archduke insisted upon first visiting the wounded spectators in the hospital.

He turned to Sophie. "You must not come. The risk is too great; there could be another attack."

Fear clutched at her heart: of dying, of losing him. "No, I must go with you," she told him, and Francis Ferdinand did not argue. When they entered their carriage again, Oskar Potiorek, the military governor, climbed in with them. His presence made Sophie feel a little safer.

The motorcade rolled back through the thronged streets. When they turned a corner, Sophie saw a sign marking Francis Joseph Street. Just as she noticed this, Potiorek sat up straighter and cried, "What's this? We've taken the wrong way!"

The driver braked. The motorcade ground to a halt. Sophie felt something graze the top of her head, a sharp stinging sensation. The Archduke's head snapped to one side. At the same time, Sophie felt something like a white-hot fist punch into her belly.

Through a haze of agony she reached for her husband. He leaned toward her, and a torrent of blood gushed from his mouth. She crumpled into his arms. Attendants swarmed around them, asked Francis Ferdinand if he was suffering. The last thing Sophie heard was her husband replying in a wet whisper, "It is nothing . . . it is nothing."

They were both dead before the sun had reached its apex in the blazing sky.

New Orleans, 1918

New Orleans is commonly thought of as a French and Spanish town. "Creole," a word now used to describe rich food of a certain seasoning and humans of a certain shade, first referred to the inevitable mixture of French and Spanish blood that began appearing several years after the city's founding. The buildings of the Vieux Carré were certainly shaped and adorned by the ancestry of their builders: the Spanish courtyards and ironwork, the French cottages with their carved wooden shutters and pastel paint, the wholly European edifice of St. Louis Cathedral.

But, block by sagging block, the Vieux Carré was abandoned by these upwardly mobile people. By the turn of the century it had become a slum. A wave of Sicilian immigrants moved in. Many of them opened groceries, imported and sold the necessities of life. Some were honest businessmen, some were criminals; most made no such clear distinction. The *onorata società* offered them a certain amount of protection from the hoodlums who roamed the French Quarter. Naturally they required a payment for this service, and if a man found himself in a position to do them a favor—legal or otherwise—he had no choice but to oblige.

The Italians gradually branched out of the Quarter into every part of the city, and New Orleans became as fully an Italian town as a French or Spanish one.

Joseph D'Antonio, formerly detective of the New Orleans Police Department, had been drinking on the balcony of his second-story hovel since late this afternoon. Bittersweet red wine, one bottle before the sun went down, another two since. His cells soaked it up like bread.

Two weeks in, this hot and sticky May portended a hellish summer. Even late at night, his balcony was the only place he could catch an occasional breath of air, usually tinged with the fetor of the Basin Canal nearby. Most nights, he had to force himself not to pass out here. These days, few things in his life were worse than waking up with a red-wine hangover and the morning sun in his eyes.

D'Antonio was forty-three. The circumstances of his early retirement had been as randomly cruel as the violence that presaged it. A crazed beat cop named Mullen walked into headquarters one afternoon and gunned down Chief Inspector Jimmy Reynolds. In the confusion that followed, an innocent captain also named Mullen was shot dead. Someone had come charging in and asked what happened, and someone else was heard to yell, "Mullen killed Reynolds!"

The yeller was Joe D'Antonio. Unfortunately, the dead Mullen had been widely known to harbor a strong dislike for Italians in general and D'Antonio in particular. No one accused him directly, but everyone wondered. His life became a hell of suspicious looks and nasty innuendo. Six months later, the new chief persuaded him to take early retirement.

D'Antonio leaned on the rickety railing and stared at the empty street. Until last year he had lived on the fringes of Storyville, the red-light district. In the confusion of wartime patriotism, somebody had decided Storyville was a bad influence on Navy boys, and all the whorehouses were shut down. Now the buildings were dark and shabby, broken windows covered with boards or gaping like hungry mouths, lacework balconies sagging, opulent fixtures sold away or crumbling to dust.

D'Antonio could live without the whores, though some of them had been good enough gals. But he missed the music that had drifted up from Storyville every night, often drawing him out to some smoky little dive where he could drink and jazz away the hours till dawn. Players like Jelly Roll Morton, King Oliver, and some new kid named Armstrong kept him sane throughout the bad months just after he left the force. He got to know some of the musicians, smoked reefer with them from time to time, warned them when undercover presence indicated a bust might be imminent.

Now they were gone. There were still jazz clubs in the city, but many of the players D'Antonio knew had moved to Chicago when Storyville closed down. They could record in Chicago, make money. And in Chicago they didn't have to sleep, drink, eat, and piss according to signs posted by white men.

Pissing sounded like a fine idea. He stood, steadied himself on the railing, and walked inside. The place had none of this modern indoor plumbing, and the odor of the slop jar filled the two airless rooms. Still, he'd never stooped so low as to piss off the balcony as some of his neighbors did, at least not that he could remember.

D'Antonio unbuttoned his fly and aimed into the jar. Behind him, the shutters on the French doors slammed shut with a report loud as a double-barreled shotgun in the airless night. His hand jerked. Urine sprayed the dingy wall.

When he'd finished pissing and cursing the freak wind, he wiped the wall with a dirty sock, then went back to the balcony doors. It was too hot in here with the shutters closed, and too dark. D'Antonio pushed them open again.

There was a man standing on the balcony, and the shutters passed right through him.

Francis Ferdinand scowled in annoyance. The first flesh-and-blood creature he'd met since his inglorious exit from this plane, and of course the fellow had to be stinking drunk.

Perhaps his drunkenness would make Francis Ferdinand's job easier. Who could know? When one had to put himself together from whatever stray wisps of ectoplasm he could snatch out of the ether, it became increasingly difficult to fathom the minds of living men and women.

Joseph D'Antonio had a shock of black hair streaked with silver and a pale complexion that had gone florid from the wine. His dark eyes were comically wide, seeming to start from their sockets. "Hell, man, you're a *ghost*! You're a goddamned *ghost*, ain'tcha?"

English had never been one of his better languages, but Francis Ferdinand was able to understand D'Antonio perfectly. Even the drunken slur and the slight accent did not hinder him. He winced at the term. "A *wraith*, sir, if you please."

D'Antonio waved a dismissive hand. The resulting current of air nearly wafted the Archduke off the balcony. "Wraith, ghost, whatever. S'all the same to me. Means I'll be goin' headfirst offa that balcony if I don't get to bed soon. By accident . . . or on purpose? I dunno . . ."

Francis Ferdinand realized he would have to speak his piece at once, before the man slipped into maudlin incoherence. "Mr. D'Antonio, I do not come to you entirely by choice. You might say I have been dispatched. I died in the service of my country. I saw my beloved wife die, and pass into the Beyond. Yet I remain trapped in a sort of half-life. To follow her, I must do one more thing, and I must request your help."

Francis Ferdinand paused, but D'Antonio remained silent. His eyes were alert, his aspect somewhat more sober than before.

"I must kill a man," the Archduke said at last.

D'Antonio's face twitched. Then he burst into sudden laughter. "That's a good one! You gotta kill somebody, but you can't, 'cause you're a goddamn ghost!"

"Please, sir, I am a *wraith*! There are *class structures* involved here!"

"Sure. Whatever. Well, sorry, Duke. I handed over my gun when I left the force. Can't help you."

"You addressed me as *Duke* just now, Mr. D'Antonio."

"Yeah, so? You're the Archduke, ain'tcha? The one who got shot at the beginning of the war?"

Francis Ferdinand was stunned. He had expected to have to explain everything to the man: his own useless assassination; the ensuing bedlam into which Europe had tumbled, country after country; the dubious relevance of these events to others in New Orleans. He was glad to discover that, at least in one respect, he had underestimated D'Antonio.

"Yeah, I know who you are. I might look like an ignorant wop, but I read the papers. Besides, there's a big old bullet hole in your neck."

Startled, the Archduke quickly patched the wound.

"Then, sir, that is one less thing I must explain to you. You have undoubtedly heard that I was murdered by Serbs. This is the first lie. I was murdered by Sicilians."

"But the men they caught—"

"Were Serbs, yes. They were also dupes. The plot was set in motion by your countrymen; specifically, by a man called Cagliostro. Perhaps you've heard of him."

"Some kind of magician?"

"A mage, yes. Also a doctor, a swindler, a forger, and a murderer. He is more than a century old, yet retains the appearance of a man of thirty. A wicked, dangerous man.

"He was born Giuseppe Balsamo in Palermo, 1743. By the time he began his scourge of Europe, he had dubbed himself Cagliostro, an old family name. He traveled the continent selling charms, potions, elixirs of youth. Some of these may have been genuine, as he himself ceased to age at this time.

"He also became a Freemason. Are you familiar with them as well?"

"Not particularly."

"They are a group of powerful mages hell-bent on controlling the world. They erect heathen temples in which they worship themselves and their accomplishments. Cagliostro formed his own 'Egyptian Order' and claimed to be thousands of years old already, reminiscing about his dalliances with Christ and various Pharaohs. It was power he sought, of course, though he claimed to work only for the 'Brotherhood of Man.'

"At the peak of his European success, he became entangled in the famous scandal of Marie Antoinette's diamond necklace. It nearly brought him down. He was locked in the Bastille, then forced to leave Paris in disgrace. He wandered back through the European cities that had once welcomed him, finding scant comfort. It has been rumored that he died in a dungeon in Rome, imprisoned for practices offensive to the Christian church.

"This is not so. His Masonic 'brothers' failed him for a time, but ultimately they removed him from the dungeon, whisked him out from under the noses of the French revolutionary armies who wished to make him a hero, and smuggled him off to Egypt.

"The practices he perfected there are unspeakable.

"Fifty years later, still appearing a young and vital man, he returned to Italy. He spent the next half-century assembling a new 'Egyptian Order' of the most brilliant men he could find. With a select few, he shared his elixirs.

"Just after the turn of the century, he met a young journalist named Benito Mussolini, who called himself an 'apostle of violence' but had no direction. Cagliostro has guided Mussolini's career since then. In 1915, Mussolini's newspaper helped urge Italy into war."

D'Antonio started violently. "Aw, come on! You're not gonna tell me these Egyptian-Dago-Freemasons started the war."

"Sir, that is exactly what I am going to tell you. They also ordered my wife's death, and my own, and that of my empire."

"Why in hell would they do that?"

"I cannot tell you. They are evil men. My uncle, the Emperor Francis Joseph, discovered all this inadvertently. He was a cowardly old fool who would have been afraid to tell anyone. Nevertheless, they hounded him into virtual retirement, where he died."

"And told you all this?"

"He had no one else to talk to. Nor did I."

"Where's your wife?"

"Sophie was not required to linger here. We were."

"Why?"

"I cannot tell you."

"You keep saying that. Does it mean you don't know, or you aren't *allowed* to tell me?"

Francis Ferdinand paused. After a moment, D'Antonio nodded. "I see how it is. So I'm supposed to dance for you like Mussolini does for Cagliostro?"

The Archduke did not understand the question. He waited to see if D'Antonio would rephrase it, but the man remained silent. Finally Francis Ferdinand said, "Cagliostro still controls Mussolini, and means to shape him into the most vicious ruler Europe has ever known. But Cagliostro is no longer in Italy. He is here in New Orleans."

"Oh-ho. And you want me to kill him for you, is that it?"

"Yes, but I haven't finished. Cagliostro is in New Orleans—*but we don't know who he is.*"

"*We?* Who's *we?*"

"Myself, my uncle."

"No one else?"

"No one else you would care to know about, sir."

D'Antonio sagged in his chair. "Yeah, well, forget it. I'm not killin' anybody. Find some other poor dupe."

"Are you certain, Mr. D'Antonio?"

"Very certain."

"Very well." Francis Ferdinand drifted backward through the balcony railing and vanished in midair.

"Wait!" D'Antonio was halfway out of his chair by the time he realized the wraith was gone. He sank back, his brain seasick in his skull from all the talk of mages and murders, elixirs and dungeons, and the famous scandal of Marie Antoinette's diamond necklace—whatever the hell that was.

"Why me?" he murmured into the hot night. But the night made no reply.

Cagliostro stood behind his counter and waited on the last cus-

236 // New Orleans Noir: The Classics

tomer of the day, an old lady buying half a pound of salt cod. When she had gone, he locked the door and had his supper: a small loaf of bread, a thick wedge of provolone, a few olives chopped with garlic. He no longer ate the flesh of creatures, though he sold it to maintain the appearance of a proper Italian grocery.

Above his head hung glossy loops of sausage and salami, rafters of wind-dried ham and pancetta, luminous globes of caciocavallo cheese. In the glass case were pots of creamy ricotta, stuffed artichokes, orbs of mozzarella in milk, bowls of shining olives and capers preserved in brine. On the neat wooden shelves were jars of candied fruit, almonds, pine nuts, aniseed, and a rainbow of assorted sweets. There were tall wheels of parmesan coated in funereal black wax, cruets of olive oil and vinegar, pickled cucumbers and mushrooms, flat tins containing anchovies, calamari, octopus. Enormous burlap sacks of red beans, fava beans, chickpeas, rice, couscous, and coffee threatened to spill their bounty onto the spotless tile floor. Pastas of every shape, size, and color were arranged in an elaborate display of bins facing the counter.

The aroma of the place was a balm to Cagliostro's ancient soul. He carried the world's weight on his back every day; he had pledged his very life to the furthering of the Brotherhood of Man; still, that did not mean he could shirk small duties. He fed the families of his neighborhood. When they could not pay, he fed them on credit, and when there was no hope of recovering the credit, he fed them for free.

He had caused death, to be sure. He had caused the deaths of the Archduke and his wife for several reasons, most importantly the malignant forces that hung over Europe like black clouds heavy with rain. Such a rain could mean the death of millions, hundreds of millions. The longer it was allowed to stagnate, the more virulent it would grow. It had needed some spark to release it, some event whose full significance was hidden at first, then gradually revealed. The assassination in Sarajevo had been that event, easy enough to arrange by providing the dim-witted Serbian anarchists with encouragement and weapons.

His name was synonymous with elaborate deception, and not undeservedly so. But some of his talents were genuine. In his cards and scrying-bowl Cagliostro could read the future, and the future looked very dark.

He, of course, would change all that.

This war was nearly over. It had drained some of the poison from those low-hanging clouds, allowed Europe to shatter and purge itself. But it had not purged enough; there would be another great war inside of two decades. In that one, his boy Benito would send thousands of innocent men to their useless deaths. But that was not as bad as what could be.

Though he had never killed a man with his own hands, Cagliostro bitterly felt the loss of the human beings who died as a result of his machinations. They were his brothers and sisters; he mourned each one as he would a lovely temple he had never seen, upon hearing it had been demolished. He could not accept that their sacrifice was a natural thing, but he had come to understand that it was necessary.

Mussolini was more than a puppet; he was a powerful orator and propagandist who would learn to yank his followers in any direction that pleased him. But he was unbalanced, ultimately no better than a fool, ignorant of the Mysteries, incapable of seeing them when a few of the topmost veils were pulled aside. He would make an excellent pawn, and he would die believing he had engineered his own destiny.

The only reason he could be allowed into power was to prevent something far worse.

Cagliostro had seen another European tyrant in his cards and his bowl, a man who made Mussolini look like a painted tin soldier. Mussolini was motivated exclusively by power, and that was bad enough; but this other creature was a bottomless well of hatred.

Given the chance, he would saturate all creation with his vitriol. Millions would die like vermin, and their corpses would choke the world. The scrying-water had shown terrifying factories built especially for disposal of the dead, ovens hot enough to reduce bone to ash, black smokestacks belching greasy smoke into a charred orange sky. Cagliostro did not yet know this tyrant's precise identity, but he believed that the man would come from Austria and rule Germany. Another good reason for the Archduke's death: Francis Ferdinand would have made a powerful ally for such a man.

Cagliostro did not think he could altogether stop this tyrant. He had not foreseen it in time; he had been occupied with other matters. It was always thus when a man wished to save the world: he never knew where to look first, let alone where to begin.

Still, he believed he could stop the tyrant short of global domination, and he believed Mussolini was his key. Members of the Order in Italy were grooming him for Prime Minister. The title would unlock every door in Europe. If they could arrange for Mussolini to become the tyrant's ally, perhaps they could also ensure that Mussolini would in some way cause the tyrant's downfall.

Cagliostro finished his simple supper, collected the day's receipts, and turned off the lights. In the half-darkness he felt his way back to the small living quarters behind the store, where he sat up reading obscure volumes and writing long letters in a florid hand until nearly dawn. Over the past century, he had learned to thrive on very little sleep.

D'Antonio was sitting up in bed, back propped against the wooden headboard, bare legs sprawled atop the sweat-rumpled coverlet, bottle nestled between his thighs. The Archduke appeared near the sink. D'Antonio jumped, slopped wine onto the coverlet, cursed. "You gotta make me stain something every time you show up?"

"You need have no fear of me."

"No, you just want me to murder somebody for you. Why should that scare me?"

"It should not, sir. What should scare you is the prospect of a world ruled by Cagliostro and his Order."

"That guy again. Find him yet?"

"We know he came to New Orleans before 1910. We know he is living as an Italian grocer. But he has covered his tracks so successfully that we cannot determine his precise identity. We have a number of candidates."

"That's good." D'Antonio nodded, pretended to look thoughtful. "So you just gonna kill all of 'em, or what?"

"I cannot kill anyone, sir. I cannot even lift a handkerchief. That is why I require your help."

"I thought I told you last time, Duke. My services are unavailable. Now kindly fuck off."

"I feared you would say that. You will not change your mind?"

"Not a chance."

"Very well."

D'Antonio expected the wraith to vanish as it had last time. Instead, Francis Ferdinand seemed to break apart before his eyes. The face dissolved into a blur, the fingers elongated into smoke-swirls; then there was only a man-shaped shimmer of gossamer strands where the Archduke had been.

When D'Antonio breathed in, they all came rushing toward him.

He felt clammy filaments sliding up his nose, into his mouth, into the lubricated crevices of his eye sockets. They filled his lungs, his stomach; he felt exploratory tendrils venturing into his intestines. A profound nausea gripped him. It was like being devoured alive by grave-worms. The wraith's consciousness was saturating his own, blotting him out like ink spilled on a letter.

"*I offered you the chance to act of your own free will,*" Francis Ferdinand said. The voice was a hideous papery whisper inside his skull now. *"Since you declined, I am given no choice but to help you along."*

Joseph Maggio awoke to the sound of his wife choking on her own blood. Great hot spurts of it bathed his face. A tall figure stood by the bed, instrument of death in his upraised hand. Maggio recognized it as the axe from his own backyard woodpile, gleaming with fresh gore. It fell again with a sound like a cleaver going into a beef neckbone, and his wife was silent.

Maggio struggled to sit up as the killer circled to his side of the bed. He did not recognize the man. For a moment their eyes locked, and Maggio thought, *That man is already dead.*

"Cagliostro?" It was a raspy whisper, possibly German-accented, though the man looked Italian.

Wildly, Maggio shook his head. "No, no sir, my name's Joseph Maggio, I just run a little grocery and I never heard of no Cagli-whoever . . . oh Jesus-Mary-and-Joseph, please don't hit me with that thing—"

The blade glittered in a deadly arc. Maggio sprawled halfway off the bed, blinded by a sudden wash of his own blood. The axe fell again and he heard his own skull crunching, felt blade squeak against bone as the killer wrenched it out. Another searing cut, then another, until a merciful blow severed his jugular and he died in a red haze.

It was found that the killer had gained access to the Maggios' home by chiseling out a panel in the back door. The chisel had belonged to Joseph Maggio, as had the axe, which was found in a pool of blood on the steps. People all over New Orleans searched their yards for axes and chisels, and locked away these potential implements of Hell.

A strange phrase was found chalked on the pavement a block from the Maggios' house: *Mrs. Maggio is going to sit up tonight, just like Mrs. Tony.* Its significance has not been discovered to this day.

Maggio's two brothers were arrested on the grounds that the Maggios were Sicilians, and Sicilians were prone to die in family vendettas. They were released by virtue of public drunkenness—they had been out celebrating the younger one's draft notice on the night of the murders, and had staggered home scarcely able to move, let alone lift an axe.

The detective in charge of the case was shot to death by a burglar one week after the murders. The investigation languished. News of the Romanov family's murder by Bolsheviks in Russia eclipsed the Maggio tragedy. The temperature climbed as June wore on.

"I detect Cagliostro's influences still at work on this plane," the Archduke said. *"We must move on to the next candidate."*

Deep inside his own ectoplasm-snared brain, which the wraith kept docile with wine except when he needed to use the body, D'Antonio could only manage a feeble moan of protest.

A clear tropical dawn broke over New Orleans as John Zanca parked his wagon of fresh breads and cakes in front of Luigi Donatello's grocery. He could not tell whether the grocer and his wife were awake yet, so he decided to take their order around to the back door. He gathered up a fragrant armful of baked goods still warm from the oven and carried them down the narrow alley that led to the Donatellos' living quarters.

When he saw the back door with its lower left panel neatly chiseled out, his arms went limp. Cakes and loaves rained on the grass at his feet.

After a moment, Zanca stepped forward—careful not to crush any of the baked goods—and knocked softly on the door. He did not want to do so, but there seemed nothing else to do. When it swung open, he nearly screamed.

Before him stood Luigi Donatello, his face crusted with blood, his hair and mustache matted with it. Zanca could see three big gashes in his skull, white edges of bone, wet gray tissue swelling through the cracks. How could the man still be standing?

"My God," moaned Donatello. "My God."

Behind him, Zanca saw Mrs. Donatello sprawled on the floor. The top of her head was a gory porridge. The slender stem of her neck was nearly cleaved in two.

"My God. My God. My God."

John Zanca closed his eyes and said a silent prayer for the Donatellos' souls and his own.

The newspapers competed with one another for the wildest theory regarding the Axeman, as the killer came to be known. He was a Mafia executioner, and the victims were fugitives from outlaw justice in Sicily. He was a vigilante patriot, and the victims were German spies masquerading as Italian grocers. He was an evil spirit. He was a voodoo priest. He was a woman. He was a policeman.

The Italian families of New Orleans, particularly those in the grocery business, barricaded their doors and fed their dogs raw meat to make them bloodthirsty. These precautions did not stop them from lying awake in the small hours, clutching a rosary or perhaps a revolver, listening for the scrape of the Axeman's chisel.

In high summer, when the city stank of oyster shells and ancient sewers, the killer returned. Two teenage sisters, Mary and Pauline Romano, saw their uncle butchered in his own bed. They could only describe the man as "dark, tall, wearing a dark suit and a black slouch hat."

Italian families with enemies began finding axes and chisels dropped in their yards, more like cruel taunts than actual threats. Some accused their enemies. Some accused other members of their families. Some said the families had brought it upon themselves. Tempers flared in the sodden August heat, and many killings were done with weapons other than axes. Men with shotguns sat guard over their sleeping families, nodding off, jerking awake at the slightest noise. A grocer shot his own dog; another nearly shot his own wife.

The city simmered in its own prejudice and terror, a piquant gumbo.

But the Axeman would not strike again that year.

D'Antonio came awake with a sensation like rising through cool water into sunlight. He tried to move his hands: they moved. He tried to open his eyes: the ceiling appeared, cracked and water-stained. Was it possible? Was the fucking monster really *gone*?

"Duke?" he whispered aloud into the empty room. His lips were dry, wine-parched. "Hey, Duke? You in there?"

To his own ears he sounded plaintive, as if he missed the parasitic murdering creature. But the silence in his head confirmed it. The wraith was gone.

He stared at his hands, remembering everything he had seen them do. How ordinary they looked, how incapable of swinging a sharp blade and destroying a man's brain, a woman's brain. For a long time he sat on the edge of the bed studying the beds of his nails and the creases in his palms, vaguely surprised that they were not caked with blood.

Eventually he looked down at himself and found that he was wearing only a filthy pair of trousers. He stripped them off, sponged himself to a semblance of cleanliness with the stale water in the basin, slicked his hair back, and dressed in fresh clothes. He left his apartment without locking the door and set off in a random direction.

D'Antonio wandered hatless in the August sun for an hour or more. When he arrived at the *States* newspaper office, his face was streaming with sweat, red as a boiled crawfish. He introduced himself to the editor as a retired police detective, an expert on both

Italians and murderers, and gave the following statement:

"The Axeman is a modern Doctor Jekyll and Mr. Hyde. A criminal of this type may be a respectable, law-abiding citizen when he is his normal self. Compelled by an impulse to kill, he must obey this urge. Like Jack the Ripper, this sadist may go on with his periodic outbreaks until his death. For months, even for years, he may be normal, then go on another rampage. It is a mistake to blame the Mafia. The Mafia never attacks women as this murderer has done."

He left the *States* office with several people staring bemusedly after him, but they printed the interview in its entirety.

After that, he lived his life much as he had before the wraith's first visit. Armistice Day brought throngs of joyous revelers into the streets, as well as a blessed wave of cool weather; it had stayed sweltering through October. The war was over, and surely the wraith would never come back and make him do those things again.

He could not forget the organic vibration that ran up his arms as blade buried itself in bone.

In fact, he dreamed about it almost every night.

Francis Ferdinand returned in the spring of 1919.

He did not muck about with appearances this time, but simply materialized inside D'Antonio's head. D'Antonio collapsed, clawing at his temples.

"*He deceived me for a time, but now I know he still walks this earth,*" said the wraith. "*We will find him.*"

D'Antonio lay curled on his side, blinded by tears of agony, wishing for the comforts of the womb or the grave.

Giacomo Lastanza was a powerful man, but he had been no match for the fiend in his bedroom. Now he lay on the floor with his head split as cleanly as a melon, and his wife Rosalia cowered in a corner of the room clutching her two-year-old daughter, Mary. Mary was screaming, clutching at her mother's long black hair. As the Axeman turned away from her husband's body, Rosalia began to scream too.

"Not my baby! Please, Holy Mother of God, not my baby!"

The axe fell. Mary's little face seemed to crack open like an egg. Rosalia was unconscious before her skull felt the blade's first kiss.

D'Antonio lay naked on the floor. The apartment was a wasteland of dirty clothes and empty wine bottles. But his body was relatively sober for once—they'd run out of money—and as a result he was sharp enough to be carrying on an argument with the wraith.

"Why in hell do we have to kill the women? You can't be worried one of *them* is Cagliostro."

"He has consorted with a number of dangerous women. When we find him, his wife will bear killing also."

"And until then, you don't mind killing a few innocent ones?"

"It is necessary."

"What about that little baby?"

"If it had been Cagliostro's daughter, he would have raised her to be as wicked as himself."

D'Antonio got control of one fist and weakly pounded the floor with it. "You goddamn monster—you're just gonna keep wasting people, and sooner or later I'll get caught and rot in prison. Or fry in the chair. And you'll go on your merry way and find some other poor sap to chase down that shadow of yours."

"The next one must be him! He is the last one on the list!"

"Fuck the list."

A bolt of excruciating pain shot through D'Antonio's head, and he decided to drop the argument.

* * *

Cagliostro was reading by candlelight when he heard the chisel scraping at his door. He smiled and turned a page.

The creature crept into his room, saw him in his chair with his head bent over a book. When it was ten feet away, Cagliostro looked up. When it was five feet away, it froze in midmotion, restrained by the protective circle he had drawn.

By looking into its eyes, he knew everything about Joseph D'Antonio and the Archduke Francis Ferdinand. But the creature upon which he gazed now was neither D'Antonio nor the Archduke; this was a twisted amalgamation of the two, and it could only be called the Axeman.

He smiled at the creature, though its eyes blazed with murderous rage. "Yes, poor Archduke, it is I. And you will not harm me. In fact, I fear I must harm you yet again. If only you had accepted the necessity of your death the first time, you would be Beyond with your beloved Sophie now.

"No, don't think you can desert your stolen body as it lies dying. You'll stay in there, my boy. My magic circle will see to that!" Cagliostro beamed; he was enjoying this immensely. "Yes, yes, I know about unfortunate ex-Detective D'Antonio trapped in there. But why do you think it was so easy for the Duke to take hold of your body, Mr. D'Antonio, and make it do the terrible things it did? Perhaps because you care not at all for your fellow human beings? *When they came for the Jews, I did nothing, for I was not a Jew* . . . ah, forgive me. An obscure reference to a future that may never be. And you will both die to help prevent it."

He reached beneath the cushion of his armchair, removed a silver revolver with elaborate engraving on the butt and barrel, aimed it carefully, and put a ball in the Axeman's tortured brain.

Then he put his book aside, went to his desk, and took up his pen.

The letter was published in the *Times-Picayune* the next day.

Hell, March 13, 1919

Editor of the Times-Picayune
New Orleans, La.

Esteemed Mortal:

They have never caught me and they never will. They have never seen me, for I am invisible, even as the ether that surrounds your earth. I am not a human being, but a spirit and a fell demon from the hottest hell. I am what you Orleanians and your foolish police call the Axeman.

When I see fit, I shall come again and claim other victims. I alone know whom they shall be. I shall leave no clue except my bloody axe, besmeared with the blood and brains of he who I have sent below to keep me company.

If you wish, you may tell the police to be careful not to rile me. Of course, I am a reasonable spirit. I take no offense at the way they have conducted their investigations in the past. In fact, they have been so utterly stupid as to amuse not only me, but His Satanic Majesty, Francis Joseph, etc. But tell them to beware. Let them not try to discover what I am, for it were better that they were never born than to incur the wrath of the Axeman. I don't think there is any need for such a warning, for I feel sure the police will always dodge me, as they have in the past. They are wise and know how to keep away from all harm.

Undoubtedly, you Orleanians think of me as a most horrible murderer, which I am, but I could be much worse if I wanted to. If I wished, I could pay a visit to your city every night. At will I could slay thousands of your best citizens, for I am in close relationship with the Angel of Death.

Now, to be exact, at 12:15 (earthly time) on next Tuesday

night, I am going to pass over New Orleans. In my infinite mercy, I am going to make a little proposition to you people. Here it is:

I am very fond of jazz music, and I swear by all the devils in the nether region that every person shall be spared in whose home a jazz band is in full swing at the time I have just mentioned. If everyone has a jazz band going, well, then, so much the better for you people. One thing is certain and that is that some of those people who do not jazz it on Tuesday night (if there be any) will get the axe.

Well, I am cold and crave the warmth of my native Tartarus, and as it is about time that I leave your earthly home, I will cease my discourse. Hoping that thou wilt publish this, that it may go well with thee, I have been, am, and will be the worst spirit that ever existed either in fact or realm of fancy.

—THE AXEMAN

Tuesday was St. Joseph's Night, always a time of great excitement among Italians in New Orleans. This year it reached a fever pitch. The traditional altars made of a hundred or more kinds of food were built, admired, dismantled, and distributed to the poor; lucky fava beans were handed out by the fistful; the saint was petitioned and praised. Still, St. Joseph's Night of 1919 would remain indelibly fixed in New Orleans memory as the Axeman's Jazz Night.

Cafés and mansions on St. Charles blazed with the melodies of live jazz bands. Those who could not afford to pay musicians fed pennies into player pianos. A popular composer had written a song called "The Mysterious Axeman's Jazz, or, Don't Scare Me, Papa." Banjo, guitar, and mandolin players gathered on the levees to send jazz music into the sky, so the Axeman would be sure to hear it as he passed over. By midnight, New Orleans was a cacophony of sounds, all of them swinging.

Cagliostro walked the streets for most of the night, marveling (if not actively congratulating himself) at how completely he had brought the city together, and how gay he had made it in the process. No one so much as glanced at him: few people were on the streets, and Cagliostro had a talent for making himself invisible.

He had left the Axeman's corpse locked in the back of the house where it wouldn't spoil the groceries. First, of course, he had bludgeoned the face into unrecognizable mush with the Axeman's own axe. Everything that suggested the murdered man might be someone other than "Mike Pepitone," simple Italian grocer, was in the satchel Cagliostro carried with him.

On the turntable of his phonograph, as a final touch, he had left a recording of "Nearer My God to Thee."

When the jazz finally began to die down, he walked to the docks and signed onto a freighter headed for Egypt. There were any number of wonderful things he hadn't gotten around to learning last time.

Italy, 1945

Toward the end, Mussolini lived in an elaborate fantasy world constructed by the loyal sycophants who still surrounded him. Whole cities in Italy were sanitized for his inspection, the cheering crowds along his parade routes supplemented by paid extras. When Hitler visited Rome, he too was deceived by the coat of sparkle on the decay, the handpicked Aryan soldiers, the sheer bravado of *Il Duce*.

He believed he had cost Hitler the war. Germany lost its crucial Russian campaign after stopping to rescue the incompetent Italian army in Albania. Hitler had believed in the power and glory of Italy, and Mussolini had failed him.

Now he had been forced into exile on Lake Garda. He was a failure, his brilliant regime was a failure, and there were no more flunkies to hide these painful truths. He kept voluminous diaries in which he fantasized that his position in history would be comparable to Napoleon or Christ. His mistress Claretta lived nearby in a little villa, his only comfort.

On April 25, Germany caved in to the Allies. The Italian people, the ones he had counted on to save him with their loyalty, turned against him. Mussolini and Claretta fled, making for Switzerland.

A few last fanatical companions attempted to help them escape by subterfuge, but they were arrested by partisans on the north shore of Lake Como, discovered hiding in a German truck, cringing inside German coats and helmets. They were shot against the iron gate of an exquisite villa, and their bodies were taken to Milan and strung up by the heels to demonstrate the evils of Fascism.

All in service of the brotherhood of man.

GDMFSOB

BY NEVADA BARR

Versailles Boulevard

(Originally published in 2006)

All Walgreen's had was a little kid's notebook, maybe four by five inches, the binding a fat spiral of purple plastic, the cover a Twiggy–Carnaby Street–white boots–flower power mess of lavender and yellow blooms.

Jeannie put it on the café table, opened it, and carefully wrote, *Goddamnmotherfuckingsonofabitch,* in her best schoolgirl cursive. The juxtaposition of sentiment and sentimentality pleased her.

Next she wrote, *Divorce Rich,* then sat back, looked at the words, and took a long luxurious sip of the cheap but not inexpensive Pinot Grigio a harried waitress in too-tight jeans had brought her.

Rich thought she drank too much. Of course she drank too much. She was married to a goddamnmotherfuckingsonofabitch. She drew a neat line through the word *divorce.*

Divorce was out of the question. Rich would never grant her a divorce. Not if it meant giving up the "income stream from the family business," as he euphemistically referred to her earnings as a sculptress.

No. Divorce wasn't happening.

That left suicide and murder.

When Rich had been particularly demeaning, Jeannie'd had the occasional fling with Dr. Kevorkian, but, in all honesty, she had to admit that she was a decent individual. She paid her taxes—and his—kept a tidy house, and got her oil changed every three thousand miles. And Rich . . .

Rich was boring.

Not casually boring; he was a bore of nuclear magnitude. More than once she had witnessed him turn entire dinner parties to stone, seen guests' eyes roll back in their heads and their tongues begin to protrude as he replaced all the available oxygen with pomposity. Not being a jobholder himself, he felt uniquely qualified to lecture on the subject. He told her cleaning lady how to clean, her gallery owner how to present art, the man who cast her work how to run a foundry, her agent how to sell sculpture.

Suicide was out. It would be wrong, un-American even, to deny the world her lovely bronzes while simultaneously condemning it to Rich's monologues.

That left murder.

In the ordinary run of things, Jeannie didn't condone murder. She wasn't even a proponent of capital punishment. But her husband wasn't in the ordinary run of things. He was extraordinarily in need of being dead.

Kill Rich, she printed carefully beneath the crossed-out *divorce*.

Another long swallow of wine and contemplation.

Over the eight years of their marriage she had shared all the nasty bits with shrinks, groups, AA, and half a dozen girlfriends. There was so much dirty laundry lining the byways of her past they rivaled the back alleys of Mexico City on wash day. Should anything untoward befall Rich, she would be the prime suspect.

There must be no evidence. None.

She scribbled out everything she'd written, then tore out the page. Feeling a fool, but being a nonsmoker and thus having no recourse to fire, she surreptitiously soaked the page in the wine and swallowed it.

As easily as that, she decided to kill her husband.

Setting her glass on the uneven surface of the wrought-iron

café table, she watched the wine tremble as minuscule earthquakes sent out barely perceptible tsunamis and she thought of the things people die of.

Drowning, burning, choking, crushing, goring by bulls, hanging, falling, dismemberment, being devoured by wild beasts, poisoning, exploding, crashing in cars, boats, planes, and motorcycles, disease, cutting, stabbing, slashing, blunt trauma to the head, dehydration, hypothermia, heatstroke, starvation, vitamin A poisoning from eating polar bears' livers, snakebite, drawing and quartering, asphyxiation, shooting, beheading, bleeding out, infection, boredom—Lord knew Rich had nearly done her in with that one.

Rumor had it people died of shame and broken hearts. No hope those would work on Rich, though over the years she had given it a go, usually at the top of her lungs with tears and snot pouring attractively down her face. A dedicated philandering deadbeat pornographer, Rich had embraced shame as an alternative lifestyle and his heart was apparently made of India rubber.

Goddamnmotherfuckingsonofabitch, she wrote on the fresh, yet-to-be-eaten page of her notebook, knocked back the last of her wine, and left the waitress a five-dollar tip.

Two hours later she was again staring at the page. The compulsion to write what she'd done was overwhelming. Vaguely she remembered there was actually a word for the phenomenon, *hyperscribblia* or something. "Don't, don't, don't," she said as she uncapped a razor-point Pilot and put the tip against the smooth paper.

Mildly fascinated and massively alarmed, she watched as the pen flickered down the page, line by line, leaving a trail the dumbest of cops couldn't fail to follow.

Went to the garage. Shoulder-deep in junk. No room for car. Found motorcycle. Put on gardening gloves. Drove roofing tack three-quarters of an inch into front tire just below fender. On the pen flew, painting the pictures so clear in Jeannie's mind: Rich's praying mantis form, clad in the endless leathers that arrived almost daily from eBay— chaps, fringed and plain, leather vests, gloves, leather pants, boots, leather jackets, leather shirts, helmets, do-rags, even a leather face guard that made Jeannie want to reread *The Man in the Iron Mask*—or rent *Silence of the Lambs*. Done up like a macho caricature of a macho caricature, the imaginary Rich pushes the bike out with his long spider's legs. Backward rolls the heavy machine, the tack slides unnoticed up beneath the fender.

Words flow across the tiny cramped pages, spinning a tale of how the tack, pounded in at an angle just so, remains static until the curve heading out onto the freeway, where the wheel turns and the bike leans and the head of the tack finally hits the pavement, driven deeper. *Bang!* The tire has blown! Out of control, the motorcycle is down. Rich is sliding. My God! My God! His helmet pops off and bounces across two lanes of freeway traffic. The motorcycle is spinning now; Rich's protective leathers begin to tear, leaving black marks on the pale concrete, hot and lumpy like a black crayon dragging across sandpaper. Leather is rasped away; flesh meets the road. Crayon marks turn from black to red. The driver of an eighteen-wheeler, high on methamphetamines, barrels down the highway, unaware of the man and motorcycle spinning toward his speeding rig. Look out! Look—

"Lover Girl? Have you been in the garage?" Rich's murmuring voice, always pitched a decibel or so lower than the threshold of human hearing, thus forcing the unfortunate listener to say "What?" several times just to make audible something not worth hearing anyway, wisps down the short hall between the garage and the kitchen, where Jeannie sits at the counter.

"The garage? No. Why?" she calls as his rubber-soled slip-ons shuff-shuffle down the hall.

The pages. She shoves them into the Osterizer and pushes *Puree*. Jammed. A pint of milk. Bingo. Pasta. "Thankyoubabyjesus."

Rich's bald head on its Ichabod Crane neck pokes around the corner. "My things. In the garage. Did you touch them?" Rich hates her to move his things.

"No, sweetheart."

"Dinner?" he asks, eyeing the Osterizer.

Jeannie nods, too scared to talk.

Rich settles on a stool, his pale bulbous eyes fixed on her. Under the blue stare Jeannie pours the mixture into a casserole dish with pasta and sauce from a bottle and sets the oven to three-fifty.

Rich likes it. "Happy tummy," he murmurs as he eats, eyes glued to *Fear Factor* contestants on the television gagging down pig bowels in cockroach sauce.

GDMFSOB, Jeannie chants in her mind as she surreptitiously makes herself a ham-and-cheese sandwich and takes it to bed.

Rich stays up till three, as he often does. Jeannie has learned to sleep. She knows if she tiptoes down the hall like a curious child on Christmas Eve night and peeks in the piled mess he calls his office, Good Old Rich will be hunkered in front of his computer screen, bald head nestled between hunched shoulders like an ostrich egg in a lumpy nest, watching the X-rated cavortings of what he insists is not pornography but Adult Content Material.

Sleep is good.

Plotting is better.

The next day, armed with information from the library's computer—so there will be no history on her own—Jeannie cultures botulism. It is surprisingly easy and naturally deadly. Perfect. Bad salmon. The GDMFSOB loves salmon. She doesn't. Perfect. Until she gets hold of the pen and out it comes: Rich reeling out of the marital bed, dragging himself to the bathroom, Jeannie pretending to sleep as his calls grow ever weaker. She dialing 911, but alas! Too late! Weeping prettily as she tells the kind, attractive, young policeman how she took an Ambien and can't remember anything until, gulp, sigh, she woke to find this. Mea culpa, mea culpa, but not really . . .

Damning, damning, damning, the words rattle over page after page.

Shuff-shuffle. The bald pate, the watery blue eyes. "Sketching a new sculpture?" Rich is oh-so-supportive of her work. He needs the money for his lifestyle.

"Sketching," Jeannie manages as she snatches up the pages.

Rich turns on the television. It's Thursday. *Survivor* is on Thursdays. Rich never misses *Survivor*.

"What's for dinner?"

"Salmon." Perfect but for the incriminating compulsion.

The Osterizer: olive oil, pesto, onion.

"Dinner is served."

"Lover Girl, the salmon smells funny. Did you get fresh?"

"Fresh."

"The pesto is great. Happy tummy."

Over subsequent days Jeannie drips acid on brake lines and writes, melts off the tips of his épées and writes. Osterizes and seasons and serves.

And Rich lives. Thrives. Like the cat who came back the very next day. Jeannie cannot get her hands on an atom bomb.

Damn.

Nothing.

Damn.

Rich is hunkered on the sofa eating lasagna of hamburger, cheese, and the pages detailing how she greased the feet of the extension ladder before asking him to take a look at the chimney, when Jeannie realizes that, as a murderess, she's a bust. Rich is protected by angels. Or demons. Or stupidity.

Suicide returns as an option. She can't love. She can't leave. She can't live.

Damn.

Guns are too messy. Hanging too painful. Pills. Being with Rich for eight years has driven her to a veritable cornucopia: Ambien, Effexor, Desyrel, Xanax—all good traceable drugs. Surely if she takes them all at once . . .

The nagging of *Big Brother* on the forty-two-inch TV whines into the bedroom, where Jeannie, tuna sandwich untouched, sits in bed, sixty-two pills in pink, white, and yellow cupped in her palm, bottled water on the nightstand. Usually she sleeps nude, but tonight she has put on a nice pair of pajamas: discreet, modest. Lord knew how she might sprawl and froth. Better to be on the safe side.

Suicide.

So be it.

Rich had won.

Jeannie tips all sixty-two pills into her mouth and reaches for the water.

"Lover Girl?" Rich stands in the bedroom door. He looks peaked, as Jeannie's mother might say.

"What?" she mumbles around the deadly sleep in her mouth.

"Unhappy tummy," he moans.

He runs for the bathroom. Jeannie spits out the pills.

"Haven't taken a dump in days," he calls genteelly through the open bathroom door. Rich never closes the bathroom door. In fact, he makes deposits while she showers, brushes her teeth, suffocating, stifling deposits.

"Oh," she calls with mechanical sympathy.

Two days later Rich is dead. Jeannie dials 911.

"Impacted bowel," the coroner tells her. "Was your husband eating anything unusual?"

"Murder," Jeannie might have said, but she didn't.

JESUS OUT TO SEA

BY JAMES LEE BURKE

Ninth Ward

(Originally published in 2006)

I grew up in the Big Sleazy, uptown, off Magazine, amongst live oak trees and gangsters and musicians and bougainvillea the Christian Brothers said was put there to remind us of Christ's blood in the Garden of Gethsemane.

My best friends were Tony and Miles Cardo. Their mother made her living shampooing the hair of corpses in a funeral parlor on Tchoupitoulas. I was with them the afternoon they found a box of human arms someone at the Tulane medical school left by the campus incinerator. Tony stuffed the arms in a big bag of crushed ice, and the next day, at five o'clock, when all the employees from the cigar factory were loading onto the St. Claude streetcar, him and Miles hung the arms from hand straps and the backs of seats all over the car. People started screaming their heads off and clawing their way out the doors. A big fat black guy climbed out the window and crashed on top of a sno-ball cart. Tony and Miles, those guys were a riot.

Tony was known as the Johnny Wadd of the Mafia because he had a flopper on him that looked like a fifteen-inch chunk of radiator hose. All three of us joined the Crotch and went to Vietnam, but Tony was the one who couldn't deal with some stuff he saw in a ville not far from Chu Lai. Tony had the Purple Heart and two Bronze Stars but volunteered to work in the mortuary so he wouldn't have to see things like that anymore.

Miles and me came home and played music, including gigs at Sharkey Bonano's Dream Room on Bourbon Street. Tony brought Vietnam back to New Orleans and carried it with him wherever he went. I wished Tony hadn't gotten messed up in the war and I wished he hadn't become a criminal, either. He was a good guy and had a good heart. So did Miles. That's why we were pals. Somehow, if we stayed together, we knew we'd never die.

Remember rumbles? When I was a kid, the gangs were Irish or Italian. Projects like the Iberville were all white, but the kids in them were the toughest I ever knew. They used to steal skulls out of the crypts in the St. Louis cemeteries and skate down North Villere Street with the skulls mounted on broomsticks. In the tenth grade a bunch of them took my saxophone away from me on the streetcar. Tony went into the project by himself, made a couple of guys wet their pants, then walked into this kid's apartment while the family was eating supper and came back out with my sax. Nobody said squat.

Back in the 1950s and '60s, criminals had a funny status in New Orleans. There were understandings between the NOPD and the Italian crime family that ran all the vice. Any hooker who cooperated with a Murphy sting on a john in the Quarter got a bus ticket back to Snake's Navel, Texas. Her pimp went off a rooftop. A guy who jack-rolled tourists or old people got his wheels broken with batons and was thrown out of a moving car by the parish line. Nobody was sure what happened to child molesters. They never got found.

But the city was a good place. You ever stroll across Jackson Square in the early morning, when the sky was pink and you could smell the salt on the wind and the coffee and pastry from the Café du Monde? Miles and me used to sit in with Louis Prima and Sam Butera. That's no jive, man. We'd blow until sunrise, then eat a bagful of hot beignets and sip café au lait on a steel bench under the palms while the sidewalk artists were setting up their easels and paints in the square. The mist and sunlight in the trees looked like cotton candy. That was before the city went down the drain and before Miles and me went down the drain with it.

Crack cocaine hit the projects in the early eighties. Black kids all over the downtown area reminded me of the characters in *Night of the Living Dead*. They loved 9mm automatics too. The Gipper whacked federal aid to the city by half, and the murder rate in New Orleans became the highest in the United States. We got to see a lot of David Duke. He had his face remodeled with plastic surgery and didn't wear a bedsheet or a Nazi armband anymore, so the white-flight crowd treated him like Jefferson Davis and almost elected him governor.

New Orleans became a free-fire zone. Miles and me drifted around the Gulf Coast and smoked a lot of weed and pretended we were still jazz musicians. I'm not being honest here. It wasn't just weed. We moved right on up to the full-tilt boogie and joined the spoon-and-eyedropper club. Tony threw us both in a Catholic hospital and told this three-hundred-pound Mother Superior to beat the shit out of us with her rosary beads, one of these fifteen-decade jobs, if we tried to check out before we were clean.

But all these things happened before the storm hit New Orleans. After the storm passed, nothing Miles and Tony and me had done together seemed very important.

The color of the water is chocolate-brown, with a greenish-blue shine on the surface like gasoline, except it's not gasoline. All the stuff from the broken sewage mains has settled on the bottom. When people try to walk in it, dark clouds swell up around their chests and arms. I've never smelled anything like it.

The sun is a yellow flame on the brown water. It must be more than ninety-five degrees now. At dawn, I saw a black woman on the next street, one that's lower than mine, standing on top of a car roof. She was huge, with rolls of fat on her like a stack of inner tubes. She was wearing a purple dress that had floated up over her waist and she was waving at the sky for help. Miles rowed a boat from the bar he owns on the corner, and the two of us went over to where the car roof was maybe six feet underwater by the time we got there. The black lady was gone. I keep telling myself a United States Coast Guard chopper lifted her off. Those Coast Guard guys are brave. Except I haven't heard any choppers in the last hour.

Miles and me tie the boat to a vent on my roof and sit down on the roof's spine and wait. Miles takes out a picture of him and Tony and me together, at the old amusement park on Lake Pontchartrain. We're all wearing jeans and T-shirts and duck-ass haircuts, smiling, giving the camera the thumbs-up. You can't believe how handsome both Tony and Miles were, with patent-leather-black hair and Italian faces like Rudolph Valentino. Nobody would have ever believed Miles would put junk in his arm or Tony would come back from Vietnam with helicopter blades still thropping inside his head.

Miles brought four one-gallon jugs of tap water with him in his boat, which puts us in a lot better shape than most of our neighbors. This is the Ninth Ward of Orleans Parish. Only two streets away I can see the tops of palm trees sticking out of the water. I can also see houses that are completely covered. Last night I heard people beating the roofs from inside the attics in those houses. I have a feeling the sounds of those people will never leave my sleep, that the inside of my head is going to be like the inside of Tony's.

The church up the street is made out of pink stucco and has bougainvillea growing up one wall. The water is up to the little bell tower now, and the big cross in the breezeway with the hand-carved wooden Jesus on it is deep underwater. The priest tried to get everybody to leave the neighborhood, but a lot of people didn't have cars, or at least cars they could trust, and because it was still two days till payday, most people didn't have any money, either. So the priest said he was staying too. An hour later the wind came off the Gulf and began to peel the face off South Louisiana.

This morning, I saw the priest float past the top of a live oak tree. He was on his stomach, his clothes puffed with air, his arms stretched out by his sides, like he was looking for something down in the tree.

The levees are busted and a gas main has caught fire under the water and the flames have set fire to the roof of a two-story house on the next block. Miles is pretty disgusted with the whole business. "When this is over, I'm moving to Arizona," he says.

"No, you won't," I say.

"Watch me."

"This is the Big Sleazy. It's Guatemala. We don't belong anywhere else."

He doesn't try to argue with that one. When we were kids we played with guys who had worked for King Oliver and Kid Orey and Bunk Johnson, Miles on the drums, me on tenor sax. Flip Phillips and Jo Jones probably didn't consider us challenges to their careers, but we were respected just the same. A guy who could turn his sticks into a white blur at The Famous Door is going to move to a desert and play "Sing, Sing, Sing" for the Gila monsters? That Miles breaks me up.

His hair is still black, combed back in strings on his scalp, the skin on his arms white as a baby's, puckered more than it should be, but the veins are still blue and not collapsed or scarred from the needlework we did on ourselves. Miles is a tough guy, but I know what he's thinking. Tony and him and me started out together, then Tony got into the life, and I mean into the life, man—drugs, whores, union racketeering, loan-sharking, maybe even popping a couple of guys. But no matter how many crimes he may have committed, Tony held on to the one good thing in his life, a little boy who was born crippled. Tony loved that little boy.

"Thinking about Tony?" I say.

"Got a card from him last week. The postmark was Mexico

City. He didn't sign it, but I know it's from him," Miles says.

He lifts his strap undershirt off his chest and wipes a drop of sweat from the tip of his nose. His shoulders look dry and hard, the skin stretched tight on the bone; they're just starting to powder with sunburn. He takes a drink of water from one of our milk jugs, rationing himself, swallowing each sip slowly.

"I thought you said Tony was in Argentina."

"So he moves around. He's got a lot of legitimate businesses now. He's got to keep an eye on them and move around a lot."

"Yeah, Tony was always hands-on," I say, avoiding his eyes.

You know what death smells like? Fish blood that someone has buried in a garden of night-blooming flowers. Or a field mortuary during the monsoon season in a tropical country right after the power generators have failed. Or the buckets that the sugar-worker whores used to pour into the rain ditches behind their cribs on Sunday morning. If that odor comes to you on the wind or in your sleep, you tend to take special notice of your next sunrise.

I start looking at the boat and the water that goes to the horizon in all directions. My butt hurts from sitting on the spine of the house and the shingles burn the palms of my hands. Somewhere up in Orleans Parish I know there's higher ground, an elevated highway sticking up on pilings, high-rise apartment buildings with roofs choppers can land on. Miles already knows what I'm thinking. "Wait till dark," he says.

"Why?"

"There won't be as many people who want the boat," he says.

I look at him and feel ashamed of both of us.

A hurricane is supposed to have a beginning and an end. It tears the earth up, fills the air with flying trees and bricks and animals and sometimes even people, makes you roll up into a ball under a table and pray till drops of blood pop on your brow, then it goes away and lets you clean up after it, like somebody pulled a big prank on the whole town. But this one didn't work that way. It's killing in stages.

I see a diapered black baby in a tree that's only a green smudge under the water's surface. I can smell my neighbors in their attic. The odor is like a rat that has drowned in a bucket of water inside a superheated garage. A white guy floating by on an inner tube has a battery-powered radio propped on his stomach and tells us snipers have shot a policeman in the head and killed two Fish and Wildlife officers. Gangbangers have turned over a boat trying to rescue patients from Charity Hospital. The Superdome and the Convention Center are layered with feces and are without water or food for thousands of people who are seriously pissed off. A bunch of them tried to walk into Jefferson Parish and were turned back by cops who fired shotguns over their heads. The white-flight crowd doesn't need any extra problems.

The guy in the inner tube says a deer was on the second floor of a house on the next street and an alligator ate it.

That's supposed to be entertaining?

"You guys got anything to eat up there?" the guy in the inner tube asks.

"Yeah, a whole fucking buffet. I had it catered from Galatoire's right before the storm," Miles says to him.

That Miles.

Toward evening the sun goes behind the clouds and the sky turns purple and is full of birds. The Coast Guard choppers are coming in low over the water, the downdraft streaking a trough across the surface, the rescue guys swinging from cables like anyone could do what they do. They're taking children and old and sick people out first and flying without rest. I love those guys. But Miles and me both know how it's going to go. We've seen it before—the slick coming out of a molten sun, right across the canopy, automatic weapons fire whanging off the airframe, wounded grunts waiting in an LZ that North Vietnamese regulars are about to overrun. You can't get everybody home, Chuck. That's just the way it slides down the pipe sometimes.

A guy sitting on his chimney with Walkman ears on says the president of the United States flew over and looked down from his plane at us. Then he went on to Washington. I don't think the story is true, though. If the president was really in that plane, he would have landed and tried to find out what kind of shape we were in. He would have gone to the Superdome and the Convention Center and talked to the people there and told them the country was behind them.

The wind suddenly blows from the south, and I can smell salt and rain and the smell fish make when they're spawning. I think maybe I'm dreaming.

"Tony is coming," Miles says out of nowhere.

I look at his face, swollen with sunburn, the salt caked on his shoulders. I wonder if Miles hasn't pulled loose from his own tether.

"Tony knows where we are," he says. "He's got money and power and connections. We're the Mean Machine from Magazine. That's what he always said. The Mean Machine stomps ass and takes names."

For a moment I almost believe it. Then I feel all the bruises and fatigue, and the screaming sounds of the wind blowing my neighborhood apart drain out of me like black water sucking down through the bottom of a giant sink. My head sinks on my chest and I fall asleep, even though I know I'm surrendering my vigilance at the worst possible time.

I see Tony standing in the door of a Jolly Green, the wind flattening his clothes against his muscular physique. I see the Jolly Green coming over the houses, loading everyone on board, dropping bright yellow inflatable life rafts to people, showering water bottles and C-rats down to people who had given up hope.

But I'm dreaming. I wake up with a start. The sun is gone from the sky, the water still rising, the surface carpeted with trash. The painter to our boat hangs from the air vent, cut by a knife. Our boat is gone, our water jugs along with it.

The night is long and hot, the stars veiled with smoke from fires vandals have set in the Garden District. My house is settling, window glass snapping from the frames as the floor buckles and the nails in the joists make sounds like somebody tightening piano wire on a wood peg.

It's almost dawn now. Miles is sitting on the ridge of the roof, his knees splayed on the shingles, like a human clothespin, staring at a speck on the southern horizon. The wind shifts, and I smell an odor like night-blooming flowers in a garden that has been fertilized with fish blood.

"Hey, Miles?" I say.

"Yeah?" he says impatiently, not wanting to be distracted from the speck on the horizon.

"We played with Louis Prima. He said you were as good as Krupa. We blew out the doors at the Dream Room with Johnny Scat. We jammed with Sharkey and Jack Teagarden. How many people can say that?"

"It's a Jolly Green. Look at it," he says.

I don't want to listen to him. I don't want to be drawn into his delusions. I don't want to be scared. But I am. "Where?" I ask.

"Right there, in that band of light between the sea and sky. Look at the shape. It's a Jolly Green. It's Tony, man, I told you."

The aircraft in the south draws nearer, like the evening star winking and then disappearing and then winking again. But it's not a Jolly Green. It's a passenger plane and it goes straight overhead, the windows lighted, the jet engines splitting the air with a dirty roar.

Miles's face, his eyes rolled upward as he watches the plane disappear, makes me think of John the Baptist's head on a plate.

"He's gonna come with an airboat. Mark my word," he says.

"The DEA killed him, Miles," I say.

"No, man, I told you. I got a postcard. It was Tony. Don't buy government lies."

"They blew him out of the water off Veracruz."

"No way, man. Not Tony. He got out of the life and had to stay off the radar. He's coming back."

I lie on my back, the nape of my neck cupped restfully on the roof cap, small waves rolling up my loins and chest like a warm blanket. I no longer think about the chemicals and oil and fe-ces and body parts that the water may contain. I remind myself that we came out of primeval soup and that nothing in the earth's composition should be strange or objectionable to us. I look at the smoke drifting across the sky and feel the house jolt under me. Then it jolts again and I know that maybe Miles is right about see-ing Tony, but not in the way he thought.

When I look hard enough into the smoke and the stars behind it, I see New Orleans the way it was when we were kids. I see the fog blowing off the Mississippi levee and pooling in the streets, the Victorian houses sticking out of the mist like ships on the Gulf. I see the green-painted streetcars clanging up and down the neutral ground on St. Charles and the tunnel of live oaks you ride through all the way down to the Carrollton District by the levee. The pink and purple neon tubing on the Katz & Besthoff drugstores glows like colored smoke inside the fog, and music is everywhere, like it's trapped under a big glass dome—the brass funeral bands marching down Magazine, old black guys blowing out the bricks in Preservation Hall, dance orchestras playing on hotel roofs along Canal Street.

That's the way it was back then. You woke in the morning to the smell of gardenias, the electric smell of the streetcars, chicory coffee, and stone that has turned green with lichen. The light was always filtered through trees, so it was never harsh, and flowers bloomed year-round. New Orleans was a poem, man, a song in your heart that never died.

I only got one regret. Nobody ever bothered to explain why nobody came for us. When Miles and me are way out to sea, I want to ask him that. Then a funny thing happens. Floating right along next to us is the big wood carving of Jesus on his cross, from the stucco church at the end of my street. He's on his back, his arms stretched out, the waves sliding across his skin. The holes in his hands look just like the petals from the bougainvillea on the church wall. I ask him what happened back there.

He looks at me a long time, like maybe I'm a real slow learner.

"Yeah, I dig your meaning. That's exactly what I thought," I say, not wanting to show how dumb I am.

But considering the company I'm in—Jesus and Miles and Tony waiting for us somewhere up the pike—I got no grief with the world.

LAST FAIR DEAL GONE DOWN

BY ACE ATKINS
Warehouse District
(Originally published in 2010)

I 've always been one to keep an eye open during a church prayer—not because of my lack of faith in God but because of my lack of faith in people. What I learned by watching was that others were doing the same. People mistrust people. Each of us pulses with our own agenda. In New Orleans, and particularly in the French Quarter, those agendas cross frequently.

That night I was in my own house of worship—JoJo's Blues Bar—with both eyes closed tight as I chased a shot of Jack with a cold Dixie. Fats's band banged out the last few chords of "Blue Monday," his lazy sax matching my own black mood. Each drink softened that black mood into brown melancholy.

A December drizzle rained outside. Cold droplets fell a muted pink along the window lit by JoJo's neon sign, only a few regulars in the bar with ragged fedoras pulled low. JoJo's niece Keesha, the only waitress on duty, tapped her foot slowly to Fats's music. While she smoked, she read the Bible by dim candlelight.

"Keesha, how 'bout another Dixie?"

"You know where they're at."

And I guess I did. JoJo was my best friend and this was my second home. I took off my trench coat and old scarf and walked behind the bar. Pushing up my shirtsleeve, I reached into the slushy ice bin and grabbed a beer. My hand instantly went numb.

"Who's closing up?" I asked.

"Felix," she answered, stuck somewhere in the middle of Corinthians. "JoJo and Loretta went to Baton Rouge."

The set finished and the sparse crowd clapped. Most of them were old men like JoJo who had frequented this place since the early sixties. JoJo's was the only decent blues bar in a city dominated by jazz. *A Little Delta on the Bayou*, is what the sign outside read.

Fats pulled up a stool next to me. His face grayed under the tiny Christmas lights strung over the bar's mirror. I looked across at both of our reflections and tilted my head. He said my name dully back to me.

"How ya been, Fats?"

"*Hmm.*"

"You know why JoJo's in Baton Rouge?" I asked, for lack of anything better.

"Naw." Fats shifted in his seat and coughed, politely turning his head away. He looked over at Keesha with her head close to the Bible.

"What? You got religion now or somethin'?"

"Seek and ye shall find," Keesha said, blowing smoke in his face.

"*Hmm,*" Fats said. "Ain't that some shit?"

Someone opened the two rickety Creole doors and a cold breeze rushed in off Conti. A horse-drawn tourist carriage clopped by with a guide pointing out famous sites. Fats popped a handful of salted peanuts into his mouth, shell and all.

"You hungry, Fats?"

He looked at my face for the first time, right in the eyes. "Yeah, I could eat."

Fats was known for gambling or drinking away his weekly profits every Friday. He usually lived on Loretta's leftover gumbo or handouts from JoJo.

We walked over a few blocks to the Café Du Monde. I asked for a couple orders of beignets and two large café au laits. A Vietnamese waiter set down the square donuts covered in powered sugar, and within a minute Fats ate them all.

"Hungry?"

His coffee sat empty before him. I ordered another round for him.

Fats didn't say a word. He leaned an arm on the iron railing and looked across the street at St. Louis Cathedral. Or maybe he was looking at the bronze statue of Andrew Jackson. I've always liked to think it was the church, with the spotlight beams illuminating the simple high cross.

"Is it the track?"

"Naw." He laughed.

"You need help?"

"No," Fats said. "What I got, pod'na, is a fair deal. Just like Robert Johnson said, *Last fair deal goin' down.* You know about Johnson?"

"Sure."

"He sure played a weird guitar. I've always tried to make my sax do that. But it just ain't the same."

"What's the deal, Fats?"

He laughed again and shook his head. He looked up. "You ever been in love, Nick?"

"Every Saturday night."

"No, man. I mean really in love. Where it make you sick jus' to think you ain't gonna get no more."

"I guess." I looked at him as he brushed a hand over his gray suit to get off the fallen powdered sugar.

"Let's just say I found somethin', all right, big chief."

"That's where the money went?"

"Thanks for the eats, Nick."

And with that, Fats reached down, grabbed the handle of his battered sax case, patted it like a child, and was gone. I sipped on another café au lait, warming my hands on the steaming mug.

Two days later, JoJo called to tell me that Fats was dead.

The sleet played against the industrial windows of my loft, a 1920s lumber storage in the Warehouse District, on the blackest early afternoon I could remember. Tulane was on Christmas break and instead of teaching blues history, I found extra time to loaf. I was practicing some of Little Walter's harp licks on my Hohner Special 20 when JoJo buzzed me from Julia Street.

"I've already joined the Moonies," I said, pressing the button on my intercom. "Fuck off."

"Goddammit, open the door."

I went to the kitchen portion of the second floor's open space, lit the stove with a kitchen match, and began to make coffee. I left the sliding metal door ajar and JoJo walked in, tramping his feet and muttering obscenities under his breath.

"You don't even know my mother," I said.

"I need you to go with me to clear out Fats's shit. That's if you want him to have a proper funeral. Man died without a cent. And no family that anyone knows about. Loretta said we should do it."

"She's right."

It was a bullet through a clouded mind that killed him. A self-inflicted wound. Or so read the coroner's report that my friend, Detective Jay Medeaux, shared with me. He told me a pink-haired runaway found Fats's body on the Riverwalk, his back broken from a final fall onto the jagged rocks lining the Mississippi River.

All I could imagine was the grayness of those rocks and the grayness of his face among the damp paper bags and broken multicolored bottles as we climbed the stairs to his apartment. It was on Decatur, not far from the French Market—a sign outside asked for fifty bucks a week.

The apartment manager met us on the stoop, thumbing through the sports section of the *Times-Picayune*. Wordless, with an impassive face, he led us to a second-floor efficiency. Hazy white light sprouted through rust-flecked metal blinds onto a rat's nest of dirty clothes, an empty bottle of Captain Morgan's spiced rum, a rumpled black suit on a bent hanger, a book called *The Real Israelites*, a juke joint poster, a toothbrush with a box of baking soda, and a pack of sax reeds on an unmade bed.

No sax.

"Mmhmm," JoJo said.

"It's not here."

"*Mmhmm.*"

"Hey, buddy," I said to the manager, "where's his saxophone?"

"What's here is here. I ain't responsible."

"Where's his goddamned sax?"

I felt JoJo's strong hand on my shoulder. "Man doesn't know."

The manager bit his lower lip, turned on a heel, and left us. We spent five minutes packing everything in the room into a cardboard box made for Colt 45 malt liquor. I took the rumpled black suit from the hanger, folded it, and handed it to JoJo. He nodded.

I heaved the box up into the crook of my elbows and walked down a urine-scented staircase. My ears rang, full of Fats's sax, those deep full notes that bled the man's life and loss. He never cheated, putting all he was into every note. And now someone had taken the one thing he cared about even more than his own life.

That afternoon I started searching all around the Quarter. I looked into any painted window using the words MUSIC, PAWN, or ANTIQUE. I learned his sax was a classic made in the forties, a collector's item that could pay for a dozen caskets and burial plots.

I found nothing.

The cool day turned into colder night as the setting sun turned burnt orange over the Mississippi. Driving down St. Charles Avenue, mottled shadows played over my face. Leaves turned end over end from the knurled water oaks dripping with Spanish moss.

I parked off Prytania, where Fats's drummer lived in a rotting carriage house among mansions.

He was stoned when he opened the door. Red-eyed, sunken-shouldered, giggly stoned. Tom Cat usually wore his hair in a greasy ponytail, but tonight it hung wild in his face. Clutching a bag of Cheetos in his skinny white arms, he wiped orange dust from the corner of his mouth and invited me in.

"Hey, dude."

I pulled a crumpled pair of jeans and a foul-smelling T-shirt off a chair and sat down. The place reeked of marijuana. He'd be lucky if the paint didn't start to peel.

"Want a smoke?"

"No thanks," I said, smiling and pulling a pack of Marlboros from my jean-jacket pocket.

"Jesus, Nick, I'm a mess." He started to giggle. "Why'd he do it, man? Didn't he realize it wasn't just him, man, that . . ." He laughed uncontrollably.

I smoked my cigarette and looked outside. Two kids played touch football in the street.

"I'm sorry," he said. His laughing died like a cold engine. "I just can't handle the shit now. Ya know?"

"Yeah."

"Your band need a drummer?"

"Did Fats have a girlfriend?"

"I really don't want to talk about this. It makes me feel like I'm gonna throw up."

"I need to know."

"You ain't a cop, man. Don't be a hard-on."

"Did he have a girlfriend?"

He dropped his head between his knees, black hair cascading into his face. In a few seconds he raised back up, looked at the ceiling, red-faced from the inversion, and said, "See, Fats didn't have a girlfriend. Fats . . . Fats had a whore."

Her name was Sarah. Petite hands, delicate face, soft brown skin. She was probably in her late twenties, going on fifty. Her lips quivered when she blew cigarette smoke over her head, and she liked to drink. Crushed ice, Jim Beam, and cherries. The closer I sat to her at the hotel bar, the more I smelled the cherries. The more I smelled her perfume. *I see, Fats. I see.*

On her third drink, she looked over at me and grinned widely into the left corner of her mouth. Her lips were full and thick. Her small body tight and exposed in black hot pants and black shirt tied above her stomach.

"You sure are big. You a Saint?" she said.

"No, I'm a dancer. Jazz, modern, and some tap. I used to break-dance, but I never could spin on my head."

She laughed. And even from the six feet that separated us, I could tell she had been crying. Dry streaks through her makeup. I moved closer.

She kept wiping her nose and eyes. She turned her gaze back to a book placed in front of her drink.

"How is it?" I asked.

She cocked her head at me and a thin strap fell from her shoulder.

"The book."

"Oh," she said, and closed it and showed me the cover. *Lady Sings the Blues.* "A friend gave it to me."

As I was about to pursue the thought, two guffawing men walked into the deserted bar. Laughing, smirking. Drunk, with slow-moving eyes and aggressive swaggers. One nodded at the bartender. He nodded back.

"Ready?" the bartender asked her.

"Oh. Yes."

I put my hand over hers; it was cold and shaking. "You don't have to do this."

She smiled at me with her eyes. "It's gonna be just fine. Just gonna be fine."

I kept my hand over hers.

One of the businessmen approached me. Maybe I was generalizing, but he sure fit the description. Brooks Brothers suit and a wedding ring. His hair was silver, and his expensive cologne clashed with his hundred-buck-meal onion breath. Big fun on the bayou in the Big Easy.

"We already paid," he said. "You'll have to do it yourself, son." He made a yanking motion with one hand.

The younger businessman snorted. The bartender was wise enough to shut up.

I looked for a long time at the older man. He probably had everyone in his company scared of him. Everyone called him *sir* and catered to his every egotistical whim. He'd never sweated, never done a damn thing but hang out at the fraternity house and kiss ass until he made partner. I stared.

He looked down at my tattered and faded jean jacket and sneered. "What do you want?"

I slowly reached down the side of my leg and pulled out my boot knife. I grabbed him by his tie—red with paisley patterns— cut it off at the knot, and shoved it in his mouth. The younger man moved in as the CEO took a swing at me. I caught his fist in my hand and squeezed. If I had anything, it was strong hands from shirking tackles when I played football.

I brought the guy to his knees.

"Sir, when your grandkids are sitting on your lap this Christmas and everything is all warm and fuzzy, I want you to remember this. I want you to think about it as you light the tree, cut the turkey, and pat the kids on the head. Tell the boys when they come to New Orleans to treat the ladies real nice."

I released my grip. He wouldn't think about what I said. He was not me, and I was not him. I remembered something a psychologist friend had told me years ago: *Don't expect anything from a pig but a grunt.*

She agreed to walk with me to the Quarter only after I gave her fifty bucks. It was fifty I didn't have, but it was the only way. Together we crossed Canal, dodging cars, soon smelling that cooked-onion-and-exhaust scent that floats around the old district.

I took her to a small bar off Decatur to talk, really it was just a place to sit and drink, only four feet from a sliding window. I got two beers in paper cups, and we sat down. No one around us except an elderly black waiter in a tattered brown sweater. Sarah finished half her beer in one gulp.

I asked her if she was afraid.

"No. Not of you."

"What then?"

She finished her beer and pulled a cigarette from a pack extracted from a cheap vinyl purse. I lit it.

"Tell me about you and Fats. You know he's dead?"

"I know."

She sat there for a moment just looking at me.

"Was he a regular?"

She dropped her head, kneading the palm of her hand into her forehead. The cigarette held high in her fingers.

"Did you work for him at his apartment or did he get a hotel?"

She scratched the inside corner of her mouth and took another drag of the cigarette.

"You were with him the night he died, weren't you?"

"Yes."

I exhaled a long breath and gambled with what I said next. "That man didn't have anything. Why'd you set him up? You could've rolled anybody, like those two in the hotel. You'd come up with a lot more money than what Fats had. He was a sweet old guy. He had more talent than someone like you could ever comprehend. Just tell me who helped you."

"Stop it. Just stop it. You don't know anything."

"Why?"

"You got it all messed 'round. You don't know how it was."

"How was it, Sarah? You tell me."

"I loved him."

I laughed.

"He tole me he'd marry me. Imagine that. Him marrying me. Even sold his saxophone to—" She was sobbing now.

I waited. When she stopped, she told me about how they first met. Thursday nights she would wait for him outside JoJo's, listening to his sweet music. The day he told her that he loved her, it was raining. "Real black clouds over the Mississippi," she said.

"So why'd he sell his sax?"

"To buy me."

It was two in the morning when I got back to the Warehouse District, lonely, cold, and tired. I didn't want to be alone. A light was on across Julia Street in the warehouse of a neighbor, one of the many artists who lived in the district. A ballet instructor. Beautiful girl. Good person.

I parked my Jeep, grabbed a six-pack of Abita out of the fridge, then found myself buzzing her from the street-level intercom. I could hear Shostakovich's Symphony no. 5 filtering out a cracked second-story window and reverberating off the concrete and bricks down the street. Her blurred image floating past the dim windows.

As I stood there, I suddenly felt silly because she could have company. I guess I arrogantly thought she would always just be there when I needed her. Just waiting, no need for a life of her own. But I guess she thought of me like one of the neighborhood cats that she consistently fed whenever they decided to wander by for a meal.

Sam slid back a rusted viewing slot, then opened the door smiling. Short blond hair and blue eyes. She wore cutoff gray sweatpants and a man's ribbed white tank top tied at her waist. She'd been dancing a long time—enough to build a sweat.

"I don't remember ordering a pizza," she said.

"I do. Should be here in fifteen minutes—chicken, artichoke hearts, and white cheese."

She shook her head and laughed. She slid two heavy bolts behind us, and I followed her up the stairs. I put my hand on her back. It was very warm.

The next day I played the waiting game in a little tourist café on Royal. I waited and I watched Sarah's apartment. I ate two bowls of bland gumbo and a soggy muffuletta, drank draft Abita until I got loopy, and then switched to "Authentic French Market Coffee." Tasted like Maxwell House.

I saw her walk outside to a scrolled balcony in a loose-fitting robe and lean over, sipping coffee. That was noon.

At three, she came back to the balcony. She sat down in a director's chair, propped her feet on the iron railing, and read. *The Billie Holiday book?*

At 3:43, she went back inside and did not come back out for two hours. The bright sunshine barely warming a cold day retreated, and the shadows finally returned, falling over my face.

Around six, she came out of the street entrance walking toward Esplanade. I tucked the copy of *Nine Stories* back in my jacket pocket, where I always kept it, placed a few bills under the weight of a salt shaker, and began to follow.

I had a ragged Tulane cap pulled low over my eyes and wore sunglasses—some Lew Archer I was. I pulled the collar of my trench coat tighter around my face. Not just for disguise, but also to block the cold. December wind shooting down those old alleys and boulevards can make a man want to keep inside.

She went into the A&P on Royal, and I stayed outside. In a few minutes she returned, unwrapping a pack of cigarettes and continuing toward the far end of Royal. She walked into a place with the doors propped wide open, leaned over the bar, and French-kissed the bartender. He struck an effeminate, embarrassed pose and laughed. She patted him on the face and kept walking.

At the end of the street, she went inside a bed and breakfast. Semirenovated. New awning, peeling paint on the windows. I got close enough to see through the double-door windows. She was talking to someone at the front desk. Then she turned, going deeper inside the building. I waited.

It was cold. There were no restaurants or coffee houses on this side of the district. It hadn't been civilized yet. I blew hot breath through closed fits.

I waited.

I got solicited twice. Once by a man. Once by a woman. And had a strange conversation with a derelict.

"Crack," he said.

"Gave it up for the holidays. Thank you, though."

"Naw, man. Dat's my name."

"Your name is Crack?"

"Shore."

I asked "Crack" where the nearest liquor store was. He said it was on Rampart, so I gave him a few bucks and told him to buy me a fifth of Jack Daniel's and whatever he wanted. Actually, it wasn't really a gamble to give him money. Most of those guys work on a strange ethical code when it comes to a fellow drinker.

He came back, and we sat on the other side of Esplanade watching the bed and breakfast until nearly ten o'clock. The whiskey tasted like sweet gasoline.

When Sarah came back, her hair was mussed, her jaw worked

overtime on gum, and she looked tired. She certainly did not expect what came next as she bent down to restrap a sequined stiletto.

As she pulled the buckle tight around her ankle, an early-seventies black Chrysler whipped around the corner of Chartres, speeding right toward us. I had no time to push her out of the way or yell. I could only watch as she just stayed bent over with her butt in the air. Hand still touching those ridiculous shoes. Very still.

I knew the car would hit her.

But it didn't. Instead, the car skidded to a halt next to her, and a white arm grabbed her by the hair and jerked her in. She screamed as I sprinted across the street. Because of the tinted windows I couldn't see the driver, who put the car back in gear and weaved to hit me.

I bolted away and lunged toward the curb, where Crack was standing holding his bottle of apple liquor. The car's tires smoked as it headed down Royal.

I followed.

My breath came in hard, fast spurts. I knew I was sprinting a losing race, but I followed until I saw the dim glow of the car's cracked red taillights turning somewhere near Toulouse.

And she was gone.

Whoever took Sarah dumped her body underneath the Greater New Orleans Bridge on the Algiers side of the Mississippi. Naked with a cut throat.

Jay Medeaux stood over me at police headquarters on Broad Street and slurped on a cup of black coffee. I rubbed my temples. It was nine a.m. and I hadn't slept. His wide, grinning face looked more amused with my situation than sympathetic.

"No coffee?"

"No thanks."

"Cruller?"

"Jay, do you mind?"

"Touchy. Touchy."

I regurgitated every trivial detail of what I witnessed and knew. Jay listened without asking any questions. He didn't even lecture me about conducting my own investigation—which he knew I was prone to do. Jay was a good friend.

I remember him happiest when we beat LSU. His grin wide as he held our coach high on his shoulders in a warped, fading photograph I still kept on my desk.

He pulled Sarah's file from Vice and made a few phone calls. We found out she was working for a pimp with the awful moniker of Blackie Lowery. A lowlife whose previous convictions included running a strip club staffed with twelve- and thirteen-year-olds, trucking oysters from a polluted water zone, indecent exposure at Antoine's restaurant, selling illegal Jazz Fest T-shirts, and beating the shit out of his pit bull with a Louisville Slugger. Sounded like our man.

Jay let me go with him to pick the guy up.

We found Blackie outside his Old Style Voodoo Shop spray-painting a dozen little cardboard boxes black—his back turned as he spurted out a final coat. He was a skinny guy with pasty white skin, a shaved head, and a thick black mustache curled at the end like Rollie Fingers used to wear. He stopped painting and looked sideways at us.

"Hey, Blackie, why don't you spell *shop* with two Ps and an E?" Jay said. "The tourists would like it more, I bet. Make it sound real authentic, ya know?"

Blackie had his shirt off, and a tiny red tattoo was stamped over his heart.

"We found one of your employees this morning," Jay said. "Blade sliced her throat real even."

He gave a crooked smile and threw down his paint can. "I don't have a clue."

"That's beside the point," Jay said. "Come on with us."

"Eat me," Blackie said.

I walked through a side door and into the voodoo shop. The smell of incense was strong among the trinkets, stones, and powders. A small, glass-topped casket sat in the middle of the room with a carved wooden dummy inside painted to look like a decomposing corpse.

But beyond the Marie Laveau T-shirts and the hundreds of bags of gris-gris powders, something interested me.

Fats's sax sat in a corner.

Sometimes I like to hear Dixieland jazz after several drinks. Sometimes I like to hear my boots as they clunk across a hardwood floor. Sometimes I even like to cover the tall windows of my warehouse with bedsheets and watch old movies all day. But most of all, I like to sit in JoJo's and listen to Loretta Jackson sing. Her voice can rattle the exposed brick walls and break a man's heart.

It was Christmas Eve, a week after Jay picked up Blackie. I was nursing a beer and watching Loretta rehearse a few new numbers. Old blues Christmas songs that she always mixed in with her set during the season. Growling the words to "Merry Christmas, Baby" and making my neck hairs stand on end.

"You keep babyin' that beer and it's gonna fall in love with ya," JoJo said, as he washed out a couple shot glasses in the sink.

"Everybody needs a friend."

"Mmhmm." He dried the inside of the glasses with a white towel and then hung it over his shoulder. "Why you down here today, anyway?"

"Sam's been wanting to go Christmas shopping in the Quarter all week. And I promised."

"You hear any more from Medeaux 'bout that pimp?"

284 // New Orleans Noir: The Classics

"Nah. Blackie's still in jail far as I know."

"You let me know if somethin's different."

Loretta finished the song with a great sigh into her microphone and a quick turnaround from the band. The guitar player made his instrument give a wolf whistle as Loretta stepped off stage. Running a forearm over her brow, she walked over and sat next to me.

"My boy Nicholas," she said as she rubbed my back. "My boy."

"Your boy Nicholas sittin' on his ass drinking while his new woman trudgin' 'round these old French streets lookin' for gifts."

"My boy deserves it.'

"Hmphh."

"Y'all talkin' 'bout Fats, weren't cha?"

JoJo nodded and walked back into the kitchen.

"Man had a sad life, Nick. Cain't believe he sold his sax for that girl."

"Guess he loved her."

"Hell, she was just a two-bit whore."

"Loretta."

"Naw, I'm serious. She was fuckin' half the band."

"What?"

"Sure she was. Saw her almost get her cheap ass beat by Fats's drummer out back. Havin' some kind of lover's quarrel, I guess."

"When was this?"

"Few days before he died."

I took a deep breath, and my fist tightened on top of the bar.

Tom Cat was passed out on his sofa when I kicked in the door to his apartment. Little multicolored Christmas lights had fallen on his body and face, and it gave him a festive, embalmed look. I grabbed him by a dirty Converse high top and yanked him off the sofa. His eyes sprung awake.

"Who killed him?"

"Nick, man. Merry Christmas to you too. Hey, I—"

"Who killed him?"

"You trippin', man."

I yanked him to his knees and punched him hard in the stomach. He doubled over weakly.

"Why didn't you tell me you were sleeping with her?"

"I wasn't."

"The pimp didn't kill Sarah, did he? He had no reason. You did. You loved her."

"Fuck you."

I kicked him hard in the side with my boot. I didn't enjoy it. It didn't make me feel like a man. I just did it.

"It was a mistake. Fats shouldn't been a part of it."

"Part of what?"

He rolled to his side and wiped his tears with a ragged flannel shirtsleeve. Pushing his long greasy hair, he told me.

I did not interrupt.

It was blackmail. Sarah and Tom Cat had worked out a scam on a local trial lawyer. But he wasn't just any lawyer. He was Spencer Faircloth, lawyer to the New Orleans mob. An all-star backslapper among criminals.

Their plan included a sick little videotape. Maybe it included a burro. I don't know what was on it, didn't want to know, but I took it with me.

I let Tom Cat go, drove to a nearby K&B Drugstore, and looked through a waterlogged phone book. Some of the pages were so stuck together that the book felt like papier-mâché.

There was no listing. I called information and was told he had an unpublished number.

I called a 250-pound bail bondsman I know named Tiny. He asked for the pay phone's number.

He called me back in five minutes with the address.

Faircloth lived in an ivy-covered brick mansion with a spiked iron fence and stained-glass windows. When I pulled up near the address on St. Charles, dozens of finely dressed men and women were drinking in Faircloth's hospitality.

I could see them all, like fish in an aquarium, through the tall windows. I lit a cigarette, smoked it into a nub, and then decided to go in.

Most of the men I passed were in winter wool suits, accented with the occasional silly holiday tie. Candy canes, reindeer, and elves.

I was dressed in blue jeans, boots, and a jean jacket.

I wasn't accepted.

"Sir?" a large black man asked me.

"Sí."

"Can I have your invitation?"

"I'm here to see Mr. Faircloth."

"Mr. Faircloth is spending time with his guests. Can I help you?"

The man's hair was Jheri-curled, and he wore a finely trimmed mustache.

"Aren't you Billy Dee Williams?"

He made a move toward me.

"Tell him that a friend of Sarah's is here."

He looked down at me, and then left.

I walked over to the buffet line and ate three very tiny turkey sandwiches. I didn't see any tiny quiches.

A few minutes later, a young man in his twenties walked over to me. I didn't recognize him at first. His hair seemed slicker tonight. His movements were more polished.

"Can I help you?"

"Are you Spencer Faircloth?"

"No."

"Then you can't. I'll just stay here, continue to eat, and thumb my nose at the conventions of the rich."

"I'll have you removed."

"You do and I'll propose a toast to Sarah. The finest whore that Faircloth ever had killed."

"You're insane."

"Perhaps."

Then I remembered him, the younger man from the hotel where I first met Sarah. The one who'd backed up the older man. I looked for him.

I saw the gray-headed gent laughing it up with a group of his ilk near the French doors.

I jumped upon the top of the linen buffet table, my dirty buckskin boots soiling the whiteness. I grabbed a glass and spoon and clinked the two together loudly.

"I would like to propose a toast to the hostess with the most-est. *Spence Faircloth*."

The party hesitatingly clapped. A drunk elderly man hooted his approval.

"Thank you, grandpa," I announced to the old man. "But right now, I would like to offer Mr. Faircloth a deal."

They were silent.

The two men were whispering to Faircloth, who had his arms tightly wrapped around himself.

"You might call it the last fair deal gone down, like my old friend Fats used to say. The deal, Mr. Faircloth, is that you join me on this table and announce to the party that you are a gutless turd who had a friend of mine killed."

The crowd stayed silent. A wrinkled old woman with huge breasts shook her head and breathed loudly out her nose.

"But where is the deal, you ask?" I said, reaching deep into the inner layer of my denim jacket and pulling out the videotape.

I held it high over my head like a Bourbon Street preacher does a Bible. I mimed my hands to pretend I was weighing the two.

Billy Dee Williams was trying to approach me from behind.

"What'll it be, Spence?"

Faircloth shook his head, turned on his heel like a spoiled child, and walked away.

I put the videotape back in my jacket and hopped off the table.

Just like with any other unwanted guest, no one tried to stop me as I left. I think they were waiting for me to pull a red bandanna up over my nose and ask for their jewels.

I got in my Jeep and headed back to the Warehouse District, my hands shaking on the wheel.

I returned to my warehouse only long enough to grab a fresh set of clothes, binoculars, a six-pack of Abita, a frozen quart of Loretta's jambalaya, my Browning, and Sam's Christmas present—a 1930s Art Deco watch that I bought on Royal Street a few weeks ago.

It was so silent in my darkened space that I could hear the watch's soft ticks as late-day orange light retreated through the industrial windows.

I tucked everything in a tattered army duffel bag and put it outside my door.

I used only the small lock near the doorknob, leaving the dead bolt open.

Walking across Julia Street, I felt a cold December wind coming from the Mississippi. It smelled stagnant and stale. I could almost taste its polluted, muddy water.

In the warehouse opposite mine, Sam slid back the door with a scowl on her face. Her short blond hair was tousled, and she was wearing an old gray Tulane sweatshirt of mine that hung below her knees.

"You're scowling."

"You left me wandering around the Quarter. What the hell is the matter with you?"

"I'm sorry."

She let me in and I followed her to the second floor of her

warehouse that looked down on a dance studio. The lights were dimmed on the floor below, and a stereo softly played Otis Redding.

"I'm still mad."

"I know."

She reheated the jambalaya in a black skillet, and we shared the six-pack of Abita. I told her about Tom Cat and about Spencer Faircloth's dinner party. She shook her head and tried not to laugh. When I told her I had my gun, she didn't like that at all, and walked out of the kitchen. One of her cats trailed her.

But she warmed up after a few more of Otis's ballads and a few more Abitas.

Later, we made love in her antique iron bed, Christmas lights strung over her headboard. The beer, food, and music blended into a fine holiday mood.

The next day we opened our gifts. She gave me an old Earl King record I'd wanted for years, a gunmetal cigarette lighter, a first edition of *Franny and Zooey,* and a framed picture of Tom Mix.

She loved the watch.

We returned to bed a few more times that day, only leaving the mattress for the kitchen and something to eat. It was one of the best Christmases I can remember.

They came around midnight, Sam still cradled in my arms asleep. Two cats were curled in balls at the foot of the bed. I could hear the sound of the engine and two doors closing while I carefully unentwined myself from Sam and peeked through her blinds. The car, a black sedan, was still running. Two men were at my front door with a crowbar.

I walked into the kitchen, pulled on my jeans, boots, and the Tulane sweatshirt. I inserted a clip into the Browning and pulled a black watch cap over my ears.

Before clanking down the steps to the street level, I called 911, reported a burglary and shooting at my address, and hung up.

Outside, it was cold enough to see my breath.

I could see someone seated in the back of the sedan smoking a cigarette. A tiny prick of orange light and then a smoky exhaling that clouded the windows. Without stopping, I bent at the waist and jogged behind the car. I opened the back door and climbed inside.

I was seated right next to Spencer Faircloth.

I'll never understand why he came. He was far too smart to put himself anywhere near something as dirty as this. I'm pretty sure it was just ego. The *gutless turd* remark must have gotten to him.

I poked him in the ribs with my Browning.

"Spencer, you old dog."

I reached over the driver's seat and pulled the keys from the ignition while I kept the gun pointed at him. I then motioned him outside, found the key for the trunk, and pushed him in with the flat of my palm.

My face felt cold and wind-bitten when I smiled.

They had made a real mess of my turn-of-the-century door, which had scrolled patterns around the mail slot. Splintered wood and muddy boot tracks led up my side staircase.

This time I did not run. I crept.

But I had the advantage. I knew every weakness in that staircase. Each creak. Every loose board.

I heard crashes and thuds. They were throwing my shit all around. And they must have enjoyed making a mess because they were laughing the whole time.

At the top of the landing, I straightened my right arm and fired a slug into the shoulder of the black man with curly, greasy hair. As he spun, one of my old books flew out of his hands, pages fluttering like a wounded bird before it crashed to the floor.

The young preppy white guy I'd encountered twice wasn't ready either. It took him a full four seconds before he tried to reach inside his raincoat. His eyes were wide with fear when I fired, hitting him in the thigh.

His gun slid along the floor, several feet away from him.

He was no bodyguard or the triggerman. He was just the guy fetching laundry and coffee for Faircloth.

But ole Billy Dee was the real deal.

I walked over to him, slowly. My boots clanking hard in my warehouse, the place where I slept, ate, and read.

The book he'd been tearing pages from was Robert Palmer's *Deep Blues*. The dog-eared pages littered the floor around him, some misted with blood from the bullet's impact.

He had his gun still in hand. A revolver.

"You're not a blues fan, are you?"

He looked up at me and laughed.

"You remember that old man who you shot in the head?"

"Should have been you, motherfucker."

"That old man could play 'Blue Monday' and break your heart."

"You're crazy."

"Maybe."

With my gun pressed flat against his nose, I took his revolver.

"I'll find you," he said. "I promise you that."

The police arrived a short time later, and with the coaxed testimony of Tom Cat, all three were charged with murder.

On New Year's Eve, I played "Auld Lang Syne" on Fats's tarnished sax and Loretta sang. Everyone made toasts and kissed while I placed the battered instrument in a dusty glass case, where it still remains today.

Sam came over, put an arm around my neck, and kissed me hard. I stood back and looked at Fats's picture on top of the wooden case.

She kissed me again, and I turned away.

JoJo told me I did a "real nice job" playing harp that night and handed me another Dixie. Drunk, JoJo ambled up onstage and professed his love for his wife. She watched him and smiled, then gave him a kiss too.

I wish I could've kept the moment, everything the way it was right then. But that was the year I met Cracker and went looking for the lost recordings of Robert Johnson in the Mississippi Delta. And my life was never the same.

PIE MAN

BY MAURICE CARLOS RUFFIN
Central City
(Originally published in 2012)

The Pie Man tells Baby that a man has got to grab his own future for his own self. The City of New Orleans pays good to work disaster cleanup and Baby would do well to cash in before all the money gets carted off. A lot more sensible, the Pie Man says, than running around punching on Spanish dudes. The Pie Man walks across the living room in his chef's jacket. He plops down on the couch, making himself at home. The walls have been stripped naked to the studs. Baby doesn't know which way his future is, but he's damn sure it's got nothing to do with scooping mold out of some abandoned school.

Baby sits at the plastic folding table in white briefs and a tank top, fingering the dry skin around his bulky, plastic ankle bracelet. He plucks a Vienna sausage from its tin and tosses the wiener in his mouth. Baby eyes the Pie Man. The Pie Man doesn't seem to get that he has no claim on this place or anyone in it. Baby may be only fourteen, but this is his house. He's the man here.

The Pie Man's eyes are red. He kneads his face with both hands and looks around like he doesn't remember why he's there. Sauced out of his mind before noon. Probably spent the night with the winos back in Gert Town.

Baby's mom doesn't notice because she's too busy flapping around the room like a hen with a case of colic. As she gathers her things for the day care center, she keeps clucking at him about making the right choices in life. Her standard rave.

She's on Baby because a Latino day-jobber got jumped outside the package liquor last night, the latest in a string of black-on-brown beatdowns in retaliation for what happened to Baby's boy, Chaney. Baby's mom thinks Baby is part of the jump squad. He's not. Yet. He doesn't tell her this. If she and everyone else think he's in on the attacks, it beats the alternative. Better to be feared than understood.

Baby's mom checks her hair in a handheld mirror before placing it on the table he's sitting at. It doubles as her dresser and the couch is her bed. Baby sleeps on the floor in his fleece blanket, wrapped up tight as a papoose. A portable stovetop makes the bathroom their kitchen. All their real stuff was destroyed in the flood from the levee breech after Hurricane Katrina passed nearly three years ago. They live in the front half of the house since the back is sealed off with blue tarp to keep the fungus odor out. It doesn't work. Everything smells like old people's feet to Baby.

Sanchez, the carpenter Baby used to gopher for, shot Chaney in cold blood, but the police called it self-defense—as if Chaney's back had a chance against Sanchez's .38. Baby's mom called the Pie Man in to odd-job their General Pershing Street home three months ago because Sanchez and the rest of the Latinos are afraid to work in Baby's neighborhood. She can't afford a contractor with papers or real tools.

Baby's mom didn't confirm the Pie Man was his pops until old man Sanchez quit. Baby told his mom and the Pie Man that it didn't make any difference that the drunk was his father. The Pie Man has no business making any claims after all this time. Either way, Baby sometimes finds himself staring into the Pie Man's face, wondering what life might have been like if the man had always been around.

Chin on the table, eyes clamped shut, Baby realizes the Pie Man and his mom have been jabbering at him the whole time.

Who knew? He wonders what they were like when they met each other back in the Stone Age. During the time of Public Enemy and parachute pants. Back when the Pie Man's uneven flattop fade was in style. Back before they became voices in the wall.

They have a similar way of phoning in their rants. No commitment. They talk at him like they're being watched. As if they'll get in big trouble for failing to pay the right amount of lip service.

The Pie Man tells Baby he ought to respect his mom, man, because that's the least she deserves for bringing him into this unbalanced world, and if Baby's going to keep driving her every which way like he's been doing, then Baby ain't no kind of man. The whole issue could be that Baby's not thinking, says the Pie Man, but he can start anytime now. He tells Baby to sit up and pay attention. Because he doesn't know the Pie Man well, Baby does as he's told. The Pie Man could be crazy or something, like Baby's friend Touché.

"What, am I supposed to call you *Daddy* or something?" Baby nudges the skateboard under the table with his bare foot.

The Pie Man's slacks, shoes, and neckerchief match his jacket, dingy white from head to toe. He mismatched the cloth buttons so that his collar is higher on one side than the other. To Baby the Pie Man looks like a homeless chocolate Chef Boyardee. There's no trace of the freckles Baby got from his redheaded mom. The ones he catches hell for at school. The ones he tried to scrub off after reading the Dred Scott decision in American history the year before. Yet even though Baby's freckles won't come off, that doesn't mean he can't become the next great civil rights leader like Malcolm X, Tupac Shakur, or Lil' Wayne. Holding it down for the people. Real niggas.

Baby scratches the oval scab on his shin, thinking it's going to leave a mark when it heals. If it heals. Maybe he'll cover it with a black fist tattoo when Mom's not looking. The tattoo is Touché's idea. Touché wants everyone in the Mighty Black Ninja

Krew to get black fist tattoos after they find and stomp Sanchez today. Baby's heard through the grapevine that Sanchez feels bad about what he did to Chaney, and it might be true. Sanchez never held back telling Baby when he'd screwed up, but he was quick to give Baby props for good work, and he always gave Baby a cold can of soda at the end of the day.

Baby gets up to leave. But his mom yells at him and makes him sit his rear back in that chair right this instant. He's a target, she says, and Baby feels she's right. The Latinos have been dishing out hard-core payback. Curtis Thompson, the running back at Baby's school, got whacked in the knee with a galvanized-steel pipe the other day. Curtis is out for the season, and with him any shot at the state championship. They say he never saw the guys who did it, but they had Spanish accents. Nobody's safe, thinks Baby. Baby's mom thinks she can protect him by sending him to the barber. His hair makes him look like a maniac, she says.

But Baby's Afro is a matter of pride for him. It's a fuzzy crown that radiates out six inches, going from black at the scalp to reddish brown at the tips. Like a halo made of rabbit's fur. Most of his friends think it's pretty cool. It counteracts the freckles.

One thing at a time, says the Pie Man to Baby's mom. Baby follows the Pie Man's lips. The way they form words. Inner-tube round one second, then flat like a pair of rotten bananas. The Pie Man says he knows Baby doesn't want to go back on full house arrest. The Pie Man says Baby's free lawyer, Mr. Bates, already told them Baby was out of chances. The Pie Man looks at Baby as if expecting a response, which Baby doesn't give. Baby stares at those bananas.

The Pie Man tells Baby to get up because it's time to go to work.

Baby looks out the window. Orange traffic barrels flank a *Do Not Enter* sign at the end of the block.

"Nope," Baby says. "I ain't doing your slave work. If that means I'm stuck inside, then so what?"

Baby's mom sprays air freshener at him. She tells him she'll turn him in herself if he doesn't get that haircut. And he better be home before the streetlights come on. If he's more than a half-inch from the front door by then, the SWAT team will come after him, she reminds him for the umpteenth-and-a-half time. She kisses him on the forehead and leaves.

The Pie Man says he'll bring Baby to the barber now but doesn't get up from the couch. He continues to stare at the empty space behind Baby.

"I'll get ready." Baby rides his skateboard to the bathroom where he straps on his Chuck Taylors and a pair of brown plaid shorts before climbing out the window.

The outside of Lawrence D. Crocker Elementary isn't much different from how Baby remembers it growing up. Lots of brick walls and stucco pillars. Plenty of rectangles. Gravel lot. The narrow Plexiglass windows were faded opaque even before Baby and his friends went here, but the interior is totally different since Hurricane Katrina turned it out. Dried gack coats the tile and baseboards. Green paint curdles from the floodwater pox. Rivulets of rust and mold syrup drool down the walls. Waterlogged books, tiny chairs coated in sludge, poster boards covered in blue-black fungus. The dump smells like anchovies pickled in urine.

Baby hasn't cut his hair but figures skipping the job would be going too far. He does skateboarding tricks on the retaining wall outside of the school, knowing it will be some time before the Pie Man puts his brain on and figures out to come. But the van appears at the street corner within minutes. The clunker has one headlight and *Nobody Starves When the Pie Man's Around* scrawled in faded orange letters across the side. Ever since the Pie Man decided he's Baby's pops again, he's begun following Baby around in that death trap even when they're not working.

The Pie Man used to sell gumbo ya-ya, greens, and bread pudding at barbershops and car washes. Sometimes he makes pies—pecan, apple, and sweet potato—all with his own two hands. Baby can tell the Pie Man had been real proud of his business selling catballs to the citizenry. Baby chuckled when he remembered the web video he'd seen of a stupid toothless cat doing its best to gum a mouse to death. The mouse kept plopping out—pissed, but pretty much okay. The Pie Man said he got shut down when the health inspector caught him selling reconstituted meat. Baby asked him, reconstituted from what? Meat mostly, said the Pie Man.

Now two-by-fours and tangled wires choke the van's bay. The Pie Man must have had breakfast, thinks Baby, because he looks sober. He managed to button his jacket right and comb his flattop so that his head looks like an eraser.

"Why can't they just bulldoze this hole and start from scratch?" Baby skates toward the Pie Man, who is unloading sledgehammers in the lobby outside of the cafeteria. Sanchez's tools were used for assembling things. Baby learned, to his own amazement, how to hang a door. It was harder than it looked, Sanchez told Baby, because you had to make many little decisions to get the right fit. Baby imagines swinging one of those sledgehammers at Sanchez's head, watching it roll across the ground like an eight ball after contact.

The Pie Man shrugs and tosses his jacket on a wheelbarrow. He has ink on his bicep. An eagle, perched above an earth and anchor, flaps its wings whenever the Pie Man flexes.

"You ever shot somebody?" Baby says.

The Pie Man slings a wide shovel onto his shoulder and says he shot two people.

"Did they die?"

The Pie Man shrugs.

They work their way into the library, where red wall pennants form a frieze near the ceiling. Bookcases lean at odd angles, having dominoed during the flooding. All the books are on the floor, mush. As little boys, Baby and Chaney filed these books for the librarian as punishment after starting a food fight. Today, the books look like cream of wheat.

They both died, says the Pie Man, but he's not entirely sure about whether he killed the second dude. The second dude he shot was an insurgent with his finger on a trip wire. The whole convoy unloaded on him and any one of them might have gotten the kill shot, he says. Or, he tells Baby, maybe the hajji died of fear.

"What about the first one?" Baby asks.

The Pie Man shovels books into the wheelbarrow on top of his jacket. He says it was his friend Freddie Lane, the first person he met when he enlisted. He murdered Freddie dead. He tells Baby he's not sure if either situation matters because at war it's legit to kill, but if you kill one of your own you'd better have your reasons clean as a fresh latrine, which is what the Pie Man had. Freddie had flipped the fuck out and tried to mow down the boys in the mess with a fifty cal. The Pie Man capped him from behind with his M240, which took Freddie's arm clean off above the elbow.

The Pie Man says Baby and his boys shouldn't be so ready to go settle scores with that Spanish guy. Baby can go any way he wants, but that doesn't mean he has to. The Pie Man says he should just sit on his hands. Baby notices a corroded picture of Nat Turner clipped to one of the wall pennants.

"People will roll you, if you let them," says Baby as he points a finger from the Pie Man to himself. "I'm done getting rolled, you heard me?" Baby straightens to his full height. "We getting him tonight."

The Pie Man pops a pill and says he can't argue with that much. He says he can't argue with much of anything except that the VA could stop screwing around and send him better medication. The Pie Man's face is scrunched up again like he's confused. He says he ain't slept since Kirkuk.

"What made you join the Marines?" Baby asks.

The Pie Man says it seemed like a good way to go. They needed a chef, and he needed a job for the future he had mapped out. A fair exchange, he thought at the time. But he never baked a single pie in the military. When he came home, he'd forgotten how to. Whether you get Sanchez or he gets you, the Pie Man tells Baby, you end up in the same place.

The Pie Man and Baby put on respirator masks. Baby thinks the Pie Man looks like a futuristic rat. Baby grabs a sledgehammer and zeroes in on the face of Guy Bluford, the first brother launched into outer space. He swings and before long the walls are coming down all around him.

It's an hour to sundown and the Pie Man left Baby once they finished work for the day. Touché and Turtle skate up the driveway in front of the school.

Touché does a 360 from a ramp angled over a mound of bricks and stops near Baby.

"Welcome back to Genitalia." Touché's got a faux-hawk and his striped hoody makes it look like he's still spinning. General Taylor and Peniston are the streets closest to Crocker facing downtown. They've called the streets *Genitalia* and *Peniston* since the sixth grade. *Dry Ass* Street runs perpendicular to them both, a few blocks closer to the streetcar line. "You still got your Oreo 'fro, little man?"

"Man, my mama can't make a brother cut off his trademark," says Baby. He hates it when Touché makes fun of his size almost as much as he hates when he makes fun of the fact he's practically half white. It isn't Baby's fault his mom's pops wasn't black like everyone else. Touché seems to know where everyone's buttons are. He's like a video-game champ who's got all the secret codes memorized. X to kick you in the gizzards. Z plus *turbo* to take out your knees and dump you in Lake Pontchartrain. Sometimes you don't even know it was Touché who got you. Touché's manipulations bug Baby sometimes, but more often than not Baby is silently praying he learns how to do it himself.

"Yeah, I asked your mama for a haircut. She gave me a blowjob instead." Baby pokes his tongue against his cheek and pumps his fist. "The bitch still don't understand English."

"Your mama so fat," says Touché, "I pushed that ho in the Mississippi River and rode her to the other side."

"I heard in Sunday school," Baby says, "your mama so old she was Jesus' nanny."

"Your mama so fat she went to an all-you-can-eat buffet and ate the Chinese waitress," says Turtle, adjusting his thick glasses. "She be using Ethiopians as toothpicks."

"Your mama—" says Touché, but he stops and punches Turtle in the shoulder. No one makes fun of Turtle's real mom. Not even Touché. Not since the last time they saw her, dry-skinned and strung out, begging for change on Canal Street. She wore a tank top and jeans so small they could have fit a ten-year-old, but loose enough to reveal her soiled lace underwear. "We need to get that Sanchez and pop him. *Whap*." Touché clutches his board and brings it down on Sanchez's imaginary head. "Or drag him across town by a rope."

"Kill that noise," says Turtle. "We ain't getting nobody." He grabs Baby's shoulder. "I saw the Pie Man's van earlier." Turtle is nearly blind from getting his head kicked in.

Baby always thinks he's staring at him from another world through those binoculars. A scarier world. Turtle's pops is a scary dude. He's in Orleans Parish Prison for drugs and guns. Two life sentences.

"He playing camp counselor again?" Turtle asks.

Baby nods.

"Come on." Turtle skates off with his glasses in hand. He doesn't need them to get where they're going.

All three boys glide to the lot behind the school. Scraggly grass forms a crescent along the edges of the fractured concrete. Baby is reminded of the Pie Man's receding hairline. They enter a rusting cargo container where the Mighty Black Ninja Krew keeps the gas canisters.

The Mighty BNK is what Baby and his boys do when they're bored. And for fame. Like the time they went berserk-boarding through the Catholic church by the house where Turtle's foster family lives. Baby videoed the others zipping across the checkerboard floors and leaping from the altar. As Touché spray-painted *MBNK* on the wooden doors during their escape, Baby noticed statues of old men in the gallery above. They wore flowing pink sheets, one statue dangling a key, the other a sword. They looked like they wanted to kick his ass. He gave them the finger, and the Mighty BNK got away clean.

Touché posted the video, which went viral on the web. The Mighty Black Ninja Krew was right behind a video of a white guy demonstrating stupid dance moves and that toothless cat trying to slurp up that mouse.

If he were being totally honest, Baby would admit he joined the Mighty BNK for the same reason as the others: to get laid. They hide their faces on camera with white stockings, but everybody at school knows who they are. It's worked out great for the rest of the Mighty BNK. It hasn't worked at all for Baby.

He doesn't have the swagger of Touché or the brains of Turtle or the wicked determination of Chaney, shot dead when the Mighty BNK tried to loot Sanchez's garage. Baby's fourteen, but looks closer to nine since he's two heads shorter than the others and has no stubble on his chin, chest, or groin. It's caused trouble for him with the girls at school, and when they call him Baby, they mean it.

He's got a plan, though. He'll lay some pipe on Trenisha, who plays center for the girls basketball team. That shorty is over six feet tall and rough around the edges, but Baby knows he can smooth her out doggie-style like a Chihuahua on a Great Dane in the janitor's closet or, better yet, in the backseat of Principal Colton's Cadillac while the Mighty BNK cheers him on. The video would make him a legend in his own time.

But Baby doesn't know the first, second, or third thing about girls, let alone what it might be like to go to any of the bases with them. He listens to the rest of the Mighty BNK kid around and is sure they've all done it—even Chaney, who will never do it again. Baby fears he'll die without doing it. He wonders if dying without doing it means he winds up in heaven as a kid for all eternity. Or hell.

Touché snickers in the corner of the rusty cargo container, having gone first. His arms are tight against his chest. Baby knows this pose means to leave him be. Baby and the Mighty BNK jacked the nitrous oxide from Sanchez because they were tired of sniffing airplane glue and Freon, which burned the ever-loving b'jesus out of their noses.

Turtle fills a blue balloon from the nitrous oxide canister and hands it to Baby. Baby's careful not to let any gas escape. Touché's face is wet. He always cries when they fly.

Turtle tokes weed in a crouch. He offers to Baby, but Baby shakes his head. Baby takes a draw from the balloon, nearly as much as his lungs will hold. Then he sucks a bit of straight air on top to hold the gas steady. The nitrous is sweet on his tongue. Sweet like he's just licked a birthday cake. Sweet and steady, like his birthday was yesterday, is today, and will be tomorrow. Seated and holding his breath, Baby clutches the tips of his Chuck Taylors for dear life. A tingling rips up his spine like electric spiders on parade. The spiders are angry this time. They rummage through Baby's innards for flies, bad ideas, and mildew, but don't find enough.

Baby pushes the gas from his lungs. He feels like propeller blades are chopping him into finer and finer pieces. Every time he feels this, Baby wonders what it would be like to choose how he puts himself back together. Maybe in Atlanta instead of New Orleans this time. Bigger and stronger this time. Taller and darker this time. This time hung like a mutant ox. Maybe this time feared by men and loved like a widow's diamond. Baby clutches his hair and falls onto his back, shivering.

They were good until the alarm in Sanchez's garage went off. Baby saw the flash of Sanchez's gun, and Chaney's eyes open as full moons on his way to the ground. After Touché and Turtle ran away, the police found Baby frozen in place, his sneakers covered in vomit, the only member of the Mighty BNK captured alive.

Touché finishes the weed before Baby gets a second tug at the balloon. Touché is tapping the side of the cargo container with the tree limb he sometimes uses as a walking stick.

"They running a terror campaign on all the blacks in our 'hood." Touché flicks the spent bud away.

The gas has different effects on each member of the Mighty BNK. It makes Touché paranoid. Well, more paranoid than normal, Baby thinks.

"Them rednecks can't just shoot any brother they feel like," Touché says.

"That's dumb," Turtle says. "Sanchez ain't no kind of redneck." The gas brings out Turtle's argumentative side. Sober, he would let Touché carry on until he got tired of hearing himself. "Old Sanchez's Hispanic."

"I don't care if he Jesus on the cross," says Touché. "His people coming over the borders taking our space, our girls."

Baby knows Sanchez didn't come over any border. Sanchez's son went to the same school as Baby's mom.

"And what about you?" Touché asks Baby.

Baby toys with his ankle bracelet. It's a hunk of plastic in the shape of a watch, a handless, faceless watch that refuses to let him know what time it is. Baby wonders what will happen after they get Sanchez. Maybe the guy didn't mean to kill Chaney, and it's not like a smackdown will bring him back. Baby raises his eyebrows as if to say, *What about me?*

"You so fake." Touché spits. "You need to man up."

"I ain't stomping some old dude," Turtle says.

"He shot our boy. He got Baby with a tracking band on his leg. But he gets to walk around scot-free. This is our neighborhood. Shit, this is our country." Touché started saying this after Chaney died. "We about to get a black president. People can't screw with us like this anymore."

"Maybe we shouldn't have tried to take his stuff," Turtle says.

Baby skates past a one-way sign on Claiborne Avenue, his hair bouncing in the wind. A police car with its sirens going nearly sideswipes him. He salutes it, but trips to his knees in the process. That's what the gas does to Baby: it kills his balance. Baby looks around to make sure no one saw him and picks up his board. He hurries past an abandoned double the Latinos tagged with graffiti. He can't accept that his own neighborhood isn't safe anymore. The jerkholes are everywhere.

It's almost dark, and Baby's mom will start check-up calling for him from her night job scrubbing hospital bedsheets clean. She expects him to tell her he's safe and sound in their box of old people's feet.

Baby thought Touché and Turtle might fight over getting Sanchez, but Touché dropped it and skated off, muttering. Baby's relieved. He feels like there might be a better way to get payback for Chaney but doesn't know what that way might be.

A Latino in overalls is perched on a ladder, applying stucco to the side of a two-story house. The lawn is littered with empty stucco bags. Baby hums a stone at the man, but misses. The man waves at Baby. Baby searches for another good rock, but the world disappears. His head is covered by a bag and he can't breathe. Something hard whacks him senseless, and even though he's defenseless, whoever's on top of him is having too much fun to let up. He kicks Baby in the stomach and twice in the face. Baby pulls the bag off his head, but the attacker is gone. He knows he's in trouble when he wipes his mouth and finds blood and tooth fragments.

When Baby gets home, the Pie Man is asleep on the side steps, using a paint can for a pillow. Baby goes inside and looks in his mom's hand mirror. He's glad she's not around to see his nose is smashed or that he's missing half an eyetooth. Blood coats his chin, and the dust from the stucco bag makes him look like a spook. He doesn't want to wash the dust off, though. He's afraid water will activate the stucco mix and turn his head to stone.

Even his mom would agree somebody has to pay for this. If the Mighty BNK let this go, pretty soon Baby, Touché, and every other kid in the neighborhood would be swinging from trees like piñatas at Sunday picnics. Baby runs outside and fingers the van keys from the snoring Pie Man's pocket. Every color in the rainbow is on the Pie Man's grungy jacket. Baby hops into the Pie Man's van and cranks the ignition. The van is hard to drive since the pedals are so far from the seat, but it's only a couple of blocks to Touché's.

The van seems fake, like one of those twenty-five-cent rides you plunk your kid brother into outside of a grocery store. The kind with two doughnut-sized steering wheels that don't do anything.

"They rolled you like a blunt." Touché purses his lips in a mock whistle after he climbs into the passenger seat. He almost seems to be enjoying this.

Baby rubs his mouth, but the sharp pain stops him. Although the bleeding has slowed, his jaw clicks when he moves it.

"Don't say I didn't try to warn you before," Touché says. "It's get or get got out here."

They stop at a gas station in Gert Town. There's a darkened church on the next lot. One of the neon cross arms is out, so it looks like a machine gun turned on its nose. Touché leaps out and disappears into the station. The station lights are painfully bright to Baby. He's starting to think taking the van was not the greatest idea.

Touché sprints from the gas station, toting a bottle. He hands it to Baby; it's a bottle of Goose.

"Should we go get Turtle?" Baby says.

"We don't need no pussies in the way. We mad dogs tonight."

Baby doesn't let the vodka bottle touch his sore lips when he drinks. Tilting his head back makes him woozy, but he recovers as his insides swelter. He tastes ashes and rust and pours some onto the van floor.

"Why'd you do that for?" Touché says.

"That's for Sanchez," Baby says. "He's going to need it."

Touché chuckles and takes the bottle. "That's what I'm talkin' 'bout."

They drive to Sanchez's garage and climb out. Touché and Baby slip white stockings over their heads. Baby's hair makes the stocking pooch out so that he looks like a lightbulb. Baby immediately wants to tear the mask off. It mashes the swollen parts of his face and sandpapers the sweat-moistened stucco coating his skin.

It's still early enough that Sanchez is bent under a hood like he's praying to the engine. Water tings as it circulates in the van radiator.

"Yo, old man Sanchez! What's up, *amigo*?" Touché calls out before they enter the wooden fence. Before Sanchez can see who's coming. Touché says *amigo* wrong. *Hi-meego*, he says.

"*Que pasa, 'migo?*" says Sanchez, stuffing a rag into his overalls. He stops in place when Touché and Baby step into view. Baby figures Sanchez will take off running or go for a gun in his toolbox, but he doesn't. He rakes a hand through his thin white hair. Baby keeps expecting the Pie Man to show up and slap Touché on the back and say they've had enough fun for one night. Instead, they stand in silence broken only by nature: crickets and toads rioting in the bushes.

Sanchez steps backward. He's short. Not Baby short, but not much taller.

"Move." Touché shoves Sanchez toward the van.

"You're Reverend Goodman's son?" Sanchez says to Touché. The stocking mask smushes Touché's features. It flattens out his cheekbones and tweaks his nose downward. Like he's wearing a mask under his mask.

"You don't know me, *niño*," Touché says.

"Ian?" Sanchez says to Baby, calling him by the name Baby's mom only uses when she's about to lay down the law. Sanchez can see Baby's face through the mask. "Why are you here to do this?"

Touché cracks Sanchez in the back of the head with the shaft of his stick. Sanchez is out cold. Baby smells copper. Blood.

"It's on and popping," Touché laughs.

Baby thinks it's over, that they'll drive off and put this behind them, but Touché stoops and wraps twine around Sanchez's wrists and ankles. Within minutes, they're speeding toward the levee on the back side of City Park. When they reach the muddy access road that shadows the levee, Touché nearly rolls the van. Sanchez clutches his knees on the floor. A dark landscape whizzes by as Baby grips the metal handles in the van bay.

The van pitches when they scale the levee, causing a box of nails to fall on Sanchez. He yelps. Baby wants to catch the next box to fall, but doesn't. He feels like he's on a conveyer belt, heading toward an open furnace. Touché stops near the concrete floodwall, which sits atop the levee. He takes Sanchez's ankles, Baby his armpits, and they haul him from the van. Sanchez is heavier than he looks. They drop him in the moist grass at the foot of the wall.

"Maybe we can just leave him," Baby says.

Touché remains silent and switches on his video camera. The

van's headlights flood the scene so there's no color. Sanchez prays into his bound hands.

"You first." Touché hands his walking stick to Baby.

Baby steps toward Sanchez and water snakes in through the seams of his Chuck Taylors, sending a jolt up his spine. Sanchez looks up at him. The stick is covered with spikes. Touché added nails to it, Baby realizes.

"Take your shot, little man."

Crooked nails glisten like fingers in the moonlight. Baby brings the stick up high above Sanchez's head. Some of the nails are angled at the van. Others slant toward Touché, Sanchez, and the night sky. One points straight at Baby.

Acknowledgments

Many thanks to all the writers who so kindly contributed excellent work, especially James Lee Burke and his team—the nice people at the Philip G. Spitzer Literary Agency, Simon & Schuster, and Pamala Burke—for making it possible to include "Jesus Out to Sea."

Also to Johnny Temple and his incomparable staff for amazingly efficient work, as always; and a special shout-out to the scholars I consulted: Kenneth Holditch, who introduced me to "Desire and the Black Masseur," and who reminded me of "Mussolini and the Axeman's Jazz," already a longtime favorite; and to Nancy Dixon, whose remarkable collection, *N.O. Lit: 200 Years of New Orleans Literature*, confirmed many of my choices and introduced me to others, notably Tom Dent's *Ritual Murder* and the writers of *Les Cenelles*. Nancy, thanks for a lovely morning at the Fair Grinds, and for Armand Lanusse.

ABOUT THE CONTRIBUTORS

Joe Worthem, Carrefour Ltd.

ACE ATKINS is the *New York Times* best-selling author of seventeen novels, including the forthcoming *The Redeemers* and *Robert B. Parker's Kickback*. He has been nominated for every major award in crime fiction, including the Edgar Award twice. A former newspaper reporter and SEC football player, Atkins also writes essays and investigative pieces for several national magazines including *Outside* and *Garden & Gun*. He lives in Oxford, Mississippi, with his family.

Donald Paxton

NEVADA BARR's first novel, *Bittersweet*, was published in 1983. The first book in her Anna Pigeon series, *Track of the Cat*, was brought to light in 1993 and won both the Agatha and Anthony awards for best first mystery. In the years since, sixteen more Anna Pigeon novels have been published, twelve of them *New York Times* best sellers. At present Barr lives in New Orleans with her husband, four cats, and two dogs.

Harold Baquet

JOHN BIGUENET's seven books include *The Torturer's Apprentice* and *Oyster*, a novel. His work has appeared in the *Atlantic, Granta, Esquire, Playboy, Storie* (Rome), *Tin House, Zoetrope*, and many anthologies. He is the author of such award-winning plays as *Wundmale, The Vulgar Soul, Rising Water, Shotgun, Mold, Broomstick*, and *Night Train*. An O. Henry Award winner, he is currently the Robert Hunter Distinguished University Professor at Loyola University in New Orleans.

Grey Cross Studios

POPPY Z. BRITE is the author of eight novels, several short story collections, and some nonfiction. Brite now goes by the name Billy Martin and lives in New Orleans with his partner, the artist Grey Cross.

Frank Veronsky

JAMES LEE BURKE, a rare winner of two Edgar Awards, and named Grand Master by the Mystery Writers of America, is the author of more than thirty novels and two collections of short stories, including such *New York Times* best sellers as *Light of the World, Creole Belle, Swan Peak, The Tin Roof Blowdown*, and *Feast Day of Fools*. He lives in Missoula, Montana.

KATE CHOPIN (1850–1904), born Katherine O'Flaherty, was the author of two published novels and about one hundred short stories, and lived in New Orleans for over ten years. She is widely considered one of the first feminist authors of the twentieth century. She is best known for her short story collections *Bayou Folk* (1894) and *A Night in Acadie* (1897), and her novel *The Awakening* (1899).

JOHN WILLIAM CORRINGTON was raised in Shreveport, Louisiana. He received a JD at Tulane University School of Law (1971), but after a few years left the practice of law and began writing full time. Before his death in 1988 he had published four books of poetry, four novels, three books of short fiction, two anthologies, and, with his wife, had written a four-book mystery series, six feature movies, and numerous television episodes.

O'NEIL DE NOUX writes in multiple genres with twenty-nine books published and hundreds of short story sales. His mysteries have won Shamus and Derringer awards and his novel *John Raven Beau* was the 2011 Police Book of the Year. His historical novels include *Battle Kiss* and *USS Relentless*. *The French Detective* is De Noux's latest, a historical mystery novel set in 1900 New Orleans. A former homicide detective, De Noux is currently a police investigator at Southeastern Louisiana University.

TOM DENT (1932–1998) was a New Orleans–born poet, essayist, playwright, and teacher, and was an active participant in the Black Arts and civil rights movements. He was a leading literary figure in New Orleans and spearheaded the Free Southern Theater community workshop program to cultivate local talent within the New Orleans community. His work as an oral historian culminated with his book *Southern Journey: A Return to the Civil Rights Movement* (1997).

ELLEN GILCHRIST won the National Book Award for her 1984 collection *Victory Over Japan*. She is the author of more than twenty books, including novels, short stories, essays, and poetry, most recently her story collection *Acts of God*. Gilchrist lives in Fayetteville, Arkansas, and Ocean Springs, Mississippi, and teaches creative writing at the University of Arkansas.

SHIRLEY ANN GRAU is the author of nine novels and short story collections who was raised in Alabama and Louisiana. Her first novel, *The Hard Blue Sky* (1958), portrayed the descendants of European pioneers living on an island off the coast of Louisiana. Her public profile rose during the civil rights movement, when her dynastic novel *Keepers of the House* (1964), which dealt with race relations in Alabama, earned her a Pulitzer Prize.

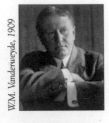

O. HENRY (1862–1910), born William Sydney Porter, was an American writer of short stories known for his wit, wordplay, and plot twists. He lived briefly in New Orleans in 1896 while fleeing embezzlement charges before eventually settling in New York City, where he would spend the remainder of his life. His most notable stories include "The Ransom of Red Chief" (1910), "The Duplicity of Hargraves" (1902), and "The Gift of the Magi" (1905).

GRACE KING (1852–1932) was a New Orleans novelist and historian whose writing captured Louisiana's complex racial identity. Her writing career began when the editor of *Century* challenged her to counter negative depictions of mixed-race slave owners. King's short fiction appeared in major national magazines before being collected in *Tales of a Time and Place* (1892) and *Balcony Stories* (1893). Her most notable work of nonfiction is *New Orleans: The Place and the People* (1895).

> No
> Author
> Photo

ARMAND LANUSSE (1812–1867) was an educator and poet who lived in New Orleans his entire life. In 1845 he edited and contributed to *Les Cenelles*, a collection of eighty-five poems written by seventeen free black Louisiana poets and the first collection of poems by African Americans ever published in the United States. In 1848 he helped establish a school for orphans of color and worked as its director until his death.

VALERIE MARTIN is the author of ten novels, including *Trespass*, *Mary Reilly*, and *Property*, three collections of short fiction, and a biography of St. Francis of Assisi titled *Salvation*. She has been awarded a grant from the National Endowment for the Arts and a John Simon Guggenheim Fellowship, as well as the Kafka Prize (for *Mary Reilly*) and Britain's Orange Prize (for *Property*). Her most recent novel is *The Ghost of the Mary Celeste*.

MAURICE CARLOS RUFFIN is a graduate of the University of New Orleans Creative Writing Workshop and a member of the Peauxdunque Writers Alliance and the MelaNated Writers Collective. His work has appeared in *Redivider, Callaloo,* the *Massachusetts Review,* and *Unfathomable City.* He is the winner of the 2014 Iowa Review Fiction Award, the 2014 *So to Speak Journal* Short Story Award, and the 2014 William Faulkner Competition for Novel in Progress.

JULIE SMITH is an Edgar Award winner for best novel, and the author of four mystery series set in New Orleans and San Francisco. A former journalist, she has worked for newspapers in both those cities and now lives in New Orleans. She is the owner of booksBnimble, which publishes mysteries and other quality works digitally. In 2007 Smith edited the bestselling anthology *New Orleans Noir* for Akashic Books.

EUDORA WELTY (1909–2001) was a National Book Award–winning author of short stories and novels that center around the American South. She was born in Jackson, Mississippi, where she lived until her death. Her most famous novel, *The Optimist's Daughter* (1973), takes place in New Orleans and won her the Pulitzer Prize. She is also notable for her photograph collection *One Time, One Place* (1971).

TENNESSEE WILLIAMS (1911–1983) was an American playwright and winner of two Pulitzer Prizes and four Drama Critic Circle Awards. He was born in Mississippi and in 1939 moved to New Orleans, a city that inspired much of his writing, including *A Streetcar Named Desire* (1947), which won him his first Pulitzer Prize. His most famous plays include *The Glass Menagerie* (1944) and *Cat on a Hot Tin Roof* (1955).

Permissions

NEW ORLEANS NOIR
Edited by Julie Smith, 288 pages, trade paperback original, $15.95

Brand-new stories by: Ace Atkins, Laura Lippman, Patty Friedmann, Barbara Hambly, Tim McLoughlin, Olympia Vernon, David Fulmer, Jervey Tervalon, James Nolan, Kalamu ya Salaam, Maureen Tan, Thomas Adcock, Jeri Cain Rossi, Christine Wiltz, Greg Herren, Julie Smith, Eric Overmyer, and Ted O'Brien.

"In Julie Smith, Akashic found a perfect editor for the New Orleans volume, for she is one who knows and loves the city and its writers and knows how to bring out the best in both ... It's harrowing reading, to be sure, but it's pure page-turning pleasure, too." —*Times-Picayune*

"[*New Orleans Noir*] is a vivid series of impressions of the city in moments that brought out either the best or worst in people. As part of the first wave of fiction to arrive in the wake of the storm, it's a thrilling read and a harbinger of what should be an interesting stream of works." —*Gambit Weekly*

MEMPHIS NOIR
Edited by Laureen P. Cantwell & Leonard Gill
288 pages, trade paperback original, $15.95

Brand-new stories by: Richard J. Alley, David Wesley Williams, Dwight Fryer, Jamey Hatley, Adam Shaw & Penny Register-Shaw, Kaye George, Arthur Flowers, Suzanne Berube Rorhus, Ehi Ike, Lee Martin, Stephen Clements, Cary Holladay, John Bensko, Sheree Renée Thomas, and Troy L. Wiggins.

"*Memphis Noir*, edited by Laureen P. Cantwell and Leonard Gill, captures the subtlety of the Memphis ethos, where blacks and whites, rich and poor, are intimately entwined. The collection—fifteen stories by some of the city's finest writers—bleeds the blues and calls down the dark powers that permeate this capital of the Delta." —*Commercial Appeal*

MIAMI NOIR
Edited by Les Standiford
332 pages, trade paperback original, $15.95

Brand-new stories by: James W. Hall, Barbara Parker, John Dufresne, Paul Levine, Carolina Garcia-Aguilera, Tom Corcoran, Christine Kling, George Tucker, Kevin Allen, Anthony Dale Gagliano, David Beaty, Vicki Hendricks, John Bond, Preston L. Allen, Lynne Barrett, and Jeffrey Wehr.

"For different reasons these stories cultivate a little something special, a radiance, a humanity, even a grace, in the midst of the noir gloom, and thereby set themselves apart. Variety, familiarity, mood and tone, and the occasional gem of a story make *Miami Noir* a collection to savor." —*Miami Herald*

DALLAS NOIR
Edited by David Hale Smith
288 pages, trade paperback original, $15.95

Brand-new stories by: Kathleen Kent, Ben Fountain, James Hime, Harry Hunsicker, Matt Bondurant, Merritt Tierce, Daniel J. Hale, Emma Rathbone, Jonathan Woods, Oscar C. Peña, Clay Reynolds, Lauren Davis, Fran Hillyer, Catherine Cuellar, David Haynes, and J. Suzanne Frank.

"All in all, the stories in *Dallas Noir* have an unsettling, slightly creepy presence that is not just appropriate but completely necessary for a collection of noir fiction. If you think Dallas is boring or white-bread—well, perhaps you haven't gotten out much and seen the dark edges of Big D for yourself. And if you haven't, maybe you don't even want to."
—*Dallas Morning News*

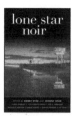

LONE STAR NOIR
Edited by Bobby Byrd & Johnny Byrd
288 pages, trade paperback original, $15.95

Brand-new stories by: James Crumley, Joe R. Lansdale, Claudia Smith, Ito Romo, Luis Alberto Urrea, David Corbett, George Wier, Sarah Cortez, Jesse Sublett, Dean James, Tim Tingle, Milton T. Burton, Lisa Sandlin, Jessica Powers, and Bobby Byrd.

"Crime, like politics, is local. The folks at Akashic Books understand this . . . *Lone Star Noir* is a solid collection. Heck, it better be—the state's red clay looks like dried blood. Noir grows out of the ground here."
—*Austin American-Statesman.*

BROOKLYN NOIR
Edited by Tim McLoughlin
320 pages, trade paperback original, $15.95

Brand-new stories by: Pete Hamill, Nelson George, Sidney Offit, Arthur Nersesian, Pearl Abraham, Neal Pollack, Ken Bruen, Ellen Miller, Maggie Estep, Kenji Jasper, Adam Mansbach, C.J. Sullivan, Chris Niles, Norman Kelley, Nicole Blackman, Tim McLoughlin, Thomas Morrissey, Lou Manfredo, Luciano Guerriero, and Robert Knightly.

Edgar Award finalist for "The Book Signing" by Pete Hamill; winner of the MWA's Robert L. Fish Memorial Award for "Can't Catch Me" by Thomas Morrissey; a Shamus Award winner for "Hasidic Noir" by Pearl Abraham; an Anthony Award winner for Best Cover Art.